FATHERS AN

SLOBODAN SELENIĆ was born in C
and a number of plays, and was
Science and Arts. Winner of the prestigious NIN ...
Belgrade's Poet Laureate, Slobodan Selenić died in 1995.

ELLEN ELIAS-BURSAĆ is a literary translator and a South Slavic scholar
who teaches Bosnian/Croatian/Serbian at Harvard University. Her
translation of David Albahari's *Words Are Something Else* (1996) won
the AATSEEL translation award.

Also by Slobodan Selenić in English translation

PREMEDITATED MURDER

Slobodan Selenić
FATHERS AND FOREFATHERS

Translated from the Serbian by
Ellen Elias-Bursać

Surprise Surprise!!,
Dec 04.

THE HARVILL PRESS
LONDON

Published by The Harvill Press 2003

2 4 6 8 10 9 7 5 3 1

Originally published with the title *Očevi i oci* by Prosveta, Belgrade, 1985

First published in Great Britain in 2003 by
The Harvill Press
Random House, 20 Vauxhall Bridge Road,
London SW1V 2SA

Random House Australia (Pty) Limited
20 Alfred Street, Milsons Point, Sydney
New South Wales 2061, Australia

Random House New Zealand Limited
18 Poland Road, Glenfield,
Auckland 10, New Zealand

Random House South Africa (Pty) Limited
Endulini, 5A Jubilee Road, Parktown 2193, South Africa

The Random House Group Limited Reg. No. 954009
www.randomhouse.co.uk/harvill

A CIP catalogue record for this book is available from the British Library

ISBN 1 84343 018 5

Papers used by Random House are natural, recyclable products made from
wood grown in sustainable forests; the manufacturing processes conform
to the environmental regulations of the country of origin

Typeset in Minion by SX Composing Ltd, Rayleigh, Essex
Printed and bound in Great Britain by
Mackays of Chatham Ltd, Chatham, Kent

TRANSLATOR'S FOREWORD

It is December 1925. The Englishwoman Elizabeth Blake writes in halting Serbian to Rashela Alkalaj, a friend in England, describing her new life in Belgrade, where she has moved with her Serbian husband, Stevan Medaković: "Now, my dear Rachel, I had been here maybe one or two weeks, and Stevan said to me that we must go to a party at the Glišić family. Good. I think – I sit, I am silent, I survive." Besieged by family and friends at the party, Elizabeth – Elizabeta, as she is known among her Yugoslav friends and family – valiantly tries out her Serbian, but no amount of language practice can have prepared her for Gordana: "Gordana was asking me now if I wanted, as she wanted, for us to be blood sisters. I hadn't the slightest idea what this 'blood sister' meant, but Stevan was far away, couldn't help me quickly." Elizabeta agrees to Gordana's suggestion but quickly realizes that this "was a big mistake, because then Gordana started to cry, she said, now we are together to death, she and I, and she kissed me, hugged, tears rolling down her face, she said that never had such happiness been hers." With a sigh of relief, Elizabeta catches sight of her husband: "Luckily Stevan came over, said we've had the coffee, we can leave. I was glad, it was over."

Elizabeta met Stevan in England, where he was studying constitutional law at the University in Bristol. She was attending classes following a difficult divorce. Rashela, a nurse from Belgrade, is married to Elizabeta's cousin Archibald and lives in England. Once Elizabeta moves to Belgrade, she and Rashela correspond regularly. Elizabeta uses her letters to Rashela to practise her Serbian and to air both her grievances and her amusement at the novelty of Belgrade life. Rashela in turn writes to Stevan to shed some light on Elizabeta's background and to talk about the work the young couple will have to do to reconcile their very different cultures: "Let Elisabeth stay English. I recommend the same to her: Let Stevan stay the Serb. Do not expect him to become English." Once the two have settled in Belgrade, Stevan's work as a professor at the law faculty draws him into the treacherous arena of politics. Meanwhile, Elizabeta gives herself over to raising their son, Mihajlo, to begin with a model English boy. Mihajlo, however, becomes a rebellious teenager during World War II, fascinated by the Partisan youth activists in Occupied Belgrade, a fascination that leads to his death.

Fathers and Forefathers is the story of Elizabeta, Stevan and Mihajlo, of how they perceive the world and each other, and shape each other's lives. History looms large in all that happens to the three of them. The historical and social questions treated in the novel, and the portraits of the Medakovićes and their perspectives on themselves and others, were put forward by Slobodan Selenić (1933–1995) within the turbulent context of the 1980s (the book was first published in 1985). Though never mentioned in the narrative, the '80s are as much a part of the novel as the years 1925–45, when it is set. Selenić provides a glimpse of a world that vanished after World War II – the world of bourgeois Belgrade – from the vantage point of another world – socialist Yugoslavia – that was vanishing in its turn.

Selenić (the author of six novels, several plays and three books on drama) was a writer who liked to shake things up. His first novel, *The Memoirs of Pero the Cripple*, shocked readers when it came out in 1968 with its unapologetic derision of the socialist leadership. During the crackdown of the 1970s that followed the brief cultural thaw of the late 1960s, Selenić stopped publishing fiction, devoting himself instead to teaching at the Belgrade Drama Academy. His next novel (*Friends at Kosančić Circle*) appeared in 1981, immediately after the death of Josip Broz Tito. Selenić dedicated his fiction of this period to examining perspectives which had hitherto been actively discouraged by the authorities.

Readers of the 1980s were eager to read novels that said things no-one had been able to say for decades. This thrill was by no means limited to Serbian readers. The socialist regime had only become selectively more permissive. Revisionist novels and plays appeared in Serbia and Slovenia, but the same easing of constraints did not follow in the rest of the country until the end of the '80s, guaranteeing Selenić a widespread readership.

Much of what is innovative in *Fathers and Forefathers* lies in its contextual framework. Selenić chose to narrate the novel from a middle-class, essentially élitist, point of view. His protagonist Stevan Medaković comes from a family that has been part of the Serbian bourgeoisie for several generations. Medaković feels sympathy for the plight of Prince Pavle and is sceptical of the Partisans and socialism. Both of these perspectives were still quite controversial in 1985.

In showing Yugoslavia through Serbian eyes, Selenić privileged the Serbian perspective, something the socialist authorities were usually quick to discourage. Perhaps the most sensitive question the novel explores, however, is that of the pre-World War II multi-party system. It is worth noting that in 1983, two years before *Fathers and Forefathers* appeared, Vojislav Koštunica and Kosta Čakovski published a controversial monograph (see Glossary, p. 284) discussing monism and pluralism and focusing on the years 1944–9, when Tito's party was in the process of doing away with the multi-party system altogether. This monograph sparked the debate that inspired Selenić to address pluralism in *Fathers and Forefathers*, a topic much on the minds of those hoping to promote a more diverse political scene in the years following the demise of Tito's regime.

Selenić did not limit himself, in his desire to raise eyebrows, to questioning the socialist version of Yugoslav history. In a move designed to prod the newly bold nationalists of the 1980s, he provided a sharply critical capsule history of Serbian nationalism in the novel. Many Belgrade readers had been swept up in a love affair with Serbia in the 1980s. Elizabeta's dispassionate gaze as a foreigner, drawing attention to the seamy, even comical, aspects of Belgrade and Serbian life, nudged not only her husband, Stevan, but also the novel's Serbian readers to see themselves through a different set of eyes.

Selenić didn't stop there. The novel has its jabs at Slovenes and Croats, mostly in the way it describes historical figures such as Radić and Korošec (see Glossary). And there are a few wry comments at the expense of the English as well.

It was precisely the electrifying combination of Selenić's irreverence and his flair for telling a good story that made *Fathers and Forefathers* a runaway bestseller throughout Yugoslavia in 1985. We all know what followed. In the context of the wars of the 1990s, this novel only gains in relevance, describing as it does with uncanny precision the tension that ominously divergent perspectives create in a society on the eve of war.

Selenić wrote his last novel, *Premeditated Murder*, published in Jelena Petrović's translation by Harvill, in 1996. The story takes place in 1990s Belgrade and on the front of the war in Croatia. The tragic denouement of that novel repeats, nearly verbatim, the most moving scenes from the final chapter of *Fathers and Forefathers*. Why pluck out these scenes and repeat them nine years later? Faced by the horror of the war of the '90s, Selenić could find no more powerful ways to voice his despair than by using repetition to show that the tragedy that is war never changes.

My heartfelt thanks to Merima Selenić for her selfless help following her husband's death; to Hortense Calisher and Curtis Harnack for their wonderful support; to Richard Burns for publishing a fragment of *Fathers and Forefathers* in "Out of Yugoslavia", *North Dakota Quarterly* (Winter 1993); to Christopher MacLehose for including an excerpt from the novel in Harvill's *Leopard IV* anthology (1999); and to Andrea Belloli for her thoughtful editing. My profound gratitude to readers Louise Askew, Caroline and Ladd Connell, Peter Elias, Anna Gessen, David Norris, Tana Pesso and Mary Thompson Popović. Historians Audrey Helfant Budding, Thomas Emmert and Dušan Djordjevich were more than generous with their help on the Glossary. Any oversights are mine alone. I found excellent resources in John Lampe's *Yugoslavia as History: Twice There Was a Country* (2000) and Stevan Pavlowitch's *Serbia: The History of an Idea* (2002), both of which I recommend to readers with a further interest in Serbian, and Yugoslav, history.

E. E.-B.
Cambridge, MA
April 2003

FATHERS AND FOREFATHERS

ONE

I am sitting rather than lying, propped up on two plump pillows, in my regally spacious, old-fashioned bed, which has been, so far as I'm concerned, the central and safest spot in our safe enclave for two decades now. I hear the ticking of the wall clock. Nine o'clock. I wonder: Why now? All over again? What is the point of upsetting the bearable stillness of our little enclave? It frightens me. Do I dare proceed any further down this frightening path? Has time made it possible for me to bear a memory that once could play havoc with me? On this particular morning, how did that thought manage to insinuate its way into our enclave, besieged on all sides but safe from the incursion of the outside world, which, if the truth must be known, has for decades shown little desire to penetrate the well-buttressed fortress? Elizabeta and I have been living in the fortress for a single day stretched out over twenty years, a day with no shape, with no name, but also with no murderous memories to poison it as a maggot would a festering wound. Instead of nightmare-racked nights in a sweltering bed – emptiness. Painless and sexless. In our little enclave.

Our enclave is perhaps best defined as a one-bedroom flat, but it eludes all the city-planning categories. The flat is on the second floor of building no. 52 on Miloš Veliki Street, and one reaches it either by going up a broad white staircase, now cracked and chipped, or by means of the reliable Schindler lift, which slowly and begrudgingly, like some wheezing old mule, lugs portly tenants to their destinations. In 1926, when we moved into this building, newly built at the time, the flat on the third floor made expressly for us was ours alone, but in 1945 they confiscated it and divided it into two unequal parts. The larger part was given to Major Šiljak. The stump was left to us. The only door connecting the parts of the divided flat has long since been walled up. The main entrance from the corridor belongs to Šiljak, while the servants' entrance, through the terrace and kitchen, is ours.

That was ages ago. I'd long since forgotten about it. And that act of partition is on the other side of the hedge I have raised between myself and life. Whenever I use the word *enclave*, it always refers only to the present, smaller size of the flat, never to the larger, original one. If I want to remember the large one, I have to close my eyes, muster all my strength and see our former habitat in my mind's eye. Far, far away.

One enters our current, one and only habitat from the staircase landing across the kitchen terrace, but that is still not our enclave; it is no man's land, a quarantine zone between the world and the planet of the Medakovićes. Our spacious, light kitchen, formerly done in white and black tiles – now half of them are gone – is the first room of the enclave. From there, two doors, one next to the other, lead to the maid's room (Elizabeta has made it her bedroom) and the pantry (now a bathroom with shower) on the left, while a much wider door to the right leads into the living room, which has a twofold function. It is my study but also the living room where we spend our time together. From the dining room, through a large double door with a stained-glass panel – the only bright remnant of former luxury – one goes into a small room (in the original flat, it led to the "small salon", which was connected, by the door now walled up, to the "grand salon"), which serves as my bedroom. It is therefore rather difficult to suggest an accurate category for the enclave: it could be treated as a two-bedroom, one-bedroom or studio flat, if the maid's room and little salon, because of their cramped size, are stripped of the status and dignity of "rooms".

But I never think of our flat as small or large, comfortable or cramped. The enclave is not subject to comparisons of this sort. Its crucial feature is that it is safe, inviolable; that with its terrace, like some medieval drawbridge over a moat two storeys deep, it is sheltered from the world that might want to penetrate our refuge; that it is ours alone, Elizabeta's and mine, from early morning in my regal bed to late in the evening, which we spend together in the living room, each reading a book by the gentle warmth of the tile stove in which the fire has already died. The Vatican amidst greater Rome. Monaco – an azure dot in endless France.

I know, of course, that the enchanted isolation of our enclave – from the flat that it used to belong to, from the building that it fits into, from the streets that surround it, from the city of Belgrade and the land of Serbia – is something we have shaped in our mind's eye, that the hedge around the enclave is spun of the finest silk, still secreted by our lives, submerged under the ashes of past events, but the impression of sovereignty conveyed by this isolation is no less effective and soothing. We are alone. It is bearable. My closer relatives all have died. The distant ones, never fond of us, were easily discouraged; for years they haven't tried to cross our threshold. Elizabeta's are all dead. Far away. In England. So here we are, my wife and I, alone.

Why now? I've already begun, in this renewed attempt to make my way through the labyrinth of my life, yet I am not able to foresee where the thread from Ariadne's skein will lead. Theseus slew the Minotaur and found a way out of his crime. Will I find mine? Will my Ariadne help me? Does she possess a skein? Should I set out on the Journey? I wonder in my spacious and safe bed, though I know that I'm already on my way.

Because, this morning, after such a long time, I awoke to a memory of the young Elizabeta. I've never been good at blocking murderous memories while letting the others stack the straws of my past life in their proper sequence. I know now that the skein of memories leads to a dark knot, which I may only be able to untangle at my own very real peril. But I'm off. Now that I've embarked. Cautiously, like a blind person, I grope, step by step, approaching the distant abyss, in hopes that the many days and years have bridged it, that under my feet, when I reach it, I'll feel a log that spans it to the other side.

I am able, then, to look at the young Englishwoman whose name, that distant evening in 1924, in the Glengyle Inn pub, I still did not know.

I am able. "Kadar". That nice, strong, solid word *kadar*. Mihajlo used to use it. He learned it from me. He and Elizabeta. He adopted that one and a few others, she, almost all the Serbian words she uses.

How stunning my Elizabeta is! Perhaps because I've done so little remembering, because I haven't probed the distant images for a while, I haven't spoiled them by frequent use. Now I see the Bristol days with a new, almost tangible vividness. As if they were not mere memories, as if the reality of four decades ago has now come tumbling into my room in all three physical dimensions, unfolding before us, numb and shut out from events as we are, sufficient unto itself. Does Elizabeta see what is happening? No, of course not, although it is often the case that we think of the same thing at precisely the same moment.

I can see it so clearly. Though she's in the midst of the general hubbub, Elizabeta strikes me as lonely in the boisterous company holding mugs of dark Guinness. She is sitting on a stool by the bar, between two friends – from this distance they seem like two little girls. She is taller than they are and more mature. A woman. The cloud of her thick, heavy red hair is twisted under the kind of hat they wore in those days: bell-shaped, tilted forward, like a little haystack, it casts a shadow on her face, but not enough to darken the gleaming whiteness of her complexion. Even then, I knew that my Englishwoman had the most beautiful colours: skin white as a peeled almond; hair red, but not the pale red that people with freckles have, rather a deeper hue; eyes green as deep ice, "bright as the precious stone in a King's ring", I once wrote. I can't see Elizabeta well, or for very long. My colleagues only pretend to pay less attention to the girls than to everyone else having a quick drink after class, but everything they are doing they do for the girls. They fight to get a word in edgewise and hog attention; they are witty, lively, pushy, too noisy and much less intoxicated than they seem.

I was, indeed, a few years older than most of them, but it seemed to me at the time that I'd turned up suddenly – an adult, bitter and experienced – among children. This was certainly far from the case, but at the Glengyle Inn I was seeing my colleagues as boys just out of short trousers. They had donned blazers, ties and kerchiefs, yet these fitted them, as Nanka would say, like a tit on a chicken. In contrast to their uniform-like clothing and University badges on their chests, I was dressed in the fashion of Viennese students, in a manner already

4

outmoded by 1924, with a cane, top hat, the gloved left hand holding the glove of the right hand. That in itself was enough to set me apart from the casual style, from what I'd call the cultivated air of carelessness, that had just begun to creep into fashion in England's red-brick universities.

From the vantage point of the present, it is easy to feel superior, but at the time my attire did cause me grave concern. Should I adapt to the unusual habits I happened upon on this eccentric island, or should I stay true to myself, which meant being both conspicuous and different? During my first ten days in London, of course, I had become aware that in my long-tailed topcoat resembling a redingote, with white gloves and a cane, I looked different from elegant Englishmen. Since my inborn shyness, inherited from my father, was ever more pronounced, I believed that the difference in my dress made me awkwardly, almost painfully conspicuous. This feeling became all the more acute when I arrived among the students in Bristol, and I would certainly have altered my wardrobe if shyness hadn't prevented me once again. One afternoon, I went to T. C. Marsh and Son Limited, a haberdashery some distance from the town centre and the University, so that I wouldn't run into anyone I knew, and there I tried on several suits recommended to me by the congenial salesman. However, when I saw my new self in the large mirror – a grey, cropped blazer with the garish University badge bearing the inscription "VIM PROMOVET INSITAM", the trousers loose, limp and wrinkled, I was mortified at the thought of how my fellow students and professors would perceive my haste to conform. So I chose the lesser of two evils: to be different – a tortuous feat of endurance given my shyness – rather than to be a frog trying to imitate a horse.

Indeed, what most overwhelmed me during those first days in Bristol was the feeling that I was completely different – and not only in dress – that I'd come from another world to join this carefree, capricious young crowd. Regardless of whether this was, in fact, the case, I felt, though only a few years their senior (there were several, of course, of my age), that I could be their father, with beard and moustache among the clean-shaven, upright, tall and stiff among the boyishly playful. Even if I'd wanted to, I couldn't have joined in their monkey-like pranks or laughed at the grimaces that announced their boyish folly and revealed their buoyant vitality. Not yet 22, only just emerged from boyhood, I had already tasted tragedy unknown to these children of peacetime, for at least two reasons. During the war, they had been under the age of 10, while I had been 15 by the time it ended; and English boys had fallen bravely on land and at sea, in Flanders and on the Somme, but had not endured war on their own soil. The difference was vast, the gap irreconcilable. The fact that I felt older and more experienced imparted not a sense of security but one of discomfort, because I couldn't behave as they did, couldn't be wayward and frivolous. My rigidity in the face of unfamiliar customs, and my halting conversation due to my meagre vocabulary, did not strike me as reasonable in this unfamiliar world; they seemed shameful. I would pretend to understand things that I did not, to follow rather than obstruct the easy flow of conversation. This was often without consequence, but I remember the miserable awkwardness when, asked directly how I stood on some topic, I had to admit that I hadn't understood what they were talking about.

Bristol University was, when I arrived, a small school, so everyone, both undergraduates and postgraduates, in particular those from the same department, would congregate at the Victoria Rooms, local tearooms, inns and playing fields. I was enrolled in the Department of History, doing a course in the history of British parliamentarism, but I met many colleagues from other departments. All of them, especially during the first few weeks, treated me like a wild animal, with curiosity, at a distance, without understanding. I can hardly blame them. I must have looked strange, always aloof, impeccably turned out, ever serious, melancholic and taciturn. Because I was foreign, a native son of the barefoot people who had fought at the battles of Cer and Kolubara, with my bushy black beard, slightly older, different in every respect, they would invariably have sneered at me sooner or later with boyish cruelty, to justify themselves and the rules of prestige (amusing, wise, proper) that each generation lays down and follows. I soon became the butt of jokes, undoubtedly because difference always excites either intolerance or taunts (something I did not, unfortunately, know at the time, so it was of no help to me), but also because I was far too serious for my years, and always brooding. I see myself, without a trace of humour, amidst that youthful, overly cynical crowd that considered everything good for a laugh, the more sacred the better. So there I was with my exaggerated sense of responsibility for every minute spent at my studies, for which my fatherland was paying vast sums, among oversexed adolescents proclaiming irresponsible idiosyncrasy to be the fundamental principle of society. I was literal-minded among the ironic; a newcomer among natives – no wonder I had to undergo several weeks of purgatory, all the more insufferable because I was unable to conceal my sensitivity with ease.

They started to ape the way I spoke English, first behind my back, then to my face, savouring it when they noted that I was unaware of what they were doing. And how could I be aware, those first few weeks, with an ear unattuned to this foreign tongue? Since idiomatic phrases are the most lively and difficult to grasp in jokes, I often took a simple pun seriously, only realising my error once the laughter had subsided following my untimely rejoinder. It soon became a habit among my young fellow students to pronounce "th" with a Slavic hardness; they would say "It struck my mind" as I had once said, instead of "It struck me", or "Edinburg" instead of "Edinboro".

Today I know that their behaviour was unruly, improper; the older and more serious of them knew as much from the start, but that didn't help me. The small Leslie Hayes was the bane of my existence (he was killed in an automobile accident, most unusual in those days, so whenever I think of him, the feeling of insult mingles with some sort of guilt), Leslie with the curly blond hair, a face like rubber, in constant motion, restless, childish, with an exaggerated need to be the centre of attention at all times. I must admit that he so caught my turn of speech, the way I twiddled my moustache when I hesitated in mid-sentence seeking an elusive word (I didn't even know I did this until I saw Leslie doing it), the way I adjusted my impeccably creased trousers when taking a seat, how I held my cane, my gloves – that it reduced to tears even those who felt that jibes at an odd, stand-offish and literal-minded Serb were crude and impolite. No matter how witty and talented an imitator Leslie may have been, success and unrestrained boyish glee went to his head. He lost sight of the limits dictated by taste, which

7

though somewhat understated in England are nonetheless as righteous as a sword blade and deadly for those who blunder. He did himself in through no merit of mine and soon found that his jibes no longer had a willing audience. The depth of my concern and the importance I placed on improving my status among these new acquaintances are conveyed by the fact that even this morning, in bed, forty years on I can still remember vividly that sinking feeling of being awkward among others so agile and quick, oafish as if hewn of a single coarse block, perhaps even stupid.

The discomfiture of my first days among strangers at the University was aggravated by the unpleasant termination of a three-week acquaintance with Robert Rackham, who had been residing for several years at Miss Trickey's boarding house, where I came on my arrival in Bristol, in the room next to the one she rented to me. As agreed beforehand, Miss Trickey was waiting for me at Temple Meads Station. The station seemed gloomy on that bleak September day; like a light rain, fog dampened the platform, the black iron columns under the curving roof, the train, benches, pigeons, people – everything my curious gaze took in as I approached two women and a man who seemed to be waiting for travellers from London. By the time I'd reached them beyond the turnstile, lugging my cumbersome trunk, worried because of my undignified posture, the younger woman was already kissing another arriving passenger, so there could be no doubt that my landlady was the elder of the two. She was in her 50s with a prominent nose and a huge smile that exposed long, large teeth and all her gums; nonetheless, it had an air of warmth and innocence about it. On that grinning head was perched a large and rather striking hat (even I, uninitiated into the nuances of fashion, could tell that it belonged to some bygone age) that did not fit with the grey double-breasted overcoat, out-sized shoes and almost mannish bearing. All the way from Bath, for almost half an hour, I had been composing an English sentence that, I would later realise, was clumsy but fortunately comprehensible.

"Are you waiting me?" I asked, in response to which large, buxom, courteously smiling Miss Trickey loudly and cheerily began to bark out

8

sentences whose meaning I couldn't begin to guess at, but in one of which I managed to make out the word *Medakovik* and so established that I had addressed the proper person. I had arrived in England with a rather high opinion of my knowledge of the language, which I had studied privately in Belgrade for over a year with a Miss Edith Lamb. I had read a number of English books both on my own and under her guidance, and had held hundreds of conversations with her on a wide range of topics. When I had bought the *Illustrated London News* at Calais, I had been delighted to discover that I could translate the captions under photographs and articles on various subjects without much difficulty. After only a few days in London, however, it became clear that I needn't divide the English into the intelligent and the stupid, or the attractive and the ugly, or the male and the female, but, at least for the time being, into those I could understand and those I was not able to understand at all. I could follow educated people kind enough to make the effort to speak simply with clearly enunciated words. It was harder to understand those who belittled everything with their mumbling, including my need to understand them. I understood not a word of what I was told on the streets, in restaurants or in shops by conductors, porters or hat-check girls. To make matters worse, for some reason – clearly simple kindness – these people were the most set on lifting my spirits with an enthusiastic rush of sentences to which I could only respond with a foolish smile and a neutral, inappropriate "Thank you". Dragging my cumbersome trunk through the waiting room towards the exit where coaches and taxis were waiting, trembling with a presentiment of trouble, I established beyond a shadow of a doubt that Miss Trickey, chatting away at my right, belonged to those English people from whose mouths gushed totally unfamiliar words, even when they were ordinary and quite familiar to me in their written forms. It was only when the large lady, grinning from ear to ear and thrilled about something or other, took her seat next to me in a coach going up steep Park Road towards the University that suddenly (I don't know why) it dawned on me what she had meant by the clutter of sounds she had produced, in the form of a query, at the station exit.

"Coach or cab, which do you prefer, Mr Medakovik," she had asked.

Admitting defeat, I had said "Yes", thus convincing my kind landlady that she would have to decide herself. I, brimming with gratitude, and buxom Miss Trickey, gazing in delight at the city and citizens moving by us as if we were part of a procession, rode at the back of the open coach, oblivious of the fog and damp. Like some great Queen Mother with a dejected Prince, an Heir Apparent ready to relinquish all worldly honours in exchange for silence, on we rode, majestic, towards Pembroke Road.

I interpreted the grand rapture which apparently had Miss Trickey in its thrall as stemming from my arrival, since here I was, someone new and strange, or perhaps it was the coach ride. But in time, I divined that ecstasy was the state in which my hostess sustained herself at all times. Miss Trickey was, simply, too, too pleased with life, the world and each individual moment. All aglow, perhaps just a trace hysterical but brimming with jollity, she would use every opportunity to exercise her unblemished merriment.

"Mr Medakovik," she would exclaim from the hallway, out of breath, the instant she caught sight of me, "a letter for you!" – beaming as if she were informing me that I had won the lottery. Even the most commonplace information – that we'd be having fish, for instance, for dinner – Miss Trickey would declare as if it were extraordinary good news, nothing short of a sensation.

"Think what we'll have for supper tomorrow!" she would say, barely able to rein in her bubbling joy. After a few, needless to say failed, attempts by the boarders to guess, Miss Trickey would erupt with the marvellous news: "Fish and chips!" – so elated that even someone unable to tolerate the sight of fish couldn't help but share in her delight. When a fine day came along, Miss Trickey would trot from room to room, beside herself with joy, and announce that it was "simply a glorious day" as if the day were her own doing, as if she had coaxed it single-handedly from her generally overcast Anglican deity.

As yet I knew nothing of this. I knew only that I understood not a single word she said. The closer we came to the boarding house, the clearer it became to me that my real troubles would begin the moment we stepped through the door. Though she had been thoughtfully spouting sentiments for which an indeterminate nod might serve as adequate response, Miss Trickey would begin, at that point, to furnish information regarding household rules, meals, rights and duties of boarders, in a language which, I knew, quite miserable and frightened, I would scarcely understand, unless something unforeseen were to transpire.

Fortuitously, transpire it did. God heard my prayers, sending me, precisely when I needed one, a guardian angel in the form of Robert Rackham. I paid the coach driver and, doubled over, dragged my trunk up the dozen steps to the front door (blue and massive, with a knocker, and a wrought-iron letter-box) where Miss Trickey was waiting for me, every bit the girl, trembling with excitement. A young man stepped out to meet me, and without waiting for my response to his "May I help you?" took hold of the trunk from the other side and assisted me in dragging the yellow pigskin monster to my quarters. Rackham I was able to understand without a hitch from our first encounter. He showed me where the bath was, where the dining room and living room were. He warned me that when I wanted to bathe, I should request it the day before, from either Miss Trickey or Mary the maid. I would be allowed to receive visitors, particularly those of the opposite sex, only in the common living room. Breakfast was served at 8.30, dinner at 6.30.

I was astonished to learn, much later, that Robert was 30 years old. He looked far younger and I assumed he was my age. He dressed rather nattily and conservatively, like a true English gentleman – striped trousers, black smoking jacket, topper, umbrella in hand – but this get-up made him seem old for his age, like someone out to mask his youth by aping adults. Slender, even slim, pale in complexion (which made his ruddy cheeks all the more eye-catching), brown hair combed to the side with the sort of irreproachable parting a boy's mother might slick him up with for the St Sava Day assembly in a Belgrade primary school. His hands were rather thin, his wrists frail, and – with his feet in irreproachably taut black silk stockings and patent-leather shoes with grey gaiters – Rackham reminded me of Jovan Jovanović Zmaj's character Pura Moca, or was it Little Jovo? I no longer remember who it was who perched his grandfather's spectacles on his nose and pretended to be a grown-up. Before I learned that Robert was 30 (which to my 21-year-old mind was as good as elderly), I recall being baffled by his title – Senior Town Hall Accountant – not by the fact that he was an accountant in Bristol Town Hall, but that he was *senior* (even once I'd realised that this word meant *higher*), since I was incapable of imagining an accountant who could possibly be *junior*, officially or age-wise, to Robert. If, however, his appearance did not convey it, his behaviour demonstrated an adult consideration which was a true salve for the initial miseries of my life abroad. Never once in the course of those three weeks did Robert ever hurry in conversation with me. Instead, with devoted patience and an evident effort to be as inconspicuous as possible about it, he would pronounce words precisely the way my Belgrade teacher, Miss Lamb, had pronounced them. For each instance of awkwardness as I faced a new and unfamiliar world, Robert found justification: it was hardly surprising that I had not understood Miss Trickey; why – he would confess to me in hushed tones – even he often found it daunting to make sense of her Gloucestershire whine ("You know she came to Bristol from Painswick in the Cotswolds!"). He had, at first, left Mary's morning porridge untouched, seeing that I did so, unaccustomed as I still was to the particular blandness of this English dish. Were he a student, he would certainly be dressing as I was, and would by no means be going about rumpled and untidy as was the novel and unseemly fashion at the University. He spotted each awkwardness of mine and with the self-sacrificing manner of a sympathetic teacher indirectly gave me to understand that the error was not mine, but lay elsewhere. It was in large part thanks to Robert that I acquired something of the English self-confidence which my colleagues, in those first few days, at least some of them, undermined rather than reinforced.

During the week, I saw Robert only at breakfast and supper, but from that first day of my stay (it was a Friday) and on through the next three weeks, we spent our weekends together, according to a plan which Robert carefully devised, consulting me and counselling how I might, in as brief a period as possible, learn about the place where I would be spending a year. Chances are I never would have developed such an acquaintance with Bristol and its environs had it not been for the solicitous senior accountant. The other students seldom stepped outside the University classrooms and dormitories. Bristol had about three thousand acres of parks and open spaces. That first Sunday, we went by car to the Durdham and Clifton Downs which stretch towards the Avon Gorge, and then along the lovely century-old Isambard Kingdom Brunel suspension bridge. The next Sunday, if I remember rightly, we were even more adventurous. We toured the City and Avonmouth docks and embankments, built as early as 1809, which had tamed the tides of the Frome and Avon, transforming their long confluence into a harbour with a constant navigational depth. Then the zoo in the vicinity of the Clifton cliffs, and then the Blaise Castle estate with its charming park and an ethnographic museum of sorts in its grounds; Brandon Hill, from which you could see the whole of Bristol and its environs stretching out at your feet; the Cabot Tower, raised as a memorial to the departure of John Cabot, otherwise known as Giovanni Cabot, a Venetian whom King Henry VII despatched on May 2, 1497, on a successful expedition to North America in the small ship *Matthew* with an eighteen-member crew. There were many other spots I have forgotten or merged with later visits in my memory.

Invariably, we'd interrupt our vigorous sightseeing at some attractively appointed tea shop Robert knew of, celebrated for its pudding, apple tart or doughnuts, which we would order with the obligatory milky tea, or in some pub where, with a glass of beer, we would take a light lunch at the bar – Scotch eggs, cold sliced meat with pickles reminiscent of our sour pickles in brine, but entirely different in flavour. Less often we would have a hot meal in a genuine restaurant, a grilled steak or a mutton chop. Robert, so kind and attentive; the cosy warmth of the fire and the pleasant dryness after the invariably damp, chilly Atlantic climate we had just come indoors from, ravenous after a long walk; the luxurious white of the tablecloth; the agreeable mixture of evaporating alcohol and the sweet fragrance of good tobacco in the pubs; the discrete smells of restaurant food which wafted over the muted chatter of the guests; the soundless approach and retreat of the waiter – these things signified England for me during those first three weeks even more than all I managed to see and experience at the University.

As agreed, we shared our expenses, but because it was easier for him to do the talking, Robert was always the one to settle the bill. I remember exactly how he did this. Pulling a handful of massive silver half-crowns out of his trouser pocket, he would pile up far more than he needed to cover the cost in a carefully ordered pillar, using his left palm as the base so that he could feel the heft of the change with evident, though concealed, pleasure. He would summon the waiter, wait to see what the total came to and then, with his index fingernail and thumb, would lift the necessary number of sturdily dignified, reassuringly solid coins and transport them in his fist as if by crane through the air, lowering them onto the tray so that they rang out when they hit the metal. Robert never spoke of it, but everything about him suggested that he knew the value of money, that he loved those silver objects which he had earned himself and that with them in the palm of his hand he felt safe, on solid island turf from which he could see the dangerously teeming sea. Or something along those lines. Never had I had such a tangible sense of worth, steady affluence or material security as I did as I watched Robert's half-crown ritual over and over again. Only after he had completed it in silence, and with an awe much like the awe in which the Serbian peasant holds bread, a Frenchman holds wine, a Russian holds the Tsar, a Greek holds the olive, Robert would resume our conversation wherever he had left it.

I would be lying if I claimed that I didn't enjoy Robert's company during those three weeks. I would even go so far as to say that with him, and only with him, did I feel relaxed and dignified. Unlike the unruly student lads among whom I found myself, Robert never let the opportunity pass to remind me of the difference between my social position and his, which were, in England, as I came to understand, further apart than they would have been in Serbia. Robert, a clerk with only a secondary degree, felt that between him and someone who "was attending the postgraduate course at University" there yawned a social abyss which only under the most fortunate of circumstances – such as our friendship – and only by sheer coincidence could he bridge. While in any other context this penchant of his for underscoring our differences would have made me exceedingly uncomfortable, I must admit that then, perhaps not fully cognisant of it myself, it suited me. It soothed the wounds which my self-esteem had suffered during those first few days spent adapting and deciphering a mysterious environment. Having learned, however, the essential facts of Robert's origins (rosy-cheeked, slicked up as if for the St Sava Day assembly, he related the sad story with too much breeze and levity, as if it were something long past and forgotten with no bearing on his present life), I saw, despite his effort to conceal it, how his solitary pain and the presumed lack of a father's love had left a void for which he would spend the rest of his life trying to compensate. His parents had apparently divorced while he was still quite small, so he had grown up extremely attached to his mother, who had died when he was 18. His uncle had helped him financially to complete school in Exeter and qualify as an accountant while giving him to know that this was the last thing he would ever do for the boy.

"Happily enough," as Robert added, to the best of my recollection, "as I'd be dead, or mad, if I had to live with the old scoundrel!"

Robert's gaiety, however, did not deceive me. I was quite certain that our friendship relied less on the hierarchical distinction which, for different reasons, suited us both, than on the fortunate affinity of Robert's feeling of isolation in the world with my feeling of isolation in Bristol. Even today, I cannot see that at that moment in our friendship I might possibly have divined the reasons which would lead to its rupture. I suppose Robert's remarkable predilection for rumour might have alerted me, the delight he took in it and the skill with which he gossiped about the other boarders, Miss Trickey, even poor old Mary. Somehow he knew all there was to know of these people's private secrets or habits, and it brought him no end of spinsterly pleasure to inform others of them with ignoble delight, with a wit which did not entirely mask his malice. I had but to utter someone's name and I would hear, for example, how old Mrs Capps never bought her own daily paper, but rather furtively pinched herself a copy of yesterday's once someone else had discarded it; how the teacher, Miss Bridges, had a lover fifteen years her junior, a common waiter; and how Mr Peele from the room across from ours was a "hairy brute of a man", as Robert put it with aversion, informing me that the gentleman bathed only once monthly. He advised me never to set foot inside Peele's "stinking lair without a gas mask". Robert's colleagues, whom I had never met, his superiors and inferiors at the Town Hall where he worked, fared no better, and he even knew the occasional choice titbit about one of my professors.

"Dr Valentine Carleton, you say? Do you know they call him a DOM?"

"No. What is a DOM?"

"A dirty old man."

"A dirty old man! Why?"

"For Christ's sake, Steven, you can imagine why!"

And though I found Robert's penchant for gossip a trifle irksome, and it often struck me as rather beneath him, nevertheless I explained, if not justified, it by his desire to entertain me, to sustain a conversation which undoubtedly would have floundered had it relied on my conversational abilities. Robert simply did what he could to put us at ease so that I should feel inadequate as seldom as possible. As youthful in appearance as he was, with ruddy cheeks which fairly burned after a pint of beer and a good dinner in a cosy restaurant, he did whatever he could to please me. Reaching far beyond mere courtesy, he was – no matter what I thought of it subsequently – a true friend such as I sorely needed just then.

I dare to use that word. After our third weekend together, we were indeed friends. I knew that we would have switched to "ti" by then in Belgrade and we would have confided our youthful troubles to each other and exchanged our most private thoughts about the future. In fact, that is precisely what we were doing in England. Our "you" to one another most definitely had the ring of the "heartfelt ti", as Pushkin would have put it, not like the "empty vi". In particularly high spirits after our third shared Saturday dinner at Miss Trickey's boarding house, dinners which were invariably better and more lively than they were on ordinary days (we would get grapefruit for starters, or a slice of melon with ham, or shepherd's pie, and then a pork roast, from which our ecstatic, prattling landlady would carve slices so thin that you could see straight through them on the table in the corner of the dining room by the window through which they passed the food from the kitchen. She would lay them on the plates we brought up and spoon gravy over them in a cultivated boarding-house way. Or we'd have lamb-chops or, less frequently, turkey with cranberry sauce, but always with the same vegetables: a few boiled peas, green beans or Brussels sprouts. For dessert, there'd be some sort of cream, a pudding, fruit cake – actually a version of *patišpanj* with raisins, almonds and candied fruit – or there'd be an array of cheeses with salty crackers, and we'd be relaxed and full, blessed after a strenuous day's walk. It was at the end of the third weekend, when we were not yet ready to retire for the night, that Robert, red-cheeked, suggested we have a drop of port in his room.

"I've had it for nearly a year. My chief's Christmas present to 'hardworking, conscientious and loyal Rackham'," he said, extracting the bottle from the cupboard, lending, as he often did, a sarcastic twist to the chief's gesture and congratulations on the card, which still hung on a golden ribbon round the neck of the bottle.

Robert's room was somewhat larger than mine and, though in the way it was furnished it was entirely identical, there was a host of his own possessions, and they gave his room the feel of home, not at all like the temporary residence my room was. A number of figurines, decorative plates with dedications, tapestries, shells, pills, his "Exeter School of Commerce and Economics" diploma, a dozen framed photographs (for the most part pictures of him and his mother, together or separate, at various seasons of the year), and a multitude of other odds and ends made the room feel ornate and yet charmingly tidy. His bathrobe and slippers were arranged in the corner as they always were, his bed was neat as a pin, everything was in its place, precisely as it ought to be, meticulously dusted. I remember thinking that if I were ever to invite Robert to my room I would have to do a major cleaning. The room was lit by a standard lamp in the corner and the bluish glow of the gas flame from the hearth. Robert sat on a pillow by the fireplace, while I took the love-seat, already knowing that such gas heaters were one of the most unpleasant things about living in modest English homes: if you turned your face towards the flame, your front roasted while your back froze; it was no good turning the other way for longer than a few minutes, because the same thing would happen behind. Heated by the good dinner and Robert's port, I was feeling comfortably warm already.

After a second glass of port, Robert asked me, during a brief lull in the conversation, whether I had ever been in love. Inquisitively. Out of the blue.

Rather startled, I explained, as decently as I could with my limited English, that I had had a single, entirely meaningless sexual experience, but that, to tell the truth, I never had been in love. I believe, if I am not sorely mistaken – it is difficult to be certain after forty years – I believe that even then, as I answered Robert's indiscreet query, the vision of the shapely, red-headed Englishwoman I had seen in my classes flashed through my head, but even if it did, I had nothing I could say about her since I hadn't made her acquaintance. It would be interesting to find out whether I did or did not think of Elizabeta at that moment only because I would like to know when I began to think of her – that is, to refresh my conviction that love, or rather an unusually powerful interest, was born the very first moment I laid eyes on her. Whatever the case, it was then that Robert, without prompting from me, began to speak of his great love which had ended unhappily two years earlier. He had been abandoned. He was aching. More out of awkwardness than curiosity I enquired, "Is she married now?"

I remember, purely from the linguistic point of view, that the way Robert chose to respond struck me as odd. "No," he said. "The person hasn't got married, so far as I know."

Despite my protestations, Robert poured me a third glass of port, sat next to me on the love-seat and began going on about how in the brief time since we had got to know each other he had grown unusually attached to me; that it seemed to him that I was one of an extremely small number of people he had grown to love in the course of his life; that his life seemed different, more meaningful and joyful, since he knew he would be seeing me at dinner every evening; since each week ended with a weekend we would spend together, alone; and on and on in that vein, using language which, for the first time in those three weeks, was unintelligible to me in places, because Robert had suddenly begun to speak too fast, and to use uncommon words and phrases. Of course, today it seems ridiculous that even then, at that moment, it did not occur to me that Robert's pronouncements might disclose his homosexuality. But in fact I had never contemplated such a thing. Of course, I knew that homosexuality existed, but it was something so bizarre that it simply could not occur among the people I knew. All I felt was a bit awkward because of the parts of his speech which I couldn't grasp; because of the agitation his trembling voice betrayed; because of his flaming countenance; because of his eyes trying to engage mine, which – baffled, even frightened – I'd lowered, staring fixedly at my hands. Had I been able to use Serbian, perhaps I might have come up with some jaunty witticism to ease the pathos of his words; I could have turned into a joke that which he intended to be entirely serious and which was, even for my Slavic soul, too emotional. But with my English, I couldn't even begin to imagine doing this, so, growing ever more bewildered, I remained silent and waited for a lull in Robert's speech to thank him for the port and be off to bed. Instead, Robert drew closer to me and took my hand. Astonished, I looked up at him and only then, for the first time, wondered, "Lord have mercy, is this man a fairy?"

The next minute, he was asking permission to kiss me, which I refused, jumping to my feet, shouting a sentence which was the best I could manage, 'No, Robert, I do not kiss men." Appalled, I asked myself, "Could this really be happening? Did I really spend three weeks with this ruddy-faced sod? Am I now alone with a bugger in his room? Drink port? Holding his hand? I see an English Puro Moca with cheeks blazing and hands trembling, his parting mussed, a lock of hair tumbling over his forehead – is all this happening?" My head buzzed with the only story about sods I had ever heard. In it, my friend, a journalist, one Jole Vukadinović, having realised that he was sharing his room at the World's Fair in Paris with a homosexual, a chap from Sarajevo, beat the bugger until he bled and then threw him down the hotel stairs. When Robert tried to cling to me, urging me to believe that love between men is purer and finer than love between people of the opposite sexes, that no woman would ever love me the way he did, I considered responding in the only way I knew, by striking him, or at least shoving him away roughly. But before I managed to do so, I was stopped, paralysed really, by the knowledge that I wasn't the slightest bit angry at Robert, that I had no urge to hurt him, but that I was terribly angry, more than I'd ever been, at myself, embittered, ashamed of the predicament in which I had embroiled myself. All I wanted was for the repulsive scene to be over, so that I could extricate myself from the semi-darkness, get the port out of my head and be left alone. So I wriggled out of Robert's embrace, barked, 'Stop it, Robert!", ashamed and hurt rather than angry, and fled towards my room.

Robert, however, did not desist. He ran after me, pleading with me to stay a moment longer, that he would explain everything, that I hadn't understood. Without heeding his words, I flew into my room and, despite his attempt to follow me, slammed and locked the door. This was not the end of that foolish, humiliating evening, though. Robert whined, whimpered through the closed door, pleading with me to let him in, that I must let him explain, that what might, in Serbia, seem offensive, in England was considered quite commonplace – all in that same agitated, even frantic, voice. I was so unprepared for the situation that not a single idea formed in my head, nothing which might bring the shameful English scene to an end. Even my sole firm resolution – not to open the door under any circumstances – began to weaken since I suddenly, with additional, horrible terror, realised that the boarding house had become silent. One of my neighbours might easily hear Robert's hissing and not so muted whispers. The very thought that this story might spread through Bristol, reach my colleagues and professors, or, heaven forbid, all the way to Belgrade, so panicked me that I nearly thought to open the door, if nothing else worked, to end the perverse performance by the fairy in the hallway. I had curled my fingers round the latch, agonising over what to do, when I heard the squeaking of unoiled hinges elsewhere on the floor. Robert, luckily, heard it too, and that is what finally convinced him to retreat, as quickly as he could, back to his room.

Soaked through, I collapsed by the door onto the floor, unable to move, overcome with shame, my eyes shut, miserable. Only miserable.

It was much later, in bed, my eyes wide open, that the first thoughts began to penetrate my sense of shame. No matter how bitter and berating they were, they did mean progress in comparison to the paralysis from which I had emerged. How could I have been so blind as not to wonder about Robert's perverted leanings! He had told me clearly, dolt that I was, that the "person" who had abandoned him hadn't married, and of course he had used the word *person* since the individual in question was a man! How could I have encouraged him to the point that the appalling thing that had just happened might not, in fact, be the end to my humiliation. Blessed Lord! Ruddy Rackham, the accountant and gossipmonger, got me, Stevan Medaković, Milutin's son and Nanka's charge, tipsy on port like some cook's under-age daughter, so that he could have his way with her! Rackham in the role of those middle-aged Belgrade tradesmen (our family barber, Živojin, a bachelor, boasted he was one of the finest) who would lie in wait at the train station for peasant women whom he, elegant and perfumed, could lure to his rooms, bewildered and frightened by the metropolis as they were, and ravish them! Did I resemble the cook's daughter or a timid peasant woman? These thoughts were so crushing that I didn't dare let them twice through my mind. I howled out loud and plunged my face into my pillow to shield my mind from those vile images with noise and feathers. Innocence unprotected! Maybe I ought to have beaten the fag and fled, leaving him with the conviction that he had nearly met with success; maybe Jole Vukadinović's treatment of that man from Sarajevo was the only suitable reaction. If he was already taking the risk of declaring his intentions so openly, Robert was risking having his teeth punched in. He must have got used to such things. Maybe it was still not too late; perhaps I should give him a sound thrashing as soon as the opportunity arose if he attempted to get close to me again.

Fortunately, no such occasion arose. There were several moments over the next few days when he tried to broach a conversation, but I cut him off, so he desisted. He abruptly became quite cold and distant. Whenever we met in the hallway or saw each other at dinner, he would turn away from me, hurt and disdainful, or would mumble greetings as if from on high. I would return his greetings, always with a sinking sense of shame which I concealed by my expressionless face and chill voice. In time, I recovered. I experienced a strong wave of revulsion when I saw Robert with a new friend. He was a little fellow, an Italian with a large bottom and with Rackham's own name – Roberto (Robert and Roberto, what a couple!) – always tossing his thick, wavy hair back from his face. I watched them through the window as they said goodbye in front of the boarding house, holding each other's hands, not letting go. Imagining, against my will, myself in the place of the large-rumped Italian chap, shame raised a blush, like a persistent rash. I felt that I couldn't wash it off for days.

Well, there's no way of escaping who you are, so I, of course, continued to live with this rash, which time and treatment did heal. There can be no doubt, however, that the need to justify myself due to the humiliating fact that someone could look at me just as Robert looked at the large-bottomed Italian fairy wearing high heels like a woman's was why I got entangled in a conversation about homosexuality which began in the Victoria Rooms common rooms of the University Student Club.

It was one evening after lectures were done for the day, when the club usually had the largest number of visitors. Some were talking, some reading the paper, others writing letters or listening to the radio (still a little strange, a recent innovation). I believe we arrived at the topic because someone asked John Downing what he was reading so attentively in a magazine – I dare say it was *Criterion* or *London Mercury*. John was reading a report, or was it a commentary on a report compiled by a commission, on homosexuality among schoolboys. While I am no longer capable of reconstructing the conversation, I remember distinctly how the way that John and another student, Barbara, spoke of homosexuality nudged me, despite my inadequate English, to offer my own opinion. John, you see, was mocking the report. He sneered at it, retelling with irony the concern which the older generation was showing for sexuality at young men's colleges, latter-day Sodoms and Gomorrahs. He was not claiming that homosexuality did or did not exist in schools, but his ridicule of the puritanical moralism of adults demonstrated that he thought the report was worthless.

Barbara asked the very question which was on the tip of my tongue: Was John ridiculing the report because he felt there was no homosexuality in men's colleges in England or because he viewed homosexuality as something which did not merit such treatment? Barbara posed the question in a measured tone, but behind the show of academic curiosity there was, I am certain, a tiny well of rage, a razor-edged cynicism, a testy urge to quarrel which I registered at the time, but was only later able to interpret. At that moment, I understood only that the question had thrown John, who had to think for a moment before he replied, that it had stirred a little ire in our group and prompted the younger members, Leslie for example, to erupt in peals of laughter like teenagers who had heard a racy joke. All at once rather courteous and cold, John responded that he had no view into the bedrooms of English men's colleges and that he would rather leave it to the commission's voyeurs to continue their "keyhole peeping and toilet eavesdropping, the old lechers", thus provoking a round of boisterous laughter and evading Barbara's question.

Barbara later congratulated me on my courage that amid that "paederast scum", as she hissed with genuine loathing, I had said what I did, without waiting for the laughter provoked by John's response to die down, but I did not deserve her congratulations. I was not a master of even the most fundamental facts with which I might, perhaps, have been capable of divining the background of the confrontation between John and Barbara. I simply expressed what I thought of homosexuality, that it was, of course, a vile phenomenon in both the moral and the aesthetic senses. With the humiliating experience with Robert so fresh in my mind, I am certain that I presented my opinion with vehemence and revulsion. I then proceeded to explain that in Serbia people were particularly revolted by – I didn't know the English word for "guzičar", so I hesitated.

Barbara leaped to my assistance: "Poofs," she said in an icy voice, which set the younger lads off again into gales of laughter while John glowered at her. Aside from being the healthy resistance of a young and untainted nation, I explained, the revulsion Serbs felt had historical roots, since the perverse and decadent Turks were inclined to sodomy, humiliating Serbian landowners in this manner. I completed my speech in the face of an unnatural hush mitigated only by the triumphant expression on Barbara's face, which, however, did not linger. With a single sentence, enunciated slowly and with deadly irony, John brought an end to the discussion, accompanied by a deafening outburst of hilarity from his fans, by saying, "Barbara, you've heard Steven! Hurry! To Serbia!"

That same evening, as I was going down the stairs of Victoria Rooms on my way to my boarding house, John caught up with me. "Steven," he said, looking me straight in the eye, anticipating with curiosity the changes in my expression, "have I never told you?"

"What?" I asked.

"That I am irredeemably homosexual."

When he had savoured my astonishment, he added, with a charming grin, "See you tomorrow, old chap," and thumped me congenially on the shoulder, setting off triumphantly down the street without a backward glance.

Rackham had shown me that pederasty is more than just a nasty tale whispered around Turkish baths but rather something which, no matter how difficult it was for me to understand, did indeed exist. John, with his victorious admission, did far more: he presented homosexuality, or at least he wished to present it, as a socially acknowledged, almost morally desirable phenomenon. "You mean I've never told you?" Not only that, "I am irredeemably homosexual!" Just like that! As if he had said, "I am a stamp collector," or, "I am an irredeemably honest bloke."

Even today, I do not know how I might precisely describe my frame of mind at that moment and over the next few days, because my feelings, seething and contradictory, created an inconceivable muddle. My disgust grew even stronger, more combative and complex, because, unlike poor Rackham, a mere ruddy-cheeked, lonely accountant, a gossiping fag with no friends, John Downing was brilliant. Despite his youth, he was already a scholar, one of the first to earn his doctorate from Bristol in the historical sciences and, because of that, an arbiter in questions of social order and taste, a leader, an authority, particularly for the undergraduate students with whom he liked to socialise – now, after his declaration, I knew why. Aside from my growing intolerance towards the world-view that I had begun to sense behind that perversion, I seemed to feel a powerful, still inexplicable, alarm in the days following John's impertinence. It took me a while before I could find a better word for the qualms that plagued me, nor could I make much progress in my interpretation of that feeling after first naming it. I knew, of course, that it was not homosexuality itself which threatened and unnerved me, but that it seemed to be contributing to my sense of a world less steady and reliable than it had been just the day before. The outlines of a new, bizarre cause for alarm began to take shape with agony in my mind. The very fact that I was capable of and willing to discuss homosexuality, for example, with someone who spoke in its defence on an equal footing, even with superiority, threatened the very foundations of my sense of security, of everything cherished which I had brought with me from my home, from tormented Serbia and from Nanka, most of all. John's impertinence, Rackham's assumptions, tea with milk and turkey with cranberry sauce, the Library of the British Museum, Barbara fuming yet restrained, blessedly cheery Miss Trickey, green English grass, the English language were flooding realms of my spirit I had thought to be impervious to water, to be as soaked in the spirit of Serbia as a tent is with waterproofing. I began spying on myself because I discovered to my dread that with each new day, more and more of my inviolable beliefs were beginning, at least in conversation, to show – not their fallibility, not that – but certainly their openness to doubt, to a different perspective. I was shaken each and every time I caught myself in the act of betrayal, stricken with panic at each sign that I had lost my faith. Oh, how pathetically I reproached myself whenever, if only for a moment, I caught myself traitorously considering one of the inviolable Serbian values not with Serbian, but with these newly indifferent, objective, eyes.

No wonder this was happening; it would have been odd had it been otherwise. I had come to England straight out of Serbian Arcadia, straight from a fairy tale in the rolling hills of Šumadija! The time of my childhood had been a time of romantic fascination with everything

Serbian, and I was one of the most active among my peers in this regard. I knew the epic songs and stories about the heroes of the medieval battle of Kosovo and the Serbian uprisings against Ottoman rule a century ago. Especially, of course, thanks to Nanka. Tireless Nanka, Nanka the knitter, the healer. I always thought of her as Nanka Gojkovica after the woman from folk tales who was walled into a bridge to make it strong, but who nonetheless managed to nurse her baby through a gap in the stones. Nanka was Milosav Marković's widow. Milosav had been an impoverished wine merchant from Kožetina in Župa (known as Aleksandrovac today) with whom my father, Milutin, had done business for many years. It is difficult to say precisely what moved Milutin to choose Nanka when, after my mother's unexpected death in childbirth, he needed to bring a woman into the household to tend to the newborn baby, Cveta, and me, one and a half years old. When I learned, as an adult, of the morbid circumstances facing Nanka when she moved to Belgrade, it seemed peculiar to me that Father had chosen her, stricken by such grave tragedy as she was. The 28-year-old teacher from Kruševac had married Milosav who, much older than she and widowed, had no children from his first marriage. They lived well, though modestly, and Nanka often spoke to us of her husband out of a sense of duty. In this way, Milosav could live on a while longer in someone else's, rather than only her own, memories. After two happy years, Nanka found she was pregnant. As so often happened in the morality tales she told us, their presentiment of happiness so sudden and so vast that they felt themselves undeserving of it turned, in a mere two months, into a cruel, merciless punishment from God. Milosav suddenly died. His dying words were "If it is a boy, his name should be Stevan" after his father, who had fallen as a young man in the Serbian–Turkish war of 1877 on the bridge at Čečine. Two months later, the boy, ill-fated Stevan, was stillborn.

When I learned of this tragedy, I was struck by how peculiar, even bizarre, my father's notion seemed to me. To take in a woman who had lost her own son, Stevan, only days before, and with him all hope of ever having a child of her own, to nurse another woman's son, Stevan, and another woman's newborn baby, Cveta, who had survived, as she came into the world, by killing her own mother, seemed hardly a decision that my father, a conscientious merchant with his head on his shoulders and a healthy dose of conservatism, would take. What reasonable person would willingly, beyond the dictates of necessity, surround his child, in those most crucial first years of life, with so many deaths?

There had to be reasons, so I searched for them doggedly and found them, though I was torn about whether they were genuine. I believe that the first and most important reason should be sought in the character of Milutin, a merchant from Slavonia, a region across the Danube from Belgrade, outside Serbia proper in the Croatian lands. He gradually shifted his trade to Belgrade, starting well before he married and I was born. He was an old-fashioned man of few words but convinced that honesty was the best recommendation for any merchant, and that citizens should behave with honour. Even those who differed with him over some issue or who ventured to compete with him never denied his integrity and his honour. Dressed Austrian-style in a redingote with a spotless, stiff white collar, trimmed moustache and beard, he enjoyed in cosy little Belgrade where everyone knew everything about everyone, the reputation of a gentleman who could be taken at his word.

Milutin did not earn this reputation overnight. Hard-working and enterprising in sales of hardware before the war, he founded his success on the modernisation of his trading practices. He was the first merchant in Belgrade to introduce set prices, thus obviating bazaar-style bartering. He was the first to give his customers itemised receipts, which meant that he couldn't get away with weighting the scales or cheating in his calculations. He made special efforts to enhance his range of goods through lively trade with other places, particularly with Trieste, which later helped him to get out of the hardware business relatively easily when it began to decline, and switch successfully to foreign trade and finance. Even the large sums of money he began to handle did not turn the honourable Milutin's head. Even the nastiest among his acquaintances said that he would never lose out even if he worked intentionally against his own interests. God looked after him, apparently.

If one considers Milutin's decision to bring the stricken Nanka into his household, it is certainly possible to say that his action was in keeping with his character. If he had been unable to prevent his friend Milosav's ruin, the least he could do would be to help the man's widow. Perhaps Milutin realised the perversity of merging two losses into an arrangement of mutual benefit. He brought into his home a woman he imagined would be no more than a nurse for his children, feeling that the brief sojourn in Belgrade might ease the poor woman's despair.

I know, however, that every bit as consequential to Milutin was the fact that Nanka possessed precisely those virtues that permeate Serbia's epic folk songs and legends. My Serbophile father cared most of all that his children should be raised in the true Serbian spirit.

Like so many other Serbs living outside Serbia proper, Milutin had cultivated a profound devotion to and religious admiration for his heroic countrymen long before there was any real danger to him in the Croatian lands, long before the war that finally broke out in 1906 between Serbia and Austria-Hungary (he moved in time to Belgrade) would have forced him out of his birthplace of Lipik and his offices in Zagreb and Trieste. He never spoke of this, of course. He was reserved and discreet in all his dealings, but the fact that he did not marry until he had moved the hardware branch of his wholesale business to Belgrade suggests that the main reason he had for abandoning his more orderly and safe Austrian birthplace for oriental, backward Serbia was so that his children could be born among their own, in freedom. Chances are that Milutin would have undertaken the move even if he had been able to predict 1918 and the creation of Yugoslavia. His burgeoning feeling of patriotism simply did not allow him to settle down before he had planted himself in his own kingdom, which my honourable father found particularly dear to his heart once decadent Obrenović was removed from the throne along with licentious Mašinova and replaced by steadfast Petar Karađorđević.

A soldier educated in Saint-Cyr and Metz, a legionnaire in the Franco–Prussian War, a royal volunteer who had engaged in the Bosnian–Herzegovinian uprising against the Turks with a brigade of two hundred heroes, Karađorđević rode a white horse through the streets of newly liberated Belgrade on December 15, 1914, a dignified father and fellow sufferer with his subjects in the great exodus through

Albania in World War I. He was a straightforward, militarily rigorous king who fitted the ideal in the patriotic imaginations of expatriate Serbs almost perfectly. Milutin remained unswerving in this regard until the end of his days, committed to the Karađorđe dynasty ruling the state, the King as the supreme champion of national unity, the Radical party of peasant landowners, merchants, exporters, bankers and industrialists, the higher-level ecclesiastical hierarchy and officials, all with a programme unchanged from its founding in 1881 up to Milutin's death in 1932. It was Serbia's sacred obligation to strive for unification, to accelerate economic development and independence from Austria-Hungary. Time would pass and Milutin's views would seem more and more old-fashioned, even ridiculous, countered as they were by the growing cynicism and disappointment in Yugoslavia, but this steadfast patriot from Slavonia, a greater Serb than any Serb living in Serbia proper, clung to his fiery turn-of-the-century convictions. He would say, "The bones of our forefathers watch us from their tombs," an eerily sombre sentiment that chilled me, despite the fact that I didn't really understand it. I imagined how I was being watched from the dark graves in the churchyard by bug-eyed skulls draped in ancestral spiderwebs. When my father uttered the mythical words "For Kosovo – Kumanovo, for Slivnica – Bregalnica," another sentence I did not understand, but because of the way Father uttered the names of these battles, I was convinced that it was some form of incantation protecting the Serbs from harm.

Milutin's fervent Serbdom did not sit comfortably with his gentlemanly sense of moderation in all things and his European habits in everyday matters. He never spoiled us, for instance. He never spoke tenderly with us, not because he didn't love us, but because somehow he wasn't able to. When he had to kiss us, for a birthday, for Christmas, when he came home from a trip, he did so clumsily, and I remember well that his demonstrations of affection always filled me with embarrassment. Later, I understood why: the silence, the coldness, the moderation concealed Milutin's timid, boyish sense of shame, the very same sense of shame with which I have been battling my entire life.

Probably not even admitting it to himself, my father cultivated a strong, deeply rooted aversion to all things Turkish. Our first home on Karađorđe Street, the business centre of turn-of-the-century Belgrade, still had an Ottoman floor plan and appearance, but our new house, built after the war in Zorina Street, was European in design. Milutin purchased almost all the furniture himself, most of it in Trieste. The bathroom was built according to his drawings and an Austrian model, and there were no oriental kilims on the walls and floor, despite the fact that at the time they graced most of the city's prominent homes. Milutin drank café au lait every morning with *milchbrot*. He took snuff and smoked an English pipe, all of which was highly unusual at the time in Serbia. His attire, his subscription to the Viennese newspaper *Wiener Courier*, all this contributed to the fact that few people considered this patriotic Serb to be a genuine Serb at all. Milutin, of course, must have known as much, and it must have grieved him. Adhering to the habits he had acquired living in Croatia, he felt guilty before his glorious fellow citizens as they wore their moccasins with pointed toes and typical Turkish attire. Somehow Milutin reconciled the contradiction between tastes and inclination.

It was that discovery which explained Nanka's arrival in our home. Since he never insisted that his children adopt his habits, and since he handed over almost all decisions regarding our education to Nanka, Milutin must have brought her as a model for us to aspire to. What he could not offer us himself, Nanka would give us effortlessly, simply by living with us. Just as others hired French governesses so that their children could painlessly adopt foreign customs and language, Milutin brought in Nanka so that Cveta and I, without ever knowing how and when, would become Serbs, permeated with the spirit of epic poetry and patriarchal values. Faithful to his beloved café au lait, he never complained of the fact that Nanka started off each morning with a shot of juniper brandy, and that instead of *milchbrot* and butter she breakfasted on cheese and raw sliced onion. He permitted her to bring kilims into her room, but more than that, he allowed her to drape them, first in the dining room and then in the children's room, over two long, low benches, which, when so covered, resembled the Turkish *minderluk,* and all this because he knew that he would never find anyone better than Nanka in the entire Serbian kingdom.

It is enough, after all those years, merely to close my eyes, and I can see her, as she was, striking, confident, busy. She was tall and thin, craggy, her features pronounced, almost a man's profile, a large nose (from her earliest childhood, Cveta had a knack for drawing, and she was especially good at Nanka's caricature). Her bearing was dignified, yet she knew her place. Her hair was a sort of ash grey in front with a long braid twisted up into a wispy and scraggly bun at the back, her face furrowed despite the fact that she was still a young, vital woman. Nanka always dressed in muted colours as she perched on the edge of the bed and recited poems or stories. "Seeing the death of his brothers" – who knows how many times I had heard this, always dreading the inevitable gory conclusion – "Zeka Buljubaša with his barebacked sons formed a chain and implored the Serbs who had retreated to return to fight. While there was gunpowder left, using bits of wood as shields, they kept the Turks at bay with their guns. When the gunpowder was gone, he and his barebacked sons unsheathed their sharp knives, looked up at the cloudy sky over Serbia one more time, looked back at the beautiful plains of Mačva, looked over the Drina to proud Bosnia, and then, invoking God and their people, they charged the Turks. And so it was that stabbing they were stabbed to the last man."

A sob caught in my throat, but I knew I must not cry. Nanka would not tolerate it. That wasn't Serbian and it wasn't manly, and before all else I must be a Serb and a man. Nanka was merciless about this. "Disgraceful," she would say sternly. "How are you going to bear the difficult things in life if you whimper at a story?"

"But Anta Bogičević cried, didn't he? He was a hero and a Serb, wasn't he?" I argued, searching for justification.

"So he did," said Nanka seriously, "but that was when he was so overcome with misery at being unable to find the words to describe the siege of the Loznice brigade."

"What about Prince Ivo of Semberija?" I was not going to give up easily. "Three times he fell, then as he began to die burning tears coursed down his cheeks!"

"Stevan, those were men of the spirit, men of conscience. They wept for the travails of their people, not out of weakness. You do not understand the Serbian heroes and their sacrifice. I won't tell you any more about our forefathers and their exploits."

Anyone who didn't know Nanka might have thought that she was making empty threats. But no. For months she would not recount a single story with a grim ending to me until I had become firmly convinced that I was able to face the torments of my people with no tears. Indeed, I have never cried since that time.

I soon divined that Nanka was not telling us stories as entertainment but as instruction. She must have been quite selective since even today I recall fragments of the poems, legends and sayings that formed a watertight moral order. "No man may place his hopes in anyone but God and his own hands" was a sentence carved into my mind for all time. Life in Nanka's stories was harsh on the Serbian people, but precisely for that reason it was glorious. I well remember her watching the Austrian troops march into Belgrade in October 1915 from her hiding place behind the curtains. Her face frozen, her eyelids narrowed, dangerously quiet, she spoke softly (though I was standing next to her, I could barely hear her), but firmly, resolutely:

> In blood our faiths will swim,
> The better of us will be he who does not drown.

Milutin was known to declare the occasional pathetic patriotic sentiment, but never so decisively. There was something in Milutin's demeanour of the parade, something lighter than in Nanka's. Nanka's thought defied judgement. Nanka did not wonder about things. She uttered judgements. So it would be, or it would not be at all.

I remember the horrors of the brief initial Austrian occupation of Belgrade. Clinging to Nanka's skirts and peering at the great masses of soldiers who thundered along the streets, terrified by the blood in which our faiths were about to swim, I asked, "What will we do now, Nanka?"

Without looking at me, without flinching, she recited,

We will die and shed our blood
To protect our oath like heroes,
Our glorious name and our sacred freedom.

It was difficult to counter the force of Nanka's convictions, no matter how limited their intellectual scope may have been, with proofs grounded in reason. When I tried, as an adult, to do precisely that, she denied my right, swiftly and cruelly, to doubt. She would hear out my wise words, my analysis, and then she would strike it off like a head on a chopping block. "Many's the opinion, Stevan, that chills my heart," or, in her way, in verse: "'He who picks apart, shall never strike the mark', or so say the Serbian people, and the people, Stevan, know their own mind."

That was Nanka. When I was fighting for my life with a raging fever amid the impoverishment of the Occupation, even then I do not recall her, once, coddling me. For three days and three nights, she never left my bedside. Every half-hour she changed my compresses, rubbed me down with vinegar, but never did she baby me. As if we were in battle, she'd say, "Don't give in, my falcon. You are a hero. Serbia's pride and joy." She rose before sunrise, at the first signs of light, and went to bed shortly after it set, though this village custom had no real place in the city.

She had a peasant woman's modesty regarding feminine intimacy. She nursed us hidden from the eyes of others. I never saw her undress, dress or wash herself. She appeared, always the same, in her clothing of subdued hues; somewhere, off by herself, she ironed her clothes, washed, dressed and undressed.

Nanka's way of classifying people was clear-cut and dual: women and men, masters and servants, the honourable, wise and upstanding and those who had broken away to become appalling outcasts. Thanks to Nanka, I knew from my very first steps that the fact that I was a man brought with it honour but also obligations. Nanka made no mistakes. Like a skilful chief of protocol at the royal court, she knew what was to be done, and what behaviour suited whom. Milutin's orders or wishes were never open to discussion; they were immediately obeyed without thought or complaint. Nanka used "vi" with him and he used "ti" with her, but his "ti" was most respectful. Only at Father's explicit request did she acquiesce to dine with the family, but as soon as she finished eating her meal she would rise from the table, leaving Father to smoke his pipe and drink his coffee alone, deep in the newspaper or his thoughts.

I cannot help but wonder if Nanka cultivated at least a tiny suspicion about Milutin's courteous manner, if she was in any way perplexed by the absence of male arrogance in him. The comforts with which Milutin surrounded himself must have seemed a trifle indecent to her, the way in which he suited his every whim and the earnestness with which he pursued his personal hygiene. I have no proof for this, but it seems to me that Milutin had great respect for Nanka, and that somewhere, hidden from view, he even feared her a little, while Nanka was most grateful to Milutin, though somewhere, even more hidden from view, she scorned him a little. The differences between them did not jar the harmony of their relations; quite the contrary, they reinforced it. Nanka, all of a piece, her views carved in stone, without a single doubt in her stalwart mind, was the very opposite of Milutin, who, though very successful, did not succeed in concealing from the adult eye of his son and the penetrating gaze of his housekeeper his divided self, his shame, his shyness.

So how else could I have felt in England but terrified – I, the devoted cadet of Nanka's drill academy – at even the slightest hint that the convictions of my stalwart Gojkovica might be questioned, as I began to see the world through other eyes? My feeling of terror was hardly surprising. Would I betray her?

Only a few days before the evening in the Glengyle Inn, I spent a weekend, as if in a dream, at the family home of Graham Ellenborough with a compelling sense that I had stepped into some other world. Later, I saw more spacious homes and more gracious parks in England, but Graham's seemed royally lavish to me, with vast french windows through which you could venture out on to a lawn every bit as green and large as the one around Windsor Castle. Breakfast in bed, a stroll in the private wood and along the golf course slopes with two borzois, bowling after the tennis that had been cut short by rain. Relaxed people around me who said, mumbling arrogantly into their beards, a little bored, "Life, after all" (I hear Graham's voice mingling with the cheerful ring of Chinese porcelain on the silver tray the butler was using to bring in the tea) "is an affair of charm, not an affair of passion." I understood nothing. Graham's cousin explained to her friend, comfortably ensconced among the pillows in an armchair with a Persian cat in her lap, that the right gown for a particular occasion would be gold, because the event was in October, when chrysanthemums and gold would work together in the light of the setting sun to best advantage. After dinner, taking a cigarette from a shagreen box, the stately Lady Brown recounted, while the flames from the fireplace danced their shadows on her almost masculine, rugged features, an appalling scene at the home of Sir John Studdart, who dressed his servants like the waitresses in those unbearable new tearooms. Graham's father, the most famous of the English tiger hunters (a photograph in his study: tropical helmet, plus-fours, his foot on a dead beast), felt that all credit was due, though rather indifferently, to the King for his participation in the process of making Cyprus a Crown colony, relating this to the jolly good attempts (though he did not think too highly of them either) at the annexation of Mosul. When I happened, on my last day there, to find myself alone with him, we carried on a mad conversation which did not so much confuse as infuriate me. I barely masked my rage with my courteous responses to his inane questions. Out of the clear blue sky, while smoothing his grey moustache, Graham's old man suddenly declared, "I'm so glad you're not a teacher."

"A teacher?" I was astonished. "Why a teacher?"

"Well, they never seem real somehow." As if he had exhausted that topic in a single breath, he impatiently and with curiosity changed the subject completely. "Is fox-hunting very popular among the upper classes in Serbia?"

And while I mused on how things stood with fox-hunting among the Serbian aristocracy, he continued, without waiting for me to respond, never taking a breath, "Do you enjoy hunting, anyway?"

If only to keep him on his favourite subject, I decided to answer affirmatively, baffled by the volley of disjointed, ridiculous sentences and wondering, seething, whether he was genuinely mad or merely playing at it, something which the most intelligent English people held in rather high regard, as I had already managed to discern: "Yes, I do enjoy it," I said.

He was extremely pleased with my answer. As if this were a load off his mind, he breathed a sigh of relief: "Oh, hunting's all right. It's reading you should beware of. Healthy young men should not read. They end up becoming broken-winded ushers."

Only later did I check in the dictionary and learn what "broken-winded ushers" were, but, of course it never occurred to me to ask him, especially since he then rose and, like someone who has just completed some important task, left the room.

Enraged by the panic which was welling up in me despite my wishes to the contrary, I knew that nothing was entirely beyond doubt. Were these people serious, or were they toying with me? Ellenborough with his tigers, Lady Brown with her tea maids, Graham with his charm and his passion? What was it they were talking about? I fumed, but there was no single reliable answer available to any of my questions.

The first day following my return from this visit, I was sitting with Graham, John Downing and Barry Davis at the Berkeley, having tea. Merely to revive the conversation which had reached a momentary lull, John, extremely cordial towards me after our unfinished discussion of homosexuality, asked me to tell them something important about my country, something which could help them understand it. I looked slowly around the lavish, cosy room, at the tables covered with impeccably starched cloths, at the heaps of English porcelain, the silver teapots that gleamed, cluttering every inch of white surface, then at the inquisitive and polite faces of my English acquaintances. Suddenly, my shyness disappeared, and in its place I felt a huge tenderness for the grimy people I had left behind. I could see their superiority over the easygoing idiosyncrasies of people like these around me who had been taking tea at 4 for hundreds of years, in a country where there had been universities for eight centuries and a royal family which had resolved its Obrenović–Karađorđević sorts of differences in the sixteenth century. So I told the most hair-raising stories: how, as an 11-year-old in 1914, I had seen the hanging of 17-year-old Mihajlo Radojčić on Terazije Square between the Balkan and Moskva Hotels; how the body of my 7-year-old sister Cveta looked when she was struck, only a few feet from me, by a shell from an Austrian gun. In the end I told them, by now myself a little disgusted and shocked, the pearl of all stories, about Milomilj, whom Father and I had met guarding his herd somewhere above the village of Krst na Rudniku one cold November day. The earth was frozen, and Milomilj – I explained in detail to the Englishmen – was jumping up and down to keep warm.

"How do you manage, barefoot?" my father asked him.

"The first cow will shit pretty soon. What happens then is wonderful: your feet in the warm manure, there is nothing more lovely, the heat climbs straight up to your ears!"

John burst out laughing. "For goodness sake, Stephen," he said, "what a story!"

But I, suddenly emptied, somehow satisfied, capable of a gleeful grin, paid no attention to John's laughter and said instead to Graham: "Milomilj for sure does not share your belief, Graham, that 'life is an affair of charm'."

"I suppose not," he said with, it seemed to me, a little scorn.

My short-lived self-confidence, my audacious Serbian diversion at the elegant Berkeley, quickly gave way to disquiet, however, which soon became my unflagging companion and tormentor. At the Glengyle Inn, eyes fixed on a willowy Englishwoman (a dark coat with a large rose pinned to the left lapel, fur-trimmed ankle-high shoes with small heels, one leg crossed over the other, sitting tall on a stool at the bar), alone with a pint of the English national beverage in her hand (Nanka loathed beer as a contemptible incursion among the Serbs) – even from this distance I can recall my acute agitation. And loneliness. And self-pity.

I have often recalled that dinner at the Glengyle Inn and am still inclined to attribute my feelings of loneliness and isolation to a supernatural power. An interchange of thoughts does exist. If the sender is strong and the receiver sensitive, souls may commune without the two ever exchanging a glance or a word.

How else could I have divined that evening that the lovely Englishwoman with whom I had never exchanged so much as a word, whose name I did not know, was every bit as lonely as I, as preoccupied as I was with thoughts other than those she disclosed to those around her? She responded to questions, an occasional word of hers made its way to me when the hubbub subsided, she smiled a few times, declined a second round – she appeared to be licking, rather than sipping, her drink – but – somehow I am certain of this – she smiled only because she had to, sipped because the others did and, most of all, though she was concealing the fact, would have preferred to be left alone. Barry, serious, earnest Barry, with his washed-out blue eyes behind the thick lenses of his spectacles, my English friend with the greatest integrity and, I'd say, the one closest to me, had no notion, of course, that all my attention was drawn to the bar, that I was barely listening to what he was saying about the behaviouristic nature of the law and legislation.

"It is characteristic of human life," I remember Barry shouting tirelessly, "that what is done by the majority of persons in a given situation takes on the quality of what ought to be done. The 'is' becomes an 'ought'." I felt genuinely, with all my senses, that my loneliness had become powerful and acute enough to attract to itself even the finest dust of other people's melancholy, let alone an isolation as large and chill as the one I felt to be spreading around Elizabeta. I knew absolutely nothing about her, but it seemed to me that evening that I could distinctly hear her cries for help wafting through the air along with the pleasing smells of fine tobacco and alcohol fumes. The cold wave of my vulnerability (the vulnerability of a loner among people different from himself, the literal owner of a pathetic world suddenly subject to impartial perusal) reached all the way to the tall beauty sitting on the bar stool, penetrated her sense of being abandoned and returned warmed by her candid gaze. Though Elizabeta, having heard a description of the feeling that struck me at the Glengyle Inn, said, slightly vexed, perhaps with a tinge of revulsion, that my story was "unbearably romantic and sickly sweet", I kept on believing that our souls met that evening in translumination, before we were even introduced.

I do not know whether Elizabeta seemed to others as bewitching and unreachable as she did to me from the first moment I caught sight of her, but it is certain that all of us, thanks to the incomprehensible thoughtlessness of the otherwise courteous Professor Young, learned (or at least were able to divine) a key fact of her biography. Intending to introduce a more open spirit to the classroom, he proposed that we introduce ourselves one by one and answer any questions our fellow students might have about us. And so we did. Elizabeta's turn came, but when she started to say her name, Professor Young, probably intending to be kind, beat the stately, red-haired young woman to it. "Oh, I know your name," he said, underlining the "your", I guess, to emphasise the distinction from our names, which he did not know. "You're Mrs Harris, are you not?"

Elizabeta faltered for an instant. Later I would learn that despite her alabaster complexion she was slow to blush, unlike most people with that sort of colouring. She remained calm, sighed, and then with a firm voice, perhaps a bit too certain, said, "No, Professor Young. I'm Miss Blake."

From that moment, I'm convinced, Miss Blake was cloaked in the mystery that arose in the space between the two spoken surnames and the states they implied. I knew that this girl who was informing us how she had taken a gap year between graduation from the prominent women's White College and her arrival in Bristol was – despite her obvious youth – a grown woman with a life of her own about which I had already begun to surmise I would never know the whole truth. What I do know for certain is that her experience, regardless of what it comprised, set her apart from the group on every occasion when I had the opportunity to observe her clandestinely, as I had at the Glengyle Inn.

Had that not been the case, however, could I have dared to approach Elizabeta, especially as I did at the Glengyle Inn? Even if I've forgotten some of the details, surely in one regard I cannot be mistaken: that I was exceedingly shy that evening. Of course, my linguistic clumsiness was already greatly diminished; now that the semester was well under way and hierarchies had been established based on knowledge and diligence, my eagerness had situated me well within them. Nevertheless, I would never have dared address a young woman who had not been properly introduced to me had I not felt the physical attraction between our two great states of loneliness in the midst of a boisterous crowd.

As I would later discover, Elizabeta had for some time, though not for the reasons I had in mind, meant to make my acquaintance. Was I not then sensing her wish, even if I interpreted it erroneously? Whatever the case, even in this day and age I can hardly believe what I did. The pale, tall young man with a full black beard abruptly interrupted Barry in mid-sentence and with a superficial apology, as if under a spell, his back straight and dignified, his step slow, began to wend his way through the crowd towards three girls perched on bar stools. The girls had their backs to the bar and were talking with a couple of colleagues, but just as I was approaching, as if at the command of some superior force, two of them left. I went over to Elizabeta and, off the top of my head, said, "Excuse me, Miss Blake, I think we haven't been introduced."

We will never know whether my unprecedented courage would have lasted and whether I would have been equally adept at pronouncing a second sentence, had Elizabeta greeted me as absent-mindedly as she had been talking with the others. I probably would have felt tongue-tied and fallen silent. Her response, however, was beyond my wildest dreams. The beautiful, secretive girl who, though with much politeness, generally kept her conversants at an unusual distance given the student context, looked as if she had been awaiting my arrival eagerly. And though only a few minutes later I learned the reasons why she genuinely wanted to make my acquaintance, and though the reasons were not the same as, or even remotely akin to, those I had supposed, the liveliness with which she began to speak with me and her evident interest made our first encounter easy and straightforward.

"No, we have not. I am Elisabeth Blake. I'm not sure I caught your name, but I know you're Serbian."

"Yes, I am. From Belgrade. My name is Stevan Medaković. You needn't try to pronounce it lest you break your tongue. Call me Steve, as everyone else does."

"Oh, no. I'll try to say it properly. Would you please repeat it?"

"Stevan . . ."

"Es-tee-vee-aee-en?"

"Yes."

"Stevan, does that sound right?"

"Perfect."

"And now the second name."

"Medaković."

"Medakovich?"

"Yes, that's quite good, really."

"So, I got it right. You know, Mr Medakovich, ever since I learned that you were from Serbia, I wanted to tell you that my cousin, Archibald Blake, is married to a Serbian girl, Rashela – is that the way you pronounce it?"

"Well, Rašela is not exactly a Serbian name."

"Yes, I know. Rachel is Jewish, but her family has lived in Belgrade for generations, and she considers herself Serbian."

"Where did she meet your cousin?"

"In Salonika, I believe. Rachel was there with the Serbian Army and served as a nurse in an English hospital where my cousin, who was badly wounded, was recovering. I'm sure they'd love to meet you. It is not very often that you come across someone from Serbia, is it?"

So that is how it began. Like a miracle. The coincidences were strung along in such an iron-clad sequence that I never think of my days in Bristol without feeling a certain religious awe. The First World War had to happen, and Rašela, whose maiden name, as I learned, had been Alkalaj, had to leave the Belgrade Jewish quarter of Dorćol and accompany the troops to the English hospital in Salonika, and it was there that she happened upon Archibald, an Englishman. (Two specks of dust floating through space. Could a mathematician calculate the probability that they would meet each other in room 4, on the second floor of the English hospital in the Greek city of Salonika, crowded with soldiers and refugees? Two other specks of dust, carried by who knows what winds, collided at the Glengyle Inn in Bristol, England. Who stirs up human space like this?) Quirky as Puck, winged providence with the speed of the imagination flits whimsically through the spaces between

Dorćol and Bristol, Salonika and Albion, arranging encounters. The sky is criss-crossed with coincidence.

After the conversation at the Glengyle Inn, I didn't see Elizabeta for six days, and even now I am not able to say whether it was the most infuriating or the most blessed week of my love. Our brief exchange, you see, was so meagre as a basis for drawing any conclusions that I could indulge in whatever interpretations I chose, a fact of which I made merciless use. I gave myself over to reverie with a remarkable lack of moderation. How green my love, how young and madly euphoric! At happier moments, when I believed I had discovered a fondness for me in Elizabeta's behaviour, I would permit myself to begin to imagine the further course of our relations. I introduced the lovely Englishwoman to all the subtle, hidden crannies of my wounded soul, and disclosed to Eliza, rendered speechless by my shrewd insight, that I knew of the sorrow that filled her, that I knew how loneliness was drawing the two of us with its magnetic force like a horseshoe attracting two nails to a shared secret, a safe place meant only for us. In a bolt of inspiration, Elizabeta would suddenly realise she might warm herself in the glow of my Slavic melancholy as she would in the sun on a chilly day. I repeated them so often that I knew by heart the sequence of statements, questions and answers we had exchanged in our several decisive encounters. In my mind, I saw her facial expression, her posture, her gestures, as if I were seeing a film sequence again and again. With her buoyant red hair, pale complexion, full lips, pert nose with sensuous nostrils – with her green gaze – Elizabeta appeared in my reveries. I was exquisitely aware of precisely how beautiful she was. And though I insist that I was not contemplating any sort of intimacy with this lovely, slender girl, but was rather drawn to her spirit, I can still picture her with her full breasts, modestly restrained by her unassuming dress but straining to pop the buttons; her strong, curving thighs; her muddy grey silk stockings, which couldn't conceal the whiteness of her long shins. I saw her at the bar at the Glengyle Inn under her bell-like hat. I would spot her profile among the sea of heads whenever I raised my eyes from the notes I was jotting down in Professor Young's class. I saw her everywhere, constantly, and then all at once, almost startled by the abruptness of the insight, I realised that I was not able to take in all of her at once. Here were the colours, here were the details – the curving shoulder, a patch of her neck and ear, the sheath of red hair, her step as she moved down the stairs in front of me, her voice while she spoke to me of Rašela Alkalaj – but I could not assemble all of her in my mind's eye!

Dreamers are wanderers. I found that to be true while I was in Bristol. At night, when the city was entirely empty, I would go out for walks which lasted many hours in the ghostly empty streets green in the glow of gas lanterns. I wandered without a goal, transported by the feeling of a lover's happiness at the root of which lurked a seductive danger. I knew it was there but preferred not to heed it. Instead, I let the sweet ardour that I barely sensed envelop my mind in the grey smoke of hashish sensuality, suddenly too weak to wrench myself from the easy lull I'd been living in, sparked by something new and stronger than anything I'd ever known before. At times, a constable would salute me in the course of my nocturnal wanderings. On some nights, this happened several times. He would be startled by my appearance in the empty streets, resembling a sleepwalker oblivious to the world around him. Kindly but suspicious, he would ask, "Is there anything I can do for you, sir?"

Confused, I would thank him, stirred from a deep slumber, and then retreat again as swiftly as I could, to the joy of my immoderate imagination.

Those were the happy moments, but there were, during that Tantalus-like week in November, many, indeed far more, miserable ones. So many unknowns lurked in the equation I was struggling to resolve, but not a single sure toehold. Always inclined as I was to underplay my own virtues and magnify my deficiencies, always prepared to embrace the role of loser, my state of being lulled into happy presentiments would be shaken to its core in a flash, and our love would seem utterly hopeless. Whatever had prompted me to believe the girl was showing me greater kindness than she showed others? She hadn't even known my name, only that I was a Serb, which she was interested in not for my sake, but for the sake of her cousin. And what could there be in my appearance, me, someone who had come from the ends of the earth, the tensest person in our entire group, what was there to appeal to this inscrutable, reticent girl? What about Young's faux pas, had it been a faux pas! What if she was, indeed, Mrs Harris, and not Miss Blake at all, as she had claimed? And was I capable of ever ascertaining the true state of affairs when I could not conduct far simpler enquiries, such as to establish, at least, what suddenly had happened to her, where had she vanished to so abruptly? And how was it that no-one seemed surprised by her absence except me? On a number of occasions, I rushed over to enquire of one of her friends whether they knew the reasons for Miss Blake's absence, but at the last moment I invariably stopped myself, realising that my concern for her would seem odd since I had only conversed with her one single time, briefly. I was startled to discover that I had changed all my habits overnight and, furthermore, that this fact did not seem to bother me in the slightest. There can be no doubt that during those six November days I was under a spell, my thoughts blocked, all except those which galloped without restraint towards lovely Elizabeta. While I had earlier dropped my penny or tuppence rather stingily and at infrequent intervals into the gas heater in my rented room, now, indifferent and absent-minded, I kept the fire going constantly, insensitive to the cost. While before I had generally been the first down to breakfast, now I would arrive in the dining room once Miss Trickey had already started tidying up after that most important of English meals. While I had hardly ever been into the Glengyle Inn, now I became their most devoted habitué, and I was always the last to leave, hoping up to the last moment that the cloud of red hair drawn in by a little bell-like hat would appear from somewhere.

Elizabeta did not appear, but ultimately the very thing I was hoping beyond hope to learn made itself known to me without any effort on my part: on the sixth day, as if mentioning some detail of absolutely no significance, through the bustle of the crowd in front of the amphi-theatre classroom, I heard someone called Susanne telling someone else, "You'll be able to borrow that from Elisabeth Blake. She will be back in Bristol tomorrow."

Into the classroom she walked the next day, the last to do so, looking, or so she seemed to me, like a queen among her subjects, beautiful and distantly kind. She looked to me as if she were possessed with thoughts taking her far away into a life about which I, naturally, knew absolutely nothing. There could, however, be no doubt. Back from her excursion, my Eliza was distracted and burdened with worries. I was genuinely pleased with myself when this served to confirm that my assessment of the situation was not merely the product of an imagination working overtime. As I was walking down one of the corridors, I heard Susanne asking, worriedly, "Elisabeth, what's the matter with you? It's as if you were somewhere else all the time. Is something wrong?"

"Oh, no, nothing's wrong," I heard Elizabeta say, too hastily and far too breezily, but I knew, and I am certain that Susanne thought so, too, that the inscrutable Mrs or Miss was concealing something serious and consequential from us, from the world.

Evidently, Elizabeta did not chat readily with fellow students. She seemed actually to avoid them. Hello and goodbye. She was always reticent and apart, she came to class at the last moment (sometimes she wouldn't come at all), and she would leave, alone, as soon as class ended, not half a metre behind the instructor, whether he was Young, Brandt or Kitto, while the rest of us were still collecting up our notes, screwing on the caps of our fountain pens. As if she had completely forgotten about my conversation with her, her cousin Archibald, the woman from Belgrade called Rašela. My alert observer's eye also did not miss the fact that during the hiatus in the day's lectures, she would carefully arrange things so that she was by herself. She would stroll around the square in front of the classroom building, or she would walk down to the Tea Room and have tea.

It was there, in the Tea Room, that the question first crossed my mind which, at least temporarily, would direct my thoughts in a new, but really rather predictable direction. On that day, blaming first her reticence and then my shyness for the fact that since her return we hadn't exchanged a single word, I emboldened myself enough to enter the Tea Room only a minute or two after she had done so. She was the only customer there, sitting tall in her chair, her head bent swan-like over the menu, which was bound in red velvet with gold lettering. I looked towards her as I passed her table, but she was engrossed in studying, or pretended to be engrossed in studying, the list of available pastries. When I ordered tea and a doughnut from the waitress, Elizabeta swivelled her head quickly in my direction, and our gazes met. She nodded and said, "How do you do?"

No Mr Medakovich, no Stephen or Stevan. Just the most impersonal "How do you do". In England, one responds to this question with the selfsame question, which also marks the end of the exchange. English people are quite surprised if they receive a real answer. That is why I responded by saying, "How do you do?", at which she, perhaps after just a brief, the very briefest, pause, lowered her gaze to the menu again, and I set off on a mindless hunt: pursuing the thoughts of Elisabeth Blake, the ineluctable.

Had she seen me as I walked past? Yes, she had. She would not have turned her head so quickly upon hearing my voice, but then again she was staring at the velvet-covered menu with a persistence inappropriate to the interest a list of pastries might excite. Had she had, even for an instant, after her "How do you do?" the intent of continuing the conversation? Wasn't I the one, as the man, who was supposed to take the next step? Was it shyness, similar to mine, which prevented her from doing what I, too, had not dared to do?

Miserable and embarrassed in that large, empty tearoom, not knowing what was polite, and what impolite, to do, not actually knowing anything, like a young ox I poured milk into my tea, stirred the sugar in and vacillated as to whether shyness, decency or indifference was the reason we were sitting there so close to each other, yet so mute. I was saddened to realise that if Elizabeta were a Serbian woman, I would have known what to do next. Since she was not, I had no choice but to agonise over everything. Then, for the first time, I thought: What a shame she's a foreigner. And immediately thereafter, like some sort of *coup de théâtre*, a matador's sword striking the spine of a bull: What is it that I want from this beautiful foreign woman?

The cup of tea stopped halfway to my lips. I was so thunderstruck by the simplicity and potential devastation of this question that I completely forgot the discomfort oozing over Elizabeta and me, petrified at adjacent tables in this quiet torture chamber. Since this question, which ought logically to have occurred to me the very first time I had thought of the beautiful Englishwoman, had posed itself considerably later, it had the impact of a surprise but also was proof of the extent to which I had been under a spell for the last few days. In my wildest flings of fancy I had overcome all obstacles to our love with the marvellous grace of an Olympic athlete, but this one I had completely ignored. It had never so much as crossed my mind that what I wanted was to take Elisabeth Blake back with me to Belgrade. Was it friendship I was hoping for? No. Not friendship, and not, God help us!, a scandalous affair! What then? Would I be able to marry a foreign woman and bring her home to Nanka and Milutin? Right there, in the Tea Room, dumbstruck at the discovery of something so obvious – that Elisabeth Blake was from another country – I was able to answer several crucial questions in a reasonable fashion.

Was it then that I experienced a change of faith? I realised that I had been living in a Belgrade advanced by half a century from the city to which the writer Laza Lazarević had thought to bring his German love Ana Gutjar. By now it was a Belgrade that aspired to echo Europe in every respect (and my Nanka in nothing), embracing each Parisian, London, Viennese or Berlin innovation with an enthusiasm far outstripping my own. The steps of the "Ripanjac", "Muvanjac", "Srbijanka" and "Kokonješte" dances gave way like a broken phalanx before the "vanstep", "blek-botom", "ingliš-vals", "fokstrot" and "slofoks", as they were called. The awareness that we were not the best in the world had penetrated. We'd better get on with it if we wished to catch the European taxicab of progress and humanity. Albeit with the best of intentions, Nanka and Milutin were the cast-off relics of a vanishing world. To be from England in Belgrade would be more of a social advantage than a drawback. Many a social climber would adore the notion of being on cordial terms with a countrywoman of Lloyd George's and a subject of King George's. I could readily picture Eliza at literary tea parties held by the Society for Building the Cvijeta Zuzorić Art Gallery, at the artists' ball attended by everyone who knew a little English (no longer an exotic language among the better-educated), or in the private circle of my friends, who would do their best to display their worldly views and their disregard for anyone capable of perceiving in someone's intent to marry a foreign woman the slightest tinge of the unpatriotic or unnatural.

But did the outside world, the majority, even if it were a progressive and educated majority, have to be the measure? Was it wise to lightly toss off morals which had been developed over hundreds of years in exchange for a novel set that we did not understand as well as we should have done? I had long been convinced that we Serbs were embracing novelty impetuously, as immature children embrace the vices of adults. It seemed honourable to be old-fashioned in one's habits and demeanour precisely because it had become so easy to be a man of the world in Belgrade. I suddenly recalled my last conversation with my father, on the platform of the Belgrade railway station. We were overcome with awkwardness, he and I, as always when circumstances required that we parade our emotions. I was at the train window, and Milutin and Nanka were on the platform waiting for the train to depart. Nanka was silent, because that was appropriate. Milutin was quiet, motionless, but I sensed his awkwardness, the agitation behind his stiffness. Since he had already made all the necessary practical pronouncements ("If you need money in a pinch, you can always get it at 'Spender and Sons'"; "Write so that we don't worry"), now was the moment to say something weighty, something I would remember off there alone among the English. Finally, he did: "You are intelligent, and you are a grown man. I have no more advice for you. You know what you must do."

After a brief pause, the bell clanged for the third time, the steam engine noisily released a moist cloud, and the levers clanged once as a test before the train pulled out of the station. "Do not forget that you are meant to return," said the old merchant. "May your journey begin well."

"May I find you happy at its end," I said, and off I went into the wide world.

Human thinking develops in leaps. Such a leap may germinate for a while in our subconscious, but then it happens in a flash, like an epiphany. Today, an unhappy, preoccupied little man stares with seasoned eyes at things he couldn't grasp until yesterday. Bergson was right. Duration is in fact a state of constant flux. There is no spiritual state identical to itself from minute to minute. With each new moment, something has been added to the one before. As he endures, a man is constantly shaping a new self. A person can stop changing only when he stops existing. Though my memory is constantly nudging thoughts, feelings, wishes from the just abandoned past into the emerging present, I am not aware of this. The changes are too minuscule for my crude perceptive apparatus, and the weight of personal dogma too great to acquiesce without resistance. So it is only when the outcome of the change is noticeable, and when the contradictions inherent to my thinking and behaviour have reshaped and reconciled themselves to a new sequence, at last, with some semblance of harmony, that I register the change as a shift from one state of mind to another.

That is what I call a leap, and for the first time in my life I became aware of it not while I was carefully studying Bergson, but in the context of my life. Who could imagine in what order the coral reefs of thought grew until an atoll, formed by millions of their dead bodies, protruded as an island above the surface of my consciousness? Who could trace what impressions, emotional and intellectual, were part of the crusty mass? How long had they been accruing in the underpinnings of the new awareness I acquired in what seemed like an instant? The City of London crowded with hurrying people wearing top hats, black jackets, striped trousers – a nightmare image from the dream of some mad character of Breton's, or a comedy act of men in tattered tails on the stage of the Finsbury Park Empire; lads in short trousers and knee socks, their knees bluish red, emerging two by two, all dressed alike, from the murky freezing fog of the park at Clifton Down; the morning aroma of café au lait and juniper brandy anchored in my nostrils since my earliest childhood; the desperate hubbub of London intersections across which I never so much as ventured to pass, with their pandemonium of double-decker buses, trams, private horse-drawn coaches and trunk-like Austins, Packards, horse-drawn freight carts with rubber wheels, darting bicyclists and crazed pedestrians; Barry's father, a distinguished judge, showing me, pathetic and proud, his collection of ducks' eggs on which he had personally engraved, in calligraphy, his most treasured thoughts, one hundred of them (should he want to add a new one, he would have to smash one of the other eggs); the grass, that moronic, lunatic English grass, a grass carpet spread out over aristocratic meadows around the castles and rolling slopes of the public parks; and John, with his offhand, mumbled sentence obviously meant as a jibe, his blasé tone intended to provoke and shame me, the provincial, pedantic yokel: "Oh, have I never told you? I am irredeemably homosexual." I had stored that sentence, frozen, at the bottom of my anguished belly and let it do its clandestine business from within. Panicked until only yesterday about how I might not so much reject one of our sacred Serbian beliefs as perceive it through foreign eyes, there I was in that Tea Room imagining Elizabeta Medaković in Belgrade, between my father, Milutin, and my nurse, Gojkovica. There was nothing in this image which unnerved me. Incredibly, damn it all, I watched it as if it were a scene that was anticipated and commonplace. Within myself, I was saying, "So what?" in the Tea Room's frozen silence, eating a doughnut that was, in fact, just another version of our Serbian *uštipak* – "so what if she is an Englishwoman? Is she not a person, a woman, cannot she, too, be a mother and a spouse, even if she isn't Serbian?" And I did not seem to be the least bit surprised that these libertine, Jacobean, scandalous thoughts were passing through my steady head. They did not excite me. "Isn't a doughnut still an *uštipak* even if it is called by some other name? Has Elizabeta no place at our table just because her name isn't Nanka and she's not partial to juniper brandy for breakfast?"

If there was something unnatural in the image in my mind's eye it was not Elizabeta's presence, but rather the stuffiness of my father cutting a slice of bread at the beginning of dinner and handing it to us ceremoniously, and the dry silence of my wolverine Nanka with her hard eyes and tightly closed lips, a stuffiness and a silence that I could see all the way from Bristol, feeling the fondness an adult might feel regarding the rather amusing and ineffectual stubbornness of two grey-haired children. It is possible, however, that the destructive component of the sudden sentence "Such a shame she is a foreigner!" was too powerful, eradicating in an instant, as if with shock therapy, my doltish attachment to the Serbian patriarchal tradition (perhaps this was the first time I had ever used such words, which in itself illuminates a new quality of my attitude) and the parochial. Yes. Though I may have applied that word to my views before that moment in the frozen silence of the Tea Room, I certainly introduced the English term "parochial narrow-mindedness" into my Serbian vocabulary for the first time there. And no matter how incredible it may have seemed to me, there was no parochial narrow-mindedness, not a trace, in the panic that struck me following the insight that Elizabeta was a foreigner. The devastation of this discovery consisted of the fact that I – in a sudden moment of enlightenment – had discovered that I loved a woman whom I could not for the life of me understand, whom, chances were, I would never understand, for I would never make my way through even the first line of defence of her intimate barricades, nor through the second line, consisting of the customs and rules that these parochial islanders had been refining for hundreds of years, people who stood with one foot on a slaughtered Bengali tiger and the other on the carpet of grass spreading out before a stone castle. Was I to spend my entire life frozen and uncomfortable, the way I had just spent the last ten minutes in the empty Tea Room in which I was addressing the simplest of tasks – whether or not I should speak to Elizabeta – with beads of sweat on my brow and anguish hanging like a stench in the agonised silence? Like some besotted, crazed ox? I remember it quite well: at that moment, I had a unique impression that my life was like some flexible substance in my hands which would not resist even the maddest shaping. I could make of it what I would: a cube or a ball, a fawn or a wolf, a priest or a defrocked priest: I could toss it out of the window, break it into halves, and yet the decisive step that would finally take me in one direction didn't frighten me; rather it filled me with a strange rapture that was similar, I believe, to that experienced by a dowser using a divining rod to find the right place to dig a well. I felt akin to God, and probably therefore superior (such a rare feeling for me) to this contradiction-ridden experience, which had been filling me until just a moment before with panicked doubts about faith and betrayal, good blood and bad blood, the hallowed Cross and golden freedom. Suddenly – or at least it seemed sudden; no-one can say just how long I had been preparing for this leap – the question of Serbs versus Turks, the black devil or the white angel, seemed far too narrow, irrelevant to the new awareness that I would describe now as a loosening of the rigid tenets that had sapped it until that moment. The either–or, *entweder–oder*, *ili–ili* acquired yet another dimension, a third 'either' beyond the 'or', which turned the uni- and bi-directionality of my thinking up to that point into a multi-directional openness to all possibilities. Perhaps this new inclination of mine, cultivated for decades, had its faults, but once it had taken hold, it would not allow me to set the truth in stone before I had considered the facts in full. The choice between café au lait with cream and juniper brandy with cheese and onion changes its essence if it is expanded to: café au lait, or juniper brandy, or porridge, not only because you now have three possibilities, but because the notion that three possibilities do exist opens the door wide to the thought that not one of them might, in fact, be the right one, but rather that it would be worth searching for a fourth, and a fifth, with much less certainty that the truth exists and that it resides in one place.

"Alzo" – as my late father would say – the prospect of facing Belgrade, my aged father and tenacious Nanka did not intimidate me, for I knew that I would be able to handle them, since my knowledge was more refined, and my understanding more profound, than theirs. The question was whether my understanding was great enough for me to make my way into Elizabeta's inscrutable soul and unlock the hidden English cupboards within it using a key designed for Serbian locks? Would I be able to spend my life by the side of a foreigner? Would she be able to be with me when what we knew of the world was so different that we didn't even see black and white with the same eyes? When, first in my leisure hours and later for the purposes of publication, I undertook the translation of Shakespeare into Serbian, I felt that Elizabeta harboured a clandestine and, for a long while, as far as I was concerned, inexplicable resistance to this activity of mine. Setting aside the extreme sense of self-abnegation to which I am otherwise, I admit, susceptible, I am able to say that my knowledge of Shakespeare's language has indeed improved over the years to really a rather professional level, but I can sense my Eliza's resistance even today, whenever I describe the translation problems I encounter. Why? For the longest time I did not know. Now I do. After thirty years of impassioned involvement in the language and work of the Swan of Avon, I certainly know Shakespeare better than my wife or most of the English do, but now I have finally understood that I read him differently from the way they do. Translating him, I Serbify him, adapt him to the way I see the world: I see him with eyes which did not perceive their first things, nature, people, in England, but rather in Serbia. The word *sea* has the same general meaning when it appears in Shakespeare and when the writer Laza Lazarević uses it, yet the sense of "sea" suggests one thing to someone from Britain and something different to a person born in rural Serbia. That is what I mean. And though in the Tea Room on Park Row it wasn't all as evident to me as it is today, even then I was enlightened and foresaw my blind man's gropings in unfamiliar terrain, the exploratory nature of the relations that would begin between Eliza and me.

If they should begin, I thought then, or, rather, if they did begin, for I was never less sure that they would begin than when I strode by her table with the cool, well-chosen phrase "See you later", which among the English means nothing at all, except, perhaps, that you are con-firming the infinite unpredictability of events, which may eventually lead to some later sighting. And that is why Elizabeta did not respond by saying, "Yes," because an affirmative response would immediately have coloured the meaningless greeting with an attitude.

Finding myself on the street, which greeted me with a whirl of traffic and rush of unknown passers-by like a welcome after the tomb-like quiet in which the two of us had been silent, I stood on my toes and, over the little curtain hung across the tearoom window, saw Elizabeta once more. She was sitting, her head lowered. She hadn't touched her tea and cake. Undone, she seemed to me, and distant, buried behind her gleaming fair complexion. I had a distinct feeling at that moment, standing a little undignifiedly on my toes, that I was surrendering her to her English destiny, and that I was headed where I belonged. It was not a nice feeling. Quite the contrary. I would have wept if Nanka hadn't trained me not to. Full of amorous longing, I did feel, on the brief walk to the Faculty, that I was coming out of a swoon, that the crisis was waning, that I was no longer delirious, that I had come back down to earth, and that I was feeling the ground with at least the tips of my toes, if not the soles of my feet. Everything subsided with a kind of sadness, as if in a healing dream. My organism culled its strengths to conquer the fever; it was fighting a winning battle with the last traces of the love virus; the arrow on the scales between collapse and recovery was inching over to my side. I still didn't know whether I was glad that I felt that way. I didn't feel myself to be a loser or a winner, but I did feel cured. Melancholic, glum, but cured, I mumbled to myself in my beard, thinking that I would believe it once I heard it aloud: it is better this way, Stevan. Full of grace as he is, God has taken steps to lead you out of temptation just in time. You were mad, Stevan, fancying what was beyond your ken, out of your reach. At that moment, I recollect it as if it were today, I remembered Milutin's sentiments expressed at the railway station. I stumbled over the words I had concealed, it must have been wilfully, from myself during my former – as I put it to myself at that moment – state of rapture, of which I was now cured: "Do not forget that you are meant to return." I had forgotten. The punishment for this transgression was the grief that darkened my face and hunched my young shoulders as soon as I remembered my old habits and my dark land.

There are moments in a man's life which always remain crystal clear in his memory. That Killer Time with all its sly tricks can do nothing to them. It heaps the sadness of everyday events on them, stretching them until the threads that connect us to them snap, but the memories do not care; they become richer and fresher with the passing of time. There, that is how I recall the one-hour storm that began raging inside my mind after the marvellous discovery that Elizabeta was a foreigner. I listened to Young, I followed his lecture rather coherently. I remember as if it were today: he was raising questions about Bergson's thesis that metaphysical principles are intuitive. Instead, he claimed that one can only divine legal principles by way of direct reality, using a special technique that would adapt the results of the Bergsonian vision to practical possibilities. Incredible but true! That is precisely what Young was saying! I can see him as he gesticulated, as from time to time he abandoned the serious tone of dispute in order to crack a joke at his own, or Bergson's, or our expense. I remember that a lad was sitting next to me whose face I can see clearly even today, though I have forgotten his name, and under the bench he was reading some literature which surely had absolutely nothing to do with the intuitionist opponent of our pragmatic professor.

My sense of coherence and presence in the lecture hall, however, in no way prevented me from following a second direction parallel to this intellectual plane which was emotional, complex, alive even when it could not be articulated. It was listing my amorous "for" and the impartial "against" on a divinely just scale, which was dropping with comfortable certainty on to my Serbian side. Divine justice tainted my new awareness of the true state of affairs with a dull ache but also with pride, because during that hour I firmly came to believe that I had succeeded; I no longer desired Elisabeth Blake! Not only was I not able to have her; I did not want her, since I had not, in the Tea Room, been able to answer the question: "What would I do with her?" I saw her sitting down in front of me, diligently taking notes, her head bent slightly to the left, her right profile turned towards me. Young brought his polemic with Bergson to a close. Elizabeta capped her fountain pen; I started moving towards the exit and reached the door at precisely the moment when she did. She was wearing a sky-blue jersey dress, a coat of the same hue, a hat that ended over the back of her head in a net that drew in the cloud of her red hair; her green eyes shone from her white face; and I lowered my own gaze, unable to sustain the greenness. I walked by without a greeting, but with the knowledge that this time my gesture was symbolic, that I had come to a crossroads in my life and had passed it by, a crossroads to which I would never return.

When I was already halfway down the hallway, I heard Elizabeta's step behind me, and then her voice. "Stevan," she said, therefore not

Steve, not Mr Medaković, "my cousin Archibald and Rachel are coming to visit me on Saturday. They asked me to pass on an invitation to lunch."

Since this had stolen my breath and since I stood there blinded by the flash of her fair complexion, mute as a "broken-winded usher", she hastily added, "That is, of course, if you happen not to have any other obligations."

No, I had no other obligations.

I went down the steps, muddled and enveloped by the crowd because of my slow stride, railing nastily at myself. "You mule," I said, "how could you not approach her in the Tea Room!" I recriminated myself bitterly for my ineptitude. "You Balkan ox, you never seem to understand anything, do you!"

Even then, however, I knew. The muddle was suddenly gone from my head.

I loved her irredeemably, Elisabeth Blake. The indiscernible.

TWO

Dear Stevan, I am answering your third letter with some delay, after deciding, this time, to reply to your many questions. As far as I can, of course. Though you didn't convince me in the first two, you have in the third that Liza will give you no answers, and I think you should know at least as much about the woman you want to spend your life with as I do. I am certain that Liza would not see my well-intended candour as betrayal, but I'd rather you didn't show her the letter. At least not now.

You see, Stevan, although Liza is my closest friend, and I've known her to apologise – in such a British way! – for burdening me with her confessions, I'm surprised, as I write to you, to realise that in fact I know very little about her, or rather I know only as much as she permits me to, and here you are right, this is never a great deal. Do not, my dear countryman, be so sensitive to Liza's closed nature. As her friend, and a subject of the English Crown for six years now, I assure you that Elisabeth's secrecy is not due to feminine coyness, nor is it a sign of a lack of trust in you. Her secrecy is her character, in part, and is also typical of her nation. In an Anglo-Saxon legend, a hero is tested to see if he is worthy of honour. Is he virtuous? Is he fearless? Is he *silent*? Do you suppose that I know more about Archibald, after six weeks of keeping watch at his hospital bedside and six years of marriage, than you do about Elisabeth? But I have understood something. I know little not because Archibald has little love for me, but because it is not proper to speak to anyone of oneself.

So you see, one does not generally confide in others here in England, which, I'd say, speaks not so much of their coldness and closed temperament, as you, admittedly with some foundation, have thought, but rather of their manners. Confidence here is seen as indecent exposure, and the capacity of a person to keep his troubles to himself is proof of resolute character and propriety. I advice you not to push Elisabeth too hard. Understand that it is difficult for her to meet your need for closeness, and accept that she can love you only as she does now.

You see, Stevan, since I am Jewish, I was born with the knowledge that we were one thing, while the Serbs were something else; I found it easy to accept that the English are something else again. You do not have that feeling. You have grown up as a part of the majority, the victors, impassioned, enamoured with yourselves as newcomers to the stage of history always are. I wasn't the least bit surprised, for instance, when you told me that you had heard, of course, of the Mahala, but had been *maybe* once in my Jewish ghetto, Ćivutani, as it was called contemptuously by the Turks, in the Sephardic kingdom of Jalija, lying between Solun, Car Uroš and Visoki Streets, all the way down to the shore of the Danube. You had no need to get to know this world with its – this will surprise you – rather English hierarchy, from the poorest people, crowded into Jalija, through *los de abajo* – to *los de arriba* Mahala above Vidinska Street, the border running between us and you, the Turkish Jews and the Turkish Slavs. My *samsars*, *rinčiperoses*, keep to their ancient Spanish and Moorish ways; they speak Ladino, eat *burekitos*, *bohus*, *alharos* (this must be the first time you're hearing these words, isn't it?), *al bundegas* and *frizaldadas*; the family gathers for Purim, Bar Mitzvahs, Passover; they sing *romances moriscos* – and you were oblivious to it all. Even when you Serbs borrow something from us, you make it so Serbian that the Sephardim can no longer recognise it. Did you know, for instance, that the word *keva* for "mother" came into Belgrade slang from Ladino? *Patišpanj*, known in every good home, is in fact our *pan de Espana*. And when my peers and I, educated in your schools, decided to move from the Sephardic Mahala into Serbian Belgrade, we did so because we found there an open-minded tolerance almost without parallel in Europe or throughout our Jewish history, a tolerance that had to be tested for centuries before our hermetically sealed ghetto would open, as it did during my generation.

We have, however, paid the price. We have adopted your language, your customs; we have become Serbs. My father was a genuine Jew. Fanatically devoted to Sephardic customs and morals, he lost his life as a Serbian soldier, a volunteer corporal, in a battle against the Turks near the village of Mlado Nagoričane in 1912. I had already finished school, a "Serbian girl of the Mosaic faith", with financial support from the state, and had gone off, a fiery patriot, to join the Serbian Army as a nurse, and yet here, as you can see for yourself, I still speak of *you* and *us*. *You* are the Serbs or the English; *we* are the Sephardim from the Mahala, who can quite adeptly become Serbs or English while still remaining Sephardim. I don't doubt that the word *mimicry* brings associations of negative, unbecoming traits to mind. Not for me. Mimicry is a skill. I am proud of it. It is proof of my inherited wisdom, perhaps – of my advantage over you. You. Unbending and unadaptable. I spent my first year in Britain observing and absorbing. Whenever I caught on to something, I would tell myself, "Aha, Rašela, now you know how they do it." Never, Stevan, never once did I ask myself, "Why do it that way?" That's their business. Mine is to watch and to conform. You asked me whether my sons understand Serbian, and I lied to you. I said that they do. They don't. I have never taught them a single Serbian word. On occasion I grieve at the fact that my children do not speak the language closest, for me, to what you'd call a mother tongue. They know a handful of Ladino words. Though I can't say why, they are fond of a verse from an old Moorish ballad:

> Mananita era manana,
> al tiempo que albordeaba,
> gran fiesta haciare los moros
> en la bella Granada.

They sing it sweetly together, yet they've never asked me what it means.

Why am I writing all this when you are so eager to find answers to the questions that interest you? Because you must realise that neither you nor Liza have the gift of adaptation, that you are brittle as steel that snaps instead of bending. You told me with a cheery grin about the little war raging between East and West at your dinner table in Belgrade, about your father who takes *milchbrot* with his café au lait, and about your nanny who insists stubbornly on juniper brandy and raw onion. She is the Serb, Stevan, not your father. Because she is unable to change. Remember how Njegoš's Draško saw the Venetians. He was filled with revulsion because instead of the *gusla* they played other instruments, and they preferred eggs and chicken to mutton; he despised them from the bottom of his soul because they'd "gone mad from their riches, infantile like small children"; their sentiments were "little improvement over the Turk", not to mention that "there could be no talk of heroics here", and that "the world has never seen such disgrace, such creatures". And since they were so different from Montenegrins, Draško came to the proper Serbian conclusion that "they gravely transgressed divine will" because the divine, naturally, is what is Serbian, "and that their empire will be struck down" – what else could be expected from something different from what Draško knew?

You and Elisabeth are, at least a little, from time to time, biased the way Draško was, each towards your own world. Difference seems like betrayal and unkindness. You believe that there can only be one truth. If in no other way, Stevan, at least through the difficulty you have encountered getting used to English customs, do try to see how strange your customs must be to such a stalwart Englishwoman. Why should your nanny be the only one with the right to her juniper brandy and raw onion? During a recent visit, Elisabeth told me that you cited my adaptability as a model for her. Wrong! I am not a model, not for you and not for her. I am Jewish, and that is why I am now English. More so even than Archibald: I exult in the fact that he knows less about me than I do about him. I am Jewish, and that is why I can be Serbian here, with you. To you I disclose realms of my soul that Archibald has never laid eyes upon. And that's it! Let Elisabeth stay English. I recommend the same to her: Let Stevan stay the Serb. Do not expect him to become English. Only in that way will you be able to go through life graciously under the same roof, in love and regard.

If it is any comfort to you, I admit that even among the more orthodox of Englishwomen there are few able to refrain from discussing a former marriage. Liza told you, "If you insist, I'll tell you all you want to know, but I'd be very grateful if you could manage to refrain from asking anything." You are not at fault for attributing this to my friend's cunning, assuming that by appealing to your sense of manliness, she had hit the bull's-eye on her Serbian target. However, I am absolutely certain that Liza is not capable of such slyness. Much too much forethought for Liza. Out of the question! I will tell you how and why Liza behaved as she has. It was from despair, Stevan. Yes, despair enlightened her because she couldn't imagine telling you about events so painfully bound to her innermost heart of hearts. That is why I will tell you everything that I saw, that I heard from others, and a bit of what I guessed.

A year and a half ago, Liza married Richard Harris. She was 18, Richard 34, but do not rush to the conclusion that this was a marriage of convenience, even if that might suit your Serbian, or perhaps merely your male, vanity. Richard is a wealthy man, from a family of much better standing than Elisabeth's (his paternal uncle became Sir Robert Harris only a few months prior to the wedding), but at 34 he was a handsome, charming man that any 18-year-old could fall in love with. Trust my female intuition. Tall, a bit too thin, narrow face, high forehead as often seen among Anglo-Saxons, attractive, light-brown hair worn somewhat longer than is fashionable these days, elegant in the English way – in other words, showing subtle signs of carelessness in attire, thus manifesting a disregard for elegance (which is only for parvenues who must prove their social status by what they wear), an Oxford graduate, a civil servant with an almost guaranteed career in the Ministry of Trade. I admit that I liked him, and I believe I envied his impeccable tact, an inborn sense for the fine line between the socially decorous and the undesirable. Sarcastic though never caustic, with a mild disdain for all that was earnest, rather satisfied with himself, even when making the harshest jokes on his own account he was slightly but comfortably bored, weary of his success in life, studied in gesture, somewhat affected in speech – the tell-tale signs of a controlled complacency. I think that Richard was the ultimate English gentleman. I was not yet close to Liza, so it is no wonder that I cannot recall whether she ever spoke of her fiancé. I had a number of occasions, however, on which to observe them. Richard treated Elisabeth like a child, taking each of her statements or questions with the mild irony of which he was a true master. Liza sometimes pretended not to hear his benevolent sarcasm, but several times she showed a little impatience with this treatment, saying, "Come on, Richard, try to be serious, I'm no child." But Richard would still manage to maintain his benevolent sarcastic tone, which he lightened only to make it palatable enough for his annoyed fiancée. He was brilliant in conversation with Liza's and Archie's tiresome aunts, while mocking their behaviour with even greater brilliance as soon as they left the company, yet never awakening the suspicions of those who stayed behind that they might meet a similar fate as soon as they moved on.

I couldn't say whether Liza was, or rather how much she was, in love, since she must have been fond of Harris to decide to marry him. Her love, however, no matter how great it may have been, was kept in check. Her feelings for Richard were hardly those of a teenager in love. Although quite young, Elisabeth had a high opinion of her own intelligence and independence. I think it unjust, Stevan, to attribute too readily all her apartness to her origin and education. Believe me, even her best English friends described my cousin as a wilful and intractable young woman. Her rather early decision to continue with her education after completing school, with the idea of having a career at a time when most girls dreamed of being carried off by a fairy-tale prince into high society, was not greeted with particular enthusiasm by her old-fashioned parents. They still believed that marriage was the one and only desirable fate for a girl. And her second, equally important and equally independent decision – to marry at the age of 18 – not only contradicted her previous professional plans (marriage implicitly meant an end to them), but confirmed once again that Elisabeth has a mind, not English in its obstinacy and decisiveness, but rather hers alone, and capable of implementing the most unexpected whim without a second thought. It is not easy, you see, not at all easy to manage Elisabeth. But all her decisions come from what I would call an honourable character, and though they may occasionally contradict custom, they never contradict the high expectations that my friend and yours has always cherished for herself and those she loves.

However, Elisabeth did not lose her head over Richard Harris; she entered into marriage sober and firm; her father was beside himself with pride and joy. The proprietor of a small estate agency, the least successful member of a large family, he was head over heels in love with his only daughter, and Robert Blake made no effort to conceal his delight at acquiring such an affluent, suave, successful son-in-law from the distinguished Harris family. While Liza's anger at Richard's patronising manner was controlled, taking the form of slight impatience, her patent annoyance was more candid and much more harsh at her father's unconcealed delight, his obsequious bearing towards his future son-in-law. She'd blush, sometimes she'd even speak sharply with her father; she'd abruptly interrupt the conversation, more humiliated than furious, or even leave the room. This, however, did nothing to ruffle Uncle Robert's joy, nor amused and ironic Richard's good spirits, for it was merely a ripple in the otherwise smooth, easy, comfortable engagement between Elisabeth Blake and prosperous, charming Richard Harris.

Of course, Archibald and I felt the difference between this match, so desirable from every vantage point, and ours, which the family still regards with undiminished disapproval, not to say rancour. I felt the happy bustle that inundated Liza's home in Reading on each of several visits as a reproach, perhaps directed more at me than at Archibald, that I, a foreigner, Jewish no less, had shoved my way into the family. Open reproach, of course, never reached me, but the hints were most frequently, may the Blakes forgive me, clear as a bell. My kind Aunt Penny, or dear Cousin Stella, were obviously aiming at poor Archie when they praised Richard's handsome figure and the reputability of the forthcoming marriage. Archie and I, of course, refused to acknowledge the malice and disdain. We've grown accustomed to it, Stevan, and their pointed comments have long since ceased to wound us. We try to see as little of them as possible, and we bear the fate of black sheep without protest. I am not boasting. It is easy to be superior to Aunt Penny and Cousin Stella.

However, although we may have been able to put up with the nasty allusions of relatives, Elisabeth, indignant, young, so very young only two years ago!, could not. It may seem a bit odd, but I probably never would have become so close to Liza if it hadn't been for the family's opposition to Archie's marriage and their English disdain towards me, a foreigner. Liza would always, in every way, show great impatience with the fatuous and unfounded nasty comments of the aunts, old maids who thought of nothing but our life, though it was none of their business. "It is so suffocating here," she'd say rudely to Aunt Penny, who was exclaiming, looking pointedly at me, at what an excellent family Richard came from, or to Cousin Stella, who spoke of the shower as a foolish European contraption, or to Archie's mother, who commented, with a sigh, how Liza's parents must be so overjoyed at the marriage, or to his father, who for no good reason, out of the blue, would talk about some bloody, stupid foreigner ignorant of local customs.

"My, it's stuffy in here," Liza would say, after trying to shield us from the poisonous darts that seemed to hurt her more than they did Archie and myself. "Rachel, let's go for a walk." Of course as soon as we went out together and were alone, she wouldn't mention the relatives' lack of tact. Not at all. We would dwell on trivia, the English way of being noble, perfected for centuries.

Elisabeth is a marvellous person, Stevan. If this letter helps to bring the two of you together, you must know that I am writing it at great personal expense. Don't be surprised that it took me so long to decide to tell you what I know. When you read everything, you'll see that it hasn't been easy.

Well, the big day arrived (I mean the precise date – March 23, year before last, that is 1923). The wedding was held at the local Anglican church, and more than a hundred people came to the Blakes' house afterwards. I think that Uncle Robert managed to ask every single guest the same question (skipping us, needless to say): "What an impressive crowd, isn't it?" – thinking certainly of the numbers, but having the eminence of the invited guests foremost in mind; Liza was quite stunning, quite young and, if I'm not mistaken, a little shaken. The newlyweds did not linger because they had to make the final arrangements before going off on their honeymoon the next morning, off to the other end of Europe, to Dalmatia. Since my part had been considerable in their decision to go to Opatija and Dubrovnik for their honeymoon, Liza caught me, just before they got into the car that was to take them to their new London flat and enquired about certain details, not because they really interested her, it seemed, but to delay departure a bit longer. I don't know, perhaps I am wrong. I never asked her whether she was, in fact, hesitating.

The fact that everything went off without a hitch made the subsequent catastrophe all the more staggering. Mr and Mrs Harris did not depart for Dalmatia, and the day after, Elisabeth came back to her parents' home and engaged a lawyer to file for divorce, with as much discretion as possible. This last part of Liza's request was, of course, logical, but most difficult to guarantee. The scandal was immense; as they say so quaintly in Serbian, they washed their mouths out with Liza and Richard in hundreds of salons at once.

Thus far, Stevan, I have written of what I know. I would now have to embark on a bit of guesswork as to what brought on such a sudden and dramatic divorce. I am not, however, prepared to do so. I could relate all sorts of gossip about the motives of one or the other spouse – and we heard versions that would stun you, goodness knows, with their inventiveness – but I am sure that they would be more likely to mislead you than steer you in the right direction. I have never asked Liza what led her to such an abrupt decision (I will disclose my certainty that it was Liza who made the decision, for which I find confirmation in the family's attitudes, both Liza's and Richard's), and she has never shown the slightest inclination to inform me of it. The fact that the two of us became close friends at that very time, so difficult for Liza, probably lies in Archibald's and my restraint from mentioning the painful event. I remember quite clearly that the word *divorce* was uttered in our household for the first time when it was legally finalised. Archie said, in passing, between gulps of beer, "I heard the business of your divorce is over."

"Yes, it is," Liza replied.

"Thank God, forget all about it as soon as you can." And that was that.

In the course of that first year following the divorce, Liza spent more time at our house than she did at her own. I believe she did so because she found it intolerable living side by side with those two utterly undone people, her father and mother. It was her father, really. Uncle Robert felt that his beloved daughter had insulted him so gravely that he could not forgive her. He barely spoke to Elizabeta. Two months after the divorce, he sold off his estate agency and retired. He barely saw a soul. As to Liza's mother, I had the impression that she was far more level-headed than her spouse. She did as much as she was able (she had bad rheumatism and a weak heart) to talk some sense into Uncle Robert and justify her daughter's action. A year ago, however, she died abruptly. The judgement passed by the family tribunal was that she had ben killed by shame, but I find that far easier to claim than to prove. Her life had been dangling by a thread for years. It could have snapped just as easily before Liza's wedding (which undoubtedly would have been attributed to an "overdose of joy") just as it did one night, in her sleep, following Liza's divorce.

That should suffice, Stevan, to allow you to imagine the hell endured by your young friend and mine, far too young for burdens so weighty. To all intents and purposes, she was excluded from those closest to her by what she had done. There she was, by the side of her crushed father, who weighed her down like a tombstone with his unvoiced reproaches in their home-tomb, by the graveside of her mother, for whose death, despite reason and all remonstrances to the contrary, she felt guilty. Tell me, how could quiet, reticent, proud Liza ever speak to you about such things? Do you still believe it was cunning rather than despair which drove her to invoke your heroic discretion? If I can say nothing about the true reason why Richard and Elizabeta separated, I can say more than anyone else how deeply wounded this person is, dearest to me, besides my sons and Archie, on this island. You have perhaps only sensed what I had many opportunities to observe (men in love are not the best at observing their beloveds) – that conscientiousness is the fundamental trait of Elizabeta's character. Watching how she writhed beneath her silence, heroically sporting a badly acted coolness and a cheery countenance, I was always sorry that she was not gifted with a trait typical of weaker people who find justification for all their blunders with ease. Liza was not able to forgive herself for a single one. I know this better than anyone, Stevan. Liza expends no effort to find easier perspectives from which she might view her scandalous divorce. Brave and sober, without a trace of generosity for herself, she faced all the consequences of her bold action. Never flinching, she paid the price of her decision without caring that she could have attributed part of the guilt to Richard and to the circumstances, error, fate, misfortune or luck, as most people skilled at such things generally do. I have not dared to be the first to broach the subject of her divorce, though I have ardently longed to do so, because Liza will not permit herself the relief of expressing her pangs in words. She will not see her blunder with my eyes, more forgiving but also more objective than hers, which are so icily impartial and accusing. It is precisely because I know all this that I reached the conclusion I wish to impart to you.

My fondest wish is to keep Liza here at my side. For selfish reasons, of course. My decision, as you will see, is to your benefit and against my better interests. I am working against myself, and I find no comfort in the fact that the motivation is unselfish. England will be a far emptier place for me if Lizica leaves it, and that is why for the longest time I tried to convince myself that time would heal her pain, that she would be able to find purpose in her studies and in work, that she might, after all – why not? – marry again, have children, leave the scandal behind just as the gossipmongers will forget it as soon as something fresher crops up, something new. Believe me, Stevan, I almost succeeded in convincing myself. And besides, dearest Stevan, without meaning to discourage you, I will tell you a truth that only superficially belies my words at the beginning of this letter. I may be Jewish with all the advantages of being a daughter of Israel, but I do not wish on anyone the fate of a woman living abroad, least of all on my steely, conscientious, intelligent Lizica. The fate of a foreign woman may be bearable, but it is not a happy one. I am not writing about myself in this letter, so I will not go into a detailed explanation of how I feel whenever you and I flee into my language and let loose there. Always the same childish longing: I'd rather not leave it and go back to alien English. When I think of Elizabeta breaking her tongue in the Dorćol shops and Belgrade living rooms while sipping her Turkish coffee and nibbling Turkish delight over awful words such as, for instance, *prst* or *smrča*, I nearly choke, and I feel at those moments that I must keep her here in England, no matter what the cost.

But I am wrong. I am sorry, but I am compelled to admit this. Almost two years have passed, and I can see that nothing has changed in Elizabeta's defiance of the world, which peppers her with scorn. I am afraid that she views her life in England as impossible, that she is finding it increasingly difficult to breathe under the wakeful scrutiny of all those condemning, cursing eyes, under the lash of sarcastic, malicious tongues, with her father's curse . . . No, Lizica cannot remain. Therefore, you see, we can call my decision to support your intended marriage unselfish and reasoned.

I should end this Serbian letter with an entirely un-British declaration: I have grown fond of you, Stevan, quickly and deeply. Only when they meet abroad can compatriots develop this kind of closeness. Looking at you, so touchingly young, sweetly awkward among the domesticated British, enchanted by Lizica's beauty and what you call her *skrovitost*, her privacy – pardon my maternal tone – you have become dear to me because of some unarticulated fragility of yours which – I don't know how to explain it better – is coupled with your goodness. Someone as honest, earnest and young as you are is likely to be vulnerable in the world of experienced, superficial, mature people, but he must also cultivate the hidden superiority of integrity, which my Lizica, actually rather like you, has sensed. I believe that it is precisely your courtesy, your goodness, the way you are in love, wholeheartedly, candidly (all traits which did not grace cynical Richard) that has enchanted my wounded Lizica. Let Liza begin a new life in a new light. On Zorina Street, where you will live, in Kalemegdan Park, through which you will stroll, around my Belgrade, where you will spend your lives. And since there is no-one in her old world, or in the new one for that matter, who can do this with love, please permit Archibald and me, unauthorised but with all our hearts, to give you Lizica's hand in marriage. To have and to hold.

May you live long and happily, Stevan.

Yours,

Rašela Alkalaj

Reading

March–April 1925

PS   I am sending you this letter by post, so as to avoid slipping it to you secretly on Saturday when you come to visit. You see I read it again, and I am absolutely certain (a) that I was meant to write it, and (b) that Lizica must not see it. Sure of your wisdom, I know that you will use the tidings I send you well, because should they be misused, they could damage you and my friend. And since, my dear countryman, the two of us now share a secret, I propose a conspiratorial sign so that we understand each other: if you address me in Serbian on Saturday, I will understand that you have embraced the spirit of my letter as I hope you will. If you greet me in English, I will be saddened by my failure. And – I will be glad for it. Now, my dear Stevan, I have told you all.

Yours,

R. A.

THREE

Dear Rachel (I know the Serbs call you Rašela, but I cannot. To me you are still Rachel), how very hard it is to begin. There is still so much I do not know. For an example – do we two use *ti* or *vi*? We are old friends and family, so I think it is *ti*. I promised to write to you, Rachel, in Serbian about everything though I am afraid of what if someone sees it because I know the language so awfully poorly. I have been writing this from my first Belgrade days. Every day a little, and I keep thinking I will write to you and send it off, but then I don't. Now, you see, I am sending it all at once from when I arrived in Belgrade until today. I know, all of this is a muddle, but the Serbian language is not the only muddle. I am confused in my thinking, too, but I know you are always intelligent, clever, and always better at understanding me than I understand myself.

My dear Rachel, please do not laugh and do keep writing to me as often as you have. Your letters are a great delight. They come to me as if from a long dead world of a thousand years ago, from a world far away by Wells's time machine. Strange. To you and cousin Archibald, I remain

Yours,

Elizabeta (my name now)
Belgrade, March 28, 1926

Oktobar–Novembar 1925
Lovely is the apartment what we will have. You know – Milosh Veliki Street number 52. Our house is still building, we stand guests in the family home. That you know also – Zorina Street. Separate standing

70

house in garden. Very nice. The square of town is near, only two–three streets away, but still with trees of plums, walnuts and quinces.

You see, Rachel, truth to tell you, how they take me here I do not know. It is not clear to me. Because of language, first. But not only. Still them I do not understand, and they watch at me. Stevan says, "They smell you out" and laughs. You can see I enjoy. And to me it is funny, when I see me, and me I see as the actress I play a role, from front row balcony at me I watch.

In the family house it is not bad, and Stevan and I will be here only a short time. Father Milutin is strict. Silent is, like our Uncle Benjamin, but different. To Stevan I do not say this but, very early when we arrive he tells me "I know my father. He is afraid of you. He is silent, to hide his worry." To me it seems Stevan here is right. But old Mr Medakovich is dear and many polite. Dignity has. Some Victorian parts has. So stiff, always serious, perfectly ironed trousers. How rolls a cigarette, this you should see, a religious ritual. With Father Milutin is all the world time. First he out takes a *dozna*, wood box with a little ivory rhombus piece. Old, from long use worn. The *dozna* he opens, slow, and puts on the table. We watch. Then the paper takes, brand "Zhob" (I not know what means this) that he stores in the *dozna* on top of tobacco of Herzegovina. Spits on his finger and careful pulls out one paper and sticks this "Zhob" paper on lip so two hands do work. Then many times he puts and takes from tobacco. First a little, then to him it seems much. When the amount is settled, the paper between thumb and finger like between two rollers and the tobacco he rolls. "Zhob" licks, the ends glues, and then one end tears off a little paper empty, at the other end long thinks, and then tears some off. The *dozna* he closes and the finished cigarette puts on top and a lighter long takes out with a wick and burns very big fire. Slow he the cigarette lights. Smokes and is silent. Only onetime through the day. After dinner. Next, a pipe he smokes. Slow, again.

The tobacco, this is fun, only you watch, but with bread is the problem. When together we dine silent is everyone around the table. At the head sits Father, opposite is nurse of Stevan, Nanka, who the black scarf only takes off for dinnertime. Stevan and I sit, facing. Only cuts bread the father, and with his hands serves one piece of bread each, a ceremony. Very muddled the first day was I, what should I do? I do not eat bread, and I worry it seems maybe now I have to. Stevan I ask after and he says it is of no importance. To Father Milutin it is all one. Like Stevan a little he is. I think they call it – *uvidzhavan*, seeing and understanding. What to me is nice, and what awkward is he sees and understands.

All over different with Nanka. One extreme strange character she is. Bones, tall, strong, like some Englishwomen looks. Such thin Englishwomen are many. But in body only, in the head not. Dark her face is and like some India woman seems in colour with grey hair. Always in black. This say I in English: Even in daylight she looks as if one were seeing her by moonlight. Like a man great nose, hook, orient cheekbones (how odd, strawberry and cheekbone!),* the deep cheek ruts, like the mountain crevice. Crosses her bread before eats. Others do not.

Stevan long ago tells me that to Nanka he is grateful how she nurses him and upbrings, but Nanka I pictured different. First, the Serbian that Nanka talks I only a little understand, actually hardly a single word do I understand. Stevan tells to me these are proverbs and sayings Nanka likes to express. Maybe, but I think she purposes to make me confused. Stevan denies, but he cannot because I know: Nanka does not me like. Well, I tell the clean truth to you, though Stevan will not hear it: I think either hates me Nanka or fears of me. In ambush she sits, it seems. Her eyes like ice behind I feel. Against me she never says anything out, but looks to me in the eyes straight, so sometimes the shiver is down my back, and I do look the first away. If the other is true – that me she fears of my strange, then Nanka against me turns her fear back, not like Father Milutin who fears only when I see something he does not want people to see. Father Milutin like Stevan has a temper, but to hate he is not able. I think that Father Milutin even likes me, not so much is he against the strange bride of his Stevan. Still I am not sure, but a little he is pleased, I think, and a little sad. Here is he like Stevan, always two minds.

*Jagoda: strawberry; *jagodice*: cheekbones.

And so, the third day, himself, stops Father Milutin giving me more bread, and makes of it nothing, but this is not the end of the story of bread. By chance, from a next room, I hear Nanka whispers to some relatives who come to drink *fildzhan* together. "That one eats no bread," she says quiet, but fierce, and the relatives are horrified and amazed: "Yuuu, blackest Nanka, could this be true! Not a crumb?"

"No," Nanka whispers, "it never passes her lips! She pushes away bread like poison."

But like that it was not. I do not eat it only because I have not the habit. Then I never tell Stevan, because this him uneasy makes the most when against Nanka I have to say, but the next day to the kitchen before breakfast I come, I ask if on the stove I may bread cook like toast. There Nanka is and at me watches from the corner while I toast. Long she watches. I toast. Then: "*Ti se od svezh hleb gadish?*" – at the end asks me, and what that means I don't know, I think, a proverb, so I say, "What is that '*svezh hleb gadish*'?" Nanka a strange look gives, as if my head she wants to see through and slow and deep speaks: "*Mislish da ye proklet ko hleb ne peche?*"*

Even not then do I understand, so I say, "Sorry still did not learn that Serb expression."

So it goes. No importance. Too much about Nanka. Such she is. With Nanka I want civilised terms for the sake of Stevan. When she sees I don't bite, no horns, as Stevan puts it, I think so she'll get used to me and relax.

December 1925

Now, my dear Rachel, it is worst when I cannot understand someone or something at all. Then I rage. Like a wild cat as Stevan says. Am I stupid? This began with that damned cousin Gordana. I had been here maybe one or two weeks, and Stevan said to me that we must go to a party at the Glišić family. Good. I think – I sit, I am silent, I survive. We got to the Glišić house, and there were a lot of people and they all knew

---

*"You have horror of fresh bread?"
"You think whoever does not toast bread is damned?"

Stevan and they wanted to meet me. I was right off terribly muddled. They all came to me and said, I am the godmother, I am the sister of an aunt, I am a cousin once removed, and I was saying left and right all I knew: "So pleased to meet you," "Delighted," but it was not enough. They were not horrible, no, no, they were kind, and all asked the same things: How do I like Belgrade? and I knew that answer. Stevan taught me. I said: Finest position in the world, the mouth of the River Danube into the River Sava. The people were so hospitable and all of them were pleased, but then, I don't know why, they all wanted me right away to drink more brandy and eat more meat and hot peppers, which I cannot, so I was even more muddled. And then, just when the commotion was largest, up came this Gordana, sat down next to me and said: I am not a close relative of Stevan's, but I love Stevan and Father Milutin very much, like my heart of hearts, because Father Milutin paid for my schooling, pocket money and everything, so I would have my crust of bread today and this Gordana was asking me now if I wanted, as she wanted, for us to be blood sisters. I hadn't the slightest idea what this "blood sister" meant, but Stevan was far away, couldn't help me quickly, and I could see someone else sitting down next to me and saying he was an old uncle, and I, completely muddled, said fine, I think it would be excellent to be a blood sister. But, that was a big mistake, because then Gordana started to cry, she said, now we are together to death, she and I, and she kissed me, hugged, tears rolling down her face, she said that never had such happiness been hers. I was so furious by then that I wasn't muddled any more, so I asked myself, oh my Lord, what is this, am I mad or is she mad, but nothing helped, because I could not hit Gordana and she would not let me go. Luckily Stevan came over, said we've had the coffee, we can leave. I was glad, it was over.

But, no.

The next day in the early morning we were still sleeping in bed when the maid Mila knocked on the door. First I thought breakfast, but I looked at the clock and I saw Mila must be mad, it was only 6. "What are you thinking, it is early, too early for breakfast." Mila was so sorry but she must because Gordana had been waiting for ages in the dining

74

room. Half asleep, I put on my dressing gown, I hardly knew what was happening, and my blood sister was kissing me again and crying, because since yesterday she was happy as she had never been before, so she had to bring me sweet watermelon rind to eat. I don't like watermelon, I don't know if the rind is eaten, but politely I said, "Thank you." I said, "I'll eat it later." I thought, now Gordana will go, but no! She sat, she took my hand, she gazed at me and said nothing, only gazed, adoring. God help me, I thought and I felt very uneasy, but I could do nothing, I could not think of one ordinary word to say. This was a nasty fix, Rachel, because ever since then she is always coming when she shouldn't and it is always the same. Then she asks me to go in the middle of the day to other houses and drink coffee, I ask, "Why?" and she says, "She is a wonderful Serbian woman, a mother."

Or, that I should go and be a benefactor to a society, and the society has such a dreadful name – try and imagine, Rachel: "Core of Bread", "Orphan", "Daily Bread", "Naked" – I couldn't tell whether the benefactors wanted to shame or to help the poor people, so because of this, I had, of course, to refuse Gordana, which one must never do, because she comes again and asks me to eat what she always brings: baklava, a lamb's foot, quince jelly moulded in the shape of a fish, a potted marinade, peppers on a string. Once she made me taste a hot pepper, just a crumb, and I spat it out flat, tears began to run, and Gordana, seeing the result, said, "Have I done this to my blood sister? I am miserable, I will punish myself at once," and before I could reply, she quickly chewed three peppers one after another. I begged her, stop, enough, but that did nothing; she chewed, sputtered and cried. With Gordana it is dreadful. I asked Stevan what to do. Stevan said, "I don't know." Trouble. Nanka who hates me is a blessing from heaven compared to Gordana who loves me. Being a blood sister, Rachel, is the worst thing in Serbia.

Yesterday Stevan came to me. He laughed. He says it will be easier for me, maybe, when I hear a story of how even Milan Stojadinović, a very important minister here, has a blood brother. Some official banquet was at the Ministry and the Croat Stjepan Radić who is a turncoat and all of a sudden loves the King and the government in Belgrade asked

Stojadinović quickly if they could be blood brothers. Stojadinović said yes, and then Radić him kissed in the mouth, and now everyone is gloating in secret because Radić has the habit of spitting when he speaks and he has spittle on his lips, so afterwards Stojadinović secretly had to wipe his mouth with a serviette many times. Stevan says I am happier with Gordana than Stojadinović is with Radić, but I am not.

Fortunately, Stevan's friends are another story from the relatives. Generally they do not push me so to eat and drink brandy merely because it is homemade. They are educated people. With some of them Stevan plays music every Thursday. Stevan's other friends will help to him to be appointed as a lecturer as soon as Stevan defends his doctorate (the defence should be in February). There, I will describe for you some who are pleasant and some who are not.

All the men who play music with Stevan on Thursday are very dear to me. Stevan did tell me long ago that he loved playing the violin, but I did not dream he played so well. The others, too. Only one of them is professional. They play, from Thursday to Thursday, only as enthusiasts. One is a lawyer (piano), another a doctor (flute, he bought it in Paris, ten thousand dinars, he could nearly have bought a house for the same sum but it is silver and has a splendid range to B flat), another again is a lecturer at the Law Faculty (cello), and there is a musician, a composer, Mr Dovžak, who plays five instruments. He is not a Serb but a Slovene from Capodistria, and lives in Belgrade. I don't know if I can analyse these friends. They do not talk, they play music, but they are so quiet, so mild-mannered, so dear, they kiss my hand and smile, and work so hard to converse with me without Stevan's help.

"First," Mr Popović, the lawyer, piano, says, "Mrs Elizabeta must learn Serbian so she feels at ease here. Mr Stevan, brother (he is not Stevan's brother, this is only the way they say it), you must tutor her as if she is a student and not your wife."

Already we have been to play at the houses of Mr Popović, Dr Simić, Professor Savić, and now it is at our house. The flat is ready, though I am still fixing it. You see, you asked me how Belgrade is. I won't tell you: "Finest position in the world, the mouth of the River Danube into the River Sava", and such, but I should confess now that I was thinking

Belgrade would be provincial and a wilderness, yet never have I seen in England that they play so much music privately and so well as they do here. And besides, there were those who said Serbs are wild, rough, but words cannot describe the courtesy – genuine, deep, not just polite – of these musicians. They are so courteous that they gave me a partitura for piano to practise in a trio composed by Mr Dovžak so that I, with my modest skill, might play music with them one Thursday. Or the moment when I asked Stevan whether it was proper that I be the only woman here? Already they had realised this and the next Thursday there was Mrs Savić with her husband, the law lecturer, to keep me company.

Of course, all of Belgrade is not this way. One day I must write a long paragraph about the Belgrade which is not so pleasant, which is deplorable. It is no disgrace to say this to you. After all, Belgrade is now more my city than yours, so the right is mine to criticise, is it not?

There are other university friends, journalists, one is a cultural worker but I am still not entirely clear on what this entails. With these friends all night one must clarify politics and drink rosé and quarrel for and against King Aleksandar. How to bring sense to the Croats? Is it good or is it a catastrophe that the peasants of Radić's party are in parliament? Is Pašić, who has a Santa Claus beard, an ordinary rascal or is he a scoundrel? This Pašić fellow, it seems to me, worries them the most. Every time there must be at least some quarrelling about Pašić. These evenings, I am finding, last too long, and the more rosé they drink, the less wisdom in what they say, the others shouting all the louder. Stevan is right. Even God in the end cannot say who is against and who is for. Of course, in England this is different completely, as you yourself know. Simple people there speak about wages, beer, football matches, and the upper classes do not talk, they only pretend to talk so as not to be vulgar like the lower classes, and I have always hated this, such a conceited pose, the fear of saying the essential things, so for me this is real theatre here which I join in with and enjoy. A person sees and knows these people – they care and they think it valuable to be trying, since change is possible. But the Englishman, personally, is a dead fish, nothing matters to him. He is only pretending, of course, that nothing matters, while at the same time he has some egotistical story about everything. I am not too harsh on

England as you write me in your letter, and am not taking it too personally. Only with the English as they say, "a noble face hides filthy ways." Here, like Nanka, I speak in sayings.

This is a big difference, and, I think, the big advantage of the Serbs over the English. Generally speaking. There are nuances, of course, and exceptions. There is one example in this company of a man who bothers me. He is so tiresome. An unfortunate case of a man who knows English well, so he besieges me in the corner and always rants about the same things. He is an anthropologist from Lika. I didn't know for ages how silly his family name is in Serbian. Šarengaća he is called. This meant nothing to me until Stevan translated it. Someone, imagine, has the surname Mr Fancypants! And, he is ridiculous in appearance, too. Small in height, a weak body, young but bald, they tell me he is not at all typical for people from Lika who are generally tall and strong. This Dane Šarengača grew up in Belgrade with cousins and so, he says, he has no accent from there, and he learned English at the home of other cousins he visited one year in Detroit. I think, personally, that he is hoping to entertain me, but he cannot, so he tells the same story each time about a glorious Serbian anthrogeographer, his professor and an idol of his, you must know this man as well, Jovan Cvijić who wrote a great deal, most importantly *The Balkan Peninsula and South Slavic Lands* and *Geomorphology*. I refused *Geomorphology*, but you are wrong if you think I could defend myself against reading *The Balkan Peninsula and South Slavic Lands*, for this Mr Dane is very stubborn. Luckily it is not so boring, to the contrary, but what is so very boring is that Mr Šarengača knows of not one thing to talk about, yet he does love to talk, and he is obsessed with anthropology.

I do know he is not purposely being a bastard and he would not insult me, but he does truly anger me sometimes. In his obsession he forgets all refinement and decorum. An example: as soon as Mr Šarengača besieged me in the corner away from the others, he paraded the skull theory for me. The Serbian and the Croatian skull, he explained, have a capacity of 1525 centimetres, but the English skull is much smaller, with only 1460. The worst? The Indians, only 1275. It is known that a microcephalic condition is a sign of idiocy.

"But, Mr Dane," I said, "I am English!"

Nothing. He does not notice that he is being a bastard, obsessed. He said to me that he has just read Lothrop Stoddart, and that I must read it, too. This Stoddart is an American psychologist who has a theory on the measurement of intelligence by a person's intellectual age, so according to this, Anglosaxons are a catastrophe – only 4.5 per cent reach the intellectual age of 18. I am silent. What can I do? On the other hand this gentleman marvels so at the Serbs. He quotes a Hans Günter (I was also meant to take this book from Mr Dane but I did not read it, I lied), that the Dinaric race has many talents, then some upheld that Slavs are the most talented in Europe, and among the Slavs, the Yugoslavs are the best. And other examples are many, he never tires. He has no notion he is insulting me. Since I am sure that no malice is intended, I chuckle to myself with no anger.

But my day of revenge came and I served him back the microcephalic condition and the 1460 English centimetres. In Ellsworth Huntington, an American book which Mr Dane put in my hands, I found a theory with a genius geography map, where Huntington drew in all the geniuses of a territory, and where the most happen to be, and he explains this by climate, history, etc. So, on this map, England is thick with geniuses, while Serbia is totally empty. I showed Huntington's map to Mr Šarengača with glee and he betrayed no surprise whatsoever, saying this was a plot, not science, because Nikola Tesla the Serbian genius was placed on the map in America where he happened to be living, not in Lika, Yugoslavia, where he was from. What we can do? Nothing I do seems to help.

I am writing this much about Mr Šarengača because this is something that I have realised. Serbs are either strongly convinced that these people are geniuses with no need of proof and they are certain about this, or again, in the same way, another time they are just as convinced that Serbia is worth nothing, that England is superior in every way. That is extremely strange and difficult to understand, but so it is. No middle ground, no reason in these considerations. In time I will begin to understand. Now I am only watching and I am surprised.

I was also most confused with Mr Barjaktarević (Mr Flagwaver, again, amusing) who, he tells me, is a cultural worker, and who is the perfect opposite of Mr Šarengača. Mr Šarengača is shy, he confides his secrets about the skull and other secrets to me, but with other people he is invariably quiet, not at all important. He wants to be liked by everyone. He reminds me of Grumpy the Dwarf in *Snow White*. He would be happy if I liked him. He does not know that he insults me, for he surely would not if he did. That is how Mr Dane is, inferior in some small way, while Mr Barjaktarević is tall, stiff, so important that he is fairly turning to stone with how important he is. He is older than most of them from this group of friends, so I asked what he does. Then I saw that Stevan was a little confused by my question. Stevan told me – a cultural worker. And what does a cultural worker do? I asked. Stevan says he does not work, he dabbles. I did not know what this meant, so then Stevan and the others said to me that Mr Barjaktarević is, well, he dabbles in a little bit of everything. He is a critic, he chairs boards everywhere, and is director of a review, wrote poems, was a young people's leader, a historian, dabbles in pedagogy, philosophy, sociology and popular pharmacology. I could not understand this, and it was a riddle to me, so I decided to ask Mr Barjaktarević personally, what he would think and what he would say he is. He laughed from up above down to me, then he pondered seriously and at the end he said, "I am a social ideologue and a popular enlightener" – you see, there are no such characters in England, but I think that this is all the best for England. Mr Barjaktarević must, surely, know nothing, since he is so busy dabbling.

Of course, many people come and talk, and as far as I can say, and so Stevan says – they are very good at what they do. The brilliant journalist Bane Petrović is one, a best friend of Stevan's from primary school, whose commentary I always read in *Politika*. He understands the situation in England excellently and brings me English magazines and newspapers. He speaks his thoughts precisely, almost always aloof in conversation and knows to hold his tongue when he sees, as he says, that "the rosé is speaking" from others. The only thing which is not so appealing with Bane is how witty he is with such irony beneath the surface, very English and nasty to me. Professor Jovanović is a wise man. He is the mentor for Stevan's doctorate. Professor Jovanović does not always come, and when he does he stays only briefly. He is so learned, I have seldom met a man so learned, and you can see that he has thought long about all he says. He never speaks off the top of his head, and says nothing of which he is not certain. I have read his comments on Stevan's thesis. It is indeed impressive how much he sees, how rich with associations in so many realms, how immediately he finds inconsistencies, contradictions, superficialities, and there were plenty of these in the first version of Stevan's thesis. It is a satisfaction to talk with Professor Jovanovic, and he is very curious, asks me all about England and about Serbia, but we speak in English for I am ashamed to speak in Serbian with him. I have not enough words yet, and I make one mistake after another (the last you must believe – you hold the proof in your hands). We see Professor Jovanović sometimes for dinner in the café, in the bookseller's "Sveslovenska knjižara" of M. J. Jovanović, and always at the bookseller's "Knjižara Petković" at no. 11 Balkanska Street. Many professors come, Stevan and I are always the youngest and the quietest. We listen to the conversation and when the bookseller's closes they talk on for a long while about everything. I have heard many things which are illuminating.

There you see, my dear Rachel, we live very intensely. In England you would not find so many people who argue, think, care. Every day there is something to do. This is hardly a slow city, in my impression, as you had told me, but, then again, everyone says that Belgrade was slow before the World War while you lived there. Now it is very dynamic socially, there is no petrified structure of class as there is in England, rather something which seems to me to be a transfusion of class which gives great energy to the life of the individual and of the people. Fine, I know, I jump to conclusions, and I have seen so little, but you asked me what I thought of Belgrade, and I have told you now what I think. Tomorrow my impressions may change.

January 1926

But, of course, I see another face, too. There is a Belgrade in which mild-mannered people play music, there is a Belgrade in which everyone cares and argues, a Belgrade which reads, clarifies debates on politics, social crises, but – all that in a surrounding which is the Orient.

Of course, I saw that immediately, and I am happy to have you to write to, for I will say nothing about this to Stevan. I will tell you why. I can feel Stevan quake at what I might say about his city. Exactly that, his city. He identifies himself with all the people, with every dog, with every cabby as if he is responsible for them all. I was not able to understand this for a long time, for I have never had that feeling, never do I wince when somebody English is a bastard, drunk or crude. Such a thing would not stir me. I could care less! But Stevan no, he is always pouncing. Did I see this or that? So I conclude: it is best that I pretend not to. It will be easier for Stevan that way and this is not always of the importance that Stevan thinks it is.

I pretend not to see, but see I do, even when I'd rather not. I am not able to forget first impressions. Our boat, the *Dušan Silni* from Bratislava, reached Belgrade from its most charming side. The sun had already fully set so the contour of Belgrade, Kalemegdan and down the hill was nicely seen against the sky. I said so to Stevan to lighten his nerves, and immediately I heard a thump, a stone fell from his heart.

But, when we stepped on to the shore – a catastrophe. Only one light bulb on the whole dock, and already it was dark, and from the dark some poor beggars in rags, barefeet, no teeth, in tatters, grabbed my *necessaire* from my hands, and to avoid them I stepped into mud, into a hole full of water, up to the knees, and I let go of the *necessaire*, and then I saw a couple of men fighting over the *necessaire*, each tugging on one side, until Stevan literally pushed one and the other and snatched it back. Then our boy Ačim came, and Father Milutin, and then we, thank God, sat in our cab and fled.

Those were the first beggars I saw, and the first mud I stepped in. Mud and beggars are no nicer now than they were then. I am the sorriest when I see a crippled beggar with a sign: "I defended my fatherland," now begging. Without a leg, or an arm. I do not know how that can be. This is so ugly to me that I cannot drop money in the Army hat. Stevan always does, and he is ashamed for a state which has no pension for a crippled war hero.

I am waging my own small war with mud. First, cobblestones are everywhere, and grass grows between the stones which they nicely call "spite". There are still many holes from shells, but also neglect. When it rains, I keep getting stuck in my narrow shoes. In the centre, near the Officers' Club, one day I got stuck, I pulled out the foot, the shoe stayed wedged, and I was barefoot. I crouched and with two hands I barely tugged out the shoe, but straightaway I went and bought galoshes. Now it is better.

But this is not so terrible, even if Stevan thinks so. Not for me. I drive in a horse-drawn cab, and then I do not get stuck, but I no longer go up Balkanska Street with a cab. I was there, but you know that street, Rachel, it is steep and pocked with holes, so the cab got stuck. Then the driver jumped down and struck the horse, the horse slipped and fell. Then he struck it again and again he, the horse, drove forward with foam in its mouth, but the poor horse could not do it! When still more beggars came and pushed, somehow we pulled out. These drivers, they are something horrible. When it was ice, I saw how a lorry full with bricks at the crossing of Nemanjina and Miloš Veliki could not pull. Instead the horses slipped, fell, and the driver with a long whip of leather, beat them until their backs were bloody, but still they could not do it. And he cursed. (Stevan would not translate this for me, but as far as I could tell, well, this is such a verbal erotic imagination that I am surprised!) Stevan says that they think of the swears themselves. For example, I heard: Fuck your father on your dead mother, which in English is revolting. Rachel, not even the Marquis de Sade would have thought of such a thing. Stevan to me says that the municipality wanted to buy two, three strong work horses to stand in Balkanska, in Nemanjina, to help when people get stuck and slip, but then they decided no, because they understand. If these drivers expect the work horses to come and help, they will load on even more bricks and wood, and fall and slip all the same.

One more thing in Belgrade that is not so pleasant. Many times I have seen groups of young men. They stand at a corner or they sit on a wall and they spit. They do nothing, only sit and spit in a circle all day long. All around them there is spittle. I do not know what this means. Is this a game of youth, or a protest against society? It is not nice. On the other hand, I am fond of the ramshackle shanties which Stevan very much despises. He says they are Turkish. But they are yellow or white with windows close to the street so a person is even able to enter the house through a window, and they have a blue, or green, or pink line below with a hat-like roof, as in fairy tales with coloured pictures.

Generally, it is accurate that the houses inside are clean, but the city is filthy. I do not know why. All that is public is neglected. As in Turkey, they say here. The street is for no-one. Imagine, Rachel, that here a woman shakes out carpets through a window on to the heads of whoever goes by, and everyone sees this as normal! Or in the National Theatre, where women are in evening gowns and in the vestibule I can smell the toilet which is immediately next to the entrance to the inner courtyard, and squalid, my God, there is no way you can venture in. And this is the way with public toilets everywhere. I have not discovered a single one to be different, while in private houses they are clean. I think it is that many men here have no regard for others, they are communally blind and urban without discipline, the city is not theirs, and not a lasting residence. They are here for refuge, as if they will stay only for a little while and then they will flee. Stevan explains it to me this way: under the Turks, the Serbs kept their house and around it ugly on purpose so that a Turk would not come to him to stay. Maybe. But this is the fact. The Serb is, with some exceptions, a bad citizen.

January 27, 1925, Sava Day

Now I will tell you what I like the least: government offices and clerks. I had to go to government offices for registration, for citizenship, to import my trunks, and for everything you have to speak with clerks and they are terrible. You come to the offices and first you see a crowd in the corridor, and before the door on a chair sits a man who lets you into the office, and who is so lazy that he is not even able to say "Next", but, only as if half asleep, his eyelids shut, he nods his head so that another can go inside. Who is he? I asked Stevan, for nowhere is there even a single corridor where no lazy man is sitting like that. Stevan says a peasant has a dream that he will get a city job, and when he has a cousin in Belgrade, or holds an election assembly for one of the parties, he gets the prize: work in a government office. But it does not really function. He is poor, dressed half like a peasant in broadcloth, and half like a city beggar.

This is true for clerks, too. The man goes to his office, he sits, only a little less lazy than the man working in the government offices, and he looks gruff. Then someone says he came for this, for that, and the clerk stares through him with painful boredom. Then the telephone rings, the clerk chats with his father-in-law who has just installed a telephone in his house. This lasts, lasts, then he finishes, looks at the man at the desk, and says, "What was it you said to me?" and the man must start straight from the beginning. The clerk, too, is a half-beggar. His suit shines with age, the white collar is grimy, his shoes muddy, he is a caricature of a civil servant, and he delights in having it be seen that he is the government and can do as he pleases. And the lower the authority, I have noticed, the worse it gets. That lazy man who sits by the door when he wakes up, was so gruff once that he said to a man whose turn it was to go in, "Eh, not you, you wait until last."

"Why?"

"Because I said so."

I admit that when they hear I am from England, and who sent me, they are not bastards, but this spectacle is ugly to see.

That Belgrade is far away from me. When I say this to Stevan he feels better. It is out there somewhere, but I am living with other people, and I write to you to practise my language, and describe my impressions but not because life in Belgrade is bitter. It is good for me here now, Rachel. Already I am certain that my home city will be a nice place for me although at the beginning, and still now, I am often surprised and ask about the things I do not know.

But I know what I do not know. I do not jump to conclusions, good or bad, in Belgrade. I must watch and understand. In Vienna where Stevan and I were on New Year's Eve, we met an Englishwoman who had been in Yugoslavia, in raptures about how it was all so beautiful, so marvellous. She was weeping because they had convinced her to disinfect her Macedonian lace and dresses, and the fabric was destroyed. We spoke English, so I will tell you what we said in English: "You must not think me stupid," she said to me, "you cannot understand why I think these dresses important; you have not been there."

"Is it so wonderful there?" I asked.

"It is more wonderful than I can tell you," she answered.

"But how," I said.

She could not tell me at all clearly.

"Well, there is everything there. Except what we have. But that seems very little."

"Do you mean that the English have very little," I asked, "or the whole of the West?"

"The whole of the West," she said, "here, too."

I looked through the window at the butter-yellow baroque Viennese houses between the chestnut trees and laughed. "Beethoven and Mozart and Schubert wrote quite a lot of music in this town," I said.

"But they were none of them happy," she objected.

"So, in Yugoslavia," Stevan suggested with a smile, "everybody is happy?"

"No, no," she said, "not at all, but . . . The thing I want to tell you couldn't be told, however, because it is manifold and nothing like what one is accustomed to communicate in words. Really we are not as rich in the West as we think we are. Or, rather, there is much we haven't got which the people in the Balkans have got in quantity. To look at them you would think they had nothing. The people who made these dresses looked as if they had nothing at all. But if these imbeciles here had not spoiled this embroidery you would see that whoever did it had more than we have."

Back into Serbian. From the pavement to cobblestones. Therefore, that Englishwoman, she fabricated a Yugoslavia, an Arcadia from her dreams. I will not. I watch. I have open eyes and I do not jump to conclusions. Unlike her, Rachel, I am surprised and I ask.

March, 1926

I am, my dear Rachel, like a huge fortress. I was always large and I did not like it that I am 5 feet 10 inches large which in my shoes is 6 feet, that I have breasts like Beowulf's mother, and now they are larger still, and my stomach is like a mountain in front of me. I do not like myself at all. Stevan tries to cheer me so he says I look like a mythic mother, but I am ashamed and full of horror, but not "fresh bread horror", as Nanka said. As far as Nanka is concerned, thank God we are now in our new flat, for she believes I must do peculiar things to be sure I will have a son and not a daughter. I have known Nanka respected only sons for a while. She calls our maid Mila "Son", though she is a girl. I asked why this is so, and Nanka says that she loves Mila so that is why she calls her "Son", but she said nothing to me when I asked why, if she loves Mila, she does not call Mila "Daughter". Nanka is one strange character. When she discovered that I was, as she says, in a blessed state, she whispered to me that I must no longer share the same room with Stevan, then she went herself to pick some plant *svinjda* (Stevan does not know this plant exists) which she dried, then rubbed between hands to dust, salted it, and makes me soak fresh bread in it, then she keeps saying to me that it is a disgrace for me to go into the city and be seen with people, and that this is no good for the child either, and other stupid instructions, which, of course, I do not follow, but this is tiresome.

Of course I am mixing only seldom with crowds now, not because of Nanka's admonition, but because I am already heavy, and I know that I am huge like a monster. I am spending ages arranging our flat so that all will be ready when I go to have the baby. It may be any day.

In these last days I am very contemplative, Rachel. Now I would love you to be here. I am alone a lot, and then from nowhere I feel that everything around me is unreal, these rooms, this maid, Mila, Nanka, this language I am speaking, and I am at a loss. How did I come here? I wonder. I have a strange feeling that I have dreamed my life. Once it seemed to me that I dreamed my Reading, my late mother, Richard (did that really happen, Rachel? Did I marry a man named Richard Harris? Was I divorced after just a single day of married life?), but at the same time it seems as if I am dreaming of myself now as I sit in my armchair and look at Miloš Veliki Street and I dream that I am waiting to have a baby. Don't be wrong to think I am nostalgic. I am not. Maybe this is like nostalgia, but different, for I am precisely sure: positively I do not wish to live in England. Anywhere else. But in England, no. I cannot explain this in Serbian, for it is not ordinary. Maybe I could if we were together and talking.

But this is monumental, and then something happens, something small, someone passes, or is heard, and all at once I know again who I am and where I am. I do not know how it was for you when you had your David. I am a little disgusted by the way I look; if you have no chance to see me, like a Zeppelin. I saw a poster here for an Italian circus: a woman in shorts and shirt advertised as the strongest woman in the world, so I said that to me I look like that giant lady. Stevan gets angry, but I cannot help it, that is my feeling. I think that I already know it is a little girl, and I love her very much, and she is very important for my life even before she is born, even now while I feel the child only as discomfort in my belly. I cannot wait for it to happen, for her to come.

I hear the key. Stevan is at the door, so I will stop dwelling with my thoughts. I would say that my dwelling is your fate. It is of no importance whatsoever that you are far away. You are always my most patient "confidante" from some play by Racine.

Now Stevan will come in. We will dine. That is reality, not a dream.

FOUR

There was a man named Jeremija – his surname I have relegated to the wasteland of oblivion – who spoke to me in whispers in Banjica prison, at night, when conversation was forbidden, about the secret properties of the human mind which he had discovered when he was wounded, suffering from concussion and amnesia. I do not know why he felt that he had to recount this precisely when he did, or why he chose me to tell. I do remember quite clearly, however, that it was not so much the fact that the brain is able to tuck away the whole of a life's experience somewhere in its recesses (as I have his surname), only to retrieve it later, which so astonished sorrowful Jeremija as it was the orderly sequence by which he regained his memory, bit by bit, during his convalescence and self-regeneration, starting with his earliest child-hood. The events that transpired immediately before he was wounded were the last to come back, as if they had been the final bit of his life to be stored.

Another mind disclosed the unusual way it ticked: Nanka's. During each new visit to Aleksandrovac (before the end, I was going there at least weekly), where my Gojkovica was in rapid decline, besieged by some strange pestilence, Nanka regressed step by step towards her beginnings. By the end, she could recall only her friends from early childhood and schooldays, an uncle and neighbours who had died ages ago. She knew nothing of what had happened the day before, or who I was, or that there was a grown woman people called Nanka.

Resumed this morning, my cohabitation with my own memories is easier for me to grasp when I recall those peculiar struggles in Jeremija's and Nanka's minds: the struggle of the former to retrieve that which comprised all he was, and that of the latter to erase everything except those earliest days cosily sheltered from life and people. My mind had long been blank of memories. Never as totally as Jeremija's or Nanka's, but nevertheless in a way akin to theirs. I focused entirely on the present (just as Nanka did on the furthest past) until this morning, when I began dipping greedily, with the same orderly sequence of Jeremija's convalescence, for bit after bit of the past, cramming them into every second of my leisurely time in bed.

Will Elizabeta notice a change? Will she know that today something special has kept me in bed? Will she guess, perhaps, that I am not sleeping, eyes closed, half sitting in my royally spacious berth? The one thing I do know is that this time, as always, there will be no reliable answers to my questions, and that will fill me, as it always has done, with an edginess which is the essence of my years of longing for a way in to the privacy of my indomitable, reticent Eliza. I have grown accustomed to this longing. It is a restiveness that maddened me years ago, but is now more like a hunger, bearable, actually more agreeable than the dull sense of satiation. Fear, nevertheless, begins to stir in me that my one and only fellow traveller, the privileged captive of our enclave, will somehow understand and interpret as a betrayal my return to the memories we erased by mutual consent some twenty years ago, just as Nanka erased hers by senility.

I don't know. Eliza never did say: Let's forget the past. Nor did I establish that if memory were to creep back into our everyday lives (like those worms which work their way into the bare feet of Abyssinians), it would putrefy, produce an ungodly stench and pollute with terrible wounds the handful of shared rituals which have sustained our submerged lives with dignity. Or whatever it is that we now seem to have. The rupture with the past came naturally, like the fulfilment of a sacred oath, a healing dream, an ability earned through suffering to forget one's own life. Our break with the past ought really to be seen as our readiness for death. My Elizabeta and I, we died one day some twenty years ago. When they live on, the dead no longer recall their past lives, useless in the Thanatos of everyday existence, in the empire of a God with a heart of iron (as the legend goes) who liberates mortals of their memories. We staggered, whimpering like two turkeys pecking, for months, or was it years, around a contaminated hen house, mutely aching with life until death delivered us or, if the word *death* seems too final, the end of life. Or maybe it was death after all? Instead of "They lived happily ever after", our fairy tale ended with "They lived dead ever after". Dead in an enclave around which the River Okeanos flows.

I, of course, am not the one to say whether my Eliza has torn the murderous tangle of memories from inside her, but her acquiescence to the sacred uneventfulness of our conspiracy for two testifies to the fact that she has grown accustomed to the dead condition of her living. And that is why I worry that my foray into the past will make waves, no matter how gentle and noiseless; I shudder to contemplate that I might, like imprudent Orpheus looking back, lose my Euridika. Or Eurydice, as the English call her.

Off the top of my head, I might explain my current feelings with that third-rate line "Time heals all wounds". But time heals nothing. Time ravages. Time – the executioner. I am a ruin, dusty and buried, therefore I am able to remember again. After twenty years, I am able to remember and feel genuine surprise at my actions as if they are the vagaries of someone else who, with no self-respect, works maliciously against himself. I am not able to explain how in God's name I was drawn into politics when I had spent my entire life at a genuine and rather deliberate distance from it: not so close that it might singe me, but not so far that I couldn't warm myself, a man of the times and a Serb, over the embers of the doings of my age. If I had one fundamental conviction rooted in life experience, it was the knowledge that an honourable and wise man must resist the siren song of politics.

I am doing my best to comprehend those most distant days of my maturation, and it is obvious to me that I developed rather early on a kind of aversion towards politics and politicians which convinced me, furtively at first, that they must be kept at bay. This aversion certainly helped me overcome with ease the nihilistic turbulence of conceit at the basis of my occasional fleeting attraction to prominence and power. Chances are, this aversion dated back to the rowdy Radicalist days of my father. I remember the clumsiness I sensed behind Milutin's fake solidity and heartiness. I cannot fathom what prompted him, in 1910 or '11, to take me with him on his pre-election rounds through the Valjevo district, where he had been named a Radical candidate, but I am certain that this was when my first thoughts on politics were born – but for war the most dangerous form of entertainment among the Serbs. Though still too young to judge, I associated things with politics on that God-awful journey which may have absolutely nothing to do with them. For example, chilly, squalid rooms above village taverns in which drunken voters were draining the barrel of *rakija* Milutin had bought them, while I was busy adding new bloodstains to the coarse, homespun bedding as I squashed bloated fleas and bedbugs. That Daumier-like image of politics has never completely vanished from my conscious-ness: the low-ceilinged room in a haze of tobacco smoke, the tallow candles, the looming meaty faces of sweaty peasants, grimacing from drink as they lurched over to the table where Milutin and the local Radical front runners were sitting so that they could hold forth long and resolutely to the future representative, who was writhing inside in a painful knot of squeamish discomfort, on how he was a sterling merchant and a patriot, as if he didn't know it already. Some of them wanted to kiss such a fine man, the pride of Serbia, dedicated to his supporters, while others downed a glass of *rakija* with him, and still others, the most brazen ones, demanded that he place their son, their son-in-law, their godfather as a clerk in some office within the Belgrade bureaucracy. Milutin, the reserved gentleman merchant, trapped in the tavern in the altar-like smoke of the tallow candles, will remain for ever in my consciousness in a mythical painting entitled *A Victim of Politics at His Execution*. Times did change. As I was coming of age, the domestic political scene most resembled a royal highway with brigands crouching at every turn in the road: Pero Živković, Milan Srškić, Nikola Uzunović, Boško Jeftić, Milan Stojadinović – what a phantasmic array of wax figures – then Stojadinović and Maček wearing knickerbockers; or snivelling Radić, who one day would be singing "The Republic, Pride of the World" with a *tamburitza* ensemble to peasants and the next would be bowing and scraping before King Aleksandar; or Pribićević, who turned from royalist to republican overnight. Could any image be less appealing?

My model has always been my professor and mentor, Slobodan, from whom I learned not only all I know about politics but also perhaps, more than I dare confess, my social graces. The professor was an ironic European who ached to be part of Serbdom, but everything, from his principles to the way he spoke, betrayed his European essence. The prudence with which he pronounced his judgements was un-Serbian, as were his deliberate manner and his sarcasm. I conversed with Slobodan mostly in his office at the Law Faculty library at Topličin Venac, from which he, like some spiritual aristocrat, a latter-day Voltaire, kept an eye, as if from some observatory, on King Aleksandar, ever the irrepressible Montenegrin curmudgeon; on the Croatian question, which he compared to "those little fevers which never kill the person, but invisibly drain away his strength"; on Father Korošec and the privileged Slovenes (he held that we could have "wooed and won the Croats with less attention and resources than we squandered on the Slovenes"); on the violent shots fired in Parliament; on the Yugoslav political scene, which he followed with a lifelong passion, though hardly finding it charming. When I asked him once on a walk to his house, "Professor, have you ever felt inclined to engage directly in politics? You are always so close, yet never inside," Slobodan glared at me, so appalled that the expression on his face, more than his exclamation – "You must be joking, Stevan!" – showed just how far the notion was from his mind.

My disdain for and fear of politics was so deeply rooted that it helped me defend myself when, under rather bizarre circumstances, the mainstream currents of our marauding social system drew me with terrible force towards its foaming vortex. It is difficult among the Serbs to remain untainted by politics, whether one is a peasant or an opera singer, and especially as a professor in the faculty for the study of those generally bypassed subjects of law and jurisprudence. Outsiders find themselves hard pressed to explain the political passions of the Serbs. Having reduced complex political relations to vulgar, petty squabbles, the Serb is not inclined to weigh the contradictions between individual and common interests in the most efficient and just manner. Lust for power, a Byzantine brand of power, in a form limited by no constraints whatsoever, informs the vision of each and every political hack and local government agent as much as it moves the prime minister and leader of the opposition. Politics in Yugoslavia are not conducted for the purpose of achieving some tangible goal. Rather, Yugoslavia exists so that the parties can harangue one another to the point of exhaustion, or lunacy. One had to keep an eye on it, though, for it infiltrated those realms where no-one in a more rational nation would have expected to find it.

And so it was that when in one of my lectures in early 1937 I analysed an unusual omission in the Constitution of the Kingdom of Yugoslavia, dated September 3, 1931, it was not my desire to draw attention to myself. Section 5 of Article 36 reads, "The Kingdom of Yugoslavia is ruled by King Aleksandar I from the dynasty of the Karađorđevićes. The heir to King Aleksandar's throne shall be his male progeny, according to primogeniture." Article 37 says, "And, failing male lineal descendants, he shall name his own heir from a consanguine line. In such a case where the King has named no heir prior to his death, the National Assembly shall, in joint session, select a King from that same dynasty." I commented on the oddity that not a single article of the Constitution would be applicable to the circumstances that existed at the time. In the hypothetical case of the death of the frail child King Petar II, Article 37 would not apply because the King of Yugoslavia, a mere boy, obviously had no heirs. Instead, Article 38 would be relevant. This suggested that his younger brother, Prince Tomislav, would not become King, but that the "National Assembly, in joint session, would select a King from the same dynasty". It was even possible that the new King might come from "the next degree of consanguinity".

The first response to what I had thought was merely a passing remark came from a colleague, Professor Janković, a well-heeled expert on public and administrative, as well as constitutional, law, who mentioned that he disagreed with me. Invoking the "spirit of the Constitution" – which, as we know, was the work of King Aleksandar I, who most certainly would not have worked contrary to the interests of his own descendants – the "monarchist tradition" and, finally, the "benevolent intentions of the Regency", Janković felt that in the hypothetical case of the death of King Petar II, his brother Tomislav would most certainly be enthroned "according to the order of primogeniture". Naturally, I demurred. I admitted that Janković was attempting to find a just solution, but the "tradition", "benevolent intentions" and "spirit" he invoked I judged to be extra-legal categories and warned him that he could not name a single constitution article in support of his thesis.

I assumed that with this brief exchange of opinion in the presence of several amused fellow professors the case was closed. It had, however, only begun, and progressed with such precipitate force that even today I am amazed how I succeeded, armed only with my fortitude, to counter the efforts of the most powerful groups to draw me, at any cost, into politics.

Two months after my lecture and interchange with Professor Janković, I received a summons. Dr Korošec, the acting Deputy Prime Minister, invited me to an interview, not in his office, but in that of the absent Prime Minister Stojadinović!

Despite my best efforts, even after consulting with several colleagues who were well versed in political matters, I could not divine why this notorious figure was requesting my presence. I knew all manner of things, of course, about Dr Korošec, but little to put my mind at ease. A man who, as president of the National Council with its seat in Zagreb, had, before unification, presided over a version of Yugoslavia that had not included Serbia and Montenegro, he had been vice-president of the initial government of the Kingdom of Serbs, Croats and Slovenes and was then incarcerated by the Ministry of the Interior, only to become a minister in that very same Ministry and one of its most effective members, ruthless in his persecution of opposition politicians, particularly in Slovenia. Dr Korošec was a priest from the Maribor Seminary, yet renowned as a connoisseur of fine wines and beautiful women who, as was widely known, gave rein to these tastes in his later years (he died in a box at the National Theatre while listening to an aria sung by his then mistress). He was the last person I wished to have anything to do with.

I must confess, however, that upon entering the office of Stojadinović's Chief of Staff, I felt a prickle of curiosity, not only about why I had been summoned, but at the prospect of meeting such a colourful, prominent figure. I had met Korošec on several occasions as a colleague – he was also a professor and taught a course on the cooperative movement in Yugoslav at the Faculty of Agriculture in Belgrade – but invariably in a group. I had to admire the breadth of the man's interests. I remembered that he had spoken, fully informed, on the history of Serbia, Viennese theatres, the Soviet economy and the personality of Benito Mussolini. Seeing, however, the degree of cordiality with which I was received by the Chief of Staff, my curiosity nearly gave way to anxiety. The massive wooden door, varnished and shining, precisely as one would have imagined the entrance to the office of the Prime Minister, was opened by the courteous, dapper Chief of Staff, Mr Marjanović, who led me into a long room across which the infamous priest, lover, policeman – the most famous Slovene after Janez Evangelista Krek – was hurrying towards me. I had remembered him as being slightly shorter. With thinning grey hair, a stout, fleshy figure, a 65-year-old face and pale complexion, wearing spectacles the lenses of which had only a reinforced metal frame on the upper rim, he was dressed, as always while in Belgrade, in lay attire, a waistcoat buttoned over his rotund belly with a long row of six buttons, his dark suit more reminiscent, for some reason, of the severe garb of a Protestant minister than of a Catholic. Perhaps the association would never have struck me had I not known of his earlier calling, and if I hadn't needed to distract myself from my growing agitation. After we shook hands on the thick carpet somewhere in the middle of the long office, between the door through which I had entered and his (or rather Stojadinović's) richly carved ceremonial desk, Korošec directed me towards a couple of leather armchairs in the corner, where we sat down side by side. The degree to which I was on my guard is demonstrated by the fact that I interpreted even this seating arrangement as significant, wondering whether perhaps Korošec had resolved to use my awkward twist to the left as we spoke to render me insecure and thereby susceptible to whatever he meant to accomplish. He urged me to help

96

myself to the cigars and cigarettes on the table but did not offer me a drink, which led me to conclude that he did not wish to have a lengthy conversation.

This proved to be the case. Grinning jovially, he proceeded to address the matter at hand without a word of introduction. "I am given to understand, my esteemed colleague Medaković, that you had a hand in the re-examination of Articles 36 and 37?"

He used some Slovene words with which I was not familiar, but from the very first sentence it was clear that I had been chased straight into the minefield of high politics despite all my efforts to the contrary. Of course, I did not succumb easily. To gain time (the manoeuvre must have been transparent), I said I did not know for certain what Korošec was referring to. To my regret, he did not leave me in the dark. I had been chosen (I quailed, not knowing what the choice was for) because of my incisive observation – Korošec did not stint on the compliments – and my polemic with Professor Janković. "We are convinced, Colleague Medaković, that you will be well suited to prepare an opinion on the question of the succession, addressing every plausible eventuality which the royal family might face."

I could see at once that there was no easy way out of the minefield, but I tried to toss the hot potato into someone else's hands. "Mr Minister, I am certain that Professor Janković, and not only he, but others knowledgeable in questions of constitutional law, are far more qualified, both in terms of rank and of expertise, and I advise you to turn to the men who have the greatest authority."

I did not, of course, find Korošec unprepared. He smiled, brightly and jovially as if he had just heard something extremely naïve (as my attempt had, indeed, been), and with a sentence both natural and cunning (something I would only understand later, too late), he brought me straight to checkmate in two moves. "We have looked at every option, believe me. You are our best bet. We were unable to think of a single other expert quite as qualified as you are. Please, my dear Professor, write an exhaustive opinion, and submit it to us as punctually as possible."

There was no doubt that he (now indubitably the minister, rather than the colleague) had ordered, not asked, me to do something which I could not, without serious consequences, refuse to do. Figuring that I would need to bring to the discussion a peace of mind which I could not boast of at that moment, I decided to accept the order and then see what to do about it later. Only as I was leaving the Ministry, tremendously agitated after a warm farewell from both Minister and Chief of Staff, did I realise the tactical beauty of Korošec's final statement. The cunning priest had, with a single courteous sentiment, hit several bull's-eyes: he had complimented me, foiled my attempt at passing the hot potato, given me to know (with his use of the emphatic plural) of their, rather than his, decision, that behind the order stood a higher collective authority, while never disclosing which, and – most important and most cunning – that they wanted me, and not Professor Janković, precisely because those who had issued the order had not done so to rectify the omission in the constitutional regulation, but rather to establish with certainty that such an omission existed.

When I remember, today, the chilling panic that sank upon me, halting my reason mid-stride, surrendering it to destructive black forebodings, I see perhaps even more clearly now than I did at the time how deeply a fear of politics was rooted in my instincts. I wasn't thinking at all; I merely quaked. So Korošec's request only acquired its proper proportions and meaning in my mind when I repeated it to cool, collected Elizabeta. She was right: my fright was founded more on doubts than on facts. He was not asking me, a university professor with expertise in constitutional law, to undertake political action of any sort, but rather to provide an expert opinion in keeping with my scholarly insight and convictions. No-one was asking me, and I did not need to know, whether Prince Pavle stood behind Korošec or not, and whether the rumours of his ambitions, or his wife Olga's ambitions, to usurp the throne, even if it meant murdering his under-aged nephew Petar, were true or not. Reassured, I presented, as conscientiously as I could, on ten typed pages, all legal facets to the regulation of the succession to the throne. In order to avoid conversation and further implication, I resolved to inform the Chief of Staff (not Marjanović, but a Slovene) that the requested analysis would be delivered in the morning. Judging by the fact that Korošec did not call me over the next few days, I concluded that he was satisfied and that he was not expecting any further services from me. I began to believe that it had all ended in an honourable and simple fashion, and that the monster of politics had bypassed and forgotten me.

This, however, was only the beginning. Precisely when I had begun to put the dangerous and (I thought) insignificant episode behind me, out of the clear sky an invitation arrived from Prince Pavle and Princess Olga to the Winter Charity Ball. That invitation, the reason for which we were at a loss to explain, filled me with forebodings which were only reinforced when, upon our arrival at the Old Palace, we discovered that we had been assigned places in the double row of guests waiting to shake hands with the Prince and Princess. In the vast, solemn hall, the men lined up in one row and their wives in another row across from them. I was not acquainted with my neighbour to the right or to the left, and there was no time to make their acquaintance, for at the very moment we were hurried to our places, Their Highnesses appeared at the door.

I had seen photographs of the Regent and his Greek wife many times in the papers and film journals, so I was confident that there would be nothing to surprise us in their flesh-and-blood appearance. This, however, was not the case. I remember that for some reason I was convinced – entirely irrationally – that the Prince would appear in civilian dress, in one of his English double-breasted flannel suits, with a top hat and an umbrella hooked over his arm, when, instead, a man in a general's uniform, bedecked with ribbons, rosettes and decorations, under a busby, a sabre hanging from his belt, walked towards our line. The Serbian people were not fond of Prince Pavle, and the belief was widespread that Pavle was not fond of them. He was far too much the Englishman, apparently, and far too much the aristocrat to understand the peasant soul. Rumours circulated, probably with no basis in fact but persistent nevertheless, that he had no Serbian blood in his veins. His legal father, Prince Arsen, was rumoured not to be his true father, since Pavle's mother, the Russian Princess Aurora Demidova, a stunning beauty, had supposedly conceived him with her lover, General Mannerheim, because of which there had been a duel (never confirmed) and a divorce (an immutable fact). In person, Pavle's face with its thin lips, broad cheekbones and jutting jaw, more striking under the busby than in photographs, with noticeable shadows under his eyes, seemed typically Serbian and sickly, somehow, precisely like those peasants of ours who are born feeble, labour with effort and die young, never enjoying a day of decent health in their lives. Diminutive in stature, dark in countenance, the uniformed weakling stood at the head of our line and began shaking the hand of each man. He exchanged the occasional word with some, while with others he did not, but instead simply nodded when he heard the name and title from his head of protocol. Having reached my neighbour, the Prince spoke briefly with him about hunting in quite excellent German. Then it was my turn.

"Dr Stevan Medaković, Professor at the Faculty of Law," announced his aide, loudly enough that I, too, could hear it, and, I remember how I prayed, tense as a child pleading with God to intercede in some small matter, that the Prince would merely nod and pass on to the next man. My wish was not heeded.

"Ah, yes, Professor Medaković, I have heard of you," said the Prince, but to my elation he did not continue. Rather, he simply smiled and proceeded through the "circle", as it was called, much more rapidly than the Princess was making her way through the line of women. Freed of my worries, I now had the time to study her. Despised more than Pavle, she was famed for her beauty and known as a conniving woman of great ambition. As I watched her that day for the first time, I could not have said whether or not she was malicious, but, as tall and slender as she was with her heron-like neck, her manner was ungainly, neither beautiful nor ugly, a cultured and groomed lady in her 30s wearing a heavy grey silk ball gown with plunging neckline, her shoulders slightly stooped, a lavish tiara looking dangerously like a crown, at least to me, burdened as I was by what I knew. When I later had the opportunity to see her closer at hand, I would find that her expressive, arresting blue eyes enhanced her bird-like figure and softened her jarringly mannish hooked nose. My initial interest in her appearance was interrupted because something began to happen in the ladies' line which diverted my attention entirely.

Upon reaching Elizabeta, the Princess had halted and spoken several words which, of course, I was unable to hear. By the way Elizabeta was listening attentively, however, and then beginning to speak herself, I concluded that she had been asked something specific. This, in conjunction with the Prince's benevolent recognition of my humble self, began to worry me, but when I observed that the conversation between the two tall women in ball gowns was continuing, apparently rather congenially, I was beside myself. When the other ladies in their elegant coiffures, their mink and ermine stoles, diamond earrings and pearl necklaces began craning their necks and conferring in whispers, unable to curb their curiosity and eager to catch sight of the lady to whom the Princess was devoting so much attention, a lady most of them were seeing that evening for the first time, I was reassured that I had not, in my inordinate fear, overestimated the length of the exchange or the Princess's unusual interest in my wife.

"Whatever are they talking about," I wondered, impatient to hear Elizabeta's report which, due to court ball decorum, I would have to wait some time for. The ladies were not slated to rejoin their escorts until the beginning of the Royal Kolo, always the first dance of the evening. The Prince and Princess led it, of course, on this as on other occasions, and we joined in according to protocol, although, at least where I was concerned (I found it comforting to see I was not alone), it was a torment to stay in step.

It transpired that the conversation between Elizabeta and the Princess had been insubstantial. Like the Prince (the coincidence of their remarks made me particularly uncomfortable), the Princess commented that she had heard of us and that she knew that Elizabeta was English. She enquired as to whether Elizabeta had grown accustomed to Belgrade life, and since their experiences must, at least in some respects, have been similar, she hinted that there would presently be an occasion for a longer conversation. This "presently", however, happened with sobering speed. Scarcely had Elizabeta finished recounting her tale to me when one of the ladies-in-waiting, Jelena Todorović, came over to us with the news that the Princess, whose sister was married to the Duke of Kent, and the Prince, for whom England was a home away from home, wished to meet with me, former student of an English university, and my wife, until recently a subject of the English Crown. The lady-in-waiting underlined this aspect of the Prince's interest so emphatically that it made me twice as anxious, but naturally the invitation could not be refused.

Could not be, but indeed, in all fairness, we did not wish it to be. I had never fancied myself a member of Belgrade high society; I had never aspired to parading around the royal salons and exclusive soirées in the most elegant palaces in a jacket and striped trousers. In this respect, I was hardly an exception; a large number of people felt precisely as I did inside the circles in which I moved. Young, enthusiastic Belgrade University cultivated a strong identity of its own, and the professors, at least the finest among them, enjoyed a status so secure that they were above the skin-deep glamour of the city's snobbish élite. Without a trace of leftist inclination, I would say that the splendour of the diplomatic hunting parties, élite balls, saints' day celebrations and receptions was regarded by my colleagues with distaste. I would be lying, though, if I said that I wasn't a bit charmed by the idea of socialising with the crème de la crème of the capital's citizenry, the diplomatic corps and the royal couple. The gleam of parquet floors, the luxury of antique silver dishes, the Chinese porcelain, the valuable paintings and the impeccable service of waiters who soundlessly decanted aged, rare wines had their allure. But despite these seductive pleasures, I invariably experienced something like a twinge of conscience, even embarrassment, at the notion of embracing this world without progressing in any way towards loftier values.

Our "brief but intense bout of socialising", as my wife dubbed it, with the royal couple, however, had an unexpectedly profound effect on her, though she would never have admitted as much. Indeed, she made every effort to conceal it. She may have cloaked her eagerness from others, but from me she could not hide her excitement, her heightened attention, the care she took in carrying on the most ordinary English conversation, and, no matter how faint, a traitorous blush spread across her pale features when the Prince or Princess addressed her directly. From the moment when she related to me with a genuine thrill the first words she exchanged with the Princess, and on the countless occasions that followed, Elizabeta's reaction both amused me and gave me pause. I observed what others might well have missed: that royal pomp royally fired Elizabeta's English blood. She would be invited to a cosy luncheon at the White Palace or to a bridge party at the home of my friend Dragomir Kasidolac, whose wife, Bebeka, Milan Stojadinović's wife and the Princess were all Greek, and Elizabeta, as the fourth foreign wife, fitted perfectly into their polyglot circle. She frequently attended receptions at the residence of the English ambassador, Ronald Campbell, to which we had, indeed, been invited earlier, as we had to receptions held by his predecessor, Sir Nevile Henderson. I had sensed back in Bristol that the word *sea* did not hold the same meaning for Elizabeta, the islander, and for me, the calloused continental, that a royal family would not stir the same emotions in a person who was a fellow citizen of the Tudors and Plantagenets and someone whose King Milan had, just yesterday, sold off the State railway lines to support his gambling habit. I watched my foreigner, my stranger, as she preened herself for each of her royal audiences, the way she uttered the words "Your Highness" with carefully mastered yet evident delight, and how she responded with disproportionate and otherwise entirely atypical bile to my derisive comment that Pavle and Olga (Elizabeta referred to them as the Prince and Princess) had managed only through concerted efforts to become "Members of the Royal House of the Dynasty of the Karađorđevićes", thereby earning the right, according to the "Familial Regulations Governing Members of the Royal Household", to the title of "Royal Highness".

It was also a revelation to me that Pavle and Olga, particularly Olga, had gladly suffered the humiliation of requiring Aleksandar to include Arsen's ancillary line in Article 1 of the "Regulation", key because despite all the attention showered upon us after my unfortunate interpretation of Articles 36 and 37, I was not clear on whether the Prince genuinely coveted the throne or suffered his duties as Regent as a burden too weighty for his gentlemanly shoulders. This was the time of the *Anschluss*, the occupation of Czechoslovakia; Mussolini's and Hitler's shadows were darkening the sky over Belgrade. It was beginning to look as if Stojadinović – all-powerful Stojadinović – was leading the country straight into the iron embrace of the Axis powers, which could hardly have been the will of the English-raised and educated Prince. On the other hand, there was no valid way for Yugoslavia to defy raging Hitler, so Pavle, born wearing a top hat with English umbrella in hand, now donned his ceremonial finery and went off to court the treacherous, maniacal painter from Braunau am Inn. I know next to nothing of Pavle's true character, but from what I managed to glean in the conversations we held or in those I overheard, I can say that he was a conscientious ruler. He placed the interests of Yugoslavia before his own ambitions and will. Done up in his English suit from Savile Row, a particularly vain, yet soft-spoken, well-mannered gentleman, a connoisseur of the fine arts, he must have rejected with at least one filament of his being the foreign and domestic intrigues into which his position drew him. The allure of government may have meant that his royal vanity prevailed over the gentlemanly nature of the aesthete; it may well be that Pavle was genuinely torn asunder by the desire to rule and the desire to be freed of the heavy burden of ruling. Being King was more than Spanish court decorum and the royal treatment whenever he visited London (something he was already cognisant of during the time when we saw him, as he was well-versed by then in the trade). The decisions he was making in those grim days were serious ones, invariably taken under pressure and despite his personal resistance.

In any case, once I had grown slightly more familiar with the Regent's manner, having seen a side of him which he might not, perhaps, have wished to disclose to his subjects, I became, as early as our second encounter, certain that my trepidation at his alarming, unexpected questions was unfounded. Neither Pavle nor Olga ever mentioned the line of succession and the contentious Articles. Even I began to believe that Elizabeta, who took the dignity of the court and the significance of the Prince's behaviour so seriously, might be right in claiming with conviction (with less conviction when Olga was the individual in question) that the Prince had no intention of exploiting the failings of the Constitution. She believed instead that someone else stood behind the intrigue, someone who feared, with Petar's coming of age (or his enthronement before achieving majority), that the Queen Mother, the Patriarch and Petar Živković would become undesirably powerful: someone who felt that the civilised and European Prince Regent, who was seriously endeavouring to address the Croatian question, would be a better choice than wayward generals and vindictive, spiteful Serbian politicians.

The fact that it was Korošec who had requested my opinion on the question of succession gave Elizabeta's assessment credence, for he could expect little benefit to himself personally or to his Slovenes from General Živković. The fact that somewhat later the Prince did, indeed, have Stojadinović removed, that he approved the formation of the Croatian provincial government and Maček's government, lent Elizabeta's thesis even greater viability. But it was only after my conversation with Dragiša Cvetković that I finally grasped there was something corrupt and very large behind the sudden and unseemly interest in my interpretation of the law. Cvetković was at that point a paltry minister in the Department for Social Policy, a remarkably vulgar gentleman with the appearance of a gypsy and the manners of an oaf.

"What do you say, Professor, about how that little brat is about to nab the throne?" he began brashly, with that brand of vigorous fire which had appalled me ever since my father Milutin's election campaign years before. We were standing a little to the side of the ranks through which King Petar II in his Sokol cadet uniform was marching on his way to conduct a review on the day of the Celebration of the Royal Guard.

"I would not speak of the King in such a tone if I were you. There is no constitutional obstacle to Petar II ascending the throne as soon as he reaches majority."

I was staring straight ahead, but I felt his eyes on my face.

"For your information, Professor" – he spoke condescendingly, probably because he had known my father and considered me his junior – "the King is mentally unstable and unfit to rule. Prince Pavle would like to know what you think about the line of succession to the throne under such circumstances."

"The Prince? Have you actually spoken with the Prince on this matter?"

"Yes, I have."

"I beg your pardon, but I do not believe you."

"Listen to me, Medaković, and listen good, so later you don't miss the boat. I am the leader of the Yugorace. I've organised the whole workers' movements single-handedly. I call a Yugorace Congress right here in the middle of Belgrade, I bring in, just watch me, a hundred thousand workers from all over the place. We shout down the King. You cook up the legal hootchy kootchy to grease the wheels. We won't forget a good turn."

After a pause, looking at me sideways, "I am not joking, Stevan," he said and walked away.

I had to pinch myself to believe that the conversation had actually happened, and when it sank in I was certain that the Prince had nothing to do with this behind-the-scenes game. I would have doubted my own capacity for judging people if it were true that the wary, tight-lipped Prince had spoken frankly to a power-greedy Serbian political conniver on such a sensitive topic. I was sure. But at that moment, it was already moot whether I was right or not. As I left the grounds of the Royal compound in Topčider I took an irrevocable decision: no matter how much Elizabeta might pine for royal company and bridge parties, I knew that I must break off these newly acquired political connections. It had to be clear that no-one could rely on me in any way, shape or form.

In all fairness I should say that Elizabeta shared my determination. Her opinion of the values and nature of the political intrigues percolating among the Serbs was no more benevolent than mine, and though she did not entirely manage to swallow her disappointment, she earnestly helped me write letters to the Prince, Cvetković and Korošec which had to be composed in such a way that they insulted no-one, yet made clear to everyone that our retreat from the game, which we had never properly joined, was irrevocable. Apparently, we succeeded. Invitations ceased to arrive from court; the politicians washed their hands of me and, most likely, found others more amenable to cooperation. I was saved.

While we were still able to talk about past times, my decisive step back from the precipice was a frequent topic, and Elizabeta and I always agreed that during those days of 1938–9 I had taken hold of my fate at the very last moment. Only an instant later, we would no longer have been able to keep a lid on things. Elizabeta is not partial to the way I refer to fate with fear, as its victim, in its thrall, nor to the way I see her as the Greek Moira, or speak of the three malevolent spinners so much more powerful than we are, with their divine powers as well as their divine caprices. Insight into the workings of destiny, awareness of the arbitrary nature by which it manifests itself, the feeling of insignificance which overwhelms me when I perceive its cosmic proportions, all this invariably fills me with a religious awe that much greater since I keep it from Elizabeta, who scornfully expressed her relationship to that great manipulator of people and the world like this: "Destiny – a fool's excuse for failure!" Ever since she said that, I have hidden from her my conviction that a man is capable of guiding his own future – and that of the world – only as much as the little bird that cleans the crocodile's teeth is capable of guiding that mighty reptile's movements.

Yet while a comparison between an individual's power to influence the course of his destiny and the might of that destiny, a machine geared to the ultimate destruction of mortals, fills me with a nightmarish sense of pointless struggle, I do believe that at the most minuscule level of one's own life, a person – a mere straw in the wind – is able, two or three times in the course of wending his way through time, to make a choice by himself, not because he suddenly acquires a new power that makes this possible, but because the cosmic forces-that-be grant him this concession while they are attending a lavish banquet and are in a generous mood. "Here you go, now you choose" – I heard them tell me this back in that Bristol tearoom. "Decide this one on your own" – grinning merrily at my anguish, they tossed me this option on the day of the Celebration of the Royal Guard. In both cases, I knew that my life, like something tangible, was in my own hands, that at that moment I could do whatever I felt was right and that my decision would be irrevocable.

The three decisive letters, sent at the last possible moment, most certainly set the stage for the next two crucial phases in our lives, when Destiny despatched us Medakovićes to our hidden enclave – the fortress in which Elizabeta and I have, lo these twenty years, resided in peace. What if there hadn't been that break, so masculine and abrupt, so unlike me, spineless as I generally was, with politics or, more precisely, with the desires of others to draw me into politics? Had I not made that break, would I have been capable of resisting Slobodan Jovanović's repeated invitation to join the Serbian Cultural Club? Had I not resisted, would we have still been living in Belgrade in April 1941 when the royal family fled, or would we have left for England when they did? When I ask myself this question, I realise just how far-reaching and formative those letters were, sent at a rare moment of choice. For, had I joined the Club, and had we fled through Cetinje to London – what would have become of us? Of Elizabeta? Would our lives have been in the slightest bit similar to what they are? Would we have saved ourselves? Kept death from our door? Oh, Elizabeta, my wife! Have you never heard Destiny cackling up there, amused by our preposterous notion that by fleeing politics a person in Serbia can save himself from politics?

I would not have been able, this I know, to resist the great Slobodan had I not passed through the first circle of political hell and felt dizzying relief as I extricated myself from it unscathed, had the memory of that nightmare and my irrational phobia of politics not been so fresh in my mind. First, because my professor enjoyed an almost unbounded authority in the public eye, and for me, his student, he meant even more. Second, because he was my model and my confidant, a person who had never permitted himself to be drawn into the political sphere, so when Slobodan took his place at the helm of the Serbian Cultural Club there must have been sound reasons. And third – I could see for myself that the country was in a terrible state, and that something had to be done. One thing, at least, was clear: the Croats were unlikely to defend Yugoslavia. In a Yugoslavia centred around Karađorđević Belgrade rather than Strossmayer Zagreb within the tripartite state of Franz Ferdinand, they were interested only in becoming, and remaining, independent. I had always been startled by the way this fact seemed to infuriate and astonish His Majesty's Serbian subjects. I explained to my students, knowing full well that they were averse to hearing it, the left- or right-wing sympathisers among them, that Yugoslavia had been founded on a natural, very powerful centralist notion put forth by Serbia, but also on a natural, very strong but federalist notion put forth by Croatia. The Serbs had evolved their state-building notion out of the Serbian revolution of 1804 with an energy that had, on several occasions, earned the admiration of the entire world. The Croats based their push for autonomy – through passive resistance and lack of cooperation – on what they called the "historic right to statehood". The argument was that despite the fact that Croatia had entered into a union with Hungary as far back as 1102, the act had been a voluntary one, and therefore Croatia had never lost its identity as a state. As much as the centralist notion was of fundamental importance to the traditional ideology of the Serbian people, so the federalist idea, articulated with particular clarity after 1848, had shaped a century of the Croatian people's aspirations. Both ideas were legitimate, and from the point of view of a common state each had its advantages and its drawbacks, but they could not coexist. That was why, when the centralist idea gained ascendancy in 1918, the Croats felt that they had been inveigled. By August 26, however, they had five ministers in the government, the Banovina administration in Zagreb, Maček as head of state and detachments of Civil Protection forces – all the trappings of federalism. But, as became obvious to everyone, this did not resolve their dissatisfaction with Yugoslavia. Quite the contrary. Croatian demands grew more insistent, no longer merely for an independent Croatia and Slovenia, but for the secession of the Vojvodina and Bosnia.

Yet, instead of bringing at least the more intelligent among the Serbs to reason, all this evidence that the Croats wanted no part of Yugoslavia merely exacerbated our complacent Piedmontism. Understanding some of Slobodan's reasoning, even much of it, for a while I was surprised that he did not see how much Serbia and Serbdom had become something entirely different from what they had been before the First World War and unification. Later I understood why I might have been expected to see more clearly certain things which escaped him and so many others.

Why was I in a position to grasp things which eluded even Slobodan? Today it seems that it may have been in part due to my background and upbringing, but also in part due to Elizabeta's presence in my life. From the very first painful and immature comparisons I drew between the Serbs and the British, parallels which agonised, indeed nearly crushed, the spirit of Milutin's son and Nanka's cadet in England, the Serbian question was not political or historical but profoundly personal. Now, in my twilight years, moving among my memories like a dreamer surrounded by nightmares, I can see even more clearly how I spent my days shielding Serbia in my heart at least as much from myself as from anyone or anything out to swallow it as a greedy bird would gobble up a black worm. Surrounded by Barry, Davis and the British Museum, enthralled by Elizabeta's green gaze and mysterious charms, at the centre of the gorged Empire and amidst the bizarre nonchalance of tiger hunters wearing cricketing trousers, I felt like Adam when he realised he was naked. But, as with Adam, I held on to my longing for Nanka's lost Serbia, now strangely coupled with a sort of tortuous self-esteem due to my new, enhanced capacity for judgement. Even today, I am not able to explain why my love for my country has grown in parallel with my recognition of her deficiencies, but I know that these opposing tendencies are somehow complementary. For forty years now, I have been observing my Serbian reality the way a patient in an optometrist's office looks at the alphabet chart. In order to describe the precise strength of my vision, they keep switching lenses and asking in a colourless voice whether I can read the next line. If so, what are the letters? I reply, never certain whether I am describing the state of which I speak with complete accuracy. For forty years now, I have not been able to look around myself without donning Elizabeta's spectacles and assuming her bewitchingly dispassionate vision. On the dusty pavement, I pass by the proffered military cap of a crippled beggar and am filled not by rage, nor by disgust, but by a profound sense of disappointment when I compare him with Nanka's childhood tales of Zeka Buljubaša's heroism or the valiant deeds of Čelopek, Velika Hoča, Petraljica. But just at that moment, my in-house optometrist, right there and so nimble, switches the lenses, and suddenly I see the beggar with the green English gaze that brings with it the chill incisiveness of an outsider's lack of affect. Accustomed to reading, watching, keeping silent, defending, attacking, loving, always under the supervision of that celestial, impartial corrector of attitudes, I long believed that in England I had indeed undergone a change of spirit. I was no longer able to love my country irrationally. As far as genuine national sentiments were concerned, I had none. For what was my nation to me, compared with what his nation meant to a man who had no outsider's spectacles through which to observe it? For me, my country was the subject of scrutiny and judgement. For him, that uncritical, genetic part of me, it was a community rich in memory sharing an unquestioning readiness to preserve the value of the legacy handed down from our ancestors. Patriotism is a feeling of responsibility for all the people of one's nation, and partiality is merely its foundation. If I do not hold the insanities of my nation to be rooted in sound rationality, how can I be a good patriot? While I still believed that there was no finer people than the Serbs, while I still failed to seek any proof for my assumptions, while I wept for the slaughter of princes, knowing even before I had so much as tasted alcohol that *šljivovica* was the finest such beverage in the world, I belonged to precisely that community which I was not competent to judge.

I sobered up gradually, one stage after another. With each stage, there was a residue of pain, a twinge of betrayal, the shame of an arrogant rationalist stripped of the privileges enjoyed by the most miserable beggar of any nation. I explained the fact that I discovered at each stage the ever greater unreliability of my people, its inability to master its own destiny, by the enhanced strength of my spectacles. This heightened strength increased my need somehow to explain to Elizabeta the undignified phenomenon I was analysing and for which I felt personally responsible. It did not help that Elizabeta, sensing my embarrassment at every Serbian shortcoming, would thoughtfully suggest her own example, and her cold and unfilial attitude towards the English: "There are a lot of English people I like, and a lot I despise, but neither sentiment is because they're English. How can I consider myself fully responsible for what I am, how can I possibly feel responsible for any

English low-life's misbehaviour? Patriotism is a form of the annihilation of the individual, the last refuge of the scoundrel." She did not, I dare say, fully comprehend my condition. For a long while, I clung to my patriotism, against my better judgement. Only because I knew that Elizabeta was not able to comprehend it, or I to explain it, did I never speak to her about my dual feeling.

Until that day, chased out into the open, forced to face Serbdom head on when Slobodan invited me to join the Cultural Club, I discovered, with a modicum of surprise, with even a certain malicious glee, what it was that had evaded me. Long convinced that I had changed by looking at the world around me with the impartial gaze of my Elizabeta, suddenly I realised that it was Serbdom, in fact, which had changed. The word that had meant so much when pronounced by Nanka, brimming with sincere passion in the vocabulary of my father Milutin, now sounded like a can emptied of all its contents and dented by many kicks.

What were my new eyes uncovering on the national scene? The *Obznana* and King Aleksandar's dictatorship, aimed though they may have been at curtailing the Croatian autonomy movement, succeeded only in devastating the political life of Serbia while nourishing the political parties of Croats, Slovenes and Bosnians. One had no need of spectacles to see how Maček had become the uncrowned King of Croatia, that Korošec and Mehmed Spaho were the sovereign leaders of their peoples, while in Serbia there was not a single party vigorous enough to represent even a simple majority of the Serbian people. Sorrier yet was the sight I found when looking at Serbs who lived in Croatia and Bosnia, and who were attentive witnesses to our collapse. The love they had once felt for Serbia had sunk into indifference, then dissatisfaction and finally into a confused loathing of Belgrade. These Serbs, who were, until the unification of 1918, living abroad, had their own publishing house, Prosvjeta, and their own cultural institutions, their autonomy in questions of religion and education, their Temperance and Sokol societies, their National Defence, only to see these same institutions in their own land, thanks to the circumstances about which I needed to speak with Slobodan, fall into ruin.

"But, Stevan, that is precisely why we founded the Serbian Cultural

Club, why I joined it and why you most definitely must follow suit! You speak of the Serbs who live outside Serbia proper. Can you not see that I am merely the front for the Club? Its motivating force is Nikola, the Bosnian leader, member of the London Yugoslav Committee. The general secretary is also a Serb from across the Danube: Vlada Ćorović, from Herzegovina, and on the Board is Vasa Čubrilović, who did not hesitate to attack royalty for the sake of liberating the Serbs!"

We were sitting in the professor's office at Topličin Venac. Twilight had seeped into the room, but, carried away by conversation, we hadn't switched on the lights. Slobodan was at his desk, his chair swivelled to the right towards the armchair where I, no longer as obedient pupil but rather as dismayed gainsayer, was pouring out what I have been collecting and turning over in my head. I had come to see Slobodan once I had straightened things out in my mind, but I had no way of predicting how the Professor would respond. He might hold himself, as he was wont to do, aloof from my distress (I often wondered why: did the world beyond books truly seem worthy of nothing but sarcasm, or was it that he used sarcasm to fortify his superiority?), above controversy, even above the topic of the conversation, employing irony to do so. He might take affront and bring our encounter to a close with a brusque "That is your opinion". He might set out in a systematic manner all the weak links of my line of reasoning, elucidating the contradictory points. I expected all that. But I did not expect the Professor to be thrilled. Slobodan did nothing to hide behind a mask of indifference. I understood immediately. Slobodan felt that his efforts at the Serbian Cultural Club and my ruminations were important, and this encouraged me to pose the central question far more candidly than I had meant to. "Professor," I said, meekly, I think, yet resolutely, "what went wrong, and whom do you blame? The Croats? Unification? Historical mishap? Or us – the Serbs?"

He stared straight into my eyes for a time without responding. Then he dropped his eyes to his desktop piled with papers and began drumming his fingers on the title page of some thick volume. After a lengthy pause, he said, "Well, what do you think?"

I had resolved to tell the Professor everything. Only in this way could

I, on the one hand, seriously lay out the reasons why I was unwilling to join the Club and, on the other, see my findings through Slobodan's knowing eyes. He did not interrupt, only flicking the light on at his desk, so that now he was well-lit, while I was in the semi-dark. I do not know how long my speech lasted, but I do know that I put my doubts forward cogently. Over the ten-day hiatus I had granted myself before responding to Slobodan's invitation, I had come to believe that an enlightened man had the right, indeed the duty, to look at the national scene around him with open eyes, but that it was far too easy simply to separate himself from that scene when it turned out to be pitiful in comparison with that of France or Austria. I had always known that the Serbs were my fathers and my forefathers on whom I could not turn my back even when they were monstrous and evil, and certainly not when I saw them as deserving of pity.

Suddenly, without feeling for the first time that I was an outcast, I saw how vast the rift was between the culture produced by the Serbian people and the pathetic ornamentation so readily flourished by the defenders of its honour and its future. I realised that the valiant Serbian warrior from the battles of Cer, Suvobor, Kajmakčalan and Dobro polje was virtually impossible to reconcile with the toothless, tattered Serbian peasant who after that long winter, from 1939 to 1940, frozen to the bone, smudged with soot, bent over the black soil, worrying anxiously whether he would have any bread to look forward to with his livestock and his children, bread being the very celestial summit of his heart's desire. "If we look around ourselves, Professor, what do we see? Do love and respect for Belgrade come easily? Migrants from Vlasotin, Lužnica, Niš, Belopalanka, Svrljig, Zaglavak, Timok, Reka, Brsjak, on the one hand, miserable souls willing to take any job, even the most gruelling, at which point it ceases to be work and becomes, instead, a labour of torment, grief, suffering, spiritual pain and humiliation, a prolonging of indenture and serfdom, the travail of the lowest of the low, beast-like subsistence. On the other hand we have the psychosis of insatiable greed, charm and profit from as little work as possible, dabbling in 'business' in order to evade work. It is hardly unusual that both these – subsistence labour and greedy work, therefore every form of work – excite Serbs to scorn. Belgrade has become a city in which there is not a single man in his proper place. Students work as waiters. Pensioned clerks hawk gewgaws and mend umbrellas; people who cannot write their names properly build many-storeyed palaces, accrue capital and real estate, and no-one knows how they manage to do this. At the same time, many are the scholars, professors, craftsmen who wonder what they will eat tomorrow. Everyone is in a breathless rush to grab more, using as little merit and effort as possible. The uneducated and incompetent are stealing the places of the skilled and learned. Society is separated into groups which support each other through filial, clannish, tribal and political connections, and everything outside that oriental tangle of I-help-you, you-help-me is swept brusquely aside. Belgrade seems to be mushrooming, a temporary refuge, the Wild West, with all manner of phantoms and phantasms streaming in to take the best positions. It is the least scrupulous, rather than the most capable, who are moving into the highest places. Arriving from the provinces, dazed and disorientated by the strange new city, they are liberating a biology of self-defence, of fads, of impatience. Peasant atavisms, the rudiments of tribal patriarchalism, are struggling with the latest Western orientations among the Užice Frenchmen, the Pirot Londoners, the Bosnian Viennese."

"But, Stevan, my child" – the Professor had never before used a term of endearment in addressing me or anyone else in my presence – "doesn't all that make the urgency of rolling up our sleeves, perhaps even dirtying our hands, all the more obvious? If all is as you say it is, what gives us the right to watch our people and our state from on high, as if it is some unseemly theatrical event with evil heroes playing the star roles? I do understand the things you describe to me; what I do not understand is your conclusion!"

I tried – I don't know how successful I was at it – to explain my point of view, closely bound as it was to my relationship towards politics among the Serbs. "I am speaking out, for the first time, Professor, though I have been deliberating for ages. With Elizabeta this is precisely the subject about which I cannot speak. Whenever I broach it, I suddenly remember what I keep forgetting: she is not one of us. How can I speak ungenerously of Serbs to someone who is not a Serb? How can I even do so before Serbs? You are the only person to whom my self-torture will be intelligible. To you I can say: the social culture that Serbs have produced in the first half of the twentieth century will not appeal to anyone beyond Serbia, especially if those in Serbia who deserve the most credit for it do not respect it. Belgrade can hardly serve as an example. Serbia, in 1918, propelled itself, or was propelled, into a position that has in many ways caught up with it. A lower level of civilisation cannot impose itself upon a higher one except by force. In the unhealthy, unnatural circumstances of the kingdom's unification, Serbia and her ideas were tainted, not by unification, nor by the Croats, but because Serbian tendencies towards statehood mushroomed disproportionately to what it could muster in terms of civilisation. Serbia could swallow up Croatia and Slovenia, but it was not able to digest them. From their subordinate positions in Yugoslavia, Croatia and Slovenia have emerged more powerful than they have ever been. Here, my dear Professor, politics do not help or hinder us as much as we tend to think. For the Serbs, politics is an alibi. Politics is not a cause, it is an effect of our current national skills or lack thereof, our immaturity in terms of civilisation, the black dregs of oriental habits which cannot lead towards progress in this age of European record-breaking. Where will we find ourselves if we allow Dr Drašković to convince us that the Serbs deserve a place among the world's finest? Would it not be better to acknowledge that we are closer to third place and then organise ourselves so that gradually we move towards Europe, rupturing our umbilical bond to the Orient? We need modesty and diligence, Professor, not grandiose political schemes, and even less do we need high-handed, inflammatory speeches."

It was about here, I guess, that as abruptly as I had begun my rough-and-tumble statement, I ended it, not because I had been interrupted but because I sensed that our thoughts and feelings of guilt had converged, that I was speaking what were actually Slobodan's words. That sense, the freshness of which has not faded after all the years that separate me from that evening at Topličin Venac, in the capital city, in Serbia, at the close of the fourth decade of the twentieth century, was all the more powerful, all the more profound, all the more eloquent than what Slobodan – rather reluctantly and without conviction, as if by duty only – did say, accepting my findings, analysing my conclusions, so much so that I have forgotten the actual arguments he employed at the time. Slobodan asked me, I believe, whether the Croats would be better off outside Yugoslavia. I answered that they certainly would not be able to survive on their own. Would Serbia truly be better off without the north-western regions of Yugoslavia? For it was only by approaching Europe that we could become a serious nation. I proceeded, in turn, to remind the Professor of Goethe's sentiment that one should "leave politics to the politicians" and of Leonardo da Vinci, who was so preoccupied with studying matters of high importance that he had no time for the woes of the Florentine republic. Only here did the Professor interrupt me with a question that stood apart from the general tone of mutual courtesy: "But you are no Florentine, Stevan, nor are you a German. You are a Serb, so you must consider politics. Are you not, after all, a member of *Napred*?"

This was not precisely below the belt, but Slobodan's question was intended to worm its way under my skin. I had indeed been a member of *Napred* since its founding in 1937, but, as the Professor knew as well as I, it was a non-partisan organisation. Its members mainly included his and my colleagues from the Faculty of Law. It focused its activities on the publication of the series "Politics and Society" where in modest volumes, one per month, it discussed urgent issues from the social, political, economic and cultural realms. The group began publishing the periodical *Napred* first monthly, then weekly, which was occasionally banned for its free-thinking views (as were individual volumes from our series) but – and this was what Slobodan intentionally overlooked when posing his question, desiring victory more than truth – the fundamental principle of the group set forth in the first issue was never questioned: "a periodical for broad democratic thought and democratic spirit which stands outside all political organisations". Members of *Napred* belonged to any number of parties. They were not of a single mind except in their desire that this spiritually stagnant community begin to move onwards. Since the Professor knew all this full well, I said, as a reprimand, a little sadly, "Come now, Professor!" He continued to speak, but for the first time was disorientated, without the clarity that had always been his hallmark.

I remember fragments of what he said. When the "Croatian question" arose, the "Serbian question" always cropped up with it; the time had passed when one could talk about whether the Croats would be with the Serbs because by now it was clear that one of them could do just as well without the other if it chose to; the ivory tower could become a haven for the immoral. He spoke about Spinoza's desire to hang a placard with the words "*Ultimi barbarorum*" near the site of the De Witt murders, about Voltaire's struggle for Calas, unjustly accused, about Zola and Dreyfus. But all these were mere feeble mumblings in the face of a vast sense of misfortune which drew us together, if I am not gravely mistaken, despite our words to the contrary, in a common bond: the solidarity of orphans ashamed of the calamity of an age in which a right choice might be every bit as morally reprehensible as treason.

Of course, we said not a word about this bond which clutched at my throat like some force of nature, which choked my words and brought tears to my eyes, but that is what, I am convinced, was pounding behind Slobodan's poorly concealed heroic resignation when he ended his disjointed presentation and proposed that we walk home together. We started off towards the Monument along dark Venac, then by the National Theatre and Veterans' Home on Prince Pavle Street. We no longer spoke of politics, and I believed that the sense of futility had so powerfully engulfed Slobodan and me that he would not raise the question "Will you join the Serbian Cultural Club?", a question to which I had been trying all evening to suggest a convincing and honest answer. He seemed hunched over and aged to me in the dark, his step short, to my right, peering down at the pavement, possessed by the same thoughts – of that I am certain – that possessed me. We were already on Pavle Street – we had walked all the way from the Library without saying a word – when the chilling thought struck me that perhaps I had affronted Slobodan, that with my scholarly perfectionism I had questioned the validity of his own political activity, and now it wasn't that the Professor was feeling saddened by our futility, but rather that he was feeling saddened by my arrogance. Frantically, I sought to patch together sentences which might demonstrate how my respect for him was greater than ever, to convince him of how I perceived his political engagement after years of reticence as a necessity and a sacrifice that he must bear since he was Slobodan, just as I could not because I was not Slobodan, but no matter what I strove to arrange into dismayed and awkward sentences, it sounded far more grating than my silence. Slobodan halted, looked up at me and said, "You haven't said a word about how your family is doing!"

He seemed to be asking this in order to bring the political part of our conversation to a definite close, politely letting me know that he was not irked by our difference of opinion, but in the way he then continued to analyse the position of a foreigner amid Serbs, the respect he showed for Elizabeta's sobriety in her comprehension of what was, for her, an entirely alien milieu, I concluded that over the last dozen minutes of walking he had been thinking about me, and my fear of offending him by sneering, aristocratically, at the political efforts he was making under hopeless circumstances was aggravated all the more. I answered his queries about Elizabeta, later about Mihajlo, whom he had not met, but of whose remarkable qualities he had heard, about our manner of living between English and Serbian cultures, and all the while I was experiencing an immense, painful onset of remorse that without meaning to, perhaps foolishly or even out of cowardice, I had somehow humiliated the one man I valued more than any other.

We arrived at the corner of Cetinjska and stopped before the entrance to the Academy of Commerce because it was here, whenever he and I walked together, that we parted ways. That is when it happened: I extended my hand to him, but he would not relinquish it. He held it between his two hands. And looked straight into my eyes.

"If I were to tell you that you are right, Stevan, and nevertheless extend the invitation to you once again to join the Club, how would you respond?"

And I – broken and humiliated by how much I would hurt the great man who stood there, undone by age, belittled before me, in his light-grey coat, his hands proffered, his eyes gentle and, if I am not gravely mistaken, imploring, a strange Slobodan, not the cynic – despite all this, I mustered the strength to say, "I regret, Professor, that I would respond as I have done before. I cannot."

"I believe you. Goodbye, Stevan."

The 70-year-old man walked slowly up the hill.

"Goodbye, Professor."

If I was capable, at that moment, of plunging a dagger into the stooping back of my role model; if I managed to repel even this attempt of his to draw me into politics, even at the cost of losing his favour and affronting, indeed wounding, the most upstanding among the Serbs I knew; if my disgust at Serbian politicking prevented me from crossing the Rubicon and becoming a true Serb, what could possibly have inspired me, a few years later, of my own free will, to plunge straight into the mainstream of our tyrannical, back-stabbing political scene? Even now I do not know.

I remember how I, quietly entering the flat, convinced that Mihajlo was sleeping and Elizabeta had already retired, went to the cupboard and drank a glass of milk, disgruntled with myself, feeling guilty about Slobodan, dispirited. Passing by Elizabeta's bedroom, I saw light under the door. I stopped in the dark, hesitating about whether to knock. I remember this detail so clearly because it was part and parcel of the essence of our relations, which were passing at precisely that time into an important new phase, presenting a multitude of interesting quandaries to my intuition.

Our intimate relationship – as I can see from today's lookout tower over my life – was then moving into its third utterly distinct stage. It all began on June 9, 1925, on the narrow cot in my little room at Miss Trickey's boarding house as a two-hour catastrophe with a happy ending, roughly 120 minutes which have, with a red-hot branding iron, been seared into my memory. What was only one-twelfth of one day of my life became a memory that has reigned supreme like a black queen with a golden crown over the broad expanses of forty years. It was the last day of my year of study and – coincidentally but significantly – a day that will remain recorded in the annals of the ancient city. In Bristol on that day, King George V, in the company of the Queen, opened the Wills Memorial Hall, the University Tower. What a day to bid farewell to England! The city was a riot of flowers, Bristol Bridge, the House of Commerce, the banks and insurance companies. Temple Meads, the railway station at which the royal couple arrived precisely at noon, the Town Hall where they first stopped and all the other public buildings had become floral fortresses; white carnations and blue hydrangeas, lungwort and verbena, purple and yellow irises, evergreen and various decorative boughs erupted from the windows of every home; the city literally fluttered with tens of thousands of gold, red, blue banners, flags of all kinds, the Cross of St George, the King's colours, the Union Jack in all manner of colours and sizes, the emblems and insignia of guilds and societies; "God Save the King" blasted out in brass band and orchestral renditions; the bedecked honorary guard of the Royal Naval Volunteers Reserve and the Fourth and Sixth Battalions of the Gloucester Regiment; the deans, presidents, judges, professors, mayors in their ornate, venerable robes; the royal coach with four jet-black horses in silk, crimson and gold; the King in his grey morning dress and grey silk top hat with a white carnation in his buttonhole, and the Queen in a springtime gown of airy silk in shades of silver and blue; and all around them the elated English people, the effusive and hysterical people of Bristol who had taken over all the streets, windows and roofs hours before the royal train arrived, only to howl in incomprehensible euphoria until 4 p.m, when Their Majesties left the city.

Elizabeta and I were across from the University Tower where the opening ceremony was held, but we made no particular effort to secure a good spot because that would have required hours of patient waiting. Elizabeta was rather sharp concerning the excitement which had taken hold of the city, and she commented disparagingly on how conventional the King's speech had been (I remember one of the sentences, or a fragment of a sentence: ". . . assuredly, nothing should be more productive of enduring good than the endowments of higher learning"), and she held it to be bad taste that in all the chaos they were parading a handful of 90-year-old Bristol veterans from the Crimean War and Indian Mutiny who had fought seventy years before at

Balaclava, Inkerman and Sebastopol. It was Elizabeta, despite her sarcasm and her scathing wit, who found it difficult to resist the waves of exaltation which held the English people under the sway of royalty in a manner I found entirely baffling. With her irony and her scepticism, she was merely holding the thrill that grabbed her at bay.

We went our separate ways around 2 p.m., as soon as Their Majesties had proceeded under the impressive stone archways of the large entrance into the tower, and we met each other again around 6. I was to wait for Elizabeta in front of the Women's Hall of Residence of Clifton Hall House so that we could attend a concert of the University Chamber Orchestra at Victoria Rooms. Bristol is a rainy city, and our long walks around Tyndall Park, our bicycle tours all the way to Priory Road and Cotham Hill or our forays to Weston-super-Mare often ended with us by the fire of some café-restaurant or pub wringing out Elizabeta's kerchief and drying our clothing, bolstered by tea or sherry. We were young, not a bit concerned about our health, and our wet feet and bedraggled appearance filled us with gaiety, charged by a feeling of closeness which, to my great delight, made Elizabeta more open. My last day in Bristol as a student, however, was bright and sunny, with an Adriatic blue sky, so rare in the British Isles that, when such a day dawns, the English always become infantile.

I wended my way through the marvellous evening towards the spot where I had agreed to meet Elizabeta, and though more than two hours had passed since the King and Queen had departed, the euphoric crowd was only gradually and reluctantly dispersing, shouting to friends and acquaintances that the weather was simply marvellous, filling the mild evening with hearty cheer. The city in all its ceremonial splendour still surrounded them, but the thrill that had shaken it like a fever only hours before had vanished from the air. Tired and perspiring, students and professors in their black, salmon-pink and cardinal-red regalia still making their way back from numerous festivities and tea parties. Elizabeta and I hurried towards the Victoria Rooms. We were full of cheer. We chatted. Whenever I had an opportunity to do so without being noticed, I would slow my pace ever so slightly to walk a step behind my quick-footed red-haired beauty, so that I could delight, instantly beguiled, by her agile stride, simultaneously light and firm. Oh, how Elizabeta walked! Already of large build even as a young girl, with strong legs, a divinely long back, full upper arms, ample breasts, she walked as though she were a slender young thing, as if with each step she would spring from the ground with a bound, as if her body had no weight at all. Only when I recall how Elizabeta's walking stirred me with its sensuality on that evening, as it had on many earlier occasions, can I tell how I was longing for our physical union, though I had made no attempt whatsoever of that sort even in my boldest thoughts. There was a shade more of the lovers' fire in our first kiss when I, a month before the royal visit to Bristol, had asked for Elizabeta's hand in marriage. On a weekend visit to Rašela's and Archibald's, we were warming ourselves by a cheery fire. For a moment, we were alone in the house. Elizabeta had knelt on the floor and was drying the front of her skirt while I towelled her hair for a long time, even after there was no need to dry it any more. Then she turned, looked at me, and I instantly found, though I don't know how, yet it was clear as a bell in the almost childlike innocent welcome of the green gaze, a feeling of support so powerful that even my shyness was overcome. "Elizabeta, would you . . . could you marry me?" I said, feeling stripped of my will, my neck on the block, the axe swung high above me in the air.

"I think . . . I could," were the merciful words from the lips of my tender English executioner.

I knelt on the floor, we hugged and kissed – only that one time the way lovers do, ready to advance to further tenderness. In the days that followed, I always kissed Elizabeta whenever we met or parted, as long as someone's presence didn't prevent me from doing so, but those were kisses without passion, because of my fear of offending her by disclosing passionate desires in a manner unseemly in England. And so it was that the more I reined in my ardour, with the growing certainty that this dazzling, pale-complexioned girl would be my wife, the greater care I took to conceal my agitation, and the colder and more moderate I seemed. I have no idea how Elizabeta interpreted the restraint of her betrothed, but all that I was able to muster was the decision that I ought to leave it to her, acquainted as she was with the customs of this society so unfamiliar to me, to initiate the first move. She, however, until the very last day of my stay in Bristol, the day of our temporary parting, did nothing at all. Absolutely nothing. She would readily offer me her lips for a kiss; timidly and with a touch of melancholy she would smile; "Goodbye, Steven," she'd say; and with her buoyant step she would glide away, waving once more before she vanished from sight.

And then, whether she had noticed my sly way of slowing down, or felt my eyes on her body, or discovered how enchanted I was with her stride, or the evening was so marvellous or for some other reason, Elizabeta stopped suddenly and, with a mischievous glance, tucked her arm under mine. "Hurry," she said, "we're late."

I, of course, was blessed, feeling the thrilling pressure of her arm on mine, but the curse of my lack of certainty descended, in that golden moment, on to me like a black nightmare: instead of being supremely happy, I immediately began to wonder what would be proper, what was expected of me, how to come up with a response that would be neither too overbearing nor too withdrawn. In a panic, I tried to work my way through the dense thicket of, as our Rašela would have put it, what people, in such circumstances, did in England.

The result of my efforts was, as always, nothing, but what Elizabeta did next, instead of aggravating my quandary and anxiety, abruptly simplified everything to a basic, primeval, biblical simplicity. The quartet of musicians, two young men on the violins, a young woman on the viola and Bernard Lowell, the well-known physics professor, on the cello, performed Haydn's Russian opus 33 from 1781 in the manner of a classic string quartet; the instruments gave one another the floor with ease and charm in an equal, celestial conversation. I love music and, when it is good and well performed, it invariably brings me to a state of philosophical reconciliation with the humility of humanity. However, on this occasion, with Liza sitting at my side, my spirit did not possess its customary serenity. Rather, I was feeling with unusual acuteness a sense of bliss, the particular nature of which I can feel today with the identical intensity I felt it then, as if the concert is taking place as I speak. Barely reined joy was exulting inside me, usually so steadfast, nudging me to leap from my chair and sing along loudly with the musicians, and since I could never do something like that, in Belgrade or in Bristol, bringing my lips right to Elizabeta's ear, I whispered passionately, "Marvellous! Isn't it?"

She barely nodded to signal her consent, she curved her head, swan-like, towards her lap and the programme open on it, but at the same time, without looking towards me, she made the most tender gesture of our entire intimate life: bewitched and shaken to the core, I felt how her hand, clandestinely, as if she were embarking on an illicit affair, sneaked into mine. I thought nothing. All the brakes in my rigid Serbian identity released at once. There were no doubts, no questions in that blissful moment in which all at once I was hearing the strains of Haydn's chamber music balance as if they were a thunderous oratorio of the gift of life and requited love. Still silent, our eyes avoiding each other, we walked out into the street (Elizabeta's white-gloved hand tucked with full confidence under my arm, her eyes modestly focused on the toes of her patent-leather shoes), and set out, not for Clifton Hall, but for Miss Trickey's boarding house. Even today, as on so many occasions since, I am unable to pinpoint who it was who took the first step in the appropriate, though not customary, direction. Did I merely acquiesce, or did I set the direction myself? Probably closest to the truth is that the entire evening, and our two future lives together, and all subsequent events, were inscribed in the book of fate from the moment when Elizabeta's timid hand slipped into mine, to remain there for ever.

I am not able to explain how it is that from such crucial memories, of which I recall not only the minutes but every single second with crystalline clarity, all recollection of how we traversed the route from Victoria Rooms to my boarding house doorway has evaporated without a trace. Did we exchange any words? Or did we walk in silence, following the paths of those superimposed commands which mortals obey without access to their wishes, justice, reason? Did I squeeze Elizabeta's hand? Did I kiss her on that unpeopled, poorly lit road (because certainly Pembroke Road would have been empty after 9 at night), did I embrace her? Or did I walk, frozen and frightened, at a polite distance from my flustered, embarrassed fiancée – I cannot divine, despite repeated efforts, this last part of the short path from our first acquaintance to our shared bed.

My memory returns at the moment when the appalling thought occurred to me – my key already in the lock of the boarding-house door – that we might bump into one of my housemates, Robert Rackham or Mr Peele, or Miss Trickey herself, in the hallway, and thus our honeymoon would end with a scolding, in shame and humiliation, before it had even begun. The boarders, however, were all in their chambers, and the moment the door of my room swiftly and silently closed behind us, my fears vanished. I am sure that Elizabeta breathed a sigh of relief as well, and that she, too, was cognisant of the danger, because all at once she felt the need, as I did, to speak. Whispering, excited, we related our feelings to one another the instant we'd made it into the room, with hushed giggles, racing to be the first to describe what we felt at that moment of great, now passed, danger. Then both of us, at the same instant, as if at a command, grew solemn; we remembered why we were in my room. I sat on the arm of Elizabeta's armchair and kissed her the way I had kissed her that first time. We did not turn on the lights, but it was not fully dark. The gas street lamp cast a glow into my room. Elizabeta had taken off her hat and jacket, and when I asked her if she'd let down her hair, she complied without hesitation. I sat at her feet, embraced her knees and gazed enchanted at the luxurious redness, the torrent of flaming locks in cascades of voluptuous disarray from which her face emerged, even whiter than usual in the dark, her beautiful face, the small, stub nose, her strong, full lips – I told her what she most certainly knew already, words which lovers always hear as if they are a revelation: that I loved her madly, that it was for life, that nothing would be too difficult for me to do to ensure her happiness. Elizabeta listened with unusual calm, she looked me straight in the eyes, she said nothing. Lost in thought. As if somewhere beneath the lovely brow, she was slowing down the mayhem of my words so that she could study them up close, rearrange them into different sentences. But when we lay, a little later, in each other's arms, I felt her tremble, she received and returned my kisses with growing ardour. She burned at my touch. All in a tangle, helping her clumsily and swiftly to remove her clothes while I removed mine, we found ourselves somehow abruptly surprised – naked in each other's arms.

And then, in that moment, catching sight of the mighty female nakedness of the milk-white beauty in a darkness that was almost green from the street lamp, a thought lit me with a mallet-like thud – I do not know from which corner of my muddled mind it arrived, I do not know by what alchemy it was forged – a diseased thought, thunder-like with lightning which lit up the dark: this woman, this foreigner, who took off her clothes so eagerly, so hot and so lascivious, so naked – might Elizabeta be nothing but a wanton woman, and was I so thick, from so far away, that I hadn't even contemplated such a possibility? The thought struck out of nowhere, supported by nothing but my ignorance and the suspicious nature typical of vigilant primitivism, yet no matter what I thought later of her remarkable appearance, at that moment this notion seemed so plausible that I carried it in my head as a certainty for several minutes at least. Good Lord, what had I got myself into, towards what was I hurtling? How naked she was, how shamelessly naked before me! However had I come so far? How was I to extricate myself? Questions pelted my brain like slaps from cold hands on hot cheeks, while – borne along by the unstoppable currents of events – I lay with Elizabeta on my narrow cot, kissing her as if these malignant thoughts had never come between us.

Then a second blow of that same mallet struck me. My lips, my hands kept making the expected gestures, but my mind was drained of all substance except the oafish certainty that I was with a woman who had been married and divorced, a woman given to sensuality, that I had, without caution, promised my life away, ruined myself. I kissed Elizabeta, held her close on that narrow cot, acutely aware that I was useless as a lover and that no matter how much passion I feigned, she would notice this herself. The fear of that moment was so vast that I did not dare to stop and admit to my wilted condition, so for eternity – or so it seemed at the time – the wrestling went on which, I knew with growing alarm, was headed nowhere.

My sexual experience at this juncture was limited, consisting of what I had gleaned during several months of trysts with our maid, Vida, from

Slavonia. As I recall, she took me into her narrow room at the end of the hallway just off the kitchen not because she chose or desired to do so, but, chances are, under orders from my devoted father, Milutin. She never told me in so many words, and I never asked my father, of course, but the customs of the day and, even more, the way Vida behaved, particularly from the vantage point of my later experience, prompted this conclusion. Vida was around 30 years old at the time. She had fled the poverty of her native Bučje and a drunken husband. Quiet, fastidious, always a little sad, or perhaps she was unusually serious. In her bearing, there was something cowed, a kind of poignant air of reconciliation with fate, not tragic so much as cheerless. Though exciting for me, new as I was to sexual life, our amorous encounters were for her somehow sombre, without any sort of lascivity or flirta- tiousness. It wasn't that way, I am sure, because Vida was humiliated or dejected because of a liaison which she felt to be unseemly. Thoughts of the kind went through my mind, but never, of this I am certain, through hers. Quite the contrary, as much as she was able, I believe she enjoyed it and was grateful to me for bringing a little passion into the grey monotony of her Belgrade existence. There were no deeper feelings, therefore, neither of the beautiful, oft-sung variety or of the less pleasant kind, on either side. Timid, naturally, and suspicious of the validity of my actions during our first encounters, I rather quickly achieved an ease and a pleasant, never domineering self-confidence in Vida's bed, which was lacking from all my other interactions with people at that age. Even today, I cannot guess how she managed this in a relationship so complicated for a man of my years and insecurity, but I do know that she did what she did without a word, without fore- thought. Her confidence that we were doing something ordinary and nice, the serene, sober, natural way she received me and saw me out of her room – it sounds a bit odd even as I say it, but there was something sisterly, perhaps even samaritan, under her melancholy, and it allowed me to spend my time without self-examination of either my morals or of some even greater arrogance. And poor Vida accomplished all this through paltry exchanges of a mundane, even childish, nature or seldom, very seldom, with a story about some event from her village life which would, unpathetic as all else which came from her, make its way into our intercoital moments of repose. Our relationship was as simple and reduced as Vida's narrow room with its iron bedstead, chair, table and wash basin in the corner beneath the window. No matter how much I rummage around in my memory, I can recall only two sentences which might be said to express Vida's feelings for me. One evening, without particular cause, or at least no cause I could remember, she said to me – not as a criticism, not as a suggestion, just in an ordinary tone, "If you are getting bored, we can stop."

"Why do you say that?"

"I just did. So you'd know."

Wasps of doubt buzzed at once about my ears. "And you? Are you tired of it?"

"For me it's nice."

"Me, too," I said, believing what she said and knowing that my words were adequate to describe precisely the nature of what went on between us.

The other evidence of her feelings Vida summed up in a single word at the end of our final encounter, before she was to marry an elderly bachelor, a tailor from Bulbulder. We parted in goodwill, both of us a bit saddened, satisfied with each other, but neither of us set against the inevitable interruption of our affair. I said something quite ordinary, I wished her happiness, something along those lines. Leaving her in bed, I started for the door of the little room to tiptoe softly into the hallway as I always did, when she called to me, "Stevan!"

I stopped.

"Thanks," she said, with feeling, but mitigated by that air of weariness with life which, oddly, had its own charm.

"Thank you, too," I said, certain then, as I am now, that Vida was not thanking me for the extensive trousseau my father had given her, but rather for the simplicity of what we had had, a simplicity close to goodness, a shared goodness, something she, in particular, had met with only seldom in her life. In any case, because sex with a maid was so customary a form of initiation for young men from more affluent homes, and far more because humble, unimaginative Vida made love with the conscientious spirit of an employed lover, without great ardour but also without remorse or superfluous questions, our relationship was free and easy, leaving no real trace on my maturity as a lover.

So, as far as love and sex were concerned, at around 10 on the night of June 9, 1925, I was a virgin, dripping with cold sweat by the time Elizabeta finally caught on to the fact that our embraces had been going on too long and, shortly thereafter, why this was so. She pulled away from me and lay on her back. I did the same, admitting defeat. Since the cot was so narrow, I was dangling half off it, in danger of falling but so completely paralysed by horror that I dared do nothing to improve my posture. And then suddenly, with the same speed with which it had arrived, the thought of Elizabeta's experienced nakedness evaporated without a trace from my head, and all the space of my convulsed being was taken by a murderous shame, some sort of spiritual vacuum in which bits of words jerked about, too feeble to join up with others and fuse into any semblance of a sentence. Who knows how long we lay that way in the darkness of the room, suddenly transformed into an icy lovers' tomb filled with the phantom-like green glow of the street lamp. I shivered, bare, awkward, whether from the cold or from the great quaking of my mind which, after those two thunderous blows of the mallet, had killed all motion in my head. It was than that I heard the sobbing, painstakingly muffled, coming from Elizabeta. Even then, I could not wrench free of my paralysis, nor did I dare turn my head and look at her naked body. When I finally did so, with a gargantuan effort as if I was truly returning from the dead, Elizabeta, in a panic, yanked up from the floor (it was the first thing she got her hands on) the heavy brocade bedspread and hastily, as she sat, hid herself with it from my eyes, and began, without restraint, clutching her knees, all wrapped like a rain-drenched soldier under a tarpaulin in no man's land, to sob uncontrollably.

A void in my mind. The body shivering, paralysed. I dared not move, pull any clothes on, say a word of comfort or justification. I shivered, said nothing, heard her sobs. To this day, after forty long years, I have never been able to forget that sound, and even today I am not able to smile, gently, aloof, at the tragedy which should, at this distance, begin to fade and become insignificant. So vast is the misery, the humiliation, of the naked young man on the narrow cot that through the years he delivers the taste and colour of genuine tragedy.

And yet, after a little time had passed, I began to feel how something I do know the name for began to make its way softly into my mind. Impatient, I quickly baptised it: tenderness, a gigantic tenderness never felt before or since, both towards Elizabeta, for whose unhappiness I was responsible, and for myself, impotent, bereft for the rest of my life of such a vital part of a man's experience (at the time I felt this was inevitable); my acceptance of a tragedy so immense that it can only be expressed through tenderness – there, that is the closest I can come to the feeling, entirely beyond thought, that finally retrieved me from the dead. That which reason could not handle happened as the result of something more ancient than reason: I put my arms round Elizabeta wrapped in the brocade coverlet, I ran my fingers through her hair, I kissed her and said words, the right words, unique to the circumstances into which we had been woven by two of the three spinners, Clotho and Lachesis: "Please don't cry, don't cry, please." I asked her not to cry, I warmed my cold cheeks on the warmth of hers, with my lips I licked the salty tears off her face, white as a peeled almond, and felt suddenly, with a triumphant fanfare – easy to look back on it now with irony – that my masculinity was returning with such relish, with such fury, that I threw the brocade coverlet to the floor and perhaps even a little roughly tumbled over on to it along with Elizabeta and lost myself in the powerful curves of the tear-stained girl.

That was how it began.

Spiritually drained, we lay on the floor, covered by the duvet I pulled down off the bed, Elizabeta's red hair on my left shoulder, the palm of my right hand resting on her heated cheek, my wife pliantly peaceful in the tender shelter of her husband's arm. We said nothing of what had happened. We were quiet. For a long time. I had nearly begun to drift to sleep when Elizabeta sat up brusquely and announced, almost businesslike, efficiently, "Time to go," and immediately, swiftly, pulled on her clothes, collecting her belongings from the floor in the dark. I followed suit.

That walk to Clifton Hill remains dreamlike to me because the bizarre quality of the dream fitted the reality of the empty streets of Bristol. The banners, emblems, floral cascades, the carnival rubbish, the tossed signs and pictures on the pavements, the greenish light cast by the street lamps, and in all that bedecked and magnificently empty city, only the two of us, exhausted lovers. We walked in silence. There was no strength in either of us for any sort of conversation, any spiritual activity. We had spent all we had on the crazy day. Deflated like two children's balloons punctured by a pin, we swam through the fantastic decor of the phantom-like unpeopled city, which greeted our passing with the limp flutter of bedraggled banners.

Once back in bed and happy after the great despair, I was nevertheless chilled by the thought that, for the nth time, of my inability to penetrate any part of Elizabeta's reticence. Too exhausted to be unhappy about it, I thought, feebly, about my own idiocy. Having discovered amid our lovemaking that Elizabeta had left her first marriage a virgin, I saw, with wrenching self-abnegation, self-castigation, with new eyes, what an untrusting, primitive oaf I had been even to hold, in my Serbian head, for a split second the ludicrous notion of Elizabeta as a woman of easy virtue. Tying her chastity to what Rašela wrote in her letter about the scandalous divorce as I drifted dejectedly into sleep, I realised what Elizabeta had not wanted to tell me: that her nuptial night had surely ended the same way that this evening of ours, June 9, the royal day at Bristol University, had begun, and at once I understood (but late, late as always) why my reticent, indomitable darling had not been able to hold back her feelings, as she otherwise always did, before and after this inauspicious beginning of our life as lovers, but sobbed with such bitter abandon.

The first stage in our love life was inaugurated on that first night of our love: from sexual impotence and inconsolable sobs to a carnal pleasure that shook us like a fever for more than a year. We made love not as if we were on the threshold of a lifetime together but as if we were prisoners condemned to die, as if our days were numbered. I was bewitched by Elizabeta's body. All I had to do was think of her long, firm legs, if I so much as nudged one of her breasts and thought of how white and full it was, or of her smooth soft belly below those large breasts, among the scattered pillows and rumpled sheets – regardless of where I happened to be at the time, whether we were in company or in a public place, whether she was at my side or far away, I would feel desire so powerful that I began to fear it and took efforts to chase the lascivious scenes from my easily inflamed fancy. I was often embarrassed by the ungovernable fever of my demands, it struck me as unseemly that I was so possessed by Elizabeta's body, but there was no help for it, I could not resist. Elizabeta's thrilling curves, both soft and firm, large yet shapely, white, so white in the dim light of our bedroom, were not, however, the only reason why I hurtled into our physical pleasures and was obsessed by them all day long. To tell the truth, I thrilled to her body at least as much as I thrilled to her pleasure. Elizabeta, who reined in all other passions, thoughts and moods, went wild with sex. She was even more desirous than I. Even in the grip of passion I still kept hold of the notion that this ecstasy was going to end and that its cooled eye would, in retrospect, see what I had done. Elizabeta, on the other hand, flamed like a raging blast furnace, she bit her hand, plunged her nails into my flesh, panted, wept, gasped words which she would never, otherwise, let by her lips. She lost her mind in the most literal sense, which for me, aside from the sexual pleasure it meant, was healing compensation for the secrecy she cloaked herself with in all other aspects of our relations. It may be that my Eliza, when her fervour passed, when her reason returned, had no recollection of what she had done or said. She may have recovered from the spell of passionate sex and lost all recollection of the lasciviousness of past moments. As her breathing slowed, the heat stopped radiating from her body, she would pull herself together and assume a businesslike brusqueness with none of the gradual transition from passion to that cosy exhaustion – the most intimate moment between lovers – as on that first night in Bristol: "Time to go," and her energetic collection of pieces of clothing scattered about the floor of the dark room. If she was not forgetting the uninhibited ardour of her large white body (how could she erase such an event from her consciousness in an instant), surely she was recalling it, as soon as the ardour passed, with a cringe.

Her sober coldness, the façade of rationality, were her way of down-playing her ardour, of relegating it to the realm of the incredible. By talking about things as distant as possible from our bedside, Elizabeta actually hoped to mask, from me and from herself, the memory of the bestiality of our freshly ended physical pleasures. She dared not even contemplate with a steady head her lack of inhibition in sex, but this helped her not at all, if, but a moment later, I so much as moved my hand across her still warm, still trembling belly or slid my fingers between her resilient thighs – and she erupted again with flames which instantly melted the icy bulwark of reason.

No-one but I could possibly have divined the volcanic eroticism of her body in the otherwise serene, sober demeanour of my indomitable one. Even less could anyone believe that despite the shame she wrestled with after her unbridled flights, Elizabeta, so self-controlled in all other ways, would toss on the wild wave of her passion, helpless like a small boat swept by an Atlantic hurricane. I remember that Elizabeta was never amused by obscene jokes in company. She even let it be known that she did not like them, though not because, as others thought, the chilly English lady did not appreciate our southern vices, but rather because (only I knew this of her) the sexual innuendo of the joke reminded her of her, or rather our, erotic forays which embarrassed her, and she preferred not to be reminded of them, particularly not in my company, the company of an unpleasant witness who knew her secret.

Then, about a year after that first night in Bristol, our intimate relations moved to a second stage that I ascribed, reasonably, to Elizabeta's pregnancy. One morning, she informed me that she was well along in her pregnancy. She wanted me to move out of our bedroom and sleep in one of the other rooms, which she had furnished for the purpose. My attempts to persuade her that we needn't make love if I stayed in our bedroom she rejected summarily, giving many reasons to conceal the real one: that she was not able to control herself once the fires began to seethe in her inflammable blood. And though, of course, I missed our ardent lovemaking, I explained Elizabeta's decision perhaps too readily to myself: as vain as any woman, my wife did not want her husband's eyes on her body, disfigured by pregnancy, or the hand of her lover on her bulging belly. She said that she was starting to look like the Nebojša Tower, that it was disgusting to see her "Falstaff's belly" in the mirror. She asked me, and others, with a joke that held a germ of truth, not to look upon the mockery of herself that she had become, although naturally all this was nowhere near the truth. She had, indeed, grown large, she was heavier, her step lost its lightness, but instead of seeing her as cumbersome the way she did, I discovered the particular charm of pregnancy, something of the animal in the life that was growing, curled up, inside her. A monkey baby in a human-like she-ape. A man in a woman. Lao Tse spent sixty years in his mother's womb before he was born as a grey-haired old man. In a word, I completely shared Elizabeta's feeling that it would be a travesty to make love with a child in her belly, it would be unclean, and, contrary to my earlier eagerness, I was now able to watch her, blessed with child, peacefully, without a carnal thought.

So everything changed at once except, of course, that all my thoughts, my tenderness, my care continued to be focused on Elizabeta while she manoeuvred, large, around our home, in anticipation of the great day. Pregnancy made her even more opaque. Before my very eyes, from each day to the next, I watched how she manifested less and less interest in me, in our friends, in the whole outside world, and how she clamped shut like a shell at the slightest touch, closed herself off from all the inquisitive eyes peering into her privacy. While earlier I had never known where her gaze turned when it turned inwards and closed, now I could tell with certainty that my indomitable one was watching Mihajlo, working with him, touching him with her womb, awed by his presence, marvelling that he was there the way God, and the two of us, had made him.

So. I have arrived. Mihajlo steps into my memory. Here I must stop. Dare I proceed? Is the ban of twenty years still in force? Dare I advance towards the memory for which I eradicated all recollection from my daily life to make it at least a modicum more bearable? Am I up to this encounter? I don't know. We'll see. Soon. Too soon I am approaching the end of my own life, death in our enclave. I only know that I dare not leapfrog over memories and thoughts. Now I must watch carefully – if I wish in this repeated attempt to understand something – so that thoughts and feelings don't insinuate their way into the sequence of my experiences before they actually happened and shaped my life, to be sure that I am not the wiser in retrospect for those things which I still did not know at the time.

In truth, therefore, I anticipated the child calmly. Unburdened. I did not feel my bond clearly with my son, Mihajlo (who had stepped into our life even before he was born, cooling our passions and parting us in bed), even when he was already crying in earnest in our home. My feelings for him were a muddle. Though he was tangible, present, for a long time he did not entirely – how should I put it? – exist for me. He was merely the notion of a child, an heir, something insubstantial in my life, just as my sense of fatherhood was something outside me, only partially pertinent to my being, with uncertain consequences. I must be careful and honest. About the facts, but also to myself. This is of the utmost importance. I dare not impose later feelings on the events that preceded them. Mihajlo, therefore, was at that time an intriguing novelty in my life, a little daily discomfort, something alive and helpless which I liked to feel in my arms, and something which cried in the afternoon when I lay down to read the paper.

While I remained unrattled, in that first phase, the first year or two, by the change in our lives, Elizabeta became a mother, as soon as "we two", so focused on each other in the Serbian surroundings, had become "we three" (first in our daily conversation, later in my consciousness as well), with all her instincts, with every thought, more in those first years than at any later time. Naturally, she never spoke of her love, nor was she one of those mothers who is forever kissing and nuzzling her baby, not at all. Yet I could not help but notice her constant obsession with the tiny body, even when he was in another room, or in the nurse's care, crying helplessly or out of her hearing. No matter where she was or what she was speaking of, one segment of Elizabeta's mind – I saw this clear as day – was engaged with the child who was, perhaps, sleeping somewhere, cooing, crying, bound constantly with invisible threads to its great matrix.

I rummage around in my thoughts, shielding the time I am thinking of from all that would transpire later and that my judgement might blur. I gradually grew accustomed to the notion that he was my son. Only with time did I acquire the feeling that I was a father. I know what and how I felt then: Mihajlo is something belonging to Elizabeta not, I'd say, because she wishes to keep him to herself, but because I am not able yet to take hold of my own part as a parent.

So the weeks went by, the first, then the second, then the third month passed. Mihajlo grew, but Elizabeta showed no inclination to invite me back to our bed. The explanation, that she was restless if she wasn't by Mihajlo's bedside, if she couldn't hear his breathing, I took as it was given, but that was not the cause of Elizabeta's evident reluctance to revive our intimacy. I was patient and confused. Blushing like a young girl, Elizabeta swiftly intercepted several of my attempts to steer her into my room, visibly grateful when I retreated at the first signs of her reluctance. With Elizabeta (always the attentive listener, practical counsellor, eager to debate all quandaries which I so readily brought to her), of course, I could never discuss the subject of our love life, so even today I am not able to say with a certainty what was happening in her maternal privacy, closely sheltered from my enquiring gaze. I was even more confused when I finally discovered that her desire, despite her stubborn refusal, was actually in no way diminished from what it had been before her pregnancy. Some three months after the birth, we were together in Novi Sad at the seventh Congress of Lawyers of the Kingdom of Yugoslavia, and in the suite in Kraljica Marija Hotel we made love for the first time after long abstinence. Elizabeta's passion was every bit as tempestuous as before, perhaps even more so. Certainly, it was no less. But I am also certain that the embarrassment was now of a different order, more acute. I can explain because I understand: my lascivious Elizabeta could not permit herself what she had been able to conceal or ignore before motherhood. Instead of the bright, businesslike cheer with which she had earlier masked her discomfort, at least superficially, Elizabeta recovered with difficulty after our lovemaking in the Novi Sad hotel suite. For ever thereafter, she would avert her eyes for several days following what were rare, random amorous encounters, though they grew more frequent later on. She would try without success to keep her shame and remorse to herself and deal with them privately.

What was the right thing for me to do? For a while, I tried to imagine how I might keep Elizabeta's embarrassment, or the passion that was the source of it, within reasonable bounds. But when I saw that all I tried to do remained without a real result, I reconciled myself to the new circumstances, considering the condition of our love life, after its second stage, to be final. My restraint, I must say, did not go unrewarded. In our wordless communication, Elizabeta knew how to let me know how much she valued my sacrifice, how much I was helping to diminish our tension, trapped somehow between desire and remorse, with my heroic decency.

Had I noticed a light shining under Elizabeta's door as I passed her bedroom before my decisive conversation about the Serbian Cultural Club in Slobodan's office, I would most surely have passed by, or perhaps I would have thought, sadly, of the pleasure I was missing. Just about that time, however, I had begun to notice a change in Elizabeta's demeanour. If I am not mistaken, I had observed the first signs of the third stage during the time of our – imposed but also welcome – encounters with the Prince, Princess and cream of Belgrade society. Not knowing the reason for the change, as always, I noticed that Elizabeta acquiesced more readily to my shy invitations. After a ceremonial evening or theatre performance, a hand of bridge or a ball, she would leave her fur coat in the front hall and of her own volition would turn to my, not her, bedroom. The change was even more clearly signalled by her decision to arrange for a separate bedroom for Mihajlo and to remain alone in the room where she had been sleeping. Mihajlo was about 8 years old then, and there was truly no need for his mother to watch over him at night. Elizabeta realised this herself and she would have moved her son into his own room well before, always in everything resoundingly English, had her romantic feelings towards me changed. Since they hadn't, she felt that the fact that she was sharing a bedroom with our son prevented us being alone. I, of course, judiciously avoided being the first to suggest Mihajlo's move, which does not mean that I wasn't overjoyed when Elizabeta did it herself. Because she made the decision, she saw to it promptly, as she did everything at that time.

The change in our room arrangement could only happen after other, deeper changes had occurred within us, the inhabitants of the apartment. As it is in life, long ripening brought our relations to a point of maturity when their nature shifted to something essentially different. It seemed to happen all at once. I was the one who, rather late in the day, discovered suddenly that almost nothing in our home was the way it had seemed to me only yesterday. Not because any one of us had changed, but because none of us was the same any longer: it was not the one-way shifting of a single belt, but rather an assembly line in which the movement of each belt tugs all the others into a new, surprising relationship. Mihajlo had changed. Elizabeta had changed. And – as I was last to observe – even I had changed.

First Mihajlo.

Cautiously and accurately. With no undue haste. As objectively as possible. At this time, I did not know what sorts of things would happen to us in life. (Shut up, Stevan: you have no notion of what will come. Pull yourself together.) I knew only Mihajlo, the baby of a few years ago, now Mihajlo, the remarkable boy of about 10, on the evening of my decision not to get drawn into politics, already 12 or 13. Mihajlo, a lad. Mihajlo, my son.

For a long time every bit as attached to his mother as she was to him, as a little boy Mihajlo always yearned, it seemed to me, for more closeness and tenderness than Elizabeta was prepared to give him. Though occupied entirely by her child, Elizabeta was able without difficulty, or at least so it seemed, to raise him while being that sort of unpampering, unspoiling mother such as most mothers are in England, thanks to which generations of prominent families flourish, while in this country, now in its second generation of prosperity, the upcoming generation is going bad, growing indolent and useless. I remember how Elizabeta, overnight, all at once, as when Mihajlo was just a little boy, stopped their early morning cuddling in her bed, although she did enjoy it, I know this for a fact, at least as much as her little son did.

I have never confessed to her how, one morning, through the barely opened door of what had been our room but was now hers and Mihajlo's, I watched, in a turmoil of emotion, a scene I cannot forget, and I know why I have never been able to confess it: I always felt

139

ashamed of my own childish peevishness at not being included in their closeness, at not being Elizabeta's main preoccupation any more, at being shoved aside overnight. I as one team, the two of them as the other. The fact that I was ashamed of my inner turmoil, which I carefully concealed from Elizabeta, did not help me to rid myself of it. On the contrary. Instead of growing acclimatised over time to the existence of *our* son, with shame I must confess that watching them I felt more and more hurt as if they were some sort of opponents. So when I suddenly had the chance to observe them, unaware as they were of my presence, amid their morning ritual of waking, even though I was ashamed the entire time of the indecency of my voyeurism, I was unable to resist.

I no longer remember what it was that brought me to the bedroom door that morning, but I do know that the scene that unfolded, though entirely ordinary, enchanted me, froze my hand mid-knock. A large room with two double beds in it. In one, Elizabeta, in the other, little Mihajlo. He was sleeping. I saw Elizabeta's face framed, partly covered, by her thick and gleaming hair, tangled from sleep, red, so red on the white pillow! She was leaning over towards Mihajlo, staring at his closed eyelids. She was on her hip. She was propping her head with her arm, bent at the elbow. She was large. Sturdy as one of the Meštrović caryatids. Precisely that. When, as a very small child, Mihajlo first saw the Meštrović monument of gratitude to France raised on Kalemegdan – a mighty woman in iron – he pointed to her and said, "Mummy!" He hardly knew how to speak at that point, but he did know how to see. Mummy truly could have posed for Meštrović. Statuesque, shapely, she lay relaxed on the bed, her long, large legs, her strong thigh of fine marble which was raised, supported by her leg slightly bent at the knee. Elizabeta noticed that Mihajlo was awake, she leaned over him and kissed him on the brow. Her ample bosom, which the plunging neckline of the nightgown could barely contain, covered his little chest as she took him into her arms and carried him to her own bed. Probably because it had been so long since I'd seen her bosom, I couldn't take my eyes from it, a remarkable, almost unnatural milk-white speckled with yellow freckles, massively ponderous but elastic, only sagging a touch downwards, with large, pale-red nipples amid a darker circle. Mihajlo giggled with a baby's high chortle while Elizabeta, lying now on her back, lifted him up and over on to her bosom, until the child asked for his "nursery rhymes". Then he fell silent. He knew what was coming. His little head peeked over Elizabeta's shoulder, hugged by her left arm. He even closed his eyes. He was loving this. The crackling of the fire in the stove mingled with Elizabeta's voice. It suddenly seemed as if a golden radiance had flooded the large light room, which smelled of the child and Elizabeta. She recited the poem "Infant Joy" by William Blake, a poet she admired a great deal, perhaps because her maiden name had been Blake. She spoke the first lines in a reedier voice, as if Mihajlo were saying them:

> I have no name:
> I am but two days old.

Then she altered her voice and asked:

> What shall I call thee?

And she replied as Mihajlo:

> I happy am,
> Joy is my name.

Then in a ringing voice, but serious, cognisant of what she spoke, she continued to the end:

> Sweet joy befall thee!
> Pretty joy!
> Sweet joy but two days old.
> Sweet joy I call thee:
> Thou dost smile,
> I sing the while;
> Sweet joy befall thee!

Will I ever forget that little poem? Can this scene ever darken in my memory? Will I ever be able to distinguish among all the feelings that filled my heart at that moment and call them by their true names? Nonetheless, shame overwhelmed my enchantment and I knocked at the door hastily, fearful that I might change my mind. Elizabeta started. I said to myself: caught. An odd word under the circumstances. I remember well the haste with which she interrupted the morning ritual of cuddling when I entered the room and put Mihajlo back in his bed as if she had been caught in the middle of something forbidden, not in cuddling her little boy. As if Elizabeta were embarrassed for me to see her nakedness in front of anyone, even her son, she quickly pulled a robe over her shoulders and bosom. As if one kind of closeness, motherly affection, was ashamed before eyes which knew of another kind of physical closeness – I find it difficult to articulate this precisely – but that morning in the mother's total devotion to her son which I could see so clearly, I sensed Elizabeta's thought that her attachment to Mihajlo was something secret, perhaps something forbidden. Naturally, the likelihood that I imagined it all, fabricated it, is not small. It possibly was not at all the way I saw it, but nevertheless, I clearly recall that Elizabeta always seemed to set Mihajlo down, as if caught, from her marble lap, hastily, as soon as I appeared, that she never held him in her arms in front of me the way she did while I watched her unobserved, that she had never recited "Infant Joy" to him in front of me, though she must have loved the poem if she learned it by heart.

I sulked only briefly about the alliance between Elizabeta and Mihajlo, however, because Elizabeta quite abruptly, soon thereafter, cut off all cuddling with her child as if with an axe. That earliest childhood maternal tenderness for Mihajlo was stopped in a single day. He was chased from her skirts, dropped from her arms, by a decision as irrevocable as an imperial edict. I knew as much from Mihajlo's complaints, and I saw the resolution with which Elizabeta refused to take him into her lap, for that was not fitting for a boy of his age, although I am certain that she regretted the harsh end to her nursery tenderness even more than he did. Since I knew how attached she was to Mihajlo, only I could judge how stoically, how bravely, Elizabeta held back from every show of tenderness, how consistent she was in keeping to the castigations she would set for Mihajlo, how courageously she managed to look at his bumped nose or knee as something that a boy must bear without tears. Mihajlo would simply have to get used to an English upbringing. While in England I had noticed how unusually mannerly even the smallest children were but that good behaviour was far less striking in the British Isles because there were so many children there who were that way. Here, Mihajlo stood apart even in his earliest years with his politeness. He seemed old for his age among the spoiled little Serbian children with his exemplary manners. Manners are, after all, a notion taken from the English. In Serbian, the word has an entirely different meaning.

From his earliest years, Mihajlo felt equally at home in Serbian and English, since Elizabeta, with my delighted consent, made both languages equally available to the child. Even before he was born, we would switch back and forth, easily and without noticing, from one language to the other. When Elizabeta was learning Serbian, when she felt, mid-sentence, that she was missing the right nicely rounded phrase or sentence, she would reach for English. I did the same, only in the other direction. It is therefore no surprise that Mihajlo made no distinction between the two languages, though there is an argument which has never been resolved as to what the first word he spoke was. Elizabeta, Grandfather Milutin and I all agreed as to what word it was, or rather what cluster of syllables resembling a word, but the question remains whether it sounded more like *deda*, meaning Grandpa, or *daddy*. Proud Grandpa Milutin claimed, with Elizabeta's full support, that this was the Serbian word *deda*, while I, more to tease them than because I could have been certain of it, claimed that it was the English word *daddy*, meant for me.

In any case, until he started school, Mihajlo felt at home in both languages. He never mixed them. He spoke English as clearly as Elizabeta did, while his Serbian was without her accent, exactly as I spoke it. But no matter what language he used, there could be no doubt that you were speaking with a little English lad, that this was Elizabeta's child standing before you. Like a true little Englishman, only a couple of feet tall, always tidy, his red hair combed to the side, Elizabeta's milk-white complexion, dressed in English style: woollen knee socks, grey trousers, a blazer as if he were a grown man, sitting straight in his chair, his hands quietly crossed in his lap, he would reply to questions with unshakeable poise: "*Da, gospodine,*" "*Ne, gospodine,*" "*Ja se nadam, gospođo,*" "*Nećete mi zameriti, ako . . .*", "*Bojim se da ću vas razočarati, ali . . .*"* These sentence fragments from an inexhaustible well of British manners, so designed that in English they meant nothing, astonished Serbs who were accustomed to the way adults behave towards children here, and children towards adults. With these petrified phrases, little Mihajlo simply did not allow the Serbs to tease him, to joke. They were constantly giving him to know that he was a child, that they considered him little, and therefore a person whose right and duty it was to be wayward and headstrong. Mihajlo's decisive refusal to accept their gift of leniency most often made our acquaintances uncomfortable, or, in better instances, it amused them and made them laugh. As a rule, the polite little English lad succeeded in holding his own and imposing it on others. I may be wrong, but I had the impression that Elizabeta would intentionally await the moment when guests would begin to ask serious questions of the little red-headed boy (Nanka never forgave him the "English" hue of his hair; perhaps it was that hair that despatched her into the throes of premature senility) and respond to his questions in the same vein. Only then, when the victory of this kind of behaviour was forthcoming, did she allow her son to return to the game he had interrupted to come in and greet the company. "You may go now, Mihajlo," Elizabeta would say, and our little English lad would bow, say how pleased he was to have met the guests or how pleased he was that they had stopped by for a visit; he would ask them to give his regards to their son or daughter, if sons or daughters had been mentioned in the conversation, and then – he would withdraw.

If, in his bearing and his attire, thanks to his mother's taste and upbringing, he resembled a little English lad, this was certainly not

*"Yes, Sir," "No, Sir," "I do hope so, Ma'am," "I hope you won't mind if . . ." "I fear I may disappoint you, but . . ."

Elizabeta's conscious intention. On the contrary, she knew that this would not be good for the boy and did everything in her power to have Mihajlo grow up as a Serb and make a life for himself. I remember vividly the moment and circumstances under which Mihajlo, still quite small, first noticed that there was something unusual in his facility in two languages. At a birthday party for Uroš, Godfather Nedeljko's youngest son, we adults were sitting in the living room while the children played on a spacious covered porch and in the garden. I saw Mihajlo coming our way, grave, pensive – not, of course, to me but to his mother. He stood on tiptoe to whisper something in her ear, but he couldn't reach it, since Elizabeta was not leaning towards him; rather, she sat straight in her chair and asked, aloud, what the child obviously wished to convey to her in secret, "*Šta želiš, Mihajlo?*"

"Mummy," and unhappy Mihajlo continued whispering to her his astounding discovery, "*Uroš doesn't understand me!*"

"*Naravno da ne razume,*" answered Elizabeta, as always in her dealings with him, an equal. "*Sa Uroš treba srbski govoriti. Razumeš?*"

Mihajlo's affirmative nod seemed rather unconvincing to me. He went off with that same worried wrinkle in his child's brow which he had had when he came for the answer to his important question. That Elizabeta's explanation had not been sufficient was confirmed some ten minutes later, when he sidled over to his mother, even more perplexed.

"*Opet imaš nešto?*" she asked, but she realised at once that this time Mihajlo would not announce his troubles aloud, so she bowed her ear to him. I sharpened my ears, so that I, too, could hear it when Mihajlo, in a near-panic, said, "Mummy, no one understands English there!"

"*Ali Majkl, ti s Srbin u Srbija i u Srbija se govori srbski. Moraš govoriti srbski ako želiš biti razumeven. To je trvoj rodni jezik.*"*

In that respect, therefore, Elizabeta was adamant. Mihajlo was a Serb

*"What do you want, Mihajlo?"
"Naturally he doesn't understand you."
"With Uroš one in Serbian speaks. Understand?"
"Have you something again?"
"But Michael, a Serb you are in Serbia, and one in Serbia speaks the Serbian. Serbian you must speak if you wish being understood. This is your language native-born."

in Serbia, and his mother tongue, regardless of his mother, was Serbian. What Elizabeta did unconsciously, however, or perhaps what she was incapable of changing, had a more profound effect beyond what she intended. In making little Mihajlo a Serb, a citizen of Belgrade, she could not help but shape him, with the purest of intentions, into a person according to her views and taste, and her views and taste were English. So Mihajlo did not persevere with his English manners because Elizabeta was instructing him in the advantages of vacuous English chat, but because she was convinced that children ought to respect their elders, that they should not bother us with the usual monkeying about. Mihajlo's manners, his gravity, his politeness – a source of amazement for unaccustomed Serbs – did not conceal his child's desire always to be the centre of attention, and even less his intention to entertain the adults. Not at all. He believed that he was behaving in an ordinary way, and he would be reduced to tears when one of our acquaintances persisted with the jokes, confusing questions and baby talk customary in this country. Mihajlo was simply modest, serious and polite, and he did not know how to act when someone tried to make him out to be spoiled, headstrong and childish. He did his duty as his mother had taught him, he did not make a show, and he gladly would leave adult company as soon as his mother permitted him to do so.

While many from our circle looked askance at Mihajlo's "English" behaviour, interpreting it as an affront to Serbdom, a betrayal of our customs, we were the least bothered who should have been the most affected: me, the child's father, and Grandfather Milutin, a Serb of the oldest, most venerable kind. In different, even diametrically opposed, ways, Milutin and I gave our silent approval to Elizabeta's methods, both the conscious ones that directed Mihajlo towards Serbdom and those one might have termed unconscious, springing from Elizabeta's education and proud English spirit.

Milutin behaved in a manner entirely contrary to all my predictions. While I imagined, during my hours of indecision in Bristol, an encounter between Elizabeta and Milutin, I trembled at the thought for two reasons. One was that because of his risibly old-fashioned Serbdom, Milutin might think of the presence of an Englishwoman in his home and family as a blemish. Knowing his fine character and his mindfulness of the shortcomings of others, I felt certain that he would never show his dismay to Elizabeta and that he would defend his daughter-in-law before the rest of the world even if, in his heart of hearts, he might rankle at the fact that I had married a foreigner. After a brief spell of examination, sniffing and circling, I saw that my fears on the first point were groundless. Either Milutin – I said to myself, curious and pleased – is such a splendid actor that his concern for his daughter-in-law, his constant worry that someone might ridicule her for her foreign habits, his well-timed manoeuvres (invisible, perhaps, to others but evident to me) to rescue baffled Elizabeta from some overbearing relative only appeared to be sincere, or – as I quickly realised was the case – he had come to love this lovely, reticent, incisive daughter-in-law as if she were his own daughter in distress, out of her depth. He had to protect her, at least in the beginning, constantly. I was particularly grateful that he gave himself over generously to a task for which I was not mature enough at the time: overseeing relations between Elizabeta and Nanka. The sole reason that Nanka, distrustful and hostile from day one towards the "English princess", "gibberish-talker", "*minderpuza*", did not try Elizabeta's patience to a degree that would have been insufferable was because Father interceded, always with tact, using reason, plea or chastisement as gently as he could, but always firmly and effectively. I heard him on several occasions at the conclusion or beginning of his and Nanka's conversations, which they would interrupt when Elizabeta or I appeared. "Stuck-up, she is," I heard Nanka once say.

"You don't understand her reserve," Milutin replied calmly. Or another time, "If she does not know how, let her learn," Nanka blustered at patient Milutin's attempt to justify the fact that Elizabeta did not know how to prepare Turkish coffee.

Or, the next time: "For every habit learned there is one to be unlearned," Nanka rejecting, drily and angrily, Milutin's explanation that Elizabeta had had the habit, in her English home, of rising after, not with, the first cock crow, as my Gojkovica always did.

And then, "In Serbian homes, a husband does not place the chair under his wife's bottom," I heard her fuming, despite Milutin's explanation that in better homes, Serbian ones as well, this was done.

"The two of us, Nanka, are for the iron heap. If we cannot help the children, let us not hinder them."

"But, why . . ." Pugnacious Nanka wanted to bring forth yet another tale of woe, but Milutin, abruptly, with rare firmness, interrupted her, "That will be enough 'whys'. Do as I say . . ."

Milutin was the one who did everything to help us off on our own as soon as possible. Every day, he visited the construction site of our new home, paid the craftsmen overtime, hurried them along, in order to spare Elizabeta his own, to his mind, burdensome presence and to spare her socialising with our relatives who were constantly confusing her, still unsure in her mastery of the language, with their inept enthusiasm, but most of all to shield her from prickly, aggravated Nanka.

While Milutin did all he could to help Elizabeta, she returned the attention in equal measure. My second Bristol fear about how Milutin and Elizabeta would get along was tied to Father's rigidity, his shy awkwardness, which might, I worried, make him feel stiff and uncomfortable. I was afraid that Elizabeta would not master the knack of conversing with an old patriarchal Serb and that, despite her best intentions, she would upset him. Everything turned out differently, however. My father and wife never conversed much, at first because Elizabeta knew little Serbian. But by the time she'd learned it, they had no need. It may sound strange, but the 20-year-old Englishwoman with her university education and modern views understood this self-taught 60-year-old Serb because, I would say, their souls were alike. Understanding between two beings relies not on words but on the personal – not the historical or national – experience that gives them a special sort of rapport. As if it were palpable, I could see this point where Elizabeta's and Milutin's happiness intersected, the knot that tied their differences into a harmonious whole without contradictions. It all began, of course, with Milutin's discovery that before him he had a conscientious, quiet, lovely young woman who suffered, or might suffer, because she was not like others, but rather superior to them, and with Elizabeta's discovery that before her was a man from some murky historical place of no return, a man of great courtesy, wisdom and goodness. Though seldom shown, never confirmed in words, their mutual regard was so evident that it sometimes made me jealous, not, of course, because there was ever a hint of an unseemly thought on either side, but because I saw how Milutin, without lifting a finger, formed a closeness with Elizabeta that I could only dream of. All the things that she never gladly or easily permitted me, Milutin dared to do and was allowed in his rapport with Elizabeta. For instance, Eliza, always tight-lipped, even disapproving of the way I expressed myself, would often laugh at what she called my "flowery style". She liked it even less when I said something which would ring, to her sceptical ear, of "bathos" or "pomp". "You and your Slavic profundity," she would comment ironically. She was the least patient with expressions of feelings, descriptions of states of the soul. They threatened her for whatever reason, and often, in defence, she would pounce: "Sentimental rubbish. Will you stop it, for Christ's sake!"

But what bothered her in my expression or behaviour, she would receive from Milutin without the slightest ire or blush. She would listen, for instance, to Milutin's "sentimental", "pathetic" and "pompous" "daughter of mine" and, without a trace of discomfort, would answer, "Yes, Father," as if that patriarchal title was not coloured by unseemly emotions. When Milutin saw his grandson for the first time, he said, "Thank you, daughter, for bearing us a hero." I stood there prickling with fear that Elizabeta would be embarrassed, but to my surprise I saw how she, exhausted though she was, grinned, thanked him and lifted the "hero" so his grandfather could have a closer look. And then there was the matter of kissing the hand, which occurred only a few months after our arrival in Belgrade. I believe we were still staying in Zorina Street, in the familial home, but I am not certain. In any case, on the first day of Christmas, Nanka always came to greet the head of the household in the living room early in the morning. She announced to him that Christ was born and, according to tradition, kissed his hand. Since I had learned to catch the signs of my father's thoughts and feelings behind his defensive postures, I knew that Milutin was already worrying, even before he responded to Nanka that Christ had indeed been born, about his encounter with Elizabeta, the next in line to congratulate him. Should he extend his hand? What if he were to mortify her by making her take part in a ritual that might be strange to her, perhaps humiliating, even barbaric? Or should he not proffer his hand, making her uncomfortable by drawing a distinction between her and the other members of the household? If Nanka hadn't been there, it would have been easier for him; he could have said something soothing. But the crane-like gaze of his strict, literal keeper of Serbian traditions precluded any easing of rigid ceremoniality. By the way he withdrew his hand when Elizabeta took it in hers, I realised he had granted his daughter-in-law amnesty, that he had taken hers, and not Nanka's, side. But without a single word, a miracle unfolded before my eyes. Their eyes met, Milutin stopped withdrawing his hand, a little smile began, a smile of trust, in Elizabeta's eye, which the elderly gentleman immediately recognised. Two smiles joined in an agreement that only the two of them understood, something freeing and aimed against all the rest of the world. Without shame, Elizabeta kissed the hand of the master of the household; without awkwardness, Milutin accepted her kiss. Somewhere at some boundary I have been seeking for so many years Elizabeta and Milutin met. Both of them private, sporting carefully fashioned masks for the outside world, they found it easy, somehow, to know each other.

So, informed as I was as to the nature of their mutual regard, I did not find surprising what other Serbs were astounded by: that Milutin observed Mihajlo's English behaviour, if not with satisfaction, at least without reproach. This old-fashioned man was the first among all the modern Europeans around us to grasp the meaning of Elizabeta's strictness in bringing up her child. And though he was an elderly man, Milutin seemed able to understand the importance of manners, even when they were devoid of meaning, for the seamless functioning of social life, and thereby finally feel vindicated in his decades-old chagrin that, though a Serb, he was not arrogant.

Or am I attributing to Father thoughts which I cultivated myself? Feelings which he never had? I don't know. I can make one claim, however, with a clear conscience: both Milutin and I considered the upbringing of the family's male heir to be exemplary, and when he began to show remarkable indications of precocity (our Mihajlo was reading without help at the age of 5, solving eighth-form maths problems in the third form, and reading Shakespeare comedies in the fourth), we were a proud father and an even prouder grandfather.

The change that erupted overnight in the behaviour of Elizabeta's courteous son can therefore by no means be ascribed to our influence – a change that would alter all the relations on our family assembly line, realign all the set positions of the straps and belts. The little Englishman, Elizabeta's polite son, the modest, diligent *wunderkind*, returned enraged from a week-long school excursion to Bled while in the second form of the Second Boys' Gymnasium, defying every assertion and anyone's opinion. This was not our courteous little lad, oh no. In terse conversations about the glaring change, clearly wrenching for her, Elizabeta countered my claim that Mihajlo had changed his nature and his convictions overnight. She hinted that the change had been long in coming, that, unlike me, she was not surprised by what had happened, though she could not explain it. Suddenly or gradually, the child had changed fundamentally. He obstinately refused, for instance, to speak English. He refused even to understand a word of our everyday conversations; rather he would politely request that his mother and I speak Serbian if, as we were wont to, we switched for a moment into English. In his own restrained way, he became capricious and given to tantrums. He abruptly stopped playing the flute, though he had played it with pleasure. All our attempts to urge him to continue with his private French lessons were to no avail; he stopped riding, which he had loved to do. He would wear none of the things Elizabeta bought him at the "Engleski Magazin" on Vuk Karadžić Street. He broke off with almost every one of his close friendships and started two or three new ones. To top it off, entirely of his own volition, without consulting Elizabeta, he left the prestigious Second Boys' Gymnasium and enrolled in the recently founded Fifth Real Secondary School, poorly equipped and situated in a private home not far from us, at Miloš Veliki 33. Elizabeta was certainly right: such fundamental changes in behaviour must not have happened overnight. The fact that I only noticed them when they rammed me like a pitchfork in the eyes shows that I barely knew my son.

One thing I did understand was that none of us could stay the same if one of us changed so fundamentally. Mihajlo changed, but that change so tugged at the straps and belts of our assembly line that Elizabeta, too, was changed, though it is difficult for me to talk about the development and depth of her change because she always kept everything about herself so carefully hidden. Sometimes it seemed to me that she was rattled, crazed by the surfacing of defiance and obstinacy in her child, who had suddenly begun to throw off all, or almost all, that he had been taught for more than a decade by example and counsel. At other times, I believed that she was governing not only herself but the storm in Mihajlo's soul, and that she was letting him wear himself out the way a fisherman plays a powerful, tenacious fish racing and tugging on his line. At yet other times, I would have other thoughts, but one thing was clear: there were no longer two teams in the household. A third one had emerged. Mihajlo had become his own team, which brings me to the final change I observed: that I, too, had changed in significant ways.

Only when Mihajlo stepped away from his symbiotic union with his mother and became able to hold views independent of Elizabeta was I able to see that I had been perceiving him through some sort of watery curtain as her foreign, courteous little wonder, an English doll who, of course, since he was so remarkable, pleased my vanity. But the boy did not excite a genuine and enduring paternal bond. For the first time, I understood my obsession with Elizabeta on the one hand, and my unfatherly lassitude towards Mihajlo on the other, as something shameful, unnatural, as a sin. Am I a monster? I wondered anxiously; had I been a monster for all those years when Mihajlo seemed merely someone who advanced my position or undermined me. Now that he stood apart from his mother, he became an independent factor. Until yesterday walled up in the fortress of Elizabeta's privacy, he had suddenly – and I felt this very clearly – become accessible to me as well. I could love him. I had to love him now.

That still unstable pontoon of access to Mihajlo which I tested with the utmost caution with the tip of my shoe, not daring to advance across it, was not obstructed, but rather aided, by the bridge to Elizabeta through a mysterious web of interconnected and dependent attachments and thoughts. Only semi-passable for more than a decade, the bridge now opened without fanfare or fireworks but, without a doubt, finally in a way suitable to our age and our years of marriage. Elizabeta came back to me with some of herself – with as much of herself as she could. She came back as a lover though without ardour and stinging remorse – in other words, mellow now, adult. She returned, for better or worse, seeking some of the support she had suddenly begun to miss, for an occasional conspiratorial word which I had to choose carefully so that I wouldn't deflect her with anything too strong. She returned to our solitude, to the two of us. I dared not, of course, disclose my "bathos" and "pomp" to Elizabeta, but I felt clearly and shouted loudly to myself: Our marriage has begun, a dozen years after the church ceremony, now that the third stage has spent our youthful strength, and life has directed Elizabeta to take shelter with me, and me to lean on her loneliness.

And so, when I saw that bar of light beneath her bedroom door (which we did not yet share because I needed another two weeks to propose that we do so), I knocked without fear and heard Elizabeta's voice: "Is that you, Stevan?"

I cracked the door and poked my head round it. She was sitting on the bed leaning against two large pillows in the light of the bedside lamp, a book in her hand.

"You're not asleep? May I come in?"

Elizabeta said, "Naturally."

A "naturally" that was revolutionary. A word that even yesterday had been impossible to imagine in her vocabulary. A word she had been practising to say, in a natural way, for fourteen years.

I sat on the edge of her bed.

"What did you say to the Professor?" she asked, raising herself up a bit on the pillows, ready to listen.

"That I cannot do as he suggests."

"Was it difficult?"

"Awful. It was awful."

"Tell me, Stevan. Do."

I told my wife. Everything. Except my harsh words about the Serbs. Those I kept for myself.

FIVE

In Belgrade, March, 1940

My dear deceased Rachel,

Majkl has whiskers.

There, it sounds funny to me at once, as soon as I am reading it, for I have not written to you in so long, and now I am announcing the news of the century: Majkl has whiskers! He does indeed. The sun this morning, the pale sun, shined through the windows on them, and suddenly I saw. Like a little chick, yellow and silky, but – whiskers. I don't know why, this was sad, I nearly cried. Poor Majkl, he is no longer a child. My Majkl now will be a man. Of course, I said nothing because I would make him uncomfortable.

When he left the table after dinner, I said to Stevan, "Majkl has whiskers."

"Whiskers? Is this possible? When did you see?"

"This morning."

"I did not."

As soon as he says this, I know I must write to you, Rachel. Maybe I am mistaken when I am always so insulted if Stevan shows towards Majkl indifference. Here I have seen something ugly, what a man has no right to do. This is *podlo*. I am meaning bad, maybe *podlo* is too strong a word. Selfish, maybe this is the better word. But I would prefer Stevan being vile. Then I could be saying to him: in this way a father must live with the son. You must change. The child has the right for his father to care for him. As it is I cannot, for he would answer, "I do care for my son," and it would be the truth, he would not be lying. But that is what seems confused. He is caring as much as he must be, but he would not

155

be noticing the child for days, if I let it go this way. And it is not enough comfort, saying: as is Stevan, so are many fathers. This does not justify, I know that I have a valid reason for being insulted.

I do not know, maybe I am the *karakondžula*, demanding too much from my husband. Now I am lying. I say that only rhetorically, and I know Stevan is guilty. Wrong. He pretends he is restrained towards our son, for pedagogical reasons, but I know, Stevan cannot fool me. He is empty, he feels no fatherly concern, he makes no effort, Majkl to him is not important. Not precisely nothing at all, but only a little, less than Majkl needs. Particularly now.

Earlier I was not so angry, because it was different with Majkl. He was attached to me and he was missing less his father's caring. I was satisfied. And I am strong enough for his sureness, and occupied enough for his happiness. We would see the father at dinner or when the company, the relatives, came, and the rest of the time we spent alone. Majkl and I. From early morning until he went to bed. Little Majkl and I.

I was not writing to you, Rachel, much about our days then, because I was glad. There are no years in my life until now more beautiful than those. Only then I never wondered about anything. I had meaning. I did not have to look for it. It was not necessary constantly to check on it fighting against reality. The meaning was here at my side. Alive. Inquisitive. From morning to dark. In every season of the year. He grew, learned new words, to read. My meaning turned before my eyes into a man.

They here all said that Mihajlo was like an English child, but they were wrong because they do not know English children. First, there exists no one sort of English child, instead there exist all manner of English children. Intelligent and stupid, talkative and quiet, polite and scoundrels. Fine, it is true, in England, generally, children are not so spoiled, ruined by their upbringing as in Belgrade, although even there there are the ones who all laugh and are in the centre, because their parents train them so. I do not like these children, not in England, not in Srbija, so that is why, probably, knowing life by my tastes, Majkl was not that kind, rather polite and modest. However, those other things, the shallow-brained people also attributed to his English upbringing. It was not English, nor Serbian, it was Majkl's remarkableness. I saw that, the specialness of that child still when he was a baby. Others saw it later, so they attributed his early knowledge and habits to teaching. Well, Majkl was always years in front of his generation of boys, but not because I particularly attempted to introduce him before the normal time to knowledge. There, they all were wondering how he when he was only five years old was reading *Mali Žurnal*! My God, how amusing it was to see him! So little, red-headed, in shorts, one leg crossed over the other, he spread the paper and read. Like a grown-up. Relatives came, neighbours, even the newspaper men wanted to see him, the little English lad, the wunderkind, but that, of course, I did not allow. And I had nothing at all to do although they praised (or scolded) me everything came from itself. One afternoon I taught him which were the vowels. Immediately, he remembered. He would show the letter and say, "Mummy, here is A, here is I." Like that, he played. Then he began, of himself, every day to ask, "Which is this letter? And this one?" I always answered his questions but never forced him, even did not encourage him to learn more, so I was myself astounded when Majkl one day stared at the first page of the newspapers behind which, holding them open in his two hands, was hidden Stevan, reading them in the armchair – and said, "It says here '*Kraljica majka*' (Queen Mother)."

I am not the crazy, in-love mother. Really, Rachel. I can be towards Majkl analytically impartial. I never thought he is a wonder-child, and I know it still isn't known if he will be something special, and do remarkable things in his life. His early knowledge, the playing of the flute, the solving of riddles, the reading of Shakespeare, all those, as I call them his circus skills which astonished the whole world, did not delight me, but they did not surprise or worry me. Let's say Shakespeare. They were reporting that he read all the comedies, but this is not so. He read, with mine and Stevan's big help (I confess – and his perseverance) *A Midsummer Night's Dream*. Then he was already 10 years old, and he read, God knows, this one comedy from late autumn all the way to spring. Every day a little. What he does not know he asks. He was, it is true, very persistent. Persistent – yes, bright – certainly, inquisitive – even over the measure, but – now I know this surely, and I knew it then when Majkl, still small, seemed to everyone a true miracle – he is just an ordinary little boy. An ordinary little boy, red-haired, "a spry little man" as the also deceased Grandfather Milutin used to say, on the narrow little face only two large grey eyes. He loved everything that other "spry little men" loved: to run, ride a pony, listen to stories, be pampered too much, like all the sons who are the only children.

And that is why always when I ask the question whether Mihajlo's remarkableness could have made Stevan grow distant from him; is it because he behaves like some "English lad" (though he did not behave this way), would it be possible to make Majkl a strange child for Stevan? In all honesty I answer – no, this is not the reason, if the reason can in general be found. Stevan looked at our son, when he noticed him, as at a strange newcomer, I guess, as he looked at the red-haired setter we took care of a short time. Sometimes I had the impression that he was simply surprised when he came upon Majkl in the hallway or the living room. In all truth, as if he was wondering, "Well, so the little one is still here? How nice!" As if he had never got the habit that our son is a new organic part of our life, and our home. And Majkl, of course, what else can he do, Mihajlo, spontaneously as a child can, without thinking, was never even a little nasty to his father, but he never asked for him. In everything he was turned to me.

At first, I confess, this, too, bothered me. Stevan's absent-minded – yes that is perhaps the good word – absent-minded attitude towards Majkl, his ignoring Majkl, even more insulted because it stood right next to Stevan's great attention for me, next to his lovely, rare consideration for all my confusings, next to his simply pathetic effort for it to be good for me in Belgrade, among the strange relatives and Serbian friends.

Stevan, Rachel, is a good man. He is good to me. There. He is mine. Not precisely as Majkl, but not completely differently. Only (maybe I am cursed) he has habits, traits, that I cannot entirely help from noticing, but often, they – I cannot say bring me to rage, but they irritate. Not like pain. Like a bothersome itch. And again, they are not intentional and vile that I would openly chide Stevan. Let's say, how he constantly pretends to be so occupied, so tired of thinking and working, but it is not so. I know best. I cannot say how much he thinks, but I see how much he works. Little. For all Stevan has time. He used to say this for late Father Milutin, but he does not see that the same holds for him. In Bristol he was so different. I, and others, we were simply amazed at how diligent Stevan was. And then after a little more, until he finished the dissertation, but then, little by little, he abandoned everything, as if with the doctorate he learned everything, and finished all jobs. Now his daily habits are more important than every work for his profession. Rachel, I simply do not like Stevan's day how it looks. Every morning he drinks coffee, reads all newspapers, in his housecoat until 9. Then comes, every morning, his barber and shaves him, then trimming the beard and the whiskers, and they talk about everything because Barber Žika knows everything. When he finishes the morning toilet already it is half of eleven and he goes to the *Fakultet*, but soon we are having dinner. Then Stevan in his *kabinet* doffs his jacket and so he lies on the leather sofa and he reads the newspaper and he naps. Until four. Then together we drink tea, to five, and then – there it is, the day is passed, and Stevan did nothing. It is true that at five he will, with an important, ceremonial look on his face, go into the *kabinet*. "Off to work," he says.

To seven. But I know that even then he does not work, because I am reading all the five–six articles which he published in the last years in *Arhiv za pravne i društvene nauke* and I am seeing this is with little effort copied from foreign books, or these are leftover parts of the dissertation. And what most disappoints me in these articles as if they are about everything, just not from his work, simply he abandoned his science and what he writes is just to pass the time, no sort of scholarship; he writes all that he managed to read, from all areas, and without the effort to elaborate. All out of his head. And all pretentious. Let's say: "Bergson and Contemporary Culture". Someone might think, this is a book of at least three hundred pages, but it is an article of two and one-half pages, in large print. And then I ask, what does Stevan, a professor of Constitutional Law, have to do with the philosopher Bergson, and what is his desire to speak about culture! Stevan is extremely critical towards the Serbian mentality. He very painfully sees "the sparrow-like work capacity", "the inability to finish what we start". Stevan one hundred times said that what he most hates is the "jeremiad of our intellectuals about what is all preventing them from working". Here, Rachel, an excerpt from one of his finest articles, though this one, too, has the pompous name: "The Will and Activity of a Person in this Country": "There are few intellectuals in this country who have mastered the secret to success in work: consistency and orderly structured time are the only way to reach greater results. But our environment considers such diligent and meticulous creators spiritual aliens: 'He is not one of us,' 'He must be Germanic in origin, or someone of mixed blood,' 'Is he a Jew, do you suppose?' 'Will you look at that fellow work! He certainly has a goal in mind, you'd better believe it.' When individuals appear who with the breadth of their work plans elevate themselves above the narrow framework of the national, every person who can and cannot, will race to throw stones at them. Tesla, Jagić, Bukovac and many others were forced to flee the country, so smothered they were by their closest associates, most of them colleagues. It is difficult to find a country in which hard work is met with such suspicion. As far as actual aid, or some form of support for someone's hard work as beneficial for the entire community, this would be out of the question. 'His business', or 'his personal ambitions' – that is how work is taxed even when it is clear as day that this work is in the interests of everyone."

Listen to this part, too, Rachel: "Criticising stands in direct disproportion to diligence. The Serb is the born critic. An indolent lack of productivity and an enviable capacity for spite typify the most expeditious and rigorous of the critics. Through offhand criticism the illusion is salvaged of one's own genius. Most of the shallow, diluted know-it-alls of ours move only in tiny, confused and disparate circles of 'being occupied' with things, anything but in the profound, durable, consequent line of doing and creating, and that is why those here who do create burn out and age, as a rule, incredibly quickly."

Stevan wrote this long ago, before, I think, his doctorate, and then I told him that he was too severe, but with time I learned he was right. How quickly, in only a dozen years, and how completely, did my Stevan fit into the picture and circumstances which he so scornfully and precisely described! Stevan does not work, but he seeks an alibi for his killed, squandered time. He, let's say, for years is translating *The History of the Peace Conference of Paris* by Harold Temperley. This they all know. When they meet him, they immediately ask, "Mr Medaković, how is the translation going?" and Stevan gloomily and solemnly answers, "There are problems, but it is moving ahead gradually, painstakingly," and they all nod their heads with understandings. It is no joke, from English to translate a book! And they and Stevan speak about the translation of this history as if it is, at the very least, deciphering hieroglyphics. Stevan ventures into theoretical discussion of the nature of translating the work, telling that this *Istorija Mirovne konferencije u Parizu* is really giving him trouble. So then, how can this not irritate me when I know that for years now that translation stands somewhere between the 34th and, it seems to me, now the 65th page! Stevan, in a word, is not translating; he is "occupied with translating", like that "cultural worker" Barjaktarević was being occupied with pharmacology. Stevan found a splendid alibi in Temperley. He is a professor at Cambridge, so Stevan was corresponding with him, which again they all know, so they already are saying that he speaks with the Professor in "ti" (which does not exist in the English language), that Stevan will be invited by the Professor, that he already did invite him to Cambridge. Then, Stevan has a theme also because Temperley wrote another book *History of Serbia*, and he was the English military attaché with the Serbian army in the First World War. And that with the special mission of delineating the boundaries with Albania, he was in 1920 in Monte Negro. For a story – an excellent alibi for work – solid as the city of Varadin! Then, last year – Temperley dies. Now he has the explanation why he will not go to Cambridge (though, I must be honest, Stevan always denied this, but that is worth nothing once people start saying it), and this is the motive for conversations as many as your soul could want. There was news in the newspapers about the death of Temperley and then they all called on the phone so Stevan could receive their condolences, for after all, good Lord, he was "working on the translation" of the man's books, now not just one, since on the occasion of the death Stevan broadened his translating plans as well to the *History of Serbia.* So much there was talk about this that I believed now that he had, finally, got to work, but then I go, not so long ago, and look at the manuscript – 65 pages. I laughed, but not in a funny way.

However, Stevan has become a master, he always has the alibi and for Temperley he has the alibi. Once it was Korošec and the business about the succession to the throne: for that two years he could not work. When that passed, he said with sorrow, there, I did not manage to finish the Temperley book, because already three years ago he began to translate – *King Henry the Fourth* by Shakespeare! Then I could not be restraining myself, so I said, "For goodness' sake, Stevan, why on earth would you want to translate Shakespeare!"

However, there is no worth in it. Stevan always thinks that I am not thinking what I say, but then he excavates to discover why I am saying this. Restrained, cautious as Stevan is, he one year later, indirectly, asks me a furious question. "Why do you cultivate an aversion towards my work on Shakespeare? To make a Serb of him, Elizabeta, means to give him to my people," he says, and I see that now he anticipates from me some special explanation, stubbornly refusing to receive that real, simple one: that I am not glad for his "working on Shakespeare", because I would like him to work on his own profession. Though, Stevan did publish something from his profession. He printed up a book *Ekonomski i socijalni osnovi Deklaracije prava** in the series "Politics and Society", a slender volume, 52 pages, with some attractive thoughts, unusual ideas, they praised even in the critics, but I personally however had the impression that it was, I don't know, weak arguments, the theses were posed approximately, and that, simply, in a hurry, between Žika the Barber and dinner at one – he slapped it together. There, and when I see this, it irritates me, that itch reaches me and bothers. We, simply, are two types. Different. And I am not, of course, always in the right. Let's say, yesterday a letter arrived to Stevan to invite him to a lecture at the University in Ljubljana. And here precisely they say: if the lecture lasts one full hour, the honorarium is I don't know precisely how many dinars, if it lasts fifteen minutes shorter, the

* *The Economic and Social Foundations for the Declaration of Rights.*

honorarium is such and such many less. And Stevan immediately is grumbling, he was simply angry, he said, "These Slovene 'i Tüpflers' make me furious!"

"What is an 'i Tüpfler'?" I asked.

"Well, that is the conscientious Slovene who all he cares about is whether he has dotted all the 'i's in his letter. In a word – a person who is petty."

"Isn't the Slovene pettiness better than the Serbian slovenliness?" I asked this time, although normally I hold back, because I know how much, though he does hide it, this always insults my Serb. But yesterday he got back at me nicely. I deserved it. Quietly, after a little pause: "Don't you think the medium in between the two the best?"

Serves me right.

I do know that it must be difficult for Stevan to understand my remarks where here they all consider him a valuable, dedicated man of diligence. Even Slobodan. That Stevan is not productive, first, is not noticed, because the others are not either, and secondly, it is not important, because they all somehow know that Stevan is talented. This is here, in this country, possible because creativity is not measured by the number and value of the products of one personality, but in some other, more magnificent way.

Rachel, I am not some ambitious Lady Macbeth. I am too glad with Stevan's status. Good Lord, could I in England dream that I would meet a cousin of the Duke of Kent's at the royal court? Stevan is a professor, he enjoys good standing, we inherited from his father more money than we need. So, this is not what bothers me. To the contrary. I myself out of full conviction encouraged Stevan to hold out and not to submit, not to Korošec, not to Slobodan's invitations to politics, because politics here is a dangerous quagmire. Therefore, I do not want of Stevan some successes and honours. He has that even more than is necessary, and far more than he is deserving. The only thing is that his rhythm it irritates me, there, that is precisely it – that life is squeezed in between Žika the Barber and evening ruminations on a subject which comes up in conversation; that he enjoys the reputation of an "excellently informed" intellectual. There, excellently informed intellectuals irritate me, then the itching attacks me and in Stevan I am discovering the tracks of one of them.

I know, I am talking too much about that and I am too rigorous. I would only have the right to ask of others perfection if I were perfect myself. But I am not. No-one is. And my Stevan is not either, but he certainly has marvellous characteristics which I, spoiled, take as if they belong naturally. Stevan is, Rachel, good and in many things an excellent man. He is serious and conscientious, he has genuine self-respect regardless of the cost that he protects it. Everyone knows that Stevan is someone on whom they can rely, which will never fail them, and I am really the *karakondžula* when I cannot forgive him one so Serbian sin: that he is without an active core of will and movement, that always he wants to do more than is his duty, but rarely finishes to the end what his duty is to finish, that he is never bothered at all when the letter "i" has no dot.

So that is why I thought that maybe it was good that Majkl was so inclined to me in those years when work habits are formed for the whole life, because I have nothing against that he takes from Stevan intelligence, moral sensitivity, courtesy towards others, especially but – not his perseverance and diligence. And this perseverance and diligence of Mihajlo's, these two so un-Serbian traits, are what have astounded the Serbs who therefore called them talent, a miracle, even genius. No. Foremost it is the doggedness and a very unchildlike systematicness which are the traits that make little Majkl seem exceptional. I do not know if a man is born that way or did he learn that from me who, infuriated by Stevan's relaxed manner, probably exaggerated in cultivating diligence in Majkl. In any case, whatever influenced this and however it happened that Majkl grew so hard-working, I, myself, not just the Serbs, even I with surprise watched how that child kept all his toys in a deliberately placed order, with what patience he built a house of cards, how stubbornly he worked to translate verses from *A Midsummer Night's Dream* and he would not ask, until I took pity, since I saw that for one whole hour he was staring at the same lines, and I jumped to help. Yes, in that he did not resemble the little Serb children around him, but, God help me, not the little English children of his age, either. I do not know how many English children at ten years would last to read through all a Shakespeare play. Why, you, yourself, Rachel, were astounded when you heard how he at six years was reading English, do you remember, and what a vocabulary he had, rich, too rich for his years.

And then my Majkl began to change. First barely to be seen, then all faster and clearer. The changing started, probably when Mihajlo started into school, but the first signs were to be seen, I think, in the second form. In the third and fourth form of elementary school they were completely out in the open, and only the absent-minded father Stevan could "discover" the change "all of a sudden", "overnight", after the second year of the Gymnasium, when Majkl returned from a school excursion to Bled Lake. But the first sign had appeared four years earlier, when Majkl, on one morning, told me that he hated that he is red-haired.

"Why," I asked, surprised.

"They all think I am English."

"And then?" I say, not knowing whether Majkl thinks that is the evil thing in general or only a handicap among little Serbs.

"And then?" I repeated, but again he did not answer, so I had to try from the other side. "And there are Serbs red-haired, are there not?" I asked for him to confirm, but Majkl said nothing and walked out of the bathroom where I had happened upon him, worried, staring at his red-haired image in the mirror.

Something like that, naturally, could escape the absent-minded father Stevan, but I took Majkl's hatred very seriously. First, I asked myself, was Majkl that morning in the bathroom, while with hatred he stared at his lovely, shiny, thick hair, was he aware that I, too, am red-headed? If he is, did he want intentionally to insult me? If not, how could he forget something like that? I had to check that because immediately I understood that this is the way to come to the newest thinking of growing Majkl, so tomorrow I asked, casually, breezily, half as a joke, "Majkl, do you want me to dye my hair?"

Majkl even now does not know how, but especially then, so small and serious, he wasn't able to pretend, so I was certain that he was sincere, when he told me, astonished, "Why you?"

"Well, and my hair is red. English."

He was caught. He had a little to think, and only then to say, persuaded that he had found the real explanation, "But you are an Englishwoman."

It still, naturally, wasn't clear to me whether he dislikes red-hairedness per se, and therefore we the English, since that is our colour. Or is it with the English, and therefore with the red hair, that everything is in order, but it is not good when one Serb has English hair? Naturally, the answer interested me a great deal, but I asked nothing further, for I understood that even Majkl had not cleared all in his own little head, which new relations must have confused, and he had got mired in them as soon as stepping out of our family quarantine into the world. However, little by little I learned the things. Let's say, I noticed before Majkl that he who never made the difference between the two languages, suddenly was happier to talk *srbski*. Good, I am thinking, this is normal, every day in school, this is a new habit, and yet, I saw that there was something else, some conscious giving of advantage. When he forgets, he speaks English normally, but I simply saw how as soon as he understands he is speaking English immediately he changes over to *srbski*. Then it was naturally already clear to me that children tease him for his red hair, and the mother of his is an Englishwoman, who has behaviour which is different. Children cruelly punish every difference, they do not tolerate anyone who is remarkable. Already it was completely clear to me what is in the thing when Majkl, who adored to play with the children of Sir Nevile cricket on the cricket ground in the ambassador's garden, first began to evade, then to decisively refuse to go there when they invited him to one match.

"Why?" I asked Majkl, but he did not want to confess.

"I have played enough cricket," he would say, or, "I have other obligations."

Then I was present, unobserved, at one little drama which enough explained what is happening in Majkl's confused little head. Majkl after the first form of the gymnasium, when the summer holidays began, often went to the swimming beach for gymnasium pupils. Although I was a little fearful, for Majkl was yet still small, he was not eleven, I allowed it precisely because I knew that he needed to socialise among his peers, that he must not mature under a glass bell and with us adults. That, and aside from that it was very well organised on the part of the Second Boys' Gymnasium and their gymnastics instructor, a Czech, conscientious and capable, whom they all called, I do not know why, brother-Vanjek, and then the gymnasium factotum, Uncle Mita, but also other teachers, pupils' parents and boys from higher forms. First only a pupil could enter here who had a regular ticket "Zajednica doma i Škole". He gives the ticket at the gate, and picks it up when he goes home, so that there is evidence. There were sport fields for volley ball, for jumping long-distance and high, boats, trampolines, and always someone who keeps track, especially about those small pupils. I never would stay to watch Majkl, though some fathers and mothers did, because I knew that this he did not like. I would, therefore, bring Majkl in the morning, and saw that the on-duty from the higher forms took him over, and then I came for him after noon. I would give Majkl also two dinars. For one he would buy bread and *kajmak*, which all got at noon the same, but the poor pupils free, and for the other, if he wanted to drink *boza*, or *klaker*, or to eat melon. Majkl loved the Pupils' Beach more than he liked the seacoast, Crikvenica, to where we went every year, precisely because here he was independent, grown-up. And that is why, though I feared, yet I left him by himself.

And that day too, I did not come earlier intentionally, but I had a *fijaker* in the city, so I said to take me down to the Danube. Here was one building on posts, and in the middle were cabins for parents, the teachers. I sat here on wooden steps and watched the happy, barebacked lads, some of them frolicking in the shallow area marked off with thick logs tied by wire, and others in the deeper area for swimmers, also marked by logs. In the open river it was not allowed to go, but some did, when they would slip under the eye of the teacher or the on-duty guard. We constantly were telling Majkl, though he swam well, precisely that, not to go outside the marked area. And he did not. He would tell me, if he did.

From my lookout place quickly I saw Majkl. He was swimming in the deep area with other children and his on-duty, a Dragan from the eighth form. Then Dragan took them to sunbathe on the sand which was close enough to the place where I was sitting. Should I wave to Majkl? But I did not. I let him be. Not because I would spy on him, but that I would not bother. The on-duty was first with them, and then he left.

"Wait here for me," he said.

The boys lay in the sun, still out of breath from swimming and jumping into the water. Majkl was the littlest. I think that they all were from the second or third form, and only he from the first. There were eight of them. Five of them were shaved to the head, two had dark hair. With his red, my Majkl gleamed in the sun among them like a lampion. It is no wonder that they called him Riđi, I thought. My poor little English lad. Although all of them were wearing only bathing trunks, Majkl among them was distinct apart. He had blue swimming trunks with red and white trim around the leggings and waist. There was still only one other boy who had a real bathing suit. All the others were in ordinary leggings of grey cloth, down to the knee, and tied by the draw-string. Then, when he came over to sunbathe, Majkl from the pupils' cabin brought his terrycloth robe, matching to his bathing trunks (I bought him that set in Fiume), and with it he covered his back, which was red. Pale white among the lot of them all with the dark com-plexions, cultivated among the neglected, red-haired and courteous among the coarse – I understood suddenly looking at him among his fellows – he must feel the foreigner. I was sorry.

One of the boys, the tallest, boasted that yesterday he with his older brother swam across the Danube to the other shore and back.

"Riđi, could you?" he asked Mihajlo.

"I don't know."

"Well, you are a better swimmer than me," says Dragan.

"Maybe," said Majkl, "I haven't tried."

"When you get tired, you lie on your back, and then again," explains the fellow who carried off the feat.

"If I had to, probably I could," thought Majkl cautiously, staring critically at the other shore, guessing the distance.

"I could, too," boasted one of them, his head shaved to bald.

But the tall one wouldn't let him boast. Witheringly he silenced him. "Ihhh, you could! Why you can't go from one of the logs to the other, if Dragan doesn't help you."

They all exploded into laughing, but Majkl.

"You are lying. No-one helps me any more. I learned how to rest on my back."

"I could, and Riđi, and, maybe, Debeli. He and a barrel will never sink."

Again Majkl did not laugh, but all the others did.

Then I noticed that something was happening on the beach. They were shouting, "There it is!" and "It is coming" and "Pull it towards the shore." They were calling one another by name and racing frantically into the water, but not in the marked-off area. Instead they were all swimming out into the open. Uncle Mita ran by me.

"What happened?" I asked, and Uncle Mita, without stopping, over his shoulder said to me that a barge with watermelons capsized.

"Who is going to stop these scoundrels from fishing melons in the river!"

And really, then I myself saw it, like a caravan, a row of green and yellow fruits floating in the river, and the boys with all strength were swimming towards the middle of the river to reach the melons. That is, those boys who managed to slip by. Others were cut off by brother-Vanjek and Uncle Mita and they didn't let them into the water.

"Get back," shouted Uncle Mita.

"Onto the beach, you rascals, you are not allowed in the water," helped him brother-Vanjek, but as soon as the two of them sat in one boat and two grown boys in another boat and started towards the middle of the river, surely to be close if something, God forbid, happens to someone, again the chased boys threw themselves into the river and swam to the melons.

I was so amused by the lively scene and euphoria at the Pupils' Beach that I only turned again my attention to Majkl's group when some of the negotiations there were taking a dramatic form. The tall one, who had swum over to the other shore, and the fat one, who would never sink, were wanting to go after melons, but Majkl he did not.

"You know it is forbidden. Brother-Vanjek will catch us," he said.

"Come on, why us? Look how many kids are in the water!"

"I don't dare," Majkl balked.

"That's more like it. Scared. The English pee-in-his-pants is chicken."

I saw this hit him. My stupid son. In the centre of foreign spite. Furiously he threw his robe down on the ground, jumped to his feet like a red rooster. "You pee in your pants," he said to the tall boy and first he started to run to the river, but after two steps he stopped and, still furious, tears in his voice, he tossed to the tall one, "You are lying that you swam across the Danube," and then he continued to run.

And I? Naturally, my first instinct was to shout, "Majkl, come back!" and I almost did that, already I jumped from the step and opened my mouth. But, I did not. Thanks to God. For, that I did, I know Majkl would obey me, but how would he look in the eyes of that boaster? How would he prove he is no English pee-in-his-pants? I understood in time, I would humiliate him terribly, for, naturally, there is no greater insult than to be English. Among the little Serbs. I had to leave him to prove his Serbian heroism. And reason in me prevailed. I collected for and against: Majkl swims well, the melon is not so far from the shore, two boats are near to help . . . I clenched teeth and slowly went along the shore, at the speed that the river carried the boys. It was not difficult to follow them: my red lampion was distinct and from the green and from the yellow melon, and from the dark-haired little heads of the other boys. He swam much better and faster than the tall one and the fat one, and first he reached the watermelons, grabbed one, and pushing it in front of him he started to come back. He went quickly, without tiredness, I saw that it was not a danger. He quickly came to shore, pulled out the watermelon and turned to see what was with the friends.

What is with them, I had already earlier seen. Debeli swam quite far, but the river carried him much down, so the melon did not reach him. He then came back, but maybe one hundred metres below the spot where Majkl came out. And as far as the tall one, Majkl was surely right: someone who swims as he could not swim across the Danube. He was flailing, kicking his feet, drinking water, and then he quickly began to come back, for he saw that it was not possible. Now both Debeli and

Visoki were walking along the shore towards Majkl who was waiting for them, with his foot on the watermelon. Surely, he was keeping it from rolling, but to me it looked like that hunter whose picture is taken with the killed tiger under the victorious boot. Debeli only says, "You caught it."

"I guess so," modestly says Majkl.

Visoki, from still far away, started to shout, "Easy for you when it floated right up to where you were!"

Majkl already was controlling himself completely. Quietly he says, giving Visoki for the right, "Yes, it wasn't hard."

Debeli took the watermelon in his hands. "This one, one brother to another, is seven kilos!"

They walked over to the place where they had been sunbathing, and along the way the other boys from their group joined them.

"Who caught it?" they asked, or, "Who swam out?"

"Mihajlo," answered Debeli, hunched over with the weight, with the watermelon in his arms.

"And the two of you?"

"We nothing."

"I knew it," that one shaved bald used the opportunity to return the insult to Visoki, "this Daddy-Long-Legs would have drowned between the logs if Dragan hadn't helped him."

"Mihajlo, let us have a little," others asked.

"Take it all. I don't like watermelon," he lied, I don't know why, and I clearly saw that the triumph to Majkl did not bring unsullied happiness, because he did beat someone, instead of the formless majority. He would have been unhappy if he lost, but he was not so glad at the measly reward: they called him by name, he was Mihajlo, and not Riđi as a little earlier.

When they reached their place, then Majkl saw that his blue terrycloth robe is not there in the sand where he furiously threw it.

"Uh! Such a nice robe," Visoki was genuinely sorry.

"Grew feet," apathetically says Debeli.

"Maybe it will turn up somewhere. The beach is small."

"Their barbarian mothers."

"If we catch them, we will beat them like a cat, no matter who."

But Majkl after he heard them all and thought about all, brought the judgement, "I think we won't find it."

You see, my dear deceased Rachel, maybe this story, objectively, is not so important, but it suddenly illuminated to me what troubled my Majkl has, how and why it is not easy to him to get accustomed. For, my conscientious Majkl had to not only change his habits, but all his convictions and the character that stands behind the convictions to be the same, or similar, not to stand out. All at once it sort of burst before my eyes. Majkl is restrained and not boasting, and these little Serbs whom I watch on the sand, they are, it occurs to me, like the Irish, inclined to rhetoric, fantasy, in a moment the border between reality on the one side and the epic on the other disappears. That, let's say, does not go in any way with Majkl's empirical persistence, with his precise acquaintance with his possibilities. Then, those were mostly children of poor parents, the rich did not mix often, and Majkl did not know of poverty until he made the acquaintance of the children at school – one more difference which he had to bring into harmony in his head. And then, most of all – Majkl's dedication to work, his enjoyment in work that is finished, if it is good, his faith that with persistence and with a systematic approach results are achieved – there is nothing, absolutely not one single common link with a phenomenon which I now already for a long time am studying among his friends, little Serbs, and I call it the mania of genius.

That is, Rachel, something very strange, and I have conversed about that subject with Stevan. He understands it better, and I am still confused, I do not understand though I have the facts. Most of all I have seen this on two new friends of Mihajlo's whom he chose himself and which for already two years and more come most often to our house. One is Duško, the other Milašin. They are bad pupils, that Duško and that Milašin, but whatever I have heard from them shows that they are not ashamed of this, but something is very suspicious in Majkl being so excellent. They scorn classes very much, to them all the subjects are something stupid and petty, and all the teachers, though the Second Boys' is considered the best, are either "*degen*" or "idiot". Not one has something in the head, because if they have, they would not be occupied with the stuff and nonsense they were occupied with and which tormented them.

Fine, I say to Stevan, this I would understand that they studied everything and now they see that what the teachers know is small, but *jok*, they are very bad pupils and barely are squeaking through at the end of the second form, and at the end of the third Duško had to repeat History, and he is the one flirting precisely with History, constantly he was carrying some rare, not school, but thick books about history, and he scorned what he learned in the school, and still, there he could not pass. I simply do not understand. Him or Milašin. For Milašin I heard that he is a Communist, but I do not believe because he is still little, only one year older than Mihajlo, therefore, only now will he be fifteen, but the truth is that he writes rough articles in some pupils' paper, that he attacks the teachers, that his brother, older, is in Mitrovica prison because of subversive activity. For me they are not very attractive, but not because Milašin is maybe a Communist, nor because, as Mihajlo once unjustly told me, because they are poor, that Dušan's mother is a cook at the Romanian embassy, next door to us, on Miloš Velika Street. To me they are unattractive because they are so lazy, and so arrogant, and especially because Mihajlo before them holds himself back, not they before Mihajlo.

I am not able to understand anything except that here there is nothing I can do. Majkl, I know, would not listen to me in general, because for a long time he is already completely alien. I can only peripherally get involved, and openly I have to suffer, for Majkl already a long time does not allow that I enter into his life, especially before these two, before whom he is a little ashamed, I do not know precisely why, uncomfortable. Because I am an Englishwoman; or because I am the mother? I cannot say that Majkl hated me, or despised me, or – it is difficult to explain; he makes the effort to keep us distanced, and not like before, close. After the excursion to Bled he announced resolutely that he would no more everyday speak English (then even Stevan noticed the "sudden" change). This was not, I think, aimed against me, integrally, rather against our former closeness. Stevan says, the child has been weaned from the nursing. Good, this I understand. The adolescent growing to maturity.

But is it only this? Should I be connecting the change in behaviour in Majkl towards me to an unpleasant question with which two years ago he so shocked and overwhelmed me? Or should I not? It is precisely that all the signs of change existed before that, too, but it would be possible that the new information he learned contributed to his accelerated changing. How he learned – I did not know then, either, and I still do not know now. For me it is a mystery. Majkl was writing some assignment at the desk, or something and I was sitting behind his back, in the armchair and reading a book, I even remember what, *Put Alije Djerzeleza* by Ambassador Andrić. Majkl, without interrupting his writing, bent over his notebook, in an inquisitive voice but not agitated, asked me, in several parts, with pauses while he continued to write, "Mother . . . is it true . . . that you had been married . . . to a gentleman . . . called . . . Richard Harris . . . before you met my father?"

It was fortunate that Majkl's question lasted so long, and especially that his back was turned and that he could not see my face. I do not know how it looked, I cannot even imagine. I, of course, was thinking about that, but somehow I did not dare consult with Stevan, whether we should say something to Majkl about my first marriage. Never did Stevan and I speak about that, and in all truth and I do not know to whom, if to anyone, Stevan had told that I already was married. According to all I had experienced I could not conclude that people in Belgrade were acquainted with this. Even the closest friends. Never did anyone ask me a word. Good, so this is politeness, but yet, I thought, that if it was known, it would spread, somehow it would reach my ears. I assumed that Father Milutin knew it, but sure I am that Nanka did not know, for she would not have lasted, she would have thrown that in my face. I think, however, that they had to know the godfathers, old Godfather Nedeljko and Slobodan. But they did not say one word. Deaf silence about that, so I somehow felt that this marriage of mine had somewhere sunk, disappeared. Good God, that was so far away, lost in the fog of time, I, completely sincerely, had already forgotten that it happened, that it existed. That was someone else's past life, and another past me, a forgotten me, so I simply thought that I wouldn't even be lying if to Majkl's "Mother, is it true?" I answered, "No, how could it be true?" Or even, "No, it didn't happen."

However, I could not lie to him. I told him after a pause, *srbski*, I don't know why, "Yes, it is true."

Mihajlo continued to write the homework. He did not turn. He asked nothing more. Only he said more as if for himself, again in English, "How strange!"

And that was all. All that I know about that.

You see, at that moment I was very happy that he did not continue curiously to explore how, why, when, because I simply could not answer, so suddenly, so unprepared for the questions, but, the next few days, I immediately knew that in truth this was not good, that now kept-in questions cooked in his head and God knows into what sort of thoughts they turned. After three days, which I spent on the coals, I was resolved to say to Stevan, what Mihajlo asked me, and Stevan was marvellous. Immediately he understood all, and without waiting for me to ask him, he promised he would converse with Majkl. I knew then that he did this more for my protection than to ease Mihajlo's understanding, but, I admit, then I was only grateful to him, for he was doing something which I could in no way handle, and it had to be done. Stevan was so discreet, so considerate that he did not tell me anything about the conversation which he led when I was not at home. But I could not contain myself. I asked him in the evening when Mihajlo had gone to sleep, "Did you converse?"

"Yes, yesterday."

He did not continue so I had to. "How was it?"

"Perfect. Easier than you can imagine. He understands everything."

A stone did fall from my heart then, but suddenly I realised how bizarre it is what now Stevan and I are doing: we for the first time after the Bristol conversation, the only one on that theme, mentioned my marriage, I thought, slightly surprised, looking at my considerate Stevan in the silence, until a second truth occurred to my mind, even more bizarre: now I and Stevan have a shared secret; the first secret against Mihajlo. In this particular instance two of us make up one party, and Michael happens to be the other.

"How strange!" said Majkl, and I thought the same.

And since after these meagre words we never went further, it is difficult, Rachel, to judge whether, and if so, how, the discovery about my first marriage diminished the closeness between me and Majkl, and maybe, if he felt it, the closening to Stevan through distancing from Majkl in our little plot against him.

However, if, therefore, I understand that our closeness was eroded from both sides, and with this event, and with Majkl's growing up, I cannot seem to understand why Majkl, as he grew more distant from me, had to get closer to those boys. Why he chose to adapt, and did not choose to stand out. How is it possible that he cared to resemble them and not be different, when already he so is, in all thinking and feeling, directly opposite with the whole behaviour. "Different I am, all right, but in everything better than you. And with the best I will associate, with them I will spend my life." But no! Majkl chooses not the two best, but two who are precisely the most different from all that he is, and precisely with them he wants to prove that he is not from another world, landed from another planet. Duško and Milašin, my God, what a scene of unsolidity! What a difference from Majkl! And how much Majkl stands out despite the fact that he works not to stand out from them!

I do not know whether it was more sad or funny to watch how Majkl had to be going on the pointless walks, or to a futbol match, going – Stevan has a good word – *džabalebarenje*, loafing, when they come at every time of day and interrupt Majkl in reading or studying. Majkl gets up and goes, and I know that it does not sit well with him, but yet – he goes. Comes Duško and says, "Cramming, again?" and Majkl simply gets scared, makes excuses: "I was just looking," or even he lies, says, "I didn't touch my books." I understand that Majkl may get an A in a subject and go unpunished by the friends only if he can prove he didn't study for it. For to study, to "cram", why that is a disgrace for the genius Duško who, so young, is already "occupied" with history, or for Milašin, who never condescends to any job less than changing the entire world.

Another day I was, not angry, not disappointed, but precisely saddened when I passed next to the Second Boys' Gymnasium. I see on the steps across the way, pupils, ten of them, sitting on their school bags which they put under them on the iron railing and spitting around them. Everything for 5 metres around them was covered with saliva. I look better, and there is my Majkl, shining red between Duško and Milašin. I am sorry because I know Mihajlo does not like that, this wasting of time, this *džabalebarenje* is gruesome for him, he is not being nice to his very self, he must make an effort to be the "genius", not the "crammer". I know that because I know Majkl, for he cannot trick me, and he gave himself away when at the half-year exams he brought home in his book of grades two threes! He who had always had only fives. Good, I knew that he only did that to please, to show he is no crammer, but to me it did not pass unnoticed from which subjects my unhappy son chose to earn threes: in Mathematics and French. Why precisely these when in them he is precisely so superior? In the third form of primary school his teachers gave him problems from the matriculation examination for the eighth form, and he was able to do them before the eyes of his teachers, so how now in the third form of Gymnasium only one of three problems he gets correct in the written part? With French, this is funny, since he studied three times a week with a private professor for five years, and was excellent, better in conversation and pronunciation both than me and than Stevan, he read, let's say, Lotti's *Pecheur d'Islande*, which is not simple reading – and then in the third form he can earn only a three! That is when I stopped and asked myself: why Majkl did not choose some other subjects in which he was not so undoubtedly the best, but precisely these two. I knew immediately: Majkl wanted to be clever. With his two threes he proved to his friends that he was no "crammer", but since this grade in the depth of his reliable soul irked him, as much as did the deceit made with his own self, he chose precisely those subjects in which he knew he could not be for a three. Poor Majkl. This confirms for me what I since long ago have known (or only think I know?): that he does not have respect for these geniuses, for their wasting of time, their superficial knowledge and ignorance, for spitting in a circle and the dreariness of *džabalebarenje* around Sarajevska and Poenkareova Streets (or is it just that I am hoping?); he thinks what he thinks and loves what he always loved, but he knows that he must deceive the majority; by mimicry, if nothing else works, to join, disappear into the yellow slime of the local landscape; to change the skin in order to save the soul. Or will he lose that, too? And become the same? I see that he swims in the tempest, that he is gasping, barely keeping his chin above water, and it is terrible to me that I cannot help him, for former little Majkl no longer wants my help. Earlier I could, I was enough. Now I cannot. For, what does a big man need a mother for? Married and divorced! And why an Englishwoman for a Serb? I am, here, thrown out, gruffly pushed away with a tender hand. I can do nothing more for Mihajlo without Stevan. Stevan who is not English. Stevan who is a man. The father.

And I, my dear deceased Rachel, I have known for a long time that it is no good. I know that it is no good that I am hurt. That I must watch the falling helpless. I am afraid, Rachel, that from Stevan help will not come. Majkl has whiskers, yellow like a chick, but whiskers which Stevan does not see because he is not seeing his son grown just as he did not see him small. He says to me, "I did not notice."

The absent-minded father and the whiskered Mihajlo. Both of them speak *srbski*, and they do not understand each other. There is nothing left for me, Rachel, but to finally learn the damned language. Until now I thought it is enough as much as I know. I say "Lijublijana" like a Slovene, I make no distinction between saying "č" and "ć", I pronounce my vowels like an Englishwoman, but good God, I never meant to hide that I was not a Serb, rather I only wanted to be understandable. Now I have resolved that this is not enough. I have decided to learn to speak with no accent, with no English sounds. I will take lessons in diction. I will speak like a Serbian woman. I will be a Serbian woman, to be able to speak equally with Majkl. You will see!

No, you won't.

But thank you, Rachel. I feel better now. You are the only one who always listens to me. My patient "confidante".

SIX

Here I stand, Mihajlo, my lad, before you, as if this is Judgement Day! I cannot say whether I am guilty or not, but I do know that I am a vulnerable mortal returning, after twenty years, to a submerged memory resembling the scene of a crime. Lord, if you do exist, give me the strength to pass through purgatory now, even if I was not able to do it then! Help me not to betray the truth, not to ease, through carelessness, these harsh memories in this, my long-overdue reckoning.

Our encounter, Mihajlo's and mine, our embrace or wrestling grip, whichever it was, began somewhere in the spring of 1942 after two full years of grey and sombre incarceration in wounded and impoverished Belgrade. Those two years, with all the tribulations of the Occupation – Elizabeta's obligations to report once a month to the Gestapo, suspicious of her as a Serbian woman of English background; my fear that I might once again end up in Banjica, where I had spent two months imprisoned when I refused, in August 1941, to sign Jonić's "Appeal to the Serbian People"; the mouldy cornbread; the executions by hanging on Terazije; the horrible news of our traumatised Serbian cousins who fled to Belgrade in the face of Ustasha massacres in Lipik, Pakrac, Gradiška, Bučje; German Oberleutnant Böme quartered in a room requisitioned in our flat; the fierce, bloodthirsty winter that we barely survived. Yet we three Medakovićes were never closer, more together, more bonded, than we were then. How strange humans are, and human happiness! There are days when I recall our poverty under the Occupation with a melancholy of the sort usually prompted by memories of wonderful moments lost for ever! I, with none of my university and other obligations, Elizabeta without her translations and

English tutoring (who would want to learn the English language in that German gloom?), our Mihajlo, home all day because of his erratic school schedule, all of us together after the curfew, assembled under the light bulb at the table in the kitchen, the only heated room of our flat, we were all we had. We filled the whole world, alone in our dark dugout, like moles we dived into our family – all that was left. Yes, precisely an earthen dugout – the kitchen, where we spent our lives, was cramped and messy, often close for we rarely aired it. That is how I see it today, surrounded by devastated Belgrade, by green uniforms, by cold people standing in queues before empty shops, by fear. And yet, if I am not mistaken, through it flowed a breath of spring even during the worst freezes, which cracked open the stones on our side terrace. Clear skies burst through the greyness of our misery; terror was held at bay by hope, for during these very days, in our little dugout, from minute to minute, a being was evolving, like an enchanted prince rising from the dreams of childhood a little eagle was spreading its wings: our small, inquisitive and diligent red-haired boy was growing to maturity, becoming whole. In a peacetime milieu, this coming of age would not have been something we would have seen so clearly; we never would have known the details we followed, partly amazed, partly tender, in our occupied but radiant kitchen. Everything would have been different in peaceful, ordinary times. Mihajlo would have talked with a friend, rather than with me and his mother, about his discovery of Freud, to someone else he would have brought the freshness of his innocent enthusiasm for Darwin and Fraser, for Tolstoy's *Resurrection* and Njegoš's *Gorski vijenac*, for Julian Sorel and Nietzsche, for books and personalities imaginary and real, ideas deep and shallow, which he swallowed and digested in his young and excitable mind as if he were the first to read them, as if they had been written just for him and only here, at our kitchen table, discovered. I would not be telling the whole truth, however, if I were to present our interest in Mihajlo's experiences as merely instructional. Bending the whole day over our darling, we did our best to keep our attention on the level of adults and equals rather than teachers or parents, but one easily forgot to whom one was talking with Mihajlo. At the age of 15, he was certainly prone to naïve reasoning and to hurling out conclusions which were too bold and poorly founded, yet at the same time he might startle one with the maturity of his thinking or the unusual quality of his observations, and it is the absolute truth that he filled our empty Occupation days with sorely needed intellectual conversation just as successfully as anyone could have from the limited circle of friends with whom we still, though seldom, socialised. I do not know, for instance, whether any one of my intellectual peers would have dared to make a comparison between the plebeian, ambitious and competent Julian Sorel and Nietzsche's Dionysian man, but should one of them have embarked on this doubtful enterprise, he would certainly not have deduced more observations, conclusions and hypotheses than agile Mihajlo. Even then, during those two years of friendship with my son, he knew how to be stubborn. Once he had made a claim, inaccessible to reason, he would stick with it to the end. But I found it easy, or at least possible, to master the irritation that would tickle me at such moments without allowing Mihajlo's, greater than mine, to escalate to a nasty duel. We did argue, but we never quarrelled. As soon as I would see Mihajlo digging his heels in, as soon as he began to tousle his hair with his nervous hands, his white ears flaming red, I would take a half-step back, even if his reasoning was weak and his proof childish, or even a whole step back if a half would not do it. I had to permit him to beat me, I knew that, but it would have been no good had I handed him victory on a plate. I contested, for instance, Elizabeta's decision to submit to Mihajlo's whim that we never speak English. He could speak as he chose, that was his decision, but he could not force us into sympathetic blockheadedness. Elizabeta, of course, insisted that she ceased using English because she had resolved to learn Serbian properly, but the coincidence between her consistent usage and Mihajlo's peculiar resistance explains its true reasons. I, however, was not able to win over two strong-minded natures, two hard Anglo-Saxon pates. Sometimes I would start a conversation in English, but I would quickly desist, it being ridiculous that only I, with the weakest knowledge in that language, was trying to speak it.

Language, naturally, was merely Mihajlo's quirk, like our

disagreements, for instance, about Bergson's *Creative Evolutions*, which he read intelligently enough, but, I think, to spite me, disparaged with polemical fervour and few sound arguments; or about Dostoevsky, whom I had never cared for because of his anti-individualism and his Orthodox imperialism, but whom Mihajlo admired to the heavens, despite the fact that all he'd read was *The Possessed*. If there was anything which would provoke me, it was never Mihajlo's convictions, since he had not genuinely formed them yet, but the obstinacy with which he defended his every notion; it was his character, in other words, rather than his attitude, a parental fear that he would smash his hard head into the even harder wall of life and injure himself unnecessarily. In truth, I paid little attention to my fear in those two lovely years in our kitchen. I noticed rather than condemned it; it bothered me more than it frightened me, and, chances are, that is how things would have remained had his obstinacy not, some time in the spring of 1943, led him down a mine-strewn path.

Am I at fault here? Could I have influenced him with wiser behaviour, better reasoning, the right books, other examples? Did I take his lurching in the deadly direction too lightly too long, merely as his need to have his sport with me? How would you, Mihajlo, answer these questions? What would Elizabeta tell me, if I dared to ask her? Would Elizabeta tell me the truth?

The truth is that I did not take the first signs of Mihajlo's leftist politics seriously. I watched them with a superior and gentle smile of understanding; they were a predictable phenomenon, chicken pox which one simply got over as soon as possible. *Cupidi rerum novarum*. Our impoverished soil is Godgiven for the cultivation of leftist and revolutionary ideas. The peasants, lacking in genuine perseverance and diligence, were disinclined towards all authority and readily believed they could extricate themselves from poverty with an overnight change of government rather than with painstaking and persistent labour. At that time, however, I firmly believed that Communism could never grow deep roots among our people. What sort of Communism could take hold in our regions of archaic-patriarchal life where people still counted their origins back fifteen "generations" and where they were still divided into the haves and the have-nots? What sort of Communism when even in the larger cities and small towns there were only a handful of workers and the occasional pitiful excuse for a fledgling industry! Dogmatised socialism, I believed, was a fabrication, a foreign import, and it was enjoying a brief popularity among the younger generation and children from better families in the cities. And so it was with Mihajlo. At first, I was not the slightest bit concerned about his newest snobbish fancy.

In the spring of 1943, our kitchen citadel crumbled. Mihajlo went his own way. Elizabeta and I remained in the fortress. He spent less and less time with us, more and more with his Dedinje crowd. At first, he would tell us in the evening what had happened to him during the day and would initiate conversations about what he was reading or thinking. And so we learned, little by little, that he was spending his time on Župana Vlastimira Street, at the home of a businessman called Majstorović, with his daughter Jelena and two of her neighbours, the brothers Predrag and Nenad, sons of the late Todor Petković, a former shareholder in the Bor mines. We knew that he met them at Kolarac University, where Nenad and Jelena attended Josić's evening art classes and all of them went to lectures and concerts. His earlier interest in music became Mihajlo's addiction. He would stop by the house just before curfew, ecstatic about Beethoven's "Eroica", about the singing of Malibaški the baritone, or about lectures – I remember with particular clarity – by Brane Petronijević on Hegel's dialectic. I knew only the most general things about Hegel, so I studied with interest even the less intelligible sections of Mihajlo's notes at Petronijević's lectures, aided by my copy of the English translation of *Phenomenology of the Mind*, in the appendix of which there was a key to the philosopher's idio-syncratic, opaque terminology. I saw no special significance in the study of Hegel, and I remember this joint effort of ours mostly because Mihajlo liked precisely those aspects of Hegel's thought which sparked a bitter resistance in me: his dogmatism, the lack of explanations, the vision of an absolute truth which this German announced with a chilly self-confidence, like a judgement. Mihajlo dubbed this feature of Hegel's thought his "spiritual rigour" and delighted precisely (or was it, again, merely to spite me?) in the sententious reduction of his style. Mere consciousness, self-consciousness, reason, spirit and religion, absolute knowledge – pure and obedient, a royal highway, straight as an arrow!

I wonder, once again I wonder – could I then have assumed that Hegel would take my Mihajlo and his Dedinje crowd straight to Marx and the Communists? And if I had, what should I have done? Can a man, warned by benevolent and far-seeing gods, avoid the misfortune bearing down on him like a hail-bearing cloud from the unintelligible future? Can a well-timed, true word alter the course of fate?

Only when I began to come across mimeographed versions (he hid them from us) of *Istorija SKPb, Antidühring, Komunistički manifest* and excerpts from *Das Kapital* did I begin to take this turn of events seriously, but not because I was fearful that it might be decisive for Mihajlo's spiritual development. I continued to be convinced that this revolutionary snobbism would have the staying power of the "toque à la Lindbergh" or the "bubikopf" hairstyle. From the same direction and along the same path as Impressionism or Surrealism, Cubism or Expressionism, now Communism arrived in our Illyrian livestock-raising homeland. All of this, I said to myself, was like Kraljević Marko, who joined the Turks to spite his fellow noblemen. Mihajlo embraced everything which served his need to spite me, and now he had donned the cap of Marxism although it certainly did not suit his spiritual physiognomy.

I had known, among my students before the war, quite a number of Communists, Montagnards. They were all as like as two eggs. Socially backward, this type of student wanted to show himself precisely as he was not: as a social, a super-social man. This kind of fellow, who did not know how to walk by another man without stomping on his foot, suddenly found that nothing was social enough for his tastes. None of these types represented organic products of our social and cultural conditions. The thing that particularly irked me about these leftists was the preponderance of negativity and demagogical declarations which lacked any understanding of the Serbian sense of social justice. Faith in violent schemes imported from somewhere else does not improve, cannot advance (quite the contrary, it prevents) a real purification of egotism and the development of a genuine social sensibility. And there was so much which sorely needed to be done to reinforce precisely this sensibility among us Serbs! The leftists, however, like members of some religious sect, operated with only a few dogmatic formulae, which they applied to every possible situation with a mindless blindness. In perfect sectarian style, they excommunicated disbelievers, for only faith would bring salvation. On the basis of personal experience, I was convinced that when a half-educated person from Serbia adopted the trappings of an orthodox socialist, he would be blinder than followers are among the more progressive nations. Ancient Dinaric sensitivity and a penchant for revenge within the trivial order tend to surface in the Balkan brand of the orthodox Left; these traits cannot be hidden beneath the grotesque veneer of Marxism.

In a word, I was entirely calm, for what sort of spiritual bond could there be, other than one faddish and transitory, between these three children of Dedinje families, along with my Mihajlo, and those tribal-mountain patriarchal oafs? If it had been peacetime, I most certainly would have done nothing, even after finding the Marxist and Bolshevik brochures in our home, convinced that the fad would pass if we paid as little attention to it as possible. But this was 1943 in Occupied Belgrade, and such Dedinje games cost people's lives. Panicked and angry, I knew that if Mihajlo were caught with the *Abbreviated Version of Bolshevik Communist Party History* under his arm, Elizabeta and I could only wait, horribly helpless, until he was shot. The danger that this might happen was sickeningly real; there were searches every day on the streets of Belgrade. But I was even more frightened that, inspired by his own crazy youthful disregard, Mihajlo might get involved in some banned organisation, might become part of the underground movement, and die madly, wastefully. I was tormented by a scene I had witnessed in late 1942, frozen in a queue in front of a bakery where cornbread was supposed to be delivered. Two young blond-haired men, wearing only jackets despite the freezing temperature, with wool scarves round their necks and covering their hands, clean-shaven and resembling each other as if they were brothers, ran out of a doorway across the way from the bakery and, slipping on the icy ground, ran frantically along Takovska Street, by the Botanical Gardens, towards Dalmatinska Street. A few seconds later, an armoured car shot out of the barracks at the corner of Dalmatinska and Takovska by which there stood a German guard post and hurtled towards the boys. They stopped and stood there, baffled, but before they were able to run back, machine-gun fire spat out. First one, then the other were simply flung into the air. The blond-haired brothers flew upwards as if struck by mighty blows, and then, their skulls bloody, they dropped into the snowy shoulder by the pavement. It was all over in no more than ten seconds. Perhaps not even that. A terrible silence settled on the two blond corpses. The queue in front of the bakery vanished. I watched for a moment more, as I walked away, how the soldiers stepped out of the car and climbed up the snow-covered shoulder towards the dead boys. I went off down the street.

Was Mihajlo to end like this? And why, in God's name! I knew, however, that pleas for caution would not convince him, young and unruly as he was, of anything. I decided that an indirect approach would resonate better with his years and his nature. I began to study Marxism myself and seek proof which would make an impression on Mihajlo. I was very pleased when I happened, in the writings of Franz Mehring, a Marxist historian, upon the fact that for Marx we were the prototype of a reactionary people, the disparate fragments of what had been a Slavic whole, without any chance of achieving national synthesis. About the Hungarians, who sought only their own freedom, Marx said that they were far too lax with the "arrogant Slavs" and that the violence the Hungarians had visited upon us represented their most valuable accomplishment. Dividing nations on the basis of social temperaments, Marx recommended that "revolutionary peoples" ought to agree and destroy without mercy the "counter-revolutionary" peoples among whom we represented the greatest and most urgent evil. "The Austrian and Turkish Slavs across the Sava and Una rivers", I translated with delight for young Dedinje Marxist Mihajlo, who cared so deeply about his Serbian origins and character that he refused to speak his mother tongue of English any more, "have known each other for centuries as thieves and bandits."

Furthermore, I said, Marxist socialism, and the governmental and national reality that had developed from it in Russia, had nothing in common with the tradition of socialism among us Serbs. I quoted from Slobodan's brilliant book on Svetozar Marković: "Under the influence of Chernishevsky, Marković understood socialism not as an economic doctrine, but rather as a new philosophical view of man and life. He gave socialism what was essentially an educational goal, to change man from within and ennoble him, turning him from an egoist to an altruist." I explained to my obstinate son that his Marxism was not the "fundamental rebirth of life" described by Vasa Pelagić, the great Serbian humanist. Rather, his were shallow, nervous leftist leanings enraged by the notions of "education", "pedagogy" or "internal transformation". I know what they were, I told him, I know them by heart.

Mihajlo may still have been listening, but – as I saw more clearly with each new conversation – he heard less and less. Bewitched, he was off chasing some bird of paradise of his own. He had exchanged us for his Dedinje compatriots; he slept at home but lived on the third balcony of the National Theatre, as far as we knew, and who knows where else and with whom else.

As time passed, however, my greatest fear – that he might get actively involved in the underground movement – diminished. I was almost overjoyed when they called him up, after he completed his final exams for the gymnasium, for National Service outside bombed-out Belgrade, in a plum orchard below Avala, and he began going off in his colourless, ragged, messy uniform at dawn to the shores of the Sava; overjoyed because National Service, no matter how exhausting, took up time which he otherwise would have devoted to more perilous occupations. In mid-August, they took him from the Sava shores to build a roadway on Zlatibor Mountain, and by the time he came home, worn-out, spotty with bug bites, morose, at some point in late September, we were already hearing the guns of liberation. It was only superstition which kept Elizabeta and me from breathing a sigh of relief and telling one another, "Thank goodness, our boy is going to get through this alive!"

This sequence of events is very important. It is essential to remember that there was never a word within the family circle about Mihajlo's joining the Partisans. I swear on all that I hold most holy, I invoke Elizabeta's testimony and my good memory. We were not afraid of the Partisans, because we figured that they would never take Mihajlo at 17 years of age, even if he volunteered. My faith in civilian order kept me in the dark about the world of the future. I do not know whether Mihajlo talked about this with Jelena and the Dedinje brothers, and whether they had taken any steps in preparation for going off into the woods: I do know that we would have done everything in our power to prevent his departure, but we simply did not have the opportunity to do so.

The Partisans, from my vantage point, were entirely beyond reason. In fact, we knew very little about both the Chetniks and the Partisans in Belgrade. Especially about the Partisans. We had read in the papers that the "*Banditen*", as the Germans called them – or the "Communist scum", as they were called by General Nedić, the quisling leader of Serbia – had been surrounded and destroyed; we saw posters of Draže Mihailović and Tito, with bounties on their heads set at 100,000 Reichmarks each, in gold; we heard about trains being blown up or attacks on barracks, but where they were, how many of them there were, especially beyond the territory of New Serbia (everything else during the Occupation seemed very distant and beyond reach), were things people merely guessed at and whispered about. Radio London made no mention of the Partisans for some time, though they did report regularly on the activities of the Chetniks, so we knew more about them, enough for me to refuse involvement of any kind.

So, Mihajlo's insistence, which he kept repeating after the city was liberated, that I had prevented him from joining the Partisans was a fabrication. He announced this for the first time to my great amazement while fighting was still raging in the city, and we, hiding in the cellar, were listening to the whistle of grenades and the rattle of still distant machine-guns.

"You? In the Partisans?" I asked, incredulous.

"Well, where else should I be going? Why not?" he countered belligerently.

I bit my tongue. "I had no idea you were entertaining such a notion."

The conversation ended with this, but only a few days later, looking out of the window of our flat as people were leaping onto the tanks, hanging onto the feet of the cavalry, running out to the ragged soldiers with flasks of brandy, Mihajlo repeated his accusation, more to himself than to me, sincerely distressed: "Why didn't I just leave, what made me listen to you!"

I do not wish to criticise my son, nor do I intend to justify myself by placing the burden on him, but I sensed what drew him to this fabrication, and I always felt that these accusations did not spring from the nobler side of his character. Seeing the victors bedecked with flowers and being kissed by girls and old women alike on the podium before the vast crowds, our glory-loving son, Elizabeta's boy, ambitious in his misery, had begun to believe that the only thing worth being in life was a surviving Partisan. Anything else hardly merited attention. The worthless bourgeoisie. Only a day after the battles over Belgrade ended, it must have been October 21 (I know it was a Saturday), in the heart of the city, by the Prince's Monument, the Soviet officers and tankists who had been killed during the seven days of battles were buried. I happened to find myself in the middle of the crowd and watched the pathetic scene: 22 tanks, each one carrying the body of a hero, drove out with magnificent thunder onto the square in front of the National Theatre. They were saluted by Lieutenant-General Peko Dapčević, 30 years old; Mijalko Todorović, political commissar for the First Army Corps, 30 years old; 25-year-old colonels; General Zhdanov and the Russian officer corps; salvos; the weeping of the crowd. Quite by chance, I happened to notice a group of younger people among whom I spotted Mihajlo. I remember his face. Both his face and the thoughts clearly written on it. He was not crying. I have no impression that he was sorry for the men who had been killed. There was nothing soft in his features. All attention. Frozen. He was chewing his lower lip and standing on his toes – not to see the tanks but to see the young generals and colonels, only a few years Mihajlo's senior, and their adjutants, Mihajlo's peers. I understood him. I do not blame my son much. This was his first experience of a liberation, and there was no way he could understand that the flags would be drenched by rain, the Partisans would demobilise, the crowds would disperse and go home, and the glorious battlefield would be heaped in unsightly debris as soon as the next day, like a ballroom after drunken revelry. Mihajlo was looking at the scene at the moment of its greatest splendour; heroes were passing on carts, and he was filled with despair at the thought that he – or so it seemed to him – could so easily have been one of them, one of the chosen, the consecrated, if only he'd, if only he'd . . . but he hadn't. Stricken by the sense of an opportunity missed, Mihajlo fabricated this opportunity in its entirety for himself, from start to finish. They may well have talked about joining the Partisans over at Župana Vlastimira Street, perhaps they even made steps in that direction (though I doubt it), but he certainly never asked permission from me for such an adventure, if for no other reason than because he knew I would never have granted it. And now, when his own mistake seemed so tragically huge, with no Partisan status or insignia, Mihajlo wanted to pass the blame, or at least a part of it, on to someone else, and he thought, probably came to believe with time, that someone must have stood in the way of realising his noble plan. And who better than I to blame for Mihajlo's civilian woes among the glorious fighters his own age?

Mihajlo managed to make up for the tragic lack of a war biography through frenzied activity in the youth and other collective organisations that took devastated Belgrade under their wing. When he ran out into the street on October 16, the day our neighbourhood was liberated, my son never came back in. After diving head first into the vortex, he did not climb back out. He dug graves for the dead whom the city was not able to clear off the pavements for days. He cleared away rubble under which people were still buried alive. He rushed citizens to the Institute of Hygiene so that they could give blood; he knocked around the Russian military garage. He collected clothing for the fighters. Red-haired. Maniacal. He whinnied, he reared up on his hind legs, and all this is in no way as strange as the fact that Mihajlo's leap into the new reality drew me with him! As if we were truly connected by little belts and ties to a shared assembly line, as if I had lost my reason, forgotten all I knew, and it was because of you, Mihajlo, my son, though at first glance it may not have seemed to be, that little by little, I, who had resisted for so many years, slowly took my place in the circle dance of politics, still astonished that I could!

Never, under any circumstances, at least that much is clear today, would I have ventured to join such a band of scoundrels had it not been for my hatred – oh Lord, can I permit that word into my mind and survive? – for all that Mihajlo loved (or pretended to love?), which blinded my sight and clouded my mind – a filthy hatred I felt even for my son. There, Mihajlo. I have shamefacedly spoken the very sentence that banished all these memories, crossed them out in black ink, for my twenty years of exile, until this morning. Perhaps you would not agree with your father. I do not know whether Elizabeta would want to associate my sudden political infatuation with our mutual envies and clashes, but I do know that if it hadn't been for you, they never would have found me in the middle of that post-war encroachment of tyranny. If it hadn't been for the rage you provoked in me with all you did and thought: your new "comrades", the Communist vocabulary, your relations to your mother, your eyes red from the constant lack of sleep, your deliberately grimy fingernails as a status symbol. You, too, would see, my son, if you were to look back now on all the events of those months, which I will, believe me, lay out one by one, in all honesty and with no hidden motives, in order to make sense of them – you would see that only through my relationship with you can I explain my behaviour, and that yours, independent as it may have seemed, was nevertheless directed from that same source along secret byways. Believe me, Mihajlo, and you, Elizabeta, that I feel like a victim at the gallows, yes, like an executioner who tries to chop off his own crazy head, that too, as I set foot on the hallowed ground of these last days of our life. And – solemn. As if in church. Or in a tribal tomb.

It is true that my first contacts with politics and politicians, only seemingly separate from Mihajlo's behaviour, occurred in late October while there was still shooting going on all over liberated Belgrade. The liberators had already begun carousing, and the occasional German fanatics who had been left behind were taking pot-shots from attic strongholds at Partisan and Russian officers or, muddy, emerging from underground passageways. To tell the truth, what I referred to as my first contact with politics had a rather dramatic twist, so much so that Elizabeta and I, for good reason, thought that the occasion in question was in fact an arrest rather than an invitation to cooperate. It was past midnight, and we had been asleep for some time when we were awakened by banging on the front door. Mihajlo was not at home; he was off somewhere expiating his mortal sin of not being in the Partisans. Appalled and half asleep, over the chain, through the timidly cracked-open door, I asked, "Who are you looking for?"

"You," said the taller of the two Partisans, both looking dangerous and unkempt, with machine-guns across their chests, bombs in their belts. "Open up."

I opened. What could I do? Force doesn't wait for permission.

"You Comrade Stevan?"

"Yes, I am."

"Well, then, get your clothes on, come with us."

"Why should I?"

"Orders."

"Hey, friend, no wasting time," interrupted the other.

His "friend" did not entirely convince me of the amicable intentions of the two boorish, hairy Partisans, but I knew, no matter what the reason was for them taking me from my home at that hour, that it would be best not to argue with surly, groggy couriers or gendarmes, it didn't matter which. It made more sense to reach the people who had issued the command as soon as possible; they would, I hoped, be more accessible to reason and better informed as to my status. We drove by jeep through the city, dark as a grave. Once or twice, we passed the headlights of other military vehicles. There wasn't a soul in sight – the 6 p.m. curfew had long since chased people off the streets. On Terazije, a Red Army traffic warden gave us the sign to pass between the cannon lining the left side of the bullet-ridden Albanija palace. I was wondering, of course, where they were taking me and why, but I couldn't come up with anything. Of all the assumptions flitting through my mind as the jeep pulled up in front of the Hotel Majestic, the craziest turned out to be the closest to the truth: I had been called in on orders from Šubašić.

And though even then I could not for the life of me divine what Dr Ivan wanted with me so urgently at that hour, I was hugely relieved to hear this, certain that it was only the rough handling by my escorts that made the invitation seem more like an arrest than a summons, most probably friendly, from the President of the Yugoslav government-in-exile. Šubašić received me in his chambers and extended long and earnest apologies that his order to find me, issued that morning, had been carried out so clumsily and so late. The encounter with this attorney, a gentle man with a cultivated sense of courtesy, a follower of Maček's who had always been close to the court (I had been introduced to him in 1938 by Prince Pavle himself), was warm but brief. Warm because we had fond recollections of each other from our few pre-war encounters, brief for two reasons: first, because the gentleman who had signed the agreement to form the temporary government with Tito still had meetings to go to, regardless of the ungodly hour, and second, because I immediately agreed to participate in assembling certain legal documents.

Looking back, one might conclude that the speed with which I agreed to work with Šubašić disclosed my desire to get involved in post-war legal life. Perhaps the other people I spoke with on that crazy night thought so as well, but I well knew that many strands came together in that concise "yes". Surely the four years we had spent in the kitchen, the devastating focus on ourselves, always with the same people to talk to and with only one active organ – the ear pressed to the muted radio, so that the Oberleutnant quartered next door would not overhear the signal from London – all that surely was in total contradiction to the mad activism that thundered through the Hotel Majestic. In the dozen minutes which I spent alone with a cup of tea in an armchair in one of the corridors, dazed by the abruptness of my new position and environment, I followed the hurried and massive traffic, as if in a train station. Partisans resembling my escorts strode to and fro with envelopes; officials strolled, pensive, from one room to another; Partisan girls hurried somewhere clutching cumbersome typewriters; everyone seemed to be running somewhere; all the lights were on; I could hear reality like the thunder of some charging machine straining to the point of snapping. Alone in the armchair like a bare-chested swimmer in the sun, only just having finished my bizarre conversation with Šubašić, amidst these exhausted, hurrying figures, I felt unreal in an even more unreal dream, and somehow, viscerally, with my ear and my mind, I could hear ravaged Belgrade, spread darkly around this living point in its belly, deadened around this tiny stronghold of dynamism and light. It seemed to me that at the bottom of the corridor I saw Dr Ribar, which gave the strange building at that strange time of night an even more unreal feel. Where did he come from? I wondered, dazed, feeling as if my thought, slowed and feeble, defective, refusing to obey, was spinning pointlessly around insignificant things instead of trying boldly to face the multitude of new data with which it was suddenly wrestling. Perhaps my slowness made it easier for me to accept the next surprise with less agitation, as if it were to be expected, though Šubašić had told me it was coming: the pre-war convict and painter Moše Pijade. Pijade appeared from somewhere in the middle of that crazy night and walked over to me, his hand outstretched, and, altogether, even without that strange dazed state I was in which numbed the elasticity of my mind, was far too much for my stiff social skills, unpractised for four years, to cope with.

I had met Pijade, from a Belgrade Jewish family, once, I believe it was in 1939 or '40, in the flat of a school friend of mine, Bane, a journalist for *Politka* and a leftist though, as far as I knew at the time, not a Communist. The meeting was coincidental and of no significance for me or for Moše, so I had nearly forgotten it, but as I clasped the hand of the small, hunched-over man of rat-like, though not repulsive, appearance, one scene came back to me with great vividness: a portion of Pijade's conversation with an elderly gentleman, a conversation I had witnessed, though I do not know how or why, in Bane's flat. The greying man had been brought to meet Pijade, and, I remember this with certainty, he was not a Communist. As soon as the man was introduced to the famous Communist convict who had only recently been released from prison, the convict, without the slightest courtesy, gruffly snarled, "So, what do you want?"

I have completely forgotten what the two of them discussed, but I do remember that this introduction, involving an elderly man whom he was seeing for the first time in his life, immediately showed who Moše was – how he had been in command while in prison, how he had interrogated those who came into the prison about how they had behaved in the face of the class enemy. He determined who was all right, who should be boycotted, who was a Communist, who a Trotskyite and who an anarchist. That my first impression had not been favourable was confirmed by something I said to Bane several days after the meeting in his flat.

"What did you think of Moše?" Bane asked me.

"I would never, of my own free will, invite that gentleman to spend a summer vacation with me!"

So, as he held onto my hand, with my thoughts dazed and slow, I felt almost certain that Moše would snarl at me, "So, what do you want?" I simply froze with surprise, when instead, in no way indicating that he remembered our pre-war meeting, he began to thank me for agreeing to cooperate with them. I answered, "It will be a pleasure."

Moše also had no time to spare. He quickly described my task: "It is Mr Šubašić's express wish that you read the text of the expanded Vis Agreement between Tito and Šubašić. I, too, am asking you to do this. By tomorrow morning."

"By tomorrow morning" seemed insane to a man like me, con-scientious and thorough, but partly due to my baffled state, partly because I did not want to make trouble from the very start, I said that I would do everything in my power to meet the deadline they requested.

We parted. Moše, hunched over, walked quickly down the corridor. Some other Partisans put me back in the jeep and took me home through unpeopled, ravaged, pre-dawn Belgrade.

That was how it began.

I would be hard pressed to say what my duties were during those first few days and what jobs I did, because everything was done in Partisan style. "Tomorrow morning" was the most popular deadline, though more often it was "at once", right then, about things which were serious and complex. For more than two months I had no idea what my official position was, but one could say that most of what I was doing made me some sort of adviser to the wartime presidency called AVNOJ, the Anti-Fascist Council for the National Liberation of Yugoslavia. I wasn't needed at the first meeting of the Presidency, in the very beginning of November, because there was only one item on the agenda: the Proposal of the Great Anti-Fascist National Liberation Assembly of Serbia (we were the most zealous right from the start) to award the Order of National Hero to Marshal Tito. This was an occasion for singers and merrymakers rather than for lawyers. Once this most urgent of tasks was taken care of at the second meeting, held only two days later, when they declared the amnesty for those who had participated in the Chetnik units of Draže Mihailović and the units of Croatian and Slovene Home Guard but who had not "bloodied their hands in crimes against the people", I was asked for a legal opinion, and for the first time came into conflict with my new colleagues. I commented that the formulation "bloodied their hands in crimes against the people" was too frivolous and loosely worded, thereby creating inexhaustible possibilities for deviation from the lawmakers' intentions, allowing the judge a personal bias, incompatible with the principle of legality. But this was something which my Partisan counterparts, even those among them who had been educated as lawyers, simply could not grasp. The rift between us regarding the essence of criminal law was too wide. I did not have long to wait before I learned the truth in all its contorted nakedness. As far as the Communists were concerned, criminal law existed solely in order to protect their authority. Individual paragraphs did not serve for punishing criminals but rather for silencing, eradicating and persecuting those who did not think, politically, as they did. This was easiest to accomplish with broadly worded and indeterminate formulations which allowed those who carried out the law to include under their jurisdiction any action or inaction of any individual whose freedom of movement was politically undesirable. From the start, it was clear as day that there was no interest in making our country a legal state; rather, the laws were being made over as copies of the Bolshevik practice of settling accounts with political opponents, a transparent way of wielding terror over those who hold convictions different from yours. But was there any point in telling them that, when they knew it themselves, and when they sought their model for everything in Asiatic Russia, which had never known anything of democracy? Lenin's word on every question was final and inviolable, and he said of propaganda, plainly and clearly – while proposing the introduction of a new criminal act – that "we must give this as broad a formulation as possible, for the revolutionary conscience will more or less determine the broader application in practice". This instruction of Lenin's was the foundation of the legal system they wished to form. With the broad, limitless authorisations, for instance, of the "Court for trying felonies and misdemeanours against Serbian national honour", there were no regulations given for individual criminal acts which would be punished in court; all it said, impudently and cynically, was that these were acts which "might be qualified" (listen to that – "might be qualified"!) "as high treason". *Iustitia remota quid sunt regna nisu magna latrocinia*?

My horror was genuine and could have been predicted, but in no way could anyone have predicted my willingness to participate. No matter how glaring the Communist plot was, I continued to do so. Why was this? One reason could certainly have been my desire to help the democrats who were nominally still in the government, to save whatever could be salvaged. Grol and Jaša and many other friends of mine, Mijalko Knežević, Radmilo Stojiljković, Dragić Joksimović, courageous Dragoljub Jovanović and, from the other nations, Šutej, for instance, and Kocbek, all of them were trying to use every man of the pitiful democratically minded minority, including me, in a joint effort to preserve freedom and justice for anyone who in any way thought differently from the Communists in those ugly and perilous times. I doubt, however, that their insistence, no matter how stubborn it might have been, would have kept me in the middle of that political maelstrom for so long. My character was not such that I could acquiesce to acting like one of those lackeys who were ready to do the dirtiest work for the Communists just to avoid persecution and live comfortably. I believed too little in Serbian politics to sacrifice a single day of my life (let alone my whole life as it, alas, transpired) to it. So why did I stay when it was already clear even to fools that there were only two ways to keep your head: by knuckling under like the lackeys or by escaping. Why did I not flee?

I wondered in those days, just as I wonder now, if perhaps I saw some benefit, if I found some pleasure, in working on the most important state documents, in the presence of the highest state authorities, and with a clean conscience I can say that I felt no satisfaction whatsoever, and that there was no benefit to be gained. The famed Partisan egalitarians jealously guarded the privilege of the diplomatic warehouses and Dedinje villas. They only gave the rest of us the occasional gnawed bones, and only if we were obedient. Even their revulsion towards almost everything I did and the way I did it couldn't placate my vanity. They nearly told me to my face that my legal opinion on the documents I was framing for them interested them less than last year's snows. All they cared about were my readiness and skill at giving their Bolshevik methods the veneer of legality – smoke in the eyes of the suspicious Western allies. At every opportunity and in every way, even when they weren't openly threatening me for my grumbling, they let me know that I was no more than a necessary evil, without whom, for a while at least, they would not be able to function, but that they would banish me like a mangy sheep as soon as they had ensconced themselves more firmly in government, as soon as they had legally entrenched their omnipotence, which for tactical reasons was still being kept within the liberal shape of a parliamentary democracy. To tell the truth, the sight of those I agreed with in the government and around it was not so inspiring that it obligated me morally or moved me to remain actively involved. Once again, the rule was proven to me that in Serbian politics the lack of reliability in government is in direct proportion to the lack of reliability in the opposition. Except for a few who were soon to be arrested, even the most courageous and most honourable had to know what they did not want to admit openly to themselves: that they had been humiliated and deceived, that they were ludicrous and welcome only because they were harmless.

I wanted to weep at the St Michael's Day celebration of old Jaša Prodanović, which I remember as being an arrogant ball for the victors and a parody of my, of our, community. One had to know Jaša as I had known him to appreciate that spectral Archangel's day and to explain my great shame and despair. Prodanović was a fine professor of literature who had been involved in politics with confidence and passion his entire life. First he fought against the Kings Milan and Aleksandar. Then he attacked Pašić's Radical party and did everything in his power against the dictatorship of the second Aleksandar. He turned defiantly on the men who assassinated Apis, thereby becoming a Republican, both to avenge Apis and to punish the ungrateful Karađorđevićes who without the terrorists of the Black Hand would never have won the Serbian throne. Since his youth, he had cherished socialist leanings, and he became a Radical when that was the finest option for all progressive people. He acknowledge Petar Karađorđević as King under the condition that he obey Parliament. He was in the royal circle, but never a minister. In the Serbian political quagmire Jaša was a rare beacon of light. Someone once called him a "political dandy", recalling Jaša's favourite saying, his guiding star through the backward, dark landscape of our political life: "It is better to walk alone than walk in shame." And Prodanović walked alone whenever it was a disgrace to be part of the majority. After a stint in Banjica prison, he spent the Occupation in silence, lost a son and a grandson to the fighting, and ended his honest life in poverty, without his own roof over his head, in a rented flat.

Had they painted him in oils, the Communists never could have painted a finer portrait of a bourgeois politician than 80-year-old Prodanović. They grabbed him immediately after liberation, literally stuffed him, baffled, into an automobile and practically dragged him to Kolarac University, where 880 delegates of the Great Anti-Fascist Assembly greeted him with ovations. They barely allowed him to utter a few sentences against the monarchy and for a republic. The 80-year-old Republican was swept away by the enthusiasm of the young crowd that flooded into Belgrade, and I truly believe that it was with the most genuine conviction that he accepted the posts the Communists heaped on him – representative of the National Liberation Front of Serbia and Yugoslavia, member of the Executive Council of the Front for Serbia, Minister in the Serbian, and federal, governments – he was welcome everywhere. Jaša, as one might expect of a man of honour, was not an obedient pawn who acted against his beliefs in order to secure benefit and peace for himself, and until that spectral St Michael's celebration at 12 Račkog Street I wondered why and how they allowed him digressions which would have cost others their heads. Jaša, for instance, like Grol and Nedeljko Divac, declared openly that there was no separate Montenegrin nation, nor did he approve of the creation of a Macedonian language, but Đilas and Emanuil Čučkov attacked only Divac and Grol, omitting any mention of Jaša. He continually protested against bandit-like procedures or mafia methods. He would shout angrily about this, then that – contrary to democratic principles, parliamentary practice, the protocol, the laws they had passed themselves – there was no shortage of opportunity for protest! All these were transgressions which should have cost him seven lives, or at least he should have fallen seriously out of grace, and yet – nothing.

At the St Michael's Day celebration, I realised why; I saw to my chagrin that Jaša, permanently humiliated, was a lackey, too, though maybe he didn't even realise it. He was not a lackey out of selfish reasons, but – which seemed all the more poignant to me – out of some distorted sense of conviction.

In the second half of November, when the saint's day of the Archangel Michael falls, broken Belgrade was already under snow. Prodanović's home on Račkog Street received well-wishers in the drawing room on the first floor, the only room where there was a fire in the tile stove, which, though it had gone out, still eased the chill. The mood was festive because we were sitting without winter coats. We were still getting used to the joy of liberation like eager children, pinching ourselves to see whether we were dreaming. We ate bits of cheese and sipped brandy. All of us at the party were of the older generation. The younger Prodanovićes, fanatic just like our Mihajlo, would hear nothing of celebrating Orthodox customs. I, on the other hand, perceived Jaša's decision to celebrate his saint's day as a defiant gesture in opposition to the Communists and a demonstration of inde- pendence that could hardly have appealed to his new, intolerant political friends. The Communists were prepared to throw Party members out for similar sins, and they regarded non-members who honoured religious customs with suspicion, frequently falling back on various forms of pressure to dissuade them. I would therefore have expected just about anything other than what I saw with my own eyes that day.

Knowing the customs of saint's day celebrations, Elizabeta and I were just about to leave when Jaša's wife led into the drawing room a group of Tito's highest-ranking ministers, famous and untouchable for most people, and infamous and dangerous for most of those gathered at the party. In a fine mood, boisterous, Ranković, Đilas, Nešković, Milentije Popović are the ones I remember coming into the room, and there were another two or three I have since forgotten, either because they were less important or because I didn't know them by name. Communists at a saint's day celebration! Wonder of wonders! The saint's icon, Communist leaders and a saint's day cake on a table in the corner – to be able to take in such sights with a single glance! I immediately concluded, of course, that their appearance could not mean a change in the Communist position on church rituals and Serbian customs, nor was it a way of excepting old Prodanović from the ban in effect for all comrades. As I watched them serve themselves *slatko* and shout jovially, mouths full, "Happy saint's day, Uncle Jaša" (old Prodanović's official Partisan nickname), it suddenly dawned on me that their elation was a joy at breaking the rules, at least to a degree, and the stricter the rule, the greater the joy! I saw in their delighted faces their pleasure that, like royalty, they were above condemnation, entitled like pharaohs to break the rules they had made for everyone else. It reminded me of those three medieval knights who proved their sovereignty by one of them ordering that a plot of land be sowed with coins, a second feeding the kitchen fire with costly candles, and the third, also in the name of extravagance, roasting all his thoroughbred horses alive. "We do it because we can," their victorious faces proclaimed. "We are above judgement, others do not dare, but we can be at a saint's day celebration and lose nothing of our Communist aura!"

Whether it was because there was no room in the drawing room, or because Jaša wanted to set the Communist bosses apart for reasons and conversations of his own, the great doors were opened and the drawing room was extended into the next room. The women quickly lit another fire in the stove, and Uncle Jaša sat the newly arrived guests in armchairs and on the sofa in the adjacent room, so that our seating arrangement resembled a stage set in a theatre: there we sat in our moth-eaten pre-war suits, some of us frightened, some grinning obsequiously (two faces emerge in my memory, though there were certainly more than two people there: the old lawyer Milanče Petrović, smooth-shaven above his old-fashioned collar and bow tie, and the plump merchant Jordan Cvetković, over whose bulging belly dangled his pocket-watch chain), and all eyes were glued on the stage, where they performed, ignoring our presence and curiosity. I retained my honour in my own eyes by moving my chair a bit to the left so that I had my back half turned to the stage. While I pretended to chat with the moth-eaten elders, under a spell, unable to stop themselves from staring into the next room, I followed tensely, just as they did, everything that was going on in the circle of Communist archangels.

Jaša held the floor. He saw an opportunity to tell the power mongers things in this more conducive setting and better atmosphere which he otherwise wouldn't have dared to say, or wouldn't have had a chance to announce officially in public. In succinct and cultivated language – language as different from vulgar Communist jargon as Turkish is from French – he told them about an argument he had had with his 13-year-old granddaughter. Using every ruse in the book to find out what had been resolved at Yalta, in particular whether there would be a referendum in Yugoslavia on the return of the monarchy, he could glean no official answers to his questions from colleagues in the Party. But then he had been invited by his granddaughter to come to a talk she was giving at the Youth Centre.

The Communists found this hilarious. Lounging in the armchairs, they gleefully asked Uncle Jaša how he had responded.

"What, pray tell, will I hear?" Grandad, as he was called by everyone in his family, asked his granddaughter. "What will you be speaking on?"

"The Yalta agreement."

"Well, thank goodness, now I will be able to find out what was decided there!"

Prodanović did not intend his story to be funny. He spoke almost angrily, with barely controlled bitterness, but the Communists found his outrage irresistibly amusing, and they guffawed, though it naturally never occurred to them to explain what had been resolved at Yalta.

"Whatever are you up to with these children! What sort of comedy is this, in the name of God! Listen," the elderly republican went on, even more irate. "Several days ago, at about 5 in the afternoon, someone rang at the door and wouldn't take his finger off the buzzer – I was thinking: must be a fire in the hayloft! At the door stood a girl, hefty – even a man fifty years younger than I wouldn't be able to beat her at arm wrestling – and stern-looking. 'Comrade,' she says, 'a coference at 7' – one of the 'n's missing – and I am supposed to be there. 'Can't make it,' I say. 'You must,' says she. 'Listen, girl,' I try nicely, 'I have nothing to learn at this conference of yours,' to which she responds, 'If you're not at the coference, you won't be on the list to receive firewood and coal!' And off she goes!"

Jaša's words "I am a minister in Tito's cabinet! Why are you humiliating me and the government!" were drowned out by the Communists' gasps of laughter, they were so amused. I could no longer rein in my curiosity and glanced over my shoulder at the stage. I saw Prodanović, seething with rage, and the young power mongers, who either didn't register the old man's complaints or felt them to be utterly insignificant. The scene was bizarre, filled with reciprocal benevolence and blindness, and suddenly, as I turned away, I realised with aching clarity that Jaša's harmless railing was part of a comedy that would last only as long as all the actors kept strictly to their parts. It was Jaša's to be a good-natured buffoon who, with his old-fashioned irrationality, created for the victor the pleasing impression of his generosity. Jaša was a trophy, a parade ornament on their iconostasis. How else could they be sure that they had destroyed an entire past world if it weren't for Jaša, living and breathing proof of their victory? How could kings know their highness, if they hadn't by their sides wise fools who reminded them of their lowliness? Poor Grandad, I thought, ashamed. Grandad doesn't even know what he lost by becoming Uncle Jaša! Poor Grandad, I thought while I watched old Milanče Petrović, who was listening tensely to the conversation in the next room and trying, by joining in the boisterous laughter, to draw attention to his full support for their behaviour; and Jordan, the plump merchant, who was repeating the conversation from the next room into his beard, taking care that those who shouldn't hear him wouldn't, hushed by his wife, Mara, in a pleading whisper ("Jordan, be quiet! I beg of you! He's an old man and a lunatic"). A great sadness took hold of me, and an impatience to escape.

On the way home, saddened, I related my impressions to Elizabeta. They had inveigled him into it. The clowns. They were standing in a circle around the cheated old man, mocking him. In his own home. On his own Holy Archangel day. The mainstream was carrying the Communists along, and they mocked him and his miserable hope that he might be able to influence them. And why shouldn't they. We deserved no better. We were their lackeys.

"You are exaggerating," mused Elizabeta, putting an end to the conversation but not to the web of questions which plagued me. Had I stayed on in this unsavoury company for the same reasons as Prodanović? Did I believe that the rare moment of reason which I had indeed managed to win was worth the lackey's humiliation, the true loss of my Serbian honour?

No, I did not believe that. Or, if I did, I believed it much less than naïve Prodanović did, and after the party at his house not a stone remained standing of my belief in our supposed utility, so his avuncular deception could not have been decisive in the continuation of my own obstinate commitment.

My reason was different, and I knew its name perfectly well.

Its name was Mihajlo.

You, Mihajlo, you lost your mind, and you kept me, the imbecile, trapped in a hellish circle in an uncalled-for and hurtful way, which I will now explain to you, a trifle belatedly, I admit.

I see you, my Mihajlo, as if you are here before me now. The English military khaki blouse, the Tito cap with the five-pointed star, greasy along the rim because you bought it second-hand, a size or two too small so it doesn't really cover your head but perches atop your thick red mat like a poorly fitting lid. Naturally, your desire was to resemble a Partisan, but strange, and often vicious, are the ways of the fates that guide us: I am sorry, son, but you looked precisely the English private, a smooth-chinned conscript, as if you had come fresh from the Reading recruitment centre to war-torn Belgrade. The milk-white face, the red hair, the feather-like moustache and silky chin hairs. The only thing Partisan about you were your eyes, the bloodshot eyes of an Angora rabbit who never slept. Being short of sleep was the hallmark of you, the "activists". You flaunted your bloodshot eyes as if they were a war decoration for heroic self-sacrifice!

Dumb with bewilderment, Elizabeta and I would still be slipping our arms into our dressing gowns as we ran into the front hall, awakened by your bumbling about in the house late at night.

"Good Lord, Mihajlo," I would ask, "where can you be going at this hour?"

"To do my duty," you would say mysteriously, carelessly slamming the door behind you.

We understood quite quickly. We stopped running into the front hall, but we always attended to the sounds of your midnight departures or early-morning returns. What were you chasing after? Whom did you hope to catch? What were you fleeing from, we wondered – Elizabeta, trembling, overcome with terror; I, infuriated by your manner and by how you had changed. Today, this seems like a months-long delirium in which we floated rather than thought, unable to ask where this was headed and why. We foundered ever deeper in quicksand. Elizabeta with her silence. Mihajlo and I with our mutual lunge for the jugular.

Merciful God, why, when Mihajlo took my mind, did my will abandon me? I would taunt him with a red handkerchief. He would charge at me like a little bull. The political corrida in our flat began the moment we started talking to each other and would stop only if Mihajlo or I had somewhere to go. I admit I should have had the wisdom to retreat before his orthodoxy and wait for the moment when he would sober, which had to come at some point, soon. But Mihajlo's dogmatism was so harshly uni-directional, his imperviousness to argument so profound, his ability to replace thinking with the trumpeting of unquestioned assumptions so consistent, that even today I am not surprised that I was unable to refrain from outbursts and quarrels. The wiser man relents, but not if he is talking to a madman who wants to jump off a bridge. I remember how at the beginning of a conversation I would always present my thoughts calmly. I invested superhuman efforts in keeping my voice steady even when Mihajlo flung the worst possible banality from his arsenal in my face as if it was the ultimate, divine word of truth. But it is also true that I frequently did not succeed in remaining calm. Now I can see that quarrelling was inevitable. We were facing each other across a trench so wide that one could only be heard by firing across it.

The eternal focus of our differences was the notion of democracy and the role of political parties in the National Front, which had been designed with the sole goal of eradicating all parties other than the Communists. I knew this difference to be of defining importance for our lives as citizens and that Mihajlo's resistance to understanding precisely this difference must be broken. As God is my witness, Elizabeta can confirm how with the greatest patience and moderation I set forth the points of view dear to reason. Yet time and time again, I collided with the architrave of Mihajlo's denial. I claimed, for instance, that there can be no democracy without competition between parties – such a simple and clear position! A political system comprised of a single party is a political system that does not, in effect, exist. It can be a majority party, but the essence of every democracy is the protection of the minority, its right to exist. Public government, even to its detriment, must enable the legal life of those who hold views different from those it espouses. Democracy means acquiescing to living together with those who do not think as you do – I was telling him the most commonplace things. But for my maniacal son, this made no sense. At first, he said he would prove I was wrong. The Communists had no intention of smothering all other parties, not those which joined it in the National Front, including my group, *Napred*, or even those who held themselves apart. I have to say, however, that even Broz, Kardelj, Pijade and others in their statements from those days bore him out. The Communists with their famous cannibalistic vocabulary even attacked all who surmised that there was any likelihood that party pluralism might be abolished in the new Yugoslavia. Tito bald-facedly claimed that he had no desire to introduce the Communist system to Yugoslavia. For a long time, Mihajlo wouldn't hear of my doubts as to the reliability of these statements, nor would he accept the hypocrisy of the Communists, Machiavellians who even as they were taking an oath were planning to transgress it the very next day.

That, however, was still bearable. I would soon learn that there was worse to come.

Even when he was merely reciting his faith in the words of Tito and Kardelj, I was irked by my son's innocent simplicity of spirit, but soon enough, sooner than the Communist leaders did, he, young and orthodox, began to say openly what they most certainly were thinking, though for tactical reasons they kept swearing oaths to the contrary. Mihajlo embraced uncritically the Bolshevik position of Stalin and Lenin regarding the dictatorship of the proletariat, which, in fact, came down to the rule of a single, Communist, party. This was when gruesome sentence-slaughter began to issue forth from the mouth of our 18-year-old child, phrases of incomprehensible cruelty and vicious intolerance which, after the first shock, cast me into an unfatherly fury. Evil seething in his eyes, fully intending to silence me with the volume of his voice if there was no other way, he would shout, "The dictatorship of the proletariat is the organisation of the avant-garde of the oppressed into a ruling class for the purpose of oppressing the oppressors! Dictatorship is government relying directly on violence, which is not bound by any laws. Parties! Democracy! Democracy for whom? For you? A handful of bourgeois debris incapable of valuing the benevolence and consideration shown you by the liberators of the country and the class of the future? Instead you plot against its world and your own people. We do not care about you, we do not even notice when we march over you. This is the force of historical necessity" – then he used a phrase that in decent society would be unacceptable even from a child – "get this into your thick skull; a single-party system has no alternative, and as for the way you are playing at parliamentary comedy in your AVNOJ committees, where they let you alone as if you spent the war quaking under your duvets, you can shove that up your ass, you won't be riding on the backs of the people much longer! Wake up! Your time is over! Comrade Moša is toying with you to placate the English and the Americans. Can't you tell? Are you blind? Can't you see the excitement of the masses? A new class stepping on to the stage of history! Step aside if you don't want to be swept away like so much of yesterday's rubbish!"

He never spoke sitting down. Seated, he would listen. But as soon as he wished to respond, which would, as a rule, be immediately, he would leap up, pace the room with long strides, lunge into my face, bluster with his finger raised dictatorially, howl like a drunkard swinging a bottle over his head, off-balance, mad, possessed by evil spirits.

When I first described Mihajlo's behaviour to Elizabeta in those terms, she said, "Yes, he does seem that way," not because she was superstitious but because Mihajlo's revolutionary passion was such a departure from his nature that it did appear as though someone foreign had wormed its way into his body.

It must be said that Mihajlo had earlier demonstrated his obstinacy, fierce ambition and persistence, and these traits may have promoted his conversion to cruel revolutionary. Parallel to or overlaying them was the other part of Mihajlo's character, however: an analytical integrity rare for someone of his age, a reverence for evidence, the truth, the quest for truth. In contrast to the more typical lack of reliability among Serbs – such fertile ground for the provocation of revolutionary intolerance – his remarkable diligence was all the more pronounced. So too was his modesty, unlike the prevailing model of garrulous oafishness, his sober retreat into the world of knowledge and thinking in contrast to his present public life with street ruffians, his English restraint, which I loved, the gentlemanly reserve unlike his current propaganda-ridden bluster; his remarkable feeling for consequence, uniformity, continuity, unlike his current Montagnard views – it is no wonder that our son seemed to us to be possessed by demons, not merely altered by the crazy times in which all three of us found ourselves.

Elizabeta and I responded in entirely different ways to this new, possessed son of ours, to this vulgar demon who lashed out of Mihajlo's mouth with its flaming tongue.

Me first.

With every new day and every new quarrel, my paternal tolerance waned, and the rage grew too large for my ability to keep myself in check. I felt the malevolence grow in my gut like some new, malignant organ, superfluous and dangerous but independent of my brain's control. I felt him, physically I felt Mihajlo flexing his muscles at the peak of his strength, threatening to sweep me away along with the Medaković home, the glass globe in which we dwelled. And while this malignant new organ was, at first, a part of me, in time it became so shrewish that I began to fear it, realising that it ruled me when I should have been ruling it.

And how could it have been otherwise! For it was not only the wrangling with Mihajlo that nourished my frame of mind. Before the quarrels came my experience, and Mihajlo's behaviour, in public. Confused, still immobilised, we made way for young Bosnian women, girls who certainly longed to be women, children, even adults, who – having discovered that our large dining-room table when extended in both directions was perfect for writing slogans on large signs – took up residence there and turned it into a revolutionary sign-and-slogan-writing workshop. I naturally could have refused to allow them to come in when Mihajlo materialised at our front door at the head of a colourful band of rogues and informed me that they would be writing slogans in the dining room.

"What slogans?"

"For a demonstration."

I stepped aside and let the mob into the flat not because something unpleasant might have happened had I objected, but, first and foremost, because of Mihajlo, also because it would have been entirely out of keeping with the temper of the times to stand in the way of public activity, to give the advantage to any form of personal comfort or private inclinations. The rules of behaviour in the slogan-writing unit were dictated by a smaller, but more powerful, number of those who had grown used, during their tenure in the guerrilla army, to the thought that the roof over one's head was something provisional, no better or worse than any other quarters anywhere else, and that a house, every house, was merely a refuge one should be ready at a moment's notice to abandon. Any attempt on my part to preserve my living space as inviolable would have brought upon me – easily imaginable at the time, ridiculous though it may seem today – the reputation of an enemy of the people, an imperialist agent, a war profiteer and a Tartar. Unlike my fellow citizens of similar stature, however, I was not afraid. I was above the threat of the lynch mob. No matter what I might do, they would have to stop short of putting me in the stocks because of my high standing with the Partisan leadership. I realised in an instant that Mihajlo would never forgive my denial of access to the dining room, so without a word I stepped aside. I clenched my teeth, kept my silence and watched how the Huns and Visigoths devastated my home from one day to the next.

The substance of the slogans and their length were set by a large, tousled woman called Savina: she was Bosnian or maybe from the Sandžak, I'm not sure, I couldn't place the dialect she spoke, but it was clear that she was in charge and the only one with a mystical connection to the higher echelons who proclaimed their divine and ineluctable wisdom to the minds of mortals by way of directives. Savina, young but heavy-set, with the discordant body of a middle-aged woman, missing her left arm to above her elbow, suit jacket, blue with discreet length-wise stripes. She was a full believer in the inscrutability, the unattainable heights, of that transcendental place from which holy decrees descended. I often saw her in the middle of the night, or early in the morning, arriving in our dining room with an air of importance and, naturally, short of sleep, among the activists who were waiting for her, ready. With a practised gesture, agilely swinging the German officer's satchel off her shoulder onto the dining-room table, she'd pitch her Tito's cap into another corner of the room with her right hand, sit astride her chair like a man and pull out her notebook. Among the activists the tension rose. No-one dared so much as peek into Savina's sacred notebook, but rather with discretion, at a distance, all of them silent, they awaited the decree. Having watched how she built the dramatic tension with masterful pomp, I was incredulous when she told me that she hadn't completed primary school! Apparently, such talents came with birth! Savina would open her notebook to the appropriate page and stare for a while at the words written there. Then, briefly, lost in thought, she would look round at the assembled activists with her tired, red, attentive eyes, as if checking to see how ready they were, how able they would be to bear the revelation she was about to impart. Finally, pounding her fist on the table, she would leap to her feet and declare, "The slogan is 'Long Live Comrade Stalin, decisive fighter for the freedom of small nations, always protecting their independence'."

Savina, of course, was not allowed to change the substance of the slogans, but she was the one who decided how long they would be. It depended on whether the group was demonstrating in front of the military court, or showing support for the Tito–Šubašić agreement, or staging demonstrations against King Petar and the Queen Mother, or swearing eternal friendship with the great Soviet Union under the wise leadership of Josip Vissarionovich – and therefore whether they would be standing in rows of four, six, eight or even more. The length of the slogan had to fit the width of the row. Once they agreed on the formation of the columns, Savina would chop off the necessary chunk: "Long Live Comrade Stalin", if four demonstrators would be holding it over their heads, or "Long Live Comrade Stalin, decisive fighter for freedom", if there were six of them, and so forth. Since even our dining-room table was not long enough for the longest of the slogans, they dragged the grand piano in from the salon and used it as an extension. They did not have long enough strips of paper, of course, but made them by gluing one piece of paper to another, and it never occurred to them, of course, that they should protect the furniture, floor, walls from damage in the process. Without a shred of concern, they would lay a piece of newspaper over the glue they spilled on the varnish of the precious Steinway and go on working as if nothing had happened. One of them while talking and walking across the room would cheerfully wave a paintbrush and dribble red paint on the floor, chairs and walls. They came in wearing their muddy Army boots, never noticing the metal scraper by the front door, placed there precisely so that one could remove the mud from one's shoes. They gouged chunks of plaster out of the walls with the boards they brought in. They tore a hole in the Drobović still life without so much as a glance.

Watching them, I remembered a feeling I had had as a child at the Sava bathing beach when Nanka had given me a slice of watermelon to eat, and I, dressed only in my swimming trunks, delighted in letting the red juice drip and drizzle all over me, down my chin and neck, on to my stomach, without a care, without the caution one takes under ordinary circumstances. The Huns and the Visigoths, however, did not even delight in muddying and destroying, violating order, because they knew no order, or what I called "ordinary circumstances". With the spontaneity of jungle creatures, they would have hopped onto the sideboard if there was something to be grabbed from high in the room, plunked their muddy shoes onto the plush of the dining-room chairs to rest their legs; if they spilled paint on the upholstered love-seat, they would leave it there to dry, or sometimes they intentionally tried out nuances of colour on the white Florentine tiles of the stove until they got the blend just right; they mixed their glue in the Mexican ceramic fruit bowl, oblivious of the fact that they were doing anything the slightest bit odd. Adam and Eve were only ashamed of their nakedness when they became cognisant of it; awareness makes a human being a master of his behaviour, and the Visigoths simply had none.

To tell the truth, it was generally not the Visigoths who infuriated me. They even touched me sometimes. In all their agonies, they made me chuckle. They also, sometimes, of course, so enraged me that I could have shot them. Like that 6-foot-tall young man, for instance, after he blundered into our bedroom!

You have to understand our position, mine and Elizabeta's. Once the horde had descended upon us, our flat was no longer our own. We had made our peace with this; we understood. While I, either curious or furious, often sidled up and watched what they were doing, at once appalled and fascinated, Elizabeta literally fled from the mob, devising stratagems so that she would not meet any of our untamed visitors. Each time she left the kitchen – a space we had managed to preserve for ourselves – she would prepare herself, using all the arts of war, by listening, then scouting cautiously to ascertain enemy positions, then tiptoeing out and slipping through the enemy ranks. For Elizabeta feared, irrationally and childishly but entirely sincerely, any encounter with the members of our revolutionary sanctum.

"Hey, lady," a young Partisan girl, paintbrush in hand, all smudged with paint, a healthy young woman, pounced on her once, despite all Elizabeta's cautionary measures. There was nothing hostile in her words, only curiosity. "Are you truly an Englishwoman?"

Elizabeta, who was getting ready to slip through the dining room and sneak unnoticed out of the front door, stopped dead in her tracks as if struck by lightning. "Yes," she said and, like a schoolchild pleading extenuating circumstances, immediately added, "But I received Yugoslav citizenship in 1926."

The girl didn't understand what this meant, nor did it interest her. "You're a real live Englishwoman?" she asked, and measured Elizabeta from head to toe.

"Yes," stuttered unhappy Eliza.

"Your father and your mother, they were English, too?"

"Yes."

"So they knew Serbian?"

"No," she said and looked pleadingly at her red-headed son, seeking help, but Mihajlo wouldn't hear a word of the conversation, he wouldn't deign to notice the humiliating flailing of the frightened woman, his mother. The well-meaning Partisan girl continued, beaming and peering at this wonder of wonders, "So how come you know how to speak our language?"

"I learned," said Elizabeta, wrenching herself from the girl's question like a frog breaking free of the gaze of a snake, and lurched towards the door, nearly at a run.

I tried to talk with Elizabeta on a number of occasions about her irrational fear or unmanageable discomfort or whatever it was, but she would withdraw into her cocoon; she would fall silent, fearful, I'd say, even of my questions. During that time, feeling the weight of the Visigoth siege far more acutely than I did, Elizabeta began to arrange and tend to our bedroom with an almost maniacal dedication, the other room whose full ownership we succeeded in winning. As if obsessed, she kept changing the impeccably white linens and starching them. Every day, she cleaned the thick white carpet, one of our rare valuable possessions which we still had not traded for food. By the door she placed a mat on which we left our shoes, filthy from walking through the flat, as soon as we entered the room, in favour of slippers. A reading lamp over our heads, between our pillows; select pieces of furniture; Belgian lace curtains which covered the blackout paper on the windows – all we needed to create the impression of cleanliness and order was here. I remember how pleased Elizabeta was once when she had rushed through the flat to the room without running into any of the Visigoths. Still out of breath, she looked around our bedroom, and said, "Just like before the war!"

Indeed, it was only in those 20 square metres that we felt as if we were at home.

And then, one evening, a month or two after Mihajlo had brought the hordes to the flat, Eliza and I were lying there reading, each in our own bed, the rest of the room in warm, intimate semi-darkness. All of a sudden, some cloddish 6-foot-tall fellow – I'd never seen him before – swung open the door with one hand while unbuttoning his fly with the other and stopped, frozen, thunderstruck by the unexpected scene before him. His eyes scanned us dully yet thoroughly, taking in the whiteness of the starched sheets, the walls, Elizabeta's vanity, two armchairs, our robes thrown over the arms, our slippers on the floor next to the beds; he stared at the bedside tables, the books on them, and then again at us, as we gaped, astonished, over our spectacles at the creature in the doorway, and then, still holding his half-open fly, he howled, "Whoa, God love us!" – slammed the door and probably ran off to describe to the Visigoths the miracle he had seen. For a miracle it was – such a clean and tidy room among the ruins of our flat, the spotlessly white carpet clear up to the line beyond which you couldn't see the parquet floor for the dried mud, paint, plaster and rubbish. The Visigoth's reaction was hardly surprising. And it was hardly surprising that I wanted, at that moment, for the first time in my life, to shoot a man. Could we enjoy no privacy even in our own bedroom! Was our room no longer a haven? Why, that fellow, if by chance it had been dark, would most certainly have urinated on us, since evidently he took our room for a *pissoir*!

Yet I knew then, and know even more clearly now, that it was not their horrendous presence in our private lives, not the Visigothic fury of the horde that was responsible, or rather at fault, for the growth of the new, malignant organ secreting a disgusting and dangerous rancour within me. I was, indeed, capable of observing the horde with a genuine interest. Looking back, I can detect at the bottom of my discomfort something akin to tenderness which filled me, at times, when I looked at those village-girl Partisans, country-bumpkin Communists – those crazed kids! Goodness, look how young they are! I would say to myself. How terribly underground and important when they went creeping off after midnight to their "secret", "dangerous" Communist meetings in the heart of Communist Belgrade! How unreservedly they believed that at that very moment they were creating an entirely new world, which would be ready to go at the very latest by next Monday! How simple and earnest they were, staring wide-eyed at the paraphernalia of a civilisation strange to them, and superfluous.

I remember, one evening, when I came back late from some God-awful meeting, I wanted to get through the dining room to the hallway that led to our bedroom without turning on the light. I tripped and nearly fell, realising while I was trying to regain my balance that I had caught my foot on something alive. I turned on the light and saw – Savina! Bewildered, wrenched from sleep, she was sitting on the floor, looking around her without comprehension. I suddenly felt so sorry for her in that filthy, unheated room. On the muddy floor, she had spread nothing but a few sheets of newspaper; covered with her overcoat, she was shivering in the chill she couldn't chase out of her bones.

"Forgive me," I said, "I should have been more careful."

"What's the time, d'you know?"

I told her.

"Fine," she mumbled, got up, ran a hand once or twice over her clothing and, chilled, slipped into her overcoat. "Have you got a cigarette, Comrade?"

"I do."

"I'll have a smoke and then I'm out of here."

I lit a cigarette, too, though I rarely do, merely so that I could stay with Savina and talk with her. She suddenly seemed – crippled, betrayed, alone, here from another world – to need a kind word. "Have you nowhere to sleep but here?"

"Sure I do, Mister, but I didn't have the time to get there. There never is enough time."

"Where are you from?"

I had been right, my ear hadn't deceived me. "We are from the village of Vrana."

"Where is that, precisely?"

"Off in Bosnia, Comrade, at the foot of Devetak."

"Is that where your parents are?"

"Nope, Comrade."

"Where are they, then?"

"Killed."

She fished a chunk of cornbread, unwrapped, from the pocket of her overcoat and started chewing it.

"The Germans?"

"The Ustashas. Ustashas. Who else."

I was about to proceed with my customary use of "vi", but my stubborn refusal to acquiesce to their ubiquitous use of "ti" suddenly seemed pompous and unseemly in conversation with this sleepy girl. I noticed for the first time that Savina was not merely an untended haystack of hair under a skimpy Tito cap and an empty sleeve on a military overcoat, but a young, even very young girl whose weary eyes and sagging cheeks might fool someone trying to guess her age. She had been touched, a moment before, when I had thought that perhaps she had no place to sleep. She smiled, and at once, as if by the flick of a magic wand, the mannish Party secretary vanished and a little girl appeared, an utterly innocent peasant girl, endearing, unprotected.

"Have you any family left in the village?"

"The village is gone."

"How could it be gone?"

"Everyone left."

"What do you think, will they be back again after the war?"

She shrugged her shoulders, thought for a bit. "Maybe so," she said, and then swiftly, from the pocket where she had kept the cornbread, pulled out a torn sheet of the *Politika* newspaper. "Listen to this, Comrade," she said and started sounding out the words: "Andrej Jefimovski, contact us, we are worried, we are fine. Love, Ksenija and Stevan Hristić."

After a pause, as if it was particularly important, with victorious joy she read the last words of the advertisement: "Takovska Street number 12"! She looked at me, a little startled that she knew how to read, and then said, "Look at this one: 'Bogić Milan, Milica's brother, political commissar of the Yugoslav People's Liberation Army, sends news to Jelka: Nebojša Lozanić is wounded. Railway Hospital in Dedinje'." Savina beamed. Then her face fell. "I wrote one, too," she said. "Want to hear it?"

"Indeed I do!" I said warmly, feeling that distant politeness was inappropriate to the situation.

Savina squinted and recited, by heart, slowly, as if she were writing it out with a clumsy hand, "Savina . . . Mi-lan's sister is a-live. Wait-ing for her bro-ther. Mu-ta-po-va Street number 18." She opened her eyes and looked at me. "Think it's any good?"

"It most certainly is," I said, and when I saw that I hadn't convinced her, I added, "Maybe he will look for you through the advertisements."

"Oh, not him, you can bet your life!"

"Why wouldn't he?"

"He doesn't know how to read."

"Maybe he has learned, like you."

She shook her head, doubtfully, yet considering the possibility. "I doubt it," she concluded. "You know, that brother of mine is a dunce," she explained to me tenderly, and with one of her sleeves she brushed away a tear. Then, as if she didn't know how to finish the conversation, she leapt to her feet. "Well, to your health, Comrade, off I go to work."

My throat tightened. I was sorry I hadn't touched her cheek, put my arm round her shoulder, kissed her forehead, so young and unattractive, crippled and neglected she seemed – just then – undone, no home, no arm, no-one to call her own.

Really, most of the time I did not hate them. Rather, numb, dull, I watched the devastation with a philosophical serenity. I acquiesced to the inevitable. A Steinway could go the way of all else! No-one had played it for years. Even the Dobrović painting! We took it down, though too late. A restorer would patch it up in better days. If ever such days came. And if they never did – what good would the Dobrović do me? Or the dining room for that matter? Why clean the walls in a dining room, anyway?

That rancorous creature in my gut was aggravated mostly, if not entirely, by my maniacal and dangerous son, Mihajlo. How could it be – everything in me howled – why was he making a fool and a nobody of himself with such a passion! Mihajlo knew full well the value of the Dobrović painting. If the Visigoths didn't care, Mihajlo couldn't be enjoying spending his time in a pigsty. He simply could not stomp about on the carpet with muddy shoes with their natural disinterest. He could not, as Savina did, believe in those simplified propaganda inanities which he was painting in red on white paper. The Visigoths had truly been nothing only yesterday, so they had every reason to believe, albeit naïvely, in the notion that tomorrow they could be everything. But what was Mihajlo seeking among them?

I often watched him in that mob of people different from him. He was so distinct. A white-haired Dane among the swarthy Seljuks. He lugged in boards, glued paper. Sang along when Kaja, known for her strong voice, led a song. I read in the writings of an English anthropologist called Brown, the first white man to reach a cannibal tribe somewhere in the Brazilian forest, that the primitive men began to lick him as soon as he arrived. Later, he learned why: they wanted to ascertain whether he was truly white or whether he was painted. Establishing that he was not painted, they began spitting with revulsion. His whiteness was disgusting to them. By a host of subtle signs, I could see that the Visigoths were suspicious of Mihajlo despite his best efforts. He made every effort not to use a single unusual word, he spilled paint with the best of them, and with the humility of the faithful he listened to the sacred declaration of transcendence from Savina's mystic notebook. And yet, I could clearly see that they had licked Mihajlo, established that he was not one of them and were now spitting with revulsion at this bizarre intruder, an activist whose thoughts and intentions could not be read despite his pathetic willingness to swear loyalty on the same cross and Holy Bible.

"Ooh," I heard Savina say, with a complicated expression on her face (disgusted, pitying, cautious, inquisitive, dismissive, surprised, envious – she could conceal nothing, unaccustomed as she was to the dictates of polite behaviour). "You misery, you, red as a Kraut!"

They were right. Mihajlo in his madness was doing all these things that were as foreign as Eskimo to his white-skinned nature. He combed his hair with stinking seal oil because Eskimos liked the smell; he dressed in the skin of the caribou and suffered, ashamed that he had not been born in Labrador. The Eskimos, however, were not fooled. Even when he had advanced within their activist hierarchy and become, I assume, somewhat more important than Savina, nothing changed. He went on being the self-effacing intruder while Savina, carved of a single block of stone, was genuine and confident by contrast. So confident and aggressive in his political quarrels with me, when he was in their company Mihajlo stuttered and groped timidly for the seemly thing to say, for when he should laugh and when he was supposed to be serious, for what was orthodox and appropriate, and what would disclose his bourgeois nature or, far worse, his half-English background.

Well, this is when my pitcher cracked. It could no longer fetch water.

I must stop. I am not far from the black smudge of our lives. I can see it from here, and I know that this time I will step forward into the ink blot, even if it dissolves me. Take a deep breath. Hold your nose. Jump . . .

SEVEN

April 1945

My dear deceased Rachel,

I have no-one to write to. And write I must. Even if it means repeating myself what, obviously, is not for anyone else's ears. Even in my own ears, believe me, it sounds unreal. Like some stupidity: I became Patrick Walker's lover a month after Stevan introduced us.

I will try to tell you all that I know about how it came to be. I will try to understand and explain. I do not promise. I am not sure I will succeed. But I must try. For it is not plain and simple.

I believe it all began even before I met the Englishman in such a way that the world completely changed overnight. But I won't speak about that. That is a long story. Now that is not in my focus. That they barged into our flat, that Stevan and Mihajlo went mad, that everything turned topsy-turvy in a sense which I do not comprehend.

I got off on the wrong foot. I will not seek excuses for myself, and the way I began, in the end I would have only something along those lines. That I do not want.

It did not, therefore, begin earlier. It began when I met Patrick in our flat in a shambles. Stevan brought him with no warning, though he had asked me earlier whether I was willing to translate for the British embassy. I was willing. Why not? Four years I had been doing nothing. I was desirous of any sort of work. I was glad and I could hardly wait for them to call me. Patrick came for us to meet and he brought immediately a document which Ambassador Stephenson wished to have in good English for official use. I remember well what it was. It was the text of the expanded Vis agreement between Tito and Šubašić, which I should translate into better English. It was a bit peculiar to us because a little earlier Stevan, too, began his work precisely on this same agreement. I quickly agreed with Patrick about everything which was related to work, and then he stayed on, for he brought us real tea, which we hadn't drunk for four years, so I invited him.

I was excited, not with Patrick, but rather – it seems to me that I am not lying – because I was speaking English with one who had just come from there. I did not wish to admit to Stevan, Rachel, but since the terrible battle began for Britain, I was (otherwise so sceptical for the English) extremely proud of my countrymen who were fighting so bravely. Even, sometimes, I was ashamed that I was not there, though I knew that my place was by my son and husband. And so, perhaps, when Patrick was here, across from me, I was excited that he was telling me about the war, about England, the current shortages there, my country about which I had only been hearing over Radio London in secret for four years.

Patrick, before he entered the diplomatic service, was in the Royal Air Force, but in 1941 he was shot down and taken prisoner. Then in 1942 he escaped from Camp 2001. For that he received medals, but he was wounded and could no longer fly, so he returned to civilian service with the rank of squadron-leader. All that, Stevan had told me first, and from Patrick I heard the same later. The first day he did not speak about that. I asked him that day how England looked now, and he said after a little thinking, "Sad, I'd say."

Then he described, at length, to a detail, how he found the time, just before he arrived in Belgrade, for the first time to go to the palace in Barley where he grew up. That palace was built by his great-grandfather on his mother's side, whose name was Peregrine, I have forgotten the last name, so that he could hold orgies here which Lord Byron used to attend upon occasion. Patrick, somehow softly and thoughtfully, spoke nicely of how that building looked before. First a large iron gate at the entrance to a park which was considered the best example of Georgian ironwork in England, between two pillars on which were Peregrine's falcons, that is how they called them, and then one took a long driveway up to the palace in Palladian style which was not so large but built so perfectly that someone called its architecture "frozen music". Now when Patrick came, the iron gate had been melted down during the war, some drunken soldier, probably, with his Sten gun had shot off the falcon's wings and shot them full of holes, the drive was overgrown with weeds, the pillars cracked, the windows smashed, some were boarded over, others had gaping holes, of the three turrets two had been knocked down, and in the end Patrick, when he passed by the house, saw that only the façade was still standing, and that the back wall was half missing, and inside only rubble and collapsed beams.

Here Patrick stopped and explained, "Well, you asked me what England looked like nowadays. Sorry to disappoint you."

I really loved the way Patrick said it. He did not put feelings into his description, and even less did he show off, but rather he made an effort for us to see the picture as precisely as possible. He did not want us to feel sorry for him or for England, but rather to see how it looks today when it is described with a few words. Stevan said something about how the English would build it up again, and Patrick agreed that they would, indeed, rebuild a great deal, but not Sir Peregrine's Palace. And it was, for him – half of England. He meant that as a joke, but you could see that he was romantic and that in his words there was grief and reality.

That is how it began. You see, nothing particular. I really did not judge him as a man then at all. Probably I noticed his appearance, but I paid it no attention. Patrick, after all, is not handsome. He is not ugly, but he is not handsome. Medium height, brown-haired, thin. He cannot entirely bend his left leg, which one can barely notice, but you see when he sits. And when he lies down.

We saw each other rather often. I went to their embassy and we would work up a translation together, or I would translate something for him on the spot which was important. Once when we had been translating for a long time, he suggested to me that we go for a walk. I acquiesced, why not? We went off by tram to Topčider and walked around in the snow from the underpass to Hajduk Fountain and back. Later we often went to Topčider, and even further, for walks in different directions, wherever the paths led.

Then I thought that it was only a nice friendship, and I knew that I liked Patrick enormously, but not as a man. I wasn't thinking of that, though I did notice how I liked to see him more and more and be with him. Patrick has some traits which I had never discovered before in a man. He talks so peacefully and seriously, and looks at you always straight in the eyes, and never is it at all unpleasant. I never from the first day turned away my eyes from him, which I otherwise do more often than I'd like. Somehow, immediately I felt that I did not have to hide from Patrick, that I could tell him everything. I was very surprised, returning home alone, that I could tell Patrick that, too, and there you have it, I told him everything, how I married Richard and divorced him immediately. I even told him what I never told anyone. Not even you, Rachel. Not Stevan. That I did it because on our first night married he admitted that he was a homosexual and that was why he could not sleep with women.

I did not believe that I was telling him this, but, again, I heard myself and felt that I was doing it without pain, because most of all the people I knew he is able to listen. I cannot say precisely how – attentively, yes, but without curiosity, so that you see he has understood everything, that without explanation he sees everything precisely the way I wish to present it, that there cannot be those subtle, barely describable misunderstandings which are able to confuse to the bottom a person's powerless words. Once I told him that there could be no perfect crime if he were the investigator, because even the most hardened trespasser would admit what he had done.

"You don't feel like a trespasser, I hope," he asked me gravely, and then I was able, laughing, to say, myself, "No, I don't. I feel more of an investigator myself." Which was true, for it was probably so easy to tell Patrick the most intimate secrets because he created the impression that he, also, was hiding nothing, that he responded to confidence with a candour which quelled even the greatest shyness. I think that it was his reason. Patrick always understands everything. And goodness. For Patrick, somehow you know that he will be able to forgive everything, for he considers that all which happens to a person is human. He knows that it is not easy to live, and he knows that life is not stable, for he learned that in the RAF. I remember his stories about a plane which went up in smoke 5 metres from his, and in it friends with whom he had been drinking beer the night before till all hours. Even when events from my life were the subject, he seemed to understand them better than I, and explain them more readily.

Did he know before I did that I wanted to go to bed with him? Did I know it myself, somewhere behind my reason, before I acknowledged it?

Maybe. Now I could say that I was only cleverly pretending, and that, maybe, it wasn't so very important. For instance, I never told Stevan that I went to Topčider. Why? Then I thought it wasn't important, but now I think that maybe I was beginning to feel some guilt, which I slyly hid from myself. One more thing tells me that it was that way, and that for a long time I was not innocent. I never asked Patrick, for instance, how old he was, and for a long time I did not think about why it was I wasn't asking him, though I knew I was interested in learning this. One can deceive oneself rather dastardly. As I did. I knew, you see, that I am older than Patrick, and clearly, I did not want to hear this. Not that I am older, and not how much older I am. I am 39 now. Closer to 40. I think that Patrick is still closer to 30. Then I was thinking something: if I was not thinking of him the way a woman thinks of a man, but rather only as a friend, why would it matter to me to keep from learning what the difference in our ages was?

However, if I did manage to trick myself in terms of my attachment to Patrick, I knew very well that this attachment was not small and unimportant in my life. I suddenly understood that this is not merely work with a cordial colleague and conversation with someone intelligent, but that Patrick had become for me a need, an essential need. Really. When they come barging in, as Stevan calls them: the Huns and Visigoths, when Mihajlo is rude, when Stevan comes full of stories about the Communists, when I am alone in the kitchen, when Housemaster Ruža forces me to attend conferences, when I am sitting at the conference – I can do all of that because I am thinking that tomorrow, or in two days, I will be with Patrick. Nothing more. Just that. There, I think that I could no longer survive understanding nothing, with all of them staring at me. For Patrick it was normal that I am an Englishwoman, with him I speak English which both of us know best, that we are not talking about Grol and the People's Front but about, for instance, cheddar which they haven't got even in England right now. We had a little English plot to escape from the Serbs, into our language, to curl up in it as if in a cloud all our own and to crouch in there. I remember, as a child, we played a game which we called Royal Tent. We would make a tent out of a blanket, or a bedspread, and we would crawl into it so the grown-ups couldn't see us. When I am with Patrick at the office, or when we are on the Topčider tram, or in a meadow, or when we are drinking "Šumadija tea" in some café, always I have the impression that the two of us have hidden in the Royal Tent, that we are safe and that no-one can do anything to us. And truly we most often were playing. For instance, precisely as we did thirty years ago in the Royal Tent. Patrick would tell me the new English abbreviations, and I would guess what they mean. Doing that I saw, a bit sadly, that I am no longer an Englishwoman.

"What is a DSO?" asks Patrick, and I do not know.

"And a DFC?" and I don't know that one either, and he explains to me that those are decorations and medals.

"What is, what is," we continue the game, "what is an ARP helmet?" and I guess: "Air Raid Protection helmet!"

"Right! And an MOI poster" – I cannot guess that one.

Then Patrick teases me: "You'll know this one: IEYCT."

"What on earth is that?"

"That's simple: I Enjoy Your Company Tremendously!"

We know that this is silly, and that is why we are not ashamed, for all the time we are laughing at our silliness in that game of the English rehabilitation of one unsuccessful Serbian woman. Why shouldn't we play? But – constantly we must not forget that after the game begins life: that the game is to catch the breath, and not replace life, which makes it even more attractive and, though one might think the opposite, even easier. We, Patrick and I, speak always softly. And we laugh softly, when we are alone, and even more softly when we are in a group of others. We actually have nothing to hide, but still we have some sort of secret of our own. And the secret is that we understand each other, and we always understand things differently from how they do which we do not show them, but we inform each other, without words, over radio antenna. Everything, for instance, which seemed very Serbian to me earlier, I would observe, and then I would mark it down for myself somewhere, and store it away in my mind. Now, when Patrick, too, is in Serbian company, and I notice some behaviour, thought, trait which is very Serbian, I immediately know that Patrick noticed it, too. I look at him secretly and I see that this is true. This is a conspiracy which delights me greatly: I am no longer alone.

Only with Patrick can I talk about the Serbs, and right at this time that is very important as it was no other time before, because I understand my life among them less and less, instead of more and more. Patrick here is very reasonable. He doesn't love or hate Serbs. He wants to understand them, and he does.

"You find here dishonesty and punctiliousness, grossness and delicacy, avarice and handsomeness, coexisting in the same person. Almost every day I meet statesmen who practise extremes in patriotism and in peculation not at different times, but on the same day, brutality that took torture and bloodshed in its stride and suddenly turned to the tenderest charity. Surely this means that not only you, but anyone brought up in a surrounding as different as English, cannot pretend to understand them always, and always well." He comforted me, when I would complain, but he also explained why it is so, in reasonable terms.

"They are not yet familiar with the circumstances of urban life. It could hardly be otherwise, since forty years ago there was not a town in Serbia the size of Rockford. The Yugoslavs can't be blamed, therefore, if they haven't worked out a tradition of conduct to fit those circumstances. Urban life takes a deal of learning. When the Industrial Revolution dawned in Western Europe, the Serbs were still Turkish slaves. To this day 87 per cent of Yugoslavs are peasants. Indeed, the middle class in Yugoslavia is so near its peasant origins that everyone you meet has a shepherd or a ploughman for a cousin or nephew."

I knew all that, but it was so reassuring, so awfully good to hear it from someone else who thought as I did, alone and always only for myself. Patrick was for me like a spa, a warm bath after a hard day, a nanny. I entered our Royal Tent as if it were an English sanatorium. I would come refreshed, able to survive, from a distance and the heights, to look on with understanding. I was no longer the one black sheep in the herd. There were two of us. I was not sure how Patrick, especially at the beginning, looked at me and what he received from me in exchange. One day, for instance, he told me, while we were translating at the office, that he could have a car in the morning over the weekend, and that we could go on an excursion to see some monument. Fine, I understand that, he needs a guide, so we made all the arrangements. Then, the day before the excursion, Patrick unexpectedly had to come to our house to pick up something which I had translated. Stevan and I afterwards drank tea with Patrick and talked about everything – but Patrick did not mention with a single word to Stevan about our excursion, or invite him to join us. And then, the next morning I lied also. I told Stevan that I was going to the embassy to translate, but we went to Oplenac to see it. Then, when I came back I justified it to myself like this, remembering our morning excursion: Stevan would have misunderstood, we would have to explain to him what we understood with no words, that we certainly could not have had the conversations we had if we had had to keep in mind the Serbian feelings of my husband. Stevan, of course, is closer to me than Patrick is, but not in that English, or English-Serbian, field. For instance: while we were looking at the mausoleum of the Karađorđevićes, Patrick asked me, "But why did this King want to hold up an encyclopaedia of medieval Serbian art over his family vault? It sounds to me as if an English King had built a mausoleum full of allusions to Richard Coeur de Lion. Is there any real continuity between the medieval Serbian empire and these present-day Serbs?"

An ordinary conversation, commonplace curiosity, but Patrick could never have spoken that way in front of Stevan, nor could Stevan have accepted it as readily as I did, but rather he would have worried, to justify and explain everything, always guilty and obliged before all his Serbs. It would have been even worse if Stevan had been present at our conversation with one of the priests, with a black, huge beard, with black vestments, whom Patrick later called Rasputin. He offered to help us when he saw that we were foreigners and that I am speaking Serbian, but to my surprise, and it would have been to Stevan's horror, he said quite seriously and candidly, hearing where we were from, that he hated the English.

"Ask the priest why he hates the English," asked Patrick, and I translated for him what the priest said: "Because he says that it was Sir George Buchanan who started the Russian Revolution."

"Buchanan! English ambassador to St Petersburg in 1917?"

"Yes," I said.

"But surely he thinks that perhaps Kerensky and Lenin had a little to do with it?"

"The priest says," I translated the priest's answer to Patrick, "that's all nonsense. How could paltry men like Kerensky and Lenin do anything like starting a revolution? It must have been someone of real influence like Sir George Buchanan!"

We could barely keep our serious expressions before the priest, but then afterwards we laughed like crazy, which we could not have done with Stevan, who I know full well would have been extremely uncomfortable, because he would feel a little that we were laughing at him. That is how Stevan is.

So I deceived myself, but in the deceit Patrick took a conscious part, as well, though both of us pretended not to know. I think that Patrick was also lonely in Belgrade, and that he genuinely enjoyed being with me. I think that, maybe, he wasn't thinking, at first, as I wasn't, that we could be lovers, rather he simply wanted to be with me, alone, without Stevan, who would complicate things, without ill intent, and would destroy our little innocent English conspiracy in the middle of so Serbian a Belgrade. Perhaps, all in all, we were less clever than it seems to me now.

I know, however, when it crossed my mind that the relation with Patrick is not so innocent as I wanted, and long believed. The occasion was unimportant, but, still, a spark flew. Patrick was talking about the visit of a Serbian politician to the embassy, and describing it, he said that the politician had obviously thought their secretary to be "bedworthy". I had never heard the word before and suddenly I saw that it had embarrassed me. So I said, "Shame on you! What a pretentious male word!"

After my exclamation both of us fell silent – and I knew then without a doubt that we were thinking the same thing. Or, at least – about the same thing.

Was there in Patrick's feelings towards me pity? Did he feel, as full of soul as he was, full of understanding, that I was begging a little English love in my Serbian isolation? I am inclined to believe that. Now even more than at the beginning of our romantic liaison. That he finds me "bedworthy", if he does, was not the initial impulse for our closeness, or for our affair. Sex was something which happened along the way. Sometimes I think that we went to bed – funny, but true – out of conventional reasons. It was done. The sex was merely a confirmation, on the side, of our closeness and attachment, not the reason we were together. I do not know how to describe it precisely, but our sexual act resembled the ceremonial drinking of tea in China, for instance, or a church wedding ceremony. Or the thesis defence of a candidate for doctor of science. I am not joking. Both of us were so considerate and careful not to trespass on the strict rules which, in a way, were more important than the game for which the rules formed the framework. As soon as we are done, we immediately get dressed, feeling more comfortable later dressed and in conversation. The laughter which brought us close in Oplenac, the intimacy we feel in conversation, in translating, is much greater than in bed. I would say that in bed we are more – how can I say it – polite, reserved, than in talking; when we exchange surreptitious, conspiratorial glances; when we explain to one another events which mean the same to the two of us but something different to everyone else. I can imagine Patrick saying to himself when he thinks of us, "Sex with Elizabeta? Well, why not if she wants it that way," not out of frivolity, not cynically, but rather – out of pity, understanding, nobility.

It seems to me that this is precisely how it is. Otherwise how could I accept someone's love out of pity, without being humiliated? Patrick gives of himself to me because he is the only one who sees the magnitude of my isolation, but he is wise enough, and clever enough, to declare, without words of course, a very important aspect of our relation which both he and I must always be cognisant of: that the affair is temporary, that it is a great, mutual pleasure, but that it must end, perhaps already tomorrow, leaving us undamaged and more able to continue our different and distinct lives.

I know that. I never thought it could be otherwise. I know that Patrick knows it, for he would never acquiesce to get involved in an affair – I am surely that dear to him, and he is surely that sort of man – in which I could lose far more than I am getting temporarily.

For a long time, the longest, actually, the only thing I could not speak with Patrick about was my greatest torment, about Mihajlo, though I felt that he could see what bush the rabbit was hiding in, the only lethal wound, and that he skirted that field with courtesy – an experienced warrior – because he knew it was mined. Patrick has often tried to lead me into such a conversation, for he thought, and justly so, that talking might help. I evaded it. For a long while. Now I know that I was resisting the most valuable thing I could receive from Patrick. He simply led me to see with different eyes, realistically, not maternally, hysterical like a woman. Without sentimentality, without unnecessary, yet inevitable, sensitivity. Seriously, thoughtfully, comforting me, he showed me Mihajlo's swift exit from adolescence, and the path on which the healing of our relationship will begin, which I already knew, yet, impatient, insulted, was ignoring. However, Patrick always warned me of something that in my bewilderment I had forgotten: that I must reconcile myself to my fundamental state, for I cannot leap off the train on to which I climbed so long ago, and so determinedly. Instead of understanding Mihajlo's adaptation as betrayal, he described it as a victory which he had to win: "Michael had to take sides with the Serbs who were constantly afflicting you with their strangeness, who made bitterness of your exile. Otherwise he would have been in exile himself. It's a pity you don't fit your emotions better into the framework of their society."

"I try, though."

He kissed me on the forehead and said worriedly, "You have to try harder, old girl."

So, there can be no doubt. I am where I am. My place is here. There is no return for me. I knew that myself. That is why I accepted the rules of our little temporary conspiracy because they were for me – not for Patrick – the only rules that made the conspiracy possible. That is why Patrick's merciful answer to my plea as a fellow countryman is a gift which did not diminish dignity, but rather deepened my knowledge of the greatness and the depths of possible human intimacy.

Intimacy which excludes no theme from conversation but excludes misunderstanding. My Stevan is good. Generous. Honourable. Everything which I have that is good, I got from him. But this intimacy, this he was not able to find. Or I was not able to bring it to him. I don't know. Perhaps because we grew up in different countries. It is not our fault. We tried. It didn't work. And that is why I am entranced by the fact that I can talk about everything with Patrick. I don't even have to talk, and yet everything that we wanted, without shades and double edges, we convey.

We are sitting in the tram for Topčider, surrounded by poor people wrapped in rags, hungry. The two of us are sitting there as if we come from another world. We talk, without awkwardness, without a single unuttered thought, on a theme about which lovers who are less close, yet in our situation, would not dare even consider: about my visit to London when Patrick's term of duty ends in Belgrade. For years I have not wanted to go to England. I went only when I had to. Quickly, as quickly as I could leave it. Now, however, I want to go to that devastated city with the sad pictures on the front pages of magazines. I tell Patrick without restraint of all the places I would like to visit, and Patrick informs me, as far as he knows, whether they are in one piece or eradicated, about my trip to Reading to visit cousin Archibald; about walks around the demolished Trafalgar Square and a visit to the preserved British Museum and the National Gallery, a concert at the Albert Hall, a glass of porto in a pub in grimy Soho. We even speak of details. We know that it could be at the end of this year. Patrick knows how he will see to all the formalities and what should be undertaken in order to leave Yugoslavia without a lot of fuss.

But – the whole thing while we are planning, the way children plan their Christmas holiday, we know full well – without a single word – that my visit, if it comes about, will be the end, a lovely ending, to our affair, and by no means the beginning of something new. Our affair is a Belgrade affair. Governed by Belgrade. Entirely impossible beyond it. I know that without a sting of conscience or nerves, without feeling hurt or bitter. I may go to England with Patrick. But it is certain that I will return – as from the excursion to Oplenac – to Stevan and Mihajlo. For ever.

What I will tell you now, Rachel, is strange, but, believe me, it is true: I feel no guilt, before my son or before my husband, that I had the affair with Patrick. Even when I want to present myself in a bad light, I still do not feel that I am hurting or dishonouring them. Somehow it seems to me that I have some profound and ancient right to my end of life – for an end to both life and world is what we are talking about. That feeling of cataclysm is the soul of my romance amidst the devastated natural environment. I know that I will bear up under Patrick's departure cheerfully, I know it completely, though without our meetings, whether romantic or professional, I cannot survive right now; I am as dependent on them as a drunkard is on alcohol. In the Royal Tent I am healing my wounds, garnering strength, getting advice, and with Patrick preparing a lasting balm for my lasting wound.

I lost a son. I got Patrick. Patrick, too, will go. Soon. But not before he makes me able to live without him. Patrick is something transitory. Damned good, my dear Rachel, but with a miserable clarity, my dear, I know that Mihajlo is not. That Mihajlo is my very constancy. That is the trouble. That is a great void. Patrick, Stevan and I can briefly assuage it. But Mihajlo is the only one who can fill it, when he returns. Patrick knows that. There can be no deception. Patrick is a drug, he eases the unbearable pain, but he is not the cure to make the pain disappear for ever.

Stevan, sure. And Patrick, too. But – my dear deceased Rachel – the true word is: Mihajlo.

EIGHT

Whatever could be eating him – merciful Lord? Why should his half-Englishness rankle him so! And if it does, why can he not let it be and leave his poor mother alone?

This is where my pitcher cracked. It could no longer fetch water.

The impatience and inflammatory nature of my polemics with Mihajlo had grown with time into rancour. But my anger at Mihajlo turned to unfatherlike hatred because of his behaviour towards his mother. Towards addled, silenced Elizabeta, whose only fault was her British birth!

You drove me mad, Mihajlo! There is a limit to how much pressure a person can bear. If he succumbs, the pressure must have been greater than the stuff he's made of. He should never have been exposed to such pressure, if the intention was to keep him human. You did not consider that, Mihajlo. I obviously could not sustain the pressure.

I do not know, Mihajlo, when it was and why it was that you began to loathe your Englishness at the moment you were leaving boyhood, as if it were something shameful, like mange on your Serbian skin. But from that moment, panicked and obstinate as only you could be, you strove to become a Serb in all you did, whether it be stupid and beneath you, or reasoned and worth your while. English saw your tempestuous rejection as an adolescent stab at adapting, finding safety in numbers. Your urge to excel, your love for clearly articulated positions, your loathing for ambiguity, even the modesty that made you so uneasy about your glaring differences perhaps explain your behaviour, but they certainly do not justify, morally or otherwise, the forms it took at the close of the war, my Mihajlo. I am sorry, my son, but so it is.

One of the memories I have longed for years to forget is of a quarrel I had with Mihajlo on March 29th, 1945, at roughly 8 in the evening, after a simply awful day with Elizabeta.

It was horrible, and it was like this.

I met Ambassador Ralph Stephenson as soon as he arrived in Belgrade, even before he presented his papers to the royal officials, Budisavljević, Mandić and Srnec, only a day or two after the Temporary Government assumed authority with Josip Broz as President. Dr Budisavljević had asked me, probably because of my knowledge of the language, perhaps because of my pre-war acquaintance with the English ambassadors Nevile Henderson and Ronald Campbell, to make myself available to this ally who had just arrived in a strange land amid the uproar of war. I only met with Ambassador Stephenson once or twice after that, in part because it was not necessary and in part because I was cautiously attempting to avoid, in those crazy times, possible suspicions aroused by my English connections. My wife, my studies abroad, my association with pre-war British ambassadors, my acquaintance with Prince Pavle, all of that, of course, was in the distant past, but it was not wise to give the Communists and OZNA, the secret police force, any additional grounds for suspicion. Elizabeta and I, however, frequently saw one of Stephenson's aides, Patrick Walker. Having learned that my wife was an Englishwoman who had mastered Serbian brilliantly (and she truly had, during those war years), he asked me if she could help to translate the more important Serbian documents into English, and official English correspondence with our authorities into Serbian. I said that she could, but to be on the safe side I informed Grol, the Vice Premier, and Pijade, neither of whom saw anything unseemly in that support to an allied representative. Elizabeta therefore often went to the British embassy to do the work they needed, and Patrick would come to our house to pick up the translated material or bring new texts. He was a dear man, and we loved to talk with him unofficially. Especially Elizabeta. I may be mistaken, but it seems to me that in her behaviour I discerned a certain excitement, almost a girlish thrill, not only in learning details about English suffering during the war but, I would say, because of the simple fact that she was speaking English, after such a long hiatus, with a genuine Englishman recently arrived from her abandoned (but was it forgotten?) homeland. Who could begrudge her that satisfaction? It was as if we were stepping into a warm room out of a snowstorm whenever we left the Visigothic surroundings and embarked on a conversation with the congenial, solicitous Englishman who made no secret of the fact that he enjoyed our company. He was probably lonely, too, in Partisan Belgrade. Patrick, who had access, at that time of scarcity, to the diplomatic warehouses, never visited without some treat, the flavour and fragrance of which we had almost forgotten – English tea, coffee, chocolate for Elizabeta – which lent our encounters the charm of luxury. In more ordinary circumstances, this might have been unimportant, but in those days of terrible privation it was nearly irresistible. In a word, it was agreeable with Patrick – like before the war, as Elizabeta would say, among other things because tactful Walker took special pains never to draw us into political discussion, he never asked anything which might be awkward for me to talk about with an English diplomat, and he never brought Elizabeta a translation that anyone from either of our governments couldn't read.

Of course, Mihajlo couldn't have known all that, for he walked by Patrick, whenever he found him in our house, as if by a Turkish tombstone. He was quite put out that we maintained relations with the man at all. What was this Englishman doing in our home! Why not go to England if we were so taken with the English! We were welcoming an imperialist spy in our house, conferring with him. Had we ever considered what sort of motives he had in visiting us? Were we sure that he would not attempt to co-opt us? Will others believe that he had not done so?

I calmly explained that Patrick was no spy, but indeed one of the Allies, and that he was not visiting our home to enlist our services but for cooperation. This much Mihajlo was able to hear, but he was incensed by my statement that in these last few years, at least, it had mattered less that the English were imperialists, more that they were the people who bore, heroically, the greatest burden of the Second World War on their shoulders. In the dedicated Partisan hymn book, naturally, the war had been won entirely by the great Red Army and Stalin himself, while the thinking, and even what was being said about the English, the Americans and the other Allies, as the war was drawing to a close, was, first secretly and then openly, that they were slated to be future enemies. There was no way for me to respond to Mihajlo's insinuations of that sort other than with fury. Once again, I did not hold my tongue. I reminded him of the disgraceful Soviet pact with Nazi Germany in the days when England was left an isolated, yet invincible fortress opposing Hitler's attempts to gain control of the world. As always when faced with an irrefutable argument, Mihajlo found the always applicable Communist solution. In a Communist Party proclamation in 1940, Tito had declared that the war had been started by the English and French imperialists attacking Germany to preserve their colonies – full stop. It didn't occur to Mihajlo that this lie was the consequence of the vassaldom of the Yugoslav Communists to the Russians, who were then in love with Hitler. The quarrel, therefore, proceeded as did all of Mihajlo's and my quarrels, but at this point, for the first time – regrettably, Mihajlo, you yourself know that it was not the last! – our son went one step further. Before he slammed the door and flew, enraged, out of the kitchen, he said to us, "Just so that you know – if that spy sets foot in this house one more time, I will report the whole thing to the authorities."

Had he not fled from the kitchen, I most likely would never have said anything further to him about this. Just as we two, Elizabeta and I, were left there like two dogs whose hind legs had just been broken by someone, we fumbled, whimpering, around the kitchen, tidying up something on the stove, shifting some books from one spot to another, unable to say a word, afraid that, if one of us were to look, he would see what the other was hiding behind their eyes. In tormented silence, we strangled the thought that would have explained our son's threat. We swallowed Mihajlo's statement, and tried to take comfort in the fact that he had spoken in anger and impetuosity. Over the next few days, we felt in our stomachs and our heads that it nevertheless prompted ravaging, destructive feelings. They were far too strong for me. For the first time, they had banished me to a silence beyond words just as, I assume, they had banished my Eliza, similarly, some time earlier, to the dark cave, the last haven in her misery.

Elizabeta's response to Mihajlo's obsession, unlike my aggressive behaviour, was to retreat, to flee from the cruel battlefield in which she could not distinguish between sides and opponents. She did not understand the reasoning of the defender or the attacker; she understood only that she was no longer able to understand or explain. She would follow the quarrels between Mihajlo and me in a knot, but mute, as if they were gory tennis matches, looking panic-stricken from me to him and back again while the two of us exchanged our unfatherly and unfilial fore- and backhands. She would not champion my side nor caution our son against his pigheadedness, but by the same token she never defended Mihajlo's disregard or tried to represent it as anything other than it was.

At first, I wanted to make her an ally in the battle for the reason and dignity of our son. "Why won't you help me," I asked her. "Why won't you say something to him? Can't you see where he is headed, what he's doing?"

Elizabeta usually did not respond to my appeals. She hugged herself in fear, and each time she would retreat one step further into her cave, from which all I could still see were her two frightened eyes, anxious, green, the eyes of a wild creature sensing the nearness of a storm . . .

This was no longer like Elizabeta's earlier silences, her passionately preserved reticence. Confident, always sure that she was doing what she meant to do, Elizabeta's secrecy had been a cloak over her lavish body. She didn't conceal it as something worth preserving because of its vulnerability, but rather because it was a beauty that she was not inclined to share lightly. In a word, Elizabeta's earlier secrecy, behind which you could always sense her superiority (perhaps this was the very thing that caused me to hurl myself at her romantically, and jealously, for years, generally without success), had turned into an asylum that she discovered within herself, where she crouched like a bedraggled turtledove, fearful and disconcerted in the Visigothic empire of her son. All my attempts to nudge her towards speech, speech to heal the trauma through which she had been going during those first days after liberation, failed miserably. She did not want, dare, wish – how can I know? – she probably did not know what to say.

"I don't understand any of this," she would say sadly. "I don't understand you Serbs at all."

"What don't you understand, Elizabeta? Tell me, maybe we can figure it out together."

She wouldn't respond. Only once did she try to explain. She did not think that anything essential had changed in our political habits since 1925, when she had first arrived. When I said that she wasn't entirely right, that before the war there had been some rules which could not be broken, she shook her head, listlessly enumerating examples of Serbian political unreliability. She reminded me of wild Puniša Račić, of Aleksandar's declaration of martial law, of the arrest of Maček, Korošec, of arrests made on someone's personal whim; of the beating of ecclesiastical dignitaries ("Can you imagine such a thing in England, in France? Imagine four bobbies beating the daylights out of the Archbishop of Canterbury in front of his cathedral, before the eyes of thousands of the faithful!"). She even remembered one of Father Milutin's tales which I had completely forgotten: the radical constitution of 1888 had foreseen the independence of the judiciary, yet Aleksandar Obrenović had suspended the Constitution for a single hour, at midnight, and during that hiatus had signed decrees under which he retired or transferred all his opponents, installing supporters in their stead. As soon as he had done this, the Constitution was reinstated in its full validity. My taciturn Englishwoman kept all manner of things in her lovely head. I have to admit that I had forgotten that ploy of Obrenović's though it was indeed true.

"Stephen, you yourself said that politics is merely an alibi for the Serbs. Politics is not the cause but the effect. Can you imagine having something like the expanded AVNOJ Council anywhere else, in Sweden for example? Something far deeper than political reasoning determines the shape of your political behaviour. Just as it does for the English, and for every other people."

"If all this is so, why are you fearful now, but before the war you weren't?"

"Before the war, it was enough to stay out of politics and a person could evade their clutches. Now they have come into our home uninvited. Every house. They have taken our child."

Elizabeta felt that far deeper than I, that politics had taken our child. It wasn't that she felt it in her head or on her tongue, where my own hissing started, but rather in organs which did not heed reason. In her womb, her heart, her glands. I could see that Mihajlo's anaesthesia of reason and behaviour was temporary. Elizabeta, however, felt his cruelty as a blow to the stomach, especially when she was dealt it for being English. Without asking her and hearing her answer, I knew that this was what hurt her most. She stopped speaking English. She learned Serbian as if she were Serbian herself, having changed her citizenship. What more could she do to return her mad and evil son to reason? I knew how Elizabeta must be feeling when Mihajlo threatened to report her to the police for associating with English people, but precisely because I could see the unfeeling way he gouged her living flesh, I was incapable of comforting her, of easing Mihajlo's terrible brutality. How could one explain away, show in a better light, a son's wish to report his parents to the police? What words of comfort were appropriate to such a misdeed? What could I say to her? Knowing that I was off the mark, I tried to convince her that there was nothing to fear for she was working with the English with the express consent of the highest echelons of the Communist government.

"Yes, yes, naturally," she would say vaguely, willing me to stop lying, to end my clumsy attempts to shift the focus from the node of her pain to a sting from without.

We were in a pitiful state on the evening of March 29, 1945. Taciturn, gloomy, we were sitting and reading, or rather were making a pretence of reading, when into the kitchen burst a Partisan (the Huns generally left the front door wide open and had managed to ruin the doorbell) with a ribbon tied round his sleeve, therefore an officer, though I do not know what his rank was, clutching an order from Slobodan Penezić, head of OZNA, the secret police, summoning Elizabeta to his office.

Not believing that she had understood the message, Elizabeta asked, "Me? Summoned by Penezić?"

"You are Elizabeta Medaković?"

"Yes."

He grinned jovially. "Yes, you, summoned by Penezić. Why the long face? Comrade Krcun is no scarecrow!"

Elizabeta turned towards me, not frightened so much as baffled, as if to plead with me to take things into my own hands because she didn't understand our position or the new obstacles on our horizon.

"Do you have any idea why Comrade Penezić wishes to see my wife?" I asked, unsure myself.

"Comrade Krcun didn't say."

"Are you certain that the summons was not addressed to me?"

"Yes, I am sure of that."

Elizabeta looked at me, unblinking, away from the friendly Partisan.

"May I go with her?" I asked, miserably.

"No. Comrade Krcun did not mention you. Don't you worry about a thing. I will bring the lady back."

Elizabeta looked up, the Partisan grinned, and a terrible helplessness suddenly overcame me. Whatever could Elizabeta have done wrong? And besides, if she had done something, the Partisan certainly never would have referred to her as a "lady". I was undone by helplessness as I sat there in the kitchen for there was nothing I could do. Elizabeta, divining my helplessness, turned to the Partisan and acquiesced. "Wait just a moment while I change."

For the two hours Elizabeta was away, I eased the crushing silence in our flat (as if to spite me, even the Visigoths weren't there; I longed for their company) by recalling the stamina with which Elizabeta had borne the pressure of the Gestapo during the Occupation. Each night before she went in to report, I would see her to the door, unable to avoid the nagging question: Would she come home this time? Elizabeta would go off calmly, unusually intent, cognisant that she was an Englishwoman and even, I wager, proud that the fascists wouldn't leave her be.

"So what if they detain me," she said coolly to me, beside myself as I was. "It can hardly be worse than it was to be in London during the bombing."

Always reserved towards her fellow countrymen, during the war she was unable to conceal her pride at their heroism. When I voiced my admiration, particularly at the outset of the war, she loved to hear it, though she would respond with true English understatement. "Yes," she would note coldly, "they are rather well organised at pulling people from the rubble."

Or: "What else can they do but clench their teeth and bear it?"

Or: "Right you are, they do no worse than anyone else would do in their place."

Trying to deceive myself into believing during those two phantasmically quiet hours in our empty flat that Elizabeta's stamina would guide my Englishwoman out of this quandary, one part of my mind must have known that the nightmare of the Occupation and this one with the police were hardly similar. The Germans were enemies to the British mind of my Eliza, of course, and what does one expect from an enemy other than threatening behaviour? There was something soothingly proper in the fact that the Gestapo would bring her in, but – I rebelled against this observation – there was something shameful in it when OZNA did the same. The faith that the tyranny of the enemy was temporary, a faith without which we could never have survived those four years, magnified the defiance of the humiliated in all of us, even Elizabeta. There was something human and heroic in being on the Germans' list of suspects. I was incapable of seeing how ugly Elizabeta's present position was by comparison. My Eliza will stand firm, I said to myself, wandering aimlessly through the rooms of our ravaged flat. She has borne up under all manner of things, and so she shall again. I repeated this, knowing all the while that though her character was as hard as crystal, it was as fragile as crystal, too. Mihajlo had smashed it to bits with a cudgel, leaving emptiness and shards.

That my hopes were in vain became clear the moment I caught sight of her entering the building from the street. Opening the door to the front hall, I heard her step and knew that whatever had transpired on Kajmakčalanska, she had not borne up well under police treatment. I wanted to help her with her coat, but she walked straight past me into the kitchen, sank down onto the stool, dropped her purse into her lap and remained motionless, staring fixedly at the floor.

"What happened?" I could not bear the silence.

"Just a moment, Stevan," she said, staring at the floor. "I will tell you everything. Leave me be for a minute."

As if the last two hours had been the straw that had finally bent her back, always so straight, or perhaps this had happened earlier but had escaped my notice. The words "She is beautiful" flitted through my mind; crushed inside, but still harmonious without, her body still strong, in colours which were still enchanting: her flaming, neatly combed hair, her complexion the hue of a peeled almond, her eyes green like deep ice. "She is beautiful," I said to myself, and felt at that moment such love, such a painfully strong attachment to my Eliza that it compared only with my blinding desire in Bristol. For a brief moment, but with a marvellous tangible vitality, I was overcome by flashes of our twenty years together, merging one event with another as one does in a dream, a sort of blur which had a meaning of its own, illogical yet real, stemming, no doubt, from my disorientation, which welled up and reduced me to racking sobs, to a spasm of rage and misery. I watched her out of the corner of my eye, so lovely was my Elizabeta, bent over slightly on her stool, and I could see her, slender, sitting tall on the bar stool at the Glengyle Inn, but whether that had been before Christ or yesterday I couldn't have said. Had it been seconds ago that white-skinned Liza, my illicit lover, had sneaked her hand into mine, or had that been in another life, buried under the sediment of daily minutiae? It is I, I told myself, who am responsible for the fact that my foreigner, brought so thoughtlessly to Serbia, has been exposed to undeserved abuse. I, a helpless Serb.

I knelt before the stool, hugged her and kissed her face. "Tell me, Eliza."

No, it wasn't that they had maltreated her. Yes, at first they had been most kind, they had tried to create a pleasant mood. They had made little jokes about her fear. Then they left the room, and the only one to remain with her was Major Kovačević, who wasted no time, proposing to Elizabeta, indeed demanding, that she report to him personally, verbally, on all the translations she did for the English mission, and all the conversations, both private and official, that she conducted with Patrick Walker.

"No," said Elizabeta. "I will not do that."

Then Major Kovačević abruptly stopped being polite. "You, I see, are on their side! So I thought!" he said, pacing round the room.

"Did you deny his accusation?" I asked Eliza.

No. She had not. She had kept her silence until the Major, probably prepared for her response, came out with the second of his three demands. "In that case, you must cease cooperating with them. Fabricate some reason. Illness, exhaustion – you will come up with a better lie than I can."

Since Elizabeta did not respond to that proposal either, Kovačević stopped in front of her and asked, by this time stridently, "So, what is this?"

"I will speak with my husband, and then I will decide," said Elizabeta. Kovačević then switched to "ti" and used vocabulary which Elizabeta did not wish to repeat.

"He was vulgar," she said.

"And then?"

"He came over to the armchair where I was sitting, planted both his hands on the arm of the chair and shoved his face into mine. He particularly wanted to make certain, apparently, that I remembered what he said: 'If the English learn you were here, I will arrest you. I am sure you understand that.' He hated me. Sincerely, from some non-policing, human depth. His last sentence – 'You may go' – was so drenched in loathing that I – foolishly, I do not know how to tell you this – felt unloved in a way that made me sad, humiliated. I could have cried. I did not, of course.

"The friendly Partisan was waiting for me in the corridor, now grim and obdurate. The change in his behaviour was so apparent that I knew in an instant that he had overheard the entire conversation. His leaving the Major's office was merely a ruse. Who knows what it was calculated to accomplish. They probably thought that I would be more likely to consent to be a spy before a single witness than before a handful of them. I don't know. I stopped in front of the friendly Partisan, confused, without thinking, though he looked away as I approached. He misunderstood me, thinking that I was expecting him to drive me home again. Somehow I knew this was no longer possible. He did say, gruffly, 'The car is busy. You can walk.' He did use 'vi'.

"At least he used 'vi'. And that, I thought, says something. So I left. On foot. Now I am here."

Here she was, still in her coat, sitting on the kitchen stool, relaxing into my arms and staring at the floor. I knew that it would not be a good idea to talk about what to do next. I was certainly not able to consider the facts soberly, nor was Elizabeta. Let her sleep on it, I thought. The morning is wiser than the day.

"Are you hungry?" I asked, to mark a temporary end to the conversation.

"I could eat," said Eliza, looking up at last.

There are times when it seems to me that people's hands and minds don't get them where they are, but rather their amazing capacity for adaptation. A person can bear all manner of things because he can get used to them. What might seem unbearable when you imagine it becomes ordinary in reality. That is why distance matters. Reality is something you need to get used to, and that takes time. I was not particularly pleased with these ponderous thoughts, but I also did not underestimate their utility. Something needs to be done, I said to myself, so that Elizabeta can put this evening behind her. Tomorrow, all the evil in this world will seem smaller, as will her doubts that there is a way to escape it.

The room was chilly because I had been awaiting Elizabeta's return to stoke the stove and warm the barley frozen in a blue pot, but the gaiety of the fire and the fragrance of the warming food made our kitchen seem much more cheery when Elizabeta came back into it than when she had left. She washed her face, put on a warm housedress and looked better than she had done a moment before. I decided to keep our conversation away from the unpleasant event, and Elizabeta was glad to talk about the day's news, bread coupons and the allotment of matches. She fully regained her sense of calm, and I also did. The kitchen, now cosy and quiet, began to seem quite a safe place, protected from people and the world, a place in which a person could survive, grow old. Inundated by a wave of nearly unbearable tenderness and self-pity, I took Elizabeta's hand in my own and looked into her eyes, wishing that we could exchange, wordlessly, support and the miserable remnants of our former security – but my indomitable one did not wish to. She looked resolutely at the floor, diving back into the darkness of her cave.

At about 8 Mihajlo arrived. Chilled. Wan. Expressionless. There was absolutely no way, none whatsoever, that we could have divined in his appearance or his bearing what it was that he was carefully hiding from us: he had volunteered for the Army and would be leaving the next morning for the front at Srem. Even before this, when we had been closer and had understood each other better, I had been hard pressed to divine by signs of excitement, gesture or words any secret he was concealing, and this was certainly the case now, when my son nearly had become a stranger to me. During those mad days, I found it difficult to connect in any real way that red-headed, maniacal, cruel boy with the greasy Tito's cap on his head, hard expression on his face and incomprehensible words with our son in earlier years. What was this smooth-chinned commissar doing among us? Who was he anyway? That evening, as I watched him furtively, I was unable, despite consider-able effort, to see the whole person in him. If we were unable to divine his intent to catch the last train for his place in the company of heroes, if we had no notion of the fact that only hours separated our mad child from his departure into a war which was nearly over, and for that very reason was gory, horribly gory, wastefully indifferent to the loss of young lives, the only raw material headquarters had in abundance, Mihajlo could not say a word to us that would divert the evening, our last evening together, from its mindless course. How could he have told us he was going off to war when he knew that we would have done everything to thwart his crazed plan? That evening was, it seems, fated to happen as it did; perhaps it was written in the stars long before.

"Take a plate," said Elizabeta to Mihajlo. "Dinner is still warm."

The two of us read. Mihajlo ate. I, at the head of the table, Elizabeta across from Mihajlo. All that I could see was that he was hungry and, perhaps, dispirited. Was he? I wondered, looking at him over the top of my book. Or was he only tired? Or – I hoped – perhaps somewhere in the depth of his obsession, maybe he felt a little guilty towards us? Maybe there were passing moments when he was unsure, perhaps even anguished, about the extremes in which he was indulging so fervently. Maybe there was at least one droplet of murky doubt at the bottom of the clear well of his unquestioning commitment? Did he wonder, perhaps, at times whether the great goal of changing the world was possible to realise with Savina and our foolish and deeply committed building superintendent, Ruža?

I knew, of course, that our son had not reported to the police his mother's forays to the British embassy and Patrick's visits to our home, but rather that the Major's attempt at recruitment had been devised elsewhere. For a moment, I was suddenly overwhelmed by curiosity – I remember the moment precisely – when a question went through my mind: Would Mihajlo have been ashamed if I had told him where and how Elizabeta had spent the evening? Would he have felt a need to justify himself, to convince us that he had not said a word to anyone and that the summons to OZNA had absolutely nothing to do with his earlier threat? My possibly childish and vengeful desire to punish Mihajlo, my son, our child-warrior, with the news of how Elizabeta had been taken in grew stronger and stronger, and the only reason I managed to suppress it was because I didn't know whether Elizabeta wished me to discuss it or not. At one moment, I caught her gaze and saw that she had read my question in my eyes but could not decide herself. She quickly lowered her gaze to her book, leaving me to resolve what to do. I understood her lack of response as approval, so I asked our son, "Mihajlo, did you tell someone, anyone, about Patrick Walker's visits to our house?"

He started and looked first at me and then at his mother, immersed in her book.

"Or about Elizabeta's cooperation with the British embassy?"

He answered, his hackles up, "I did not," and went on eating.

"You told no-one?"

"If I said I told no-one, I told no-one! Why do you ask?"

"OZNA interrogated your mother today about those matters."

Here I am, Mihajlo, my son; here I am, Elizabeta; here we are, all three of us, on the brink of the black smudge, on the shore of Acheron, which it has taken me twenty years to cross.

I said to Mihajlo, "OZNA interrogated your mother as regards this question today," and I can remember how even at that moment I was galled at the intrusion of the clumsy phrase "as regards this question" from their vocabulary. Elizabeta is wrong when she judges my manner of speech to involve putting on airs, to be "flowery", whingeing. I could not have spoken differently. I could not have been the person I was, at that time, had I acquiesced to the then current manner of linguistic interchange, abbreviation and grammatical blunders. Language was not given to man so that he could ask for his slippers or to have a bit more tea. Through language, we, each in our own way, show our spirits, immortal in their uniqueness, contained in the manner, more than in the subject, of our speech.

Once I had spoken, unsettled by the intruding jargon, Mihajlo's spoon stopped in mid-air, and, quite agitated, he turned his tense face, relaxed until a moment before, to look at Elizabeta. Elizabeta, however, did not lift her head from her book. She read. All we could see was the top of her head and a bit of her brow. We could not divine the thoughts or feelings behind it.

Maybe that is why Mihajlo got up, threw his spoon into his dish and began pacing around the kitchen with his large, Partisan-like stride but, I'd say, genuinely frightened, silent because he still didn't know what to say. Did he feel remorse? Would he apologise? Start making excuses? For a while he did nothing, and since I did not wish to ease his position in any way, spiteful as I was, I, too, returned to my book, leaving my son to his troubles but curious, more and more curious, to see how he would extricate himself.

What did happen was something I had not foreseen. Instead of regret or at least a dark, taciturn admission of guilt and remorse, instead of consoling his mother and easing his conscience – a bloodthirsty, merciless onslaught on Eliza's already dangerously wounded sensitivity! Well, she couldn't say he hadn't warned her! Did she have even the slightest idea where she was living, who she was and with whom? He,

Mihajlo, would have said nothing against the OZNA police if they had gone ahead and arrested her instead of just interrogating her. This was a revolution, not "four o'clock tea!" Who had time for fatuous bourgeois manners, who cared a fig for what she did and did not say to that nasty spy who would just as soon restore the monarchy! The lady was free to choose: either she could live with this people and for it, or she could go back to the English. There was the door, what was she waiting for!

Mihajlo didn't spew out this tirade in a single breath. It took time. Mihajlo blasted insults at his mother while pacing agitatedly around the kitchen, pausing only in order to redouble his cruelty and fury. It lasted long enough that I recovered from the first blow and then was struck dumb, staring appalled at the impassioned young man, white as chalk when he was silent and thinking, then crimson as he howled at his mother, shaking that didactic finger of his at the top of her head, the veins bulging in his neck. Still blinded by hatred, I noticed something which brought it to its zenith: Mihajlo was relishing his role, fancying himself in some sort of novel, in a revolutionary legend; he saw himself as important, fanatically dedicated to a goal for which he was capable of sacrificing everything, even his own mother. I also noticed, when I turned to look at Eliza, helplessly, several times, how she was staring the entire time at her book, reading, and didn't dare raise her eyes to see what she was hearing, to see what she would not be able to bear. Then the moment came when I no longer saw anything. I did not hear. I did not know. I did not think. Later, I would recall that I thumped my fist on the table and howled, "Shut up!"

And though Mihajlo, caught off guard, had fallen silent, once again I howled, "Shut up!"

Even that was, evidently, not enough. With those two howls, I had not expelled the murderous energy accumulated during Mihajlo's speech. I flew at him, grabbed him by the shoulders and thrust him up against the wall, still blind to what I was doing but able to see, at least, Mihajlo's face, only a few centimetres from my own, terrified, or astonished, or both, vacantly white and baffled. Then, unable as I was to control myself, the sentence burst out of me. I didn't hear it as it gathered in the darkened realms of my constricted mind. Before it shook our kitchen like a dull explosion, I had no notion I would say it. I heard myself, in a voice not my own, say, in English, quietly, "I wish you were dead!"

There, that is how it happened. Here is the masked, darkly held memory, returning with vigour, physically tangible, magnificently visible in the clear morning air of our dimly lit kitchen. Every bit of it I remember, though I wanted, for so many years, to forget it. My thoughts, but also Mihajlo's face, and Elizabeta's scream, and the silence, both weighty and hollow, settling slowly like leaden dust, stirred by my howl, on three people snared in the most wretched moment of their lives.

Elizabeta's scream was brief because she stifled it by clapping her hand over her mouth. Was it that I seemed, appeared, genuinely deranged? So much so that Elizabeta believed that these were not mere threats, that I was not simply venting spleen with rhetorical flourish but rather voicing a threat I meant to act on? Language, the English language, is a part of Elizabeta's body. There is practically no distance, for her, between meaning and expression, so it is possible that to her ear the threat had an impact that was diminished for me on its way from English to my native Serbian. Was that why I, oddly clear amid the bedlam, chose to release in foreign English, into the four walls of our kitchen, these terrible son-murdering words? I don't know. Or did I do it so that Elizabeta would understand me better, fully grasp the lengths to which I was prepared to go to protect her, her and her Englishness, even against our son's harangues if I had to? Another possible explanation for the stifled scream comes to mind. It occurs to me that Elizabeta wanted to smother it so swiftly with her hand, before it pressed her distress into the open, because she was afraid that in its fullness it might disclose something that she was hiding, whatever that might have been. It may well be, furthermore, that Elizabeta had seen, as had I, our alienated son, bloodthirsty attacker, as dead to her, gone, at least in metaphorical terms, vanished, maliciously replaced by a stand-in, her scream exposing, in a sense, thoughts which she had been unwilling to admit even to herself. Or did Elizabeta scream (but why, then, stifle it with her hand?) to drown out my words on their way to Mihajlo's ears?

In any case, if her intention was to shield her son, she failed. Sobered, as if wrenched from my stupor by what I said, first by its sound, then by its substance, I began to discern the incredible sequence playing out on that face barely a foot from my eyes. Fear, astonishment, the sudden realisation of the profundity of my hatred, something of that, or, more likely, all of it together, simply shattered the Partisan, revolutionary decorum of Mihajlo's expression; the muscles of the lower part of his face sagged, giving his smooth-chinned, chick-like, boyish face an even more childish look. Gone was the troublemaker, gone that intruder who had taken the place of our son; I sought him frantically but found only Mihajlo, recognisable at this moment for the first time after so long, the offspring of our marital bed on the eve of his heroic departure for the Army. With eyes wide open, I saw a boy who was wretched at the thought that he was losing the support he had always assumed to be unconditional. I read in that awfully close childish face the fact that its owner was cognisant of the lie of his behaviour, but convinced that I must understand it, that in the ultimate reckoning of our relationship I would see him as a son whom I would forgive, whom I must always forgive, especially for his need for independent growth and maturity, no matter how mad it might seem to my parental eye. Could there actually exist something which my father would hold against me for ever? he seemed to be asking. He looked as if he were on the verge of bursting into tears. I, your child, may use words that way – said the face, exposed, helpless, lacking decorum – but you, my parent, may not! A person mustn't (even if a child brazenly does) fundamentally demolish his son's sense of security! This is no longer a game. This is real. My father – really – hates me!

The expression I read, printed on him as if on a sheet of paper, I have never forgotten. Never. Not even when it seemed I had isolated it in a darkness opaque even to the most penetrating gaze. It has always been there. The expression of a frightened, mortally wounded child needing protection. Unskilled at hiding anything. Pliant as a woman. Not a grimace of misfortune, but misfortune incarnate.

I had no idea that this was, in fact, the face of a warrior readying to leave the next morning for the battlefield, that I had wished my son to his death before he went into combat. At last, shaken to my core, I dropped my hands, with which I had been pinning him to the wall, and stepped back as if I had seen a phantom and not our Mihajlo. I may be wrongly reading my thoughts, or Mihajlo's, or Elizabeta's scream, but I remember the actions and the words with perfect accuracy. I was backing off not because I meant to flee, but because I was incapable in a few short seconds of forcing my hands into a loving embrace. If only I had! If only I had been able to do at once what I longed to do! If Mihajlo had not flown from the kitchen only an instant before I had the chance to approach him, filled with guilt, to plead for his forgiveness, the memory of the unfinished encounter of March 29, 1945, no matter how horrible, might be a bit more bearable. But it is not. It rots, unbearable, stinking in my belly. How is it possible – I wonder without hope whether I will ever know the answer – that the evening of March 29 happened at all? Who was toying with us, stripping us of our reason and, as if that were not enough, giving it back to us when we could no longer right any of the preternatural, hideous wrongs committed in the throes of madness? How was it that during the months of watching the rampage of our 18-year-old scoundrel – not any old scoundrel but my very own, our one and only scoundrel – I hadn't been able to see through to the vulnerable heart behind the rough façade until my son himself showed it to me, appalled by my murderous ferocity? I had a desire – belated, I admit, but sincere – to go to his room, not to justify myself but to speak the truth, and in a voice more like my own, paternal, calm, reliable, to say, "I wish I were dead!" – because that was more or less how I felt, collapsed onto my stool, next to Elizabeta, who had still not taken her hand from her mouth, probably afraid that the scream would erupt again. I did not go, however. Why I didn't, I do not know precisely. Everything around me seemed ruined. Probably weariness. Exhaustion. Perhaps even a sense of discretion. Perhaps I thought it best to hold off until morning. The wound would have had some time to heal a little. And time – I thought, guiltless in my awful misconception – time, at least, we had plenty of; I thought this even as it was running out, even when its end was upon us. And yet, I recall that after a dozen minutes of choking silence I asked Elizabeta, ashamed before her perhaps even more than I was before myself and Mihajlo, "Should I go to him?"

"Don't ask me," she said in a still voice, in English, just as I had used English for my awful sentence, though at that time she seldom spoke English with us any more.

"Tomorrow I will," I said. "Better we sleep it off."

It was still night, that time of night when a person senses with a strange, animal-like sense rather than with sight that something of the pale light of dawn is spinning into the blackest darkness, when I heard Mihajlo roaming around the flat, obviously preparing to go out. We were used to his departures at all times of day and night, we no longer got out of bed but we always heard them. I knew that Elizabeta was awake, though she said nothing and didn't move, so I said, "Where is he off to now?"

Elizabeta said nothing. I lay in the dark and listened to the door close behind Mihajlo, every bit as despairing (I kept thinking there was no cause for it!) as if I had known that it was the last time he would do it.

Our Mihajlo left for the killing fields without saying goodbye.

What is a father's love, I often thought, too often – or, what is it in paternal feelings that makes them different from anyone else's? I do not know whether this is true of all fathers, but from the time Mihajlo was born I had noticed that I was not able to love him unconditionally the way Elizabeta clearly did. She had to make a gargantuan effort – I was witness to this heroic undertaking – to wean him from his easy, baby's feeling that there was nothing he had to do to be loved, that he was loved for existing. My love was never to be taken for granted. Even when it became truly paternal, it seemed to me that it became extremely demanding. I am not saying that this is praiseworthy, that it is not selfish. I am merely saying what I know that in my case was true. I am not, at this moment, in search of Justice. I merely swore to speak the truth about my experience. My son was, for me, first and foremost an extension in time over the border of my own death, and because he would be walking the world in my stead, I wanted to see him shaped according to my character and my ideals. Elizabeta's love for Mihajlo was given freely; I had always known that he would have to earn mine (as I, his) by actions, by what he made of himself, and not by what he, helplessly and unconditionally, was. In the selfishness of paternity, which even today I do not consider to be unnatural, I wanted Mihajlo to be like me; let him be better than me, but in a way that I liked. Like every other profound feeling in the murky fogs of an individual's spiritual alchemy, even the feeling of paternity, of course, is never formed in isolation but rather it mixes with other feelings and invariably becomes impure. My hatred towards my son was the despair of a father's betrayed aspirations, but the tenderness I felt towards him at the moment when my murderous gaze discovered at the distance of a mere foot the vulnerability and helplessness of a child was most certainly unconditional.

Love is not a simple relation to someone else; it is always an attitude, a view of the world, a character trait. Even today, I am not ashamed of my dissatisfaction with my son, for in my eyes he was becoming the opposite of everything I valued in man's character and loved in man's soul. A son is that particle which from one age transfers to the next, from one generation to the next, not any thing, or even all that the father received from his father, ennobled and handed on, but precisely the most excellent qualities that define him as an individual, a nation, as humankind. Whenever I look at what I got from Milutin, I can easily find the thread that leads back towards some forgotten but implicit proto-witness and proto-parent. But when I look forward, all I see is interruption. I see a tree stump, I see a head, red-haired, severed from its body, and an executioner, his face hidden behind a black mask. Was this thread of our familial ties corroded and broken by this English redhead? Does Serbian salt combined with an English base produce poisonous acid? Are the matrices of social behaviour inscribed in the genes along with skin colour, meaning that the melding of two diverse systems was bound to create a smudge? Or do the contours of human behaviour take shape over time through influences, study and imitation, among others? Might the clash between genes and upbringing, upbringing and environment, produce in one instance a bastardised outcome while in another an enhancing one? Or was it that on that evening, March 29th, the time had come for everyone, and therefore for us Medakovićes, to reach a great hiatus, a new beginning with no precedents, a present without a past, a time for sons without fathers and mothers, a time for fathers with no heirs?

More easily than I ever dreamed I would be able to do so, here I am, confessing: when Mihajlo's friend Jelena from Dedinje came with the letter in which our son curtly informed us that he had been accepted by the Thirty-first Serbian Elite Brigade and that he was on the way to the Srem front, beside my fierce, maternal terror for the life of our child, that paternal monster of exasperation with the son who did everything backwards and differently from the way he should swayed in my stomach. The one and the other at the same instant and in the same man. There are all sorts of things in a person, oh strict, unknown judge, and if you truly know human nature, then no single evil thought lurking behind the granite brows of humanised bipeds will surprise you!

"Did he go alone? Without anyone he knew?" I heard Elizabeta asking, after the first shock, and Jelena answering, in a forced, cheery, comforting tone, "Of the ones you know, Predrag and Nenad are with him. You know them, my neighbours, the Petkovićes."

"But they know nothing of war," I said. "This is lunacy!"

"For more than two months, they went, every day, to military training."

"Yet we knew nothing about it. How could he not tell his father and mother such a thing!"

"Uncle Stevan," Jelena began, as if speaking to a child, "you know what you would have done if you'd learned what they intended to do, don't you?"

I had to bite my tongue. She was right. As soon as she left, Elizabeta and I began to plot how to get him back from the front, though we knew that it was not easy, and probably not even possible.

My political position – the lackey from the very start, therefore extremely uncertain and humiliating – was at that time even more shaky. It would be five more months before I would give my famous speech about Yugoslavia's vassal-like relationship to the USSR and about the arrogance of the Russian allies, who were behaving as if they were in charge, so irate was I that I felt no fear. They did not even arrest me then, but they did everything else: I ceased to be a professor and a doctor, they assigned Major Šiljak to live in our flat, and I became, overnight, a national traitor and imperialist spy. At the moment when Mihajlo went into the Army, however, they still needed me, so they kept me on, for precisely the same reason that left me so vulnerable later. They knew that the English would hear my words and honour them. So they left me to prattle on, to flail about, knowing that I could do nothing against them. They knew, but so did I, and yet, driven by Mihajlo's orthodoxy as an ox is driven by the sting of the whip, I sank deeper and deeper into a battle with Communist self-complacency, ever more lonely amid the growing mob of impassioned and intolerant supporters. From Savina in the flat, to my son in the youth leadership and Ruža in the street command of DUND, to the presidency of AVNOJ and the Provisional Government in the Green Hall of the Assembly building, every political or other form of opposition was greeted with greater animosity. In all manner of ways, they informed me, still cordial but no longer amicable: we are the one, the chosen, people who crossed the Red Sea, the proletariat, the victors; you are the other, the bourgeoisie, stripped of authority, former people, suspicious and slated for imminent execution. I sought the opportunity to speak, though I was warned at the outset by shouts in the hall that my appearance would not be met with a better reception than it had been elsewhere. No matter what I spoke about – the partitioning of the Sandžak, the exchange of Occupation money, control over speculation, personal freedom, the privacy of the home and the posts, confiscation of property, expansion of AVNOJ into new councils, the plot in Parliament which I, in a reconciliatory tone, referred to as "chance procedural errors" – it was always with the same, minimal goal: to bring them to reason, to draw their attention to the laws older than the ones the Russian hordes had brought with them out of the forest and were teaching them. But the agitated representatives of our wild people would shout, embittered by my very appearance, "Don't give him the floor! Down with him! Down with the traitors!" I would let them shout, and with the reluctant support of the chairing Communist, I would generally manage to say what I had come to say.

Even worse were the public meetings to which they dragged me in order to keep up the appearance of the National Front as a coalition of different parties. Then, behind my back, they would agitate for the audience to insult me, green with hatred, and spit on me – once they even poured shoemaker's dye on me. One time, only a few days before Mihajlo's departure for the front, when I was walking through a crowd of people who were being settled in the Vojvodina, I was hit several times on the back and shoulders with a stick, most painfully in my jaw. Looking back, I can say that I did not, like Mihajlo, have bloodshot eyes from lack of sleep. Quite the contrary. Always fresh, I set out on my official duties; I did not, as he did, cultivate dirt under my fingernails, but always went meticulously dressed in my best suit among their rumpled neglect. As if I had arrived from another planet, I did not shout or, like my son, wag my finger at them, but, quite the contrary, spoke softly and reasonably from the podium. And yet, I do not know who was the madder of the two of us Medakovićes! I, who was in it out of spite, or he, who was the genuine enthusiast. I, who wanted to teach the plebeian mob about mutual respect and democracy, or he, who wanted to merge with that same mob. I, in the highest echelons of government yet with no authority, or he, on the bottom rung of the ladder with Savina and Ruža, but often with all the authority of the world! And yet, once some settlers (raging at the suggestion that I supported the King and was against the requisitioning of wheat and its distribution to incomers) beat me up, I resolved, humiliated, to do nothing useful, to disembark from the Yugoslav political train (I should never have joined it in the first place) and to leave it to roll along its merry way under a crazed momentum all its own. Even more firmly resolved after Elizabeta's rough treatment at police headquarters, I had to retreat from my decision on the day and evening when Jelena brought the letter. A lovely girl, Jelena, intelligent, open-faced, perhaps our ill-fated daughter-in-law, she was right: Elizabeta and I read the letter, instantly, as a death sentence on our son which, through intercessions, threats and intrigues, in any way we could possibly manage, we had to convert, if nothing else, into a life sentence in prison!

I do not know why I settled on Moše Pijade, but I do recall that I began my beggar-like traipsing from office to office by visiting him. Chances are it was because he was the first person I ran into in the corridors of the Assembly building and managed to sequester in a corner, pleading for a moment of his time on a strictly personal matter.

"Not now. Are you going to be at home this evening?"

"Yes."

"I will send my chauffeur round as soon as I have the time."

The chauffeur arrived around midnight, when Elizabeta and I had lost all hope that he would come at all, and he drove me to Pijade's villa up on Senjak, which had previously belonged to a barrister, the vice-president of the Socialist Party, Aca Pavlović, who was now serving a ten-year prison sentence in Mitrovica Penitentiary. I had been there before the war as a guest and to visit Pijade two or three times, but always in his lower office. Now, however, as soon as I greeted Pijade's wife Lepa Nešić briefly, he took me to his upper office, next to his bedroom, which he, the least slept of all the New Yugoslavia's revolutionaries, used for his nocturnal work, interrupted by only two or three hours of sleep. He had ordered that he was to be awakened as soon as I arrived, but he showed no sign of grogginess when he walked over to me briskly, his hand extended in greeting. The room was lit only by his desk lamp, so most of it was in a homey semi-darkness that made Pijade seem softer and more accessible than he did at official meetings and at the Assembly. Seated at his desk, he said gravely to me, across from him in an armchair, with no formality or hostility, "Please proceed, Mr Medaković. I am listening."

Until that moment, I had felt that it was of paramount importance simply to reach Pijade and have him hear me out. I believed, foolishly, that there are few things in life more natural than the desire to rescue one's son from a place of danger. Racked by my uncertainty as to whether Pijade would be willing to consider my plea, I never for a moment considered that there might be something untoward about it. I knew that I must be skilful, not too inflexible, making every effort to preserve my dignity and independent position throughout, so stubbornly fought for on the podium, as well as in my personal polemics with the Communists, yet not too pliant and grovelling, so that he wouldn't think I was willing to sacrifice all I believed in return for the help I was asking. The moment, however, that Pijade spoke those words and settled more comfortably into his chair – he, clearly lit, I, in the semi-dark – once I had said that I was there to make a request, suddenly the words I had been meaning to say seemed inane, impossible, undignified; stripped of every logic by that rat-like little man facing me across the desk who considered his own life worthwhile only inasmuch as politics benefited from it. In a sudden state of total lassitude, amid the warm semi-darkness of Pijade's office, it struck me how impermissible it was to plead for a humiliating, unheroic favour in that epic, heroic time! It seemed impossible because I realised something which I had foolishly neglected to see: other sons, of other fathers, had been sent, either drafted or voluntarily, into the massacre; the Germans, Ustasha, Circassian fighters would not leave the country of their own volition; many people near and dear to the man facing me had already been killed in this war. And were still being killed. That he most certainly would not have done for his own son what I was asking him to do for mine. Why mine? Why shouldn't he pull someone else from the front? Why Mihajlo?

I barely kept myself from leaping to my feet, thanking Pijade and leaving without even telling him my request, but then I knew I would have to spit it out or die with it, in part because of that gratuitous, unconditional mother's love for her child, more (later I understood this), I confess, much more because of that malicious intolerance of a miserable father with betrayed hopes, guilty for wishing his son, rhetorically or sincerely, it makes no difference, nothing less than his death at the watershed moment when he hated him. How to live with the terrible sentence if the desire it voiced were to happen? What if he were killed, and I had done nothing to prevent it? How to mend what that sentence had rent in my son, in Elizabeta, in me, if Mihajlo, alive, had not given me the opportunity? It was selfishness, yes, selfishness that gave me strength. In part the selfishness of a father who wanted to keep his son alive for his own sake, but in larger part a blacker, uglier desire to save myself from the Furies of my conscience, which would, should Mihajlo die, tear me limb from limb.

"My son, not even 18 yet, volunteered to join the Army and was sent to the front at Srem. I would like to ask that you have him returned," and bowed my head, expecting the worst.

The worst, however, did not transpire. Pijade was clear in his answer, but certainly not obstinate or insulting. With a quiet voice in which I even detected some sympathy, he said that he could not do that, and that he probably would not do it even if such a decision were within his purview. This was perhaps the final battle of this war, but someone had to win it, so I must clench my teeth, like so many other fathers, and hope for the best. Seeing that I went on sitting there in silence, my head still bowed, he asked me after a pause, "When did he go?"

"Two days ago."

"To which division?"

"To the Twenty-first Serbian Elite Division. The commander is General Majo Miloje Miljoević. The Thirty-first Brigade, First Battalion, Second Company" – I rattled it off, hoping that Pijade might, after all, be able to do something.

"As far as I know, a major battle is about to happen, a breakthrough on the Srem front in the next few days. The axis of the central thrust will run from Mohovo on the Danube to Tovarnik. It is unlikely that your son, novice that he is, will be a part of that. Head high, Mr Medaković. In no time, he will be back, astride his white horse, home after a month."

Calmed after this conversation, I realised that perhaps Pijade had not been the right person to go to, that I ought to have gone much higher in the Communist hierarchy. At the peak of the pyramid stood Broz as the indubitable, widely acknowledged chief. At the second tier were Ranković and Kardelj. The third was somewhat broader, where Žujović, Hebrang, Kidrič and Đilas stood shoulder-to-shoulder. Pijade stood somewhere below the first seven, an expert on all questions, deciding on nothing. Proclamations, the systems of the first, second and third AVNOJ, laws before the Constitution, the Constitution and then subsequent laws, the federal publications from the major trials, the granting of and denial of pardons – those were his works, but he did not hold a seat on the Politburo. On my way home, I divined that the unheroic decision to pull a soldier from the front lines could only be made by someone sovereign in his authority, someone who would dare to require that the military headquarters fulfil his command. I could not reach as high as Tito, Ranković or Kardelj. In a bad moment, I resolved to try my luck with Đilas, but after the first words the Montenegrin spoke, I saw the depth of my error in judgement, the paltry nature of my petition in his eyes, his fury that I dared to request such a thing of him. Hurt, humiliated, I was able to see clearly that I would not be able to weasel my son's transfer, but I persisted nevertheless. As I pounded the pavement to their villas and offices, I accumulated more and more unarticulated rage, but had I been more prepared to analyse myself, I would have confessed to a strange satisfaction, the larger and the graver the insults that were flung at me. By the sacrifices I was bearing, the humiliations I was suffering, I was diminishing my own sin, expiating myself in my own and Elizabeta's eyes and accruing a small sum of capital which Mihajlo, when he came home and returned to reason, would value. After a dozen such visits, concluding that I had adequately humiliated myself, I resolved to cease my petitioning.

Did I do the right thing? Why didn't I go straight to Broz? Why didn't I ask my English friends for favours, when I knew that their petition might be far more effective than mine? Embarrassment? A sense of national honour? What sense of honour! What embarrassment could there be when faced with the prospect of my son's tomb! Did I conclude too hastily that I had been insulted enough and that there was no prospect whatsoever for success? Or – horrible to contemplate, but I must not suggest that it was impossible, my judge – was there a darkened part of my embittered world which malevolently wished that my son be left to fend for himself, and that with my honour and the futility of my attempts I was merely seeking an excuse for myself? To conceal my evil thoughts, my unfatherly vengeance, my murderous intent? The Furies, who never cease punishing those who violate the primeval unwritten laws against spilling the blood of kin, dog my steps with their chalk-white faces, three old hags with snakes on their grey heads, with black, bloody foam on their lips, holding a flaming torch in one hand and a whip in the other. They chase me, unbribable, all the way to the borders of Hades. They have sucked my blood, polluted my mind, turned me into a shade and cast me into the Underworld of our enclave so that even after death I will continue to pay for my guilt.

I fall short of answering these terrible questions or making a clear confession not because I wish to help myself, dead as I am, but because I do not know what I was thinking and feeling during those murky days, the murkiest, most troubled days of my life. Even from today's vantage point, it is through a mist that I see the contours of objects and people, while forebodings are every bit as tangible as thoughts and words, mingled to a point where I can no longer discern among them. Whatever I say about those few months of my life has been said. We were in a delirium. It might seem that we were resigned to our fate, resolved to follow Pijade's advice: to clench our teeth and wait.

We didn't have to wait for long. Mihajlo was killed between April 12 and 13, the thirteenth day after he left Belgrade. Near Tovarnik. Along the axis of the central thrust. Our mad little English lad.

The mists grow suddenly denser on that day, April 15, when the news reached us. I can no longer see much of anything clearly, so I am not able to comment on my immediate thoughts. From this distance, the best I can do is discern my movements. I was able to walk, and I had much to do, but I do not know what drove me in the desired direction and what feelings were nourishing my quickened activity. I said things, searched, arranged, but it was as if I was bereft of my true physical weight, as if I was afloat over the earth, as if a part of my consciousness had been sliced out by a knife. I cannot say what the words *son*, *death*, *father* meant in this new order of things. The best I can say is that it was fundamentally different from the previous order. If I see clearly from the vantage point of today, my conscience did not even bother me; I pushed away my guilt along with all other thoughts and feelings. I did what I had to do right then, without looking back, but only looking as far forward as I had to to see what was obstructing my path.

Few of those who fell at Srem were buried in cemeteries. Far more often, they were left in the trenches and scattered out on the endless fields that time would level and corn would overgrow. So many dead, so little time. Who could ever dig such large cemeteries! They would cover half of Srem! Today, they speak of thirty to forty thousand young men, but they have the honesty to admit that there is no way to be certain of the precise number. In any case, if you were resolved to bury your son yourself, you had to go to the front lines and fetch the corpse back to your house as best you could, if you had the good fortune of finding it at all. I set out on the afternoon of the 16th, thanks most of all to the wholehearted support of those very people who had curtly thwarted my attempts, only the day before, to save Mihajlo's life. One of them procured a permit for my movements at the front, another directed me to a war buddy of his at headquarters, a third, noticing my unsuitable city overcoat, lent me his military trenchcoat, still warm from his back, and then sent a soldier to my flat with a pair of German military boots. They decked me out like a bride, and I was so stupefied that I had no real sense of what was happening, where I was headed; I was not at all clear who the groom was to be at this bloody wedding, I felt nothing but the need to find the child and bring him to Belgrade.

Only half conscious of what was going on around me, I floated above the ground like a Zeppelin and found myself by a railway wagon packed with soldiers. A couple of boys, soldiers without orders, somehow managed to shove me in along with two other old men in Serbian peasant clothing made of coarse brown homespun, with fur hats. They put the older men side by side in the corner of the wagon, perched atop two crates slapped together out of roughly hewn boards which they had brought with them on their backs. They sat stiffly, their eyes bloodshot, no tears. The soldiers offered them food but they refused, with a barely noticeable shake of the head, wordlessly. With pity, the soldiers watched them, listless and speechless, incapable as they were of expressing even their thanks for the attention by which they were surrounded, but concern also registered on the smooth young faces.

"What was your grandson's name?" asked a boy who, judging by his accent, was a peasant from southern Serbia.

"Radisav," answered one of the older men.

"And yours?"

"Gliša."

"Maybe it is all a mistake. Maybe you will find them alive and well."

The old men were silent. The taller and thinner of the two started crying, shamefacedly, into his hands.

I was sitting a little way off from them, also in a privileged spot on the floor, by a side wall, so that I could lean back and rest. It was horribly stifling in the closed wagon, but I remember quite clearly, though I am not capable of explaining how this is possible, that I, hyper-sensitive as I am, found that the awful smells did not nauseate me, even when a blond soldier across from me started retching into his cap, until others let him hop over the bodies and stick his head out of the back of the transport. The train rattled along slowly. It was standing more than it moved. The soldiers fell asleep, one on top of the other, scattered haphazardly like ears of grain after a downpour. They snored. Broke wind. In their sleep, some would shout, then subside. It is my guess that the old men and I were the only ones awake. After a time, the young man asleep next to me stirred and sat up. He offered me bread and cheese. I declined with thanks.

"So where is your coffin?" he asked me, chewing, and it was only then that I realised: the crates the old men were sitting on were coffins to take their grandsons home in. Could I have been so dazed? Somewhat feverishly, I asked myself: Indeed, where was my coffin? What would I be picking Mihajlo up in? Slow, noiseless winds were wafting through my empty head, light as a hot-air balloon on my stiff shoulders. As if in a dream when you would like to jump up with all the strength of your legs but you can barely budge an inch, I began, suddenly sapped of my strength, to worry: how would I manage if that peasant wasn't waiting for me in Kukujevci?

Explosions suddenly erupted around the train. Orders, running, the soldiers all leapt from the wagon and threw themselves flat onto the embankment. "Come on, old man," my neighbour said to me as he scampered out, and the only thing to occur to me, dully, at that moment was: "Remember this. It is the first time anyone has called me old." I thought about that and didn't run out, though everyone else had already done so. The old men, I saw, were still sitting, motionless, on their coffins. Between explosions, I called out to them, "Where did you get those coffins?"

"In the village. Had them made."

"Can a person buy one?"

"I don't know, sir," said the taller of the two. The second man said nothing.

"How does he know I am a gentleman," I wondered, looking down at my Army overcoat and boots, and then asked myself again whether that Vidosav fellow would be waiting for me in Kukujevci, the pre-war milkman to Vladisavljević, a colleague of mine at the university.

In fact, he was running along by the train, shouting as loudly as he could, "Medaković! I am looking for Medaković! Professor Medaković!"

If I had been capable of amazement, this Vidosav would have seemed damned bizarre to me. He had received Vladisavljević's message thanks to Uncle Jaša's efforts, through the headquarters of the Twenty-first Serbian Elite Division. Vidosav had been in the vicinity of headquarters, or with the Thirty-first Brigade for three months now, ever since he had arrived at Srem looking for his own son, who had been killed back in January somewhere in the meander of the Bosut – he had never been able to pin down precisely where. All trace of the boy had been lost in some heap of corpses for whose proper burial there had been no time in the heat of battle. For a long time, he clung to the hope that he would find his son's corpse and bring it back to Beli Potok, at the foot of Avala. He kept looking, and as he questioned other fighters who had been in combat and local people, anyone who might direct him, he became a genuine expert about the graves and about the battles that had taken place in the bloody circle between Bapska, Šarengrad, Sotin, Orolik, Otok, Nijemci and Tovarnik. All who could not find their sons or grandsons were immediately referred to Vidosav, who, though no-one ordered him to do so, remained in the gory district, helping everyone to find their corpses since he hadn't been able to find his own. A weird calling, by any standard, but a calling much sought after and useful in those days.

A master, then, of his trade, he met me equipped with a two-wheeled cart and a single, scrawny nag known, contrary to her elderly appearance, as Girl, and a wooden coffin, which, longer than the cart, stuck out at both ends but was skilfully fastened with ropes. Realising that I was confused and clumsy, sharp-eyed Vidosav asked me the essential questions. Did I have the money to pay for the coffin and the cart he had rented, to which, thanks to Patrick Walker, I was able to answer in the affirmative. Walker had brought me fifty gold German marks before the trip and that had prompted me to collect some of the remaining jewellery and objects of value from around the house. For Nedić's dinars and Ustasha kunas had no value whatsoever. Then Vidosav asked what I knew of my son's death. It seemed little to go on – the brigade, battalion and company in which he was killed, that it was on April 13 somewhere in the area around Tovarnik – but experienced Vidosav was satisfied.

"Climb up, Professor," he said vigorously. "We are on our way!" The two of us with the old nag, Girl, in front and the coffin behind set out from Kukujevci into the mud and the darkness. It is about 24 kilometres from Kukujevci to Tovarnik, and under ordinary circumstances, with Girl and the coffin, it would have taken us about four hours, but a number of things extended our trip – or at least that is how it seemed to me – making it endless. The thick, slimy mud of Srem, first of all, and the black darkness under the cloudy and rainy sky through which only Vidosav's catlike eyes could find the way – all this slowed our progress. And beyond that, on several occasions we happened upon barbed wire, front-line trenches, ruts behind the lines, pits from explosions filled with water over which the cart wouldn't budge, so then Vidosav had to make great detours, cautiously sidestepping the minefields. Once we were off the dirt, but still passable, roads, we would invariably sink into deep mud, which meant that we had to get down off the cart and help Girl to drag the sunken wheels out of the slime.

Furthermore, Vidosav had a schedule of his own, according to which he had not planned for us to go immediately to the likely spot of Mihajlo's death. The only suggestion I managed to forge in my boggled, hot-air-balloon head, that we should catch up with Mihajlo's company and enquire where he was buried, Vidosav dismissed at once, so we proceeded to the hospital in Adaševac to find wounded soldiers, or nurses, or perhaps a volunteer among the Srem girls helping to bury the dead, and learn from one of them, at least approximately, where we should seek our dead lad. We reached Adaševac at dawn and set out to visit the houses where the wounded were bivouacked. We happened upon a wounded soldier from the second platoon of the Second Company of the First Battalion just when they were loading him onto an ox cart to transfer him to the hospital in Ruma, but he was unconscious, so though he had been in Mihajlo's company, he couldn't help us. But the nurse told Vidosav, whom she knew well, that the unconscious fighter had been visited the day before by another soldier, only slightly wounded, who was being treated in a classroom in the Adaševac elementary school. We found him. He was not from Mihajlo's Second Platoon, but he remembered Red. He remembered how he died. He couldn't say whether it was near elevation 141 or in front of Trunica salaš, or perhaps it had happened a little later, near Lovac. But their medical-corps officers, Comrade Bosa, had not left with the rest of the company. She had stayed in Ilinci at the Brigade post for changing bandages, and she would certainly know where Red was buried.

Back in the cart, we trundled along towards Ilinci. Comrade Bosa knew. How could she not know. Exhausted, she could barely speak, but she was filled with commiseration as everyone was, absolutely every-one – the soldiers, the peasants, the commissars, everyone whom I told that I was looking for my dead son. This Bosa even shed a tear, weary as she was from burying, but not inured to death and the sufferings of others. Bosa knew how I felt. She had talked with Mihajlo, for the first time, not knowing it was the last, right before the battle in which he was killed. Somewhere near the third trenches, where we broke through enemy lines. No. Not by bayonet or bullet, she knew by the wound: it was either a hand grenade or a shell. Young. Green.

"Unkissed," Bosa said, an odd word, which kept rattling, stupidly, meaninglessly, in my empty, inflamed mind all the way to Tovarnik.

"Was he afraid?" I asked.

No. No more than the others. Everyone was afraid. Every last one of them, even the ones with experience. At least as far as this tired girl who had been the last to hear Mihajlo speak was concerned, he was different only because he was a redhead. That he had schooling was no longer so strange; many like that were coming now.

Crouching, Bosa leaned back against the wall of the spacious village house where the Brigade had set up its bandaging facility; the two of us, Vidosav and I, said nothing. She was struggling with exhaustion. Around us bustled mostly peasant women who were bringing food, linen sheets to use for bandages, woollen socks for the men who still had legs, or helping with cleaning and washing. We could hear the moaning of the wounded who were being carried in and out on stretchers, the shouts of the people handling them. Flesh, rotten human flesh, bloody, dismembered, was everywhere. The healthy had moved on to keep killing or be killed, leaving behind them mangled fighters and pathways and roads strewn with rotten and red human flesh.

Bosa finally, wearily, stood up. "I have to keep going."

She explained to Vidosav where Mihajlo was interred: in a gully between Tovarnik and Lovaš, we would see a grove of acacias, beneath it . . . That was enough; Vidosav knew the spot. Once more, Bosa turned to me, once more she repeated the sentence that was threaded through her story like an apology, like a musical phrase that divided the oratorio of death into rhythmically equal parts: "I know, Comrade, how it is."

At that moment, for the first time since I had heard of my son's death, I felt guilty and worthless. In a few short moments, like an electric shock, a bitter, murderous awareness of some unnamed guilt struck me in the middle of my brain, the thought of paternal unworthiness, a sin for which there was no repentance; a murderous force that quickly dispersed in my empty head, fortunately granting me temporary mercy now that it had warned me that it was there, alive and dangerous, and ready to torment me.

On the road to Tovarnik we passed columns of ox carts transporting the wounded. They lay there motionless and gory, moaning when the carts trounced into holes in the road or turned, joggling them, stacked like logs. Nurses in Partisan uniforms and girls from Srem would hurry over to the carts and rearrange them in the positions they had been in, encouraging them. Man is an animal. He gets used to anything. I was already inured to the scene; it seemed ordinary to me. Oxen, or cattle, dragged carts loaded with rotten or bloody flesh, which despite being mangled was still alive and aware of itself. And then all of a sudden, a sight appeared that was entirely extraordinary, incomprehensible. Carts were passing full of crippled, twisted creatures. Some were lying, others had lifted themselves up a little, on an elbow, or the side of the cart; somehow they were all holding on to each other, helping each other. They looked like complicated human sculptures, like a composite living arrangement. And – they were singing! Out of tune, with great effort, their faces contorted, halting feebly, but sing they did, with great earnestness. I remember the words, and I memorised the melody, almost impossible to catch because of their lack of tunefulness and their pain:

> A red star there upon his forehead,
> On it gleam hammer and sickle . . .

They reminded me – though one mustn't treat this seriously – of the festive crèche carriers who used to go from door to door in Lipik at Christmas. I have no idea why. In any case, there was nothing gleaming here, no stars. Only stumps of legs and bandages through which blood oozed. The only colours: filthy white, bright red and brown. Around us, the bloating bodies of butchered horses, smashed tanks, scattered pieces of guns or Srem peasant carts. Vidosav grunted and swore by my side.

The phantasmal song was behind us now, but I could still hear it, far away, when we slowed to a halt. "It is down there. See the acacia grove?" asked perceptive Virgil from Beli Potok.

I see it. We can only get there on foot, up an incline on which the cart would turn over. I do what I am told. We take down the coffin, open it and lay the spade, shovel, large blanket in it – this master of his trade has thought of everything. We take the coffin between us, and we make our way to the burial ground hardly able to pull our legs from the sticky mud.

"Here it is," Vidosav says.

What I saw was not, in fact, a real burial ground, but rather a natural depression in the land used so that the corpses could be laid in it and then covered with earth. Vidosav, peasant-like, with measured, slow movements, raised a shovelful of soil and tossed it into the distance with a wide swing. I stood paralysed next to him, my gaze fixed on the earth. When he'd dug down a bit, corpses began to show. The sleeve of a shirt, or a bare foot, white as bone, mouth and teeth full of earth, a smashed shoulder, a collarbone piercing a ragged shirt. I grabbed a spade and began to scrape with it. In a moment, I stopped. I saw thick red hair full of grey soil appearing under Vidosav's shovel.

I opened my mouth to say something, but no sound came out. I realised that in some peculiar way, for hours now, all the way from the Ilinci hospital, ever since the conversation with Bosa amidst the moans of the wounded, I had been carrying in my mind's eye, without knowing it, the very image that was now before me: Vidosav wielding the shovel in a hole full of mangled corpses, white as bone, brown in uniforms covered with blood bonding clothing and body into great clotted scabs; corpses merging with earth; the battlefield a messy rubbish dump, and amidst it the flame of one red head.

"That is him," I managed to say, but only when I was afraid Vidosav might hurt Mihajlo's face with the shovel.

Vidosav stopped digging and looked at me searchingly, experienced, judging whether I'd need help or not. When he saw that I was OK, he put down the shovel and started pushing the earth from Mihajlo. The face was gone. A smudge. A cavity filled with clotted blood, brains and mud. A red fleece above a crusty mass. Suddenly, the wild thought struck me that I'd seen it somewhere once before. I remembered a dog that our cart had run over on the road to Kragujevac. A heap of mingling fur and bloody meat still shuddering. On Mihajlo, everything is dead. The body in its uniform has shrunk and is hard to distinguish from the earth that has covered and besieged it. He seems to be in one piece. His feet in socks, without my pre-war mountain-climbing boots that he left home in. One of his arms is still in the ground, buried, and the other lies, as if he is taking an oath, across his chest. I kneel and kiss it, icy and muddy. "Unkissed," the meaningless word drums once more through the empty skull. I do not get up. I cannot. I don't know whether I think anything at that moment. I don't cry. Vidosav lets me kneel like that, as long as I need to, but no longer than necessary – Vidosav knows everything.

He puts his hand on my bowed head. He says, "Come on, Professor, come on."

Without a word, then, he takes Mihajlo by the shoulder and gives me a sign to take my son's unshod feet. We place Mihajlo on the open blanket. I use the rest of the blanket to cover him – I think – the way Elizabeta covers her baby when he kicks off the covers in his sleep, so he won't catch cold. Then into the coffin. Vidosav leaves me standing over him, absent; I hover above the earth weightless, all the time in that fog that hasn't lifted from the world since we got the letter informing us of his death. Vidosav goes back alone, with those same steady movements, to bury the unearthed dead. I watch my son in the blanket, for hours, it seems. Finally, Vidosav stops working, puts down the shovel and stands above the graves. He crosses himself and begins, in his own words, to talk to the corpses as if they're alive, steady at first and then with a growing tremor in his voice. "My dear sons, don't hold it against us that we have disturbed you in your eternal rest, Stevan Medaković here, professor from Belgrade, and I, Vidosav Prokić, peasant from near Avala. It means nothing to you, but we've taken your friend, Mihajlo, we're taking him home. God willing, my fine boys, yours will find you one day, when this goddamn war is over, and they'll take you to your native black earth. I'd take you all by myself, my sons, I swear by my father's eyes, one by one I'd carry you, on my back if I had to, if I only knew who you are and where you're from, so young and dead. But I don't know," he says and then begins to sob. I watch him for a while and then do what Vidosav had taught me to do just a few minutes before.

I put my hand on his bowed head. I say, "Come on, Vidosav, come on."

When we buried the body of our faceless child, Mihajlo's red hair in the Medaković family tomb, four days later, next to his nearest kin – Granny Ilinka, Grandfather Milutin, 7-year-old Aunt Cveta, also mutilated by a German hand grenade, the thought flashed through my empty head with a strange clarity that our unhappy child was no more at home in that tomb than he was in the marshy field below the acacia grove, that he belonged no more among my family than he did among Vidosav's mangled sons. So red-haired and obsessed, our little calamity, he had never belonged anywhere, he was alone in the great, gaudy world. I suddenly felt sorry in a different way, more impartially, and I felt sorry for us because of it, too, but I was never able to move beyond this feeling, to explain it more clearly. Leaving that for better times, I filled the silence with it while listening to the chanting of the priest and the muffled sobs of the family behind Elizabeta and me. I don't know how long I'd have pondered on our Mihajlo, unsuited to his own grave, if I hadn't seen, after the chanting was over, that Elizabeta was moving towards the coffin. I didn't know what she wanted to do, but there was certainly something strange in her manner; I felt that her intention was ominous. And it was. She asked for the lid to be raised, she wanted to see her son, but I wrenched myself in time from the tense immobility and, unable to hold back my panic, screamed, "Don't!", frantic at the thought that she would see her child, whose appearance I hadn't described, the way Vidosav and I had seen him.

Elizabeta halted; people looked up at me.

"There is nothing to see," I said. "Mihajlo is gone," I added, and, calmer, I realised that it was precisely as I'd said. Mihajlo was gone. I managed at the last minute to hide from Elizabeta the horrible cavity gaping where, in mind and eye, his white face dotted with yellow hairs had been. Our little Englishman was rent asunder in Serbia.

Crippled Savina suddenly emerged, in an unbuttoned overcoat, without an Army cap perched on the haystack of hair, from behind me. "Did it rip him apart?" she asked, her face clenched to cry, breathlessly watching my lips, and, experienced as she was, when she saw that I was unable to speak, she was the only one to interpret my scream correctly. "Fuck their filthy mothers," she said, leaving the graveside abruptly, with big strides, not turning back.

I don't know how my scream sounded to Elizabeta, how she interpreted the cryptic explanation that there was nothing to see, because Mihajlo was, simply, gone, but I do know that I'm glad to this day that the remnant of Mihajlo's smashed red and crazy head has not plagued her waking and sleeping hours as it has mine. At least I did that much for her, poor woman. I have never completely managed to understand Elizabeta's silence; I've never fully penetrated the thoughts and feelings behind her stalwart front. But while in other circumstances and times, I could at least guess what she was hiding with her green-eyed steel gaze, with a good chance of being right about it, now I couldn't even begin to. For two reasons. Because Elizabeta closed completely like a seashell when it is disturbed, like a flower when the sun goes down. Being myself overly preoccupied with my own thoughts and Mihajlo, I was less involved with Elizabeta's thoughts and feelings. Not because I loved her any less in those days and months. Hardly. I loved her with a love that ached, with a new-found intensity, the way one loves a raped daughter who bears her shame and childish horror whimpering inside while like a gazelle, previously haughty but now sullied, she slinks around the house hoping most of all that she won't be noticed. My love for Elizabeta, torn apart by a bomb, was no different in those days from calamity. Calamity and love are the first and last names of my terrible helplessness. What was I to do? How to help Elizabeta, loved and pitied, when she, abused and frightened, wouldn't let me within firing range – a creature that retreated to its den as soon as it sniffed man. How to help the sad whale who did not want to be unstranded? Watching her as she wanders about the house enveloped in silence like a protective fog that she releases from her frozen soul; catching her eyes that look away in panic, eyes that reveal – it is hard to say just what – fear, certainly, but fear stemming not from an anxiety for life, rather from a lack of understanding of this world, suddenly so altered and perilous, which can't be reduced to a single familiar and safe value. Rife with Olympian fickleness and cruelty. What is happening to me! shrieks something submerged deep inside my formerly wilful and intractable young woman. Where am I, who am I, what am I doing here! I hear the cries and sit helplessly in my chair across from her, hands limp in my lap. If she had wept, if only she'd wept! I would have, too – glad to see her tears, a sign of life! If she had railed, no matter at whom – at me, Serbs, fate – her abuse would have filled our kitchen with a holiday brightness. But nothing. An expressionless face, the frightened gaze of a little creature that has been caught in a trap, knowing only one thing – that there is no way out.

Elizabeta began to avoid me before Mihajlo left and was killed, and even more after his death. She could only bear, it seems, to be alone. I assume that my presence was enough to take her back to the questions buzzing frantically around her spirit, longing for peace. I knew that my support would help her, if she wanted it, if she could take support from anyone. I offered a shoulder, like a lowly dog, begging for her trust, but I would always see the same thing: her defeat was sufficient unto itself; she did not want to leave it and venture into a world where things could only get worse.

She started to do something every day that she had never done before: she would leave the house and be away for hours, without giving me any explanation of where she had been and what she had done. Several times I asked her, "Where were you, Elizabeta? I was concerned."

And I always got the same answer: "I wandered around," which clearly meant that she'd rather not be asked because she would have to admit that there was no reason for wandering except the unmention-able reason: the desire to be somewhere far from her own life, shielded from every memory of him. I don't know what Elizabeta thought about along the dusty Belgrade streets, alone there like some dead and unrestful queen. I have never been able, then or now, to imagine the event, person, memory, incident that could chase the thought of Mihajlo out of her head and the miserable life she lived after his death. Did she go back to her English childhood, her youth? Did she perhaps accuse me, in that grisly conversation with herself, of a lack of self-sacrifice? Of an unfatherly vehemence? Or perhaps she accused Mihajlo of an unfilial cruelty, running amuck in the Malay jungle of late-war Belgrade. There is black darkness all around, and in the black darkness there are no signposts. She'd come back from her walks with that same dead face and elusive gaze, suspicious, ominously composed and distant, cold, somewhere on a blurred horizon. She was at arm's length, yet words couldn't reach her. I on one chair, she on the other; black-bearded Stevan, across from white, red and green Elizabeta, we sat and were silent. We were silent because she could not speak, and I felt that this was what, with the two of us, with me, she could bear: silence. Each staring at our own book, without even a semblance of turning the pages. We sat in the kitchen exposed to black thoughts like poison rays we couldn't run away from.

I noticed that after an interlude of many years, she started speaking English with me again, but I couldn't say whether she did it consciously, whether she was trying to tell me something, or whether she felt that there was no longer any earthly or heavenly reason to work towards any goal. I tried responding to her English sentences in Serbian, but she would continue the conversation in English indifferent to my sly test, probably not even aware of the manoeuvre. Conversation! What conversation! There was no conversation between us in those days.

"Supper's ready," she says to me. "I'll bring you a sweater," I say to her.

"I'll be back soon," she says to me if she says anything, leaving for her "wandering around", which will last for hours. And so on for days. For months.

When trivial thoughts began to seep back into my empty head, I remember that I began to loathe life as something individual, a sort of cruel and unchanging order, a tyranny that could not be overthrown. Earlier, when I stared at the sky, it used to disclose an existence to my innocent eyes, perhaps not of God but of an awareness so much more powerful than our capacity to grasp it that it filled one's spirit with a religious awe: life as something astounding, an unbelievable chance that should be revered rather than interpreted. I never thought, earlier, of death. For me, death was something hovering in the nimbus of the dangerous emanations of our spirit, something which happened to others, something evil which must not be allowed access to thoughts and mouth except by grievous necessity. At one point, however, death as an idea and a living presence of Mihajlo's demolished face in our family tomb had moved into my head as a real image and constant subject for wonder. It started to seem, this enemy of mine, like something shameful and astonishing in comparison with the order that exists in everything living, like a disorder rendering order frail, in fact non-existent. It was something easily replaceable with its opposite, death. The fact that people will continue to live for a while is no comfort for Mihajlo, who has vanished without a trace. Death, Mihajlo's death, made life abhorrent; much like a tyrant whom we must obey, the only way out being one's own death, as though life were a brief calamity for those of us granted the knowledge by some evil spirit, while we still live, that it must come to an end.

I have never tried to tell anyone of these thoughts of mine, because I knew their lack of substance would make them seem a mere generality as soon as they are spoken, yet a want of words to express the feeling that filled me with the wretched stupor of a poor creature under illegible stars hardly diminished the authenticity of the feeling, nor did it counter my readiness for death. All that life can do began to seem so paltry that the distance between truth and falsehood, justice and injustice, between happiness and unhappiness, shrank away, almost disappeared, turning my daily existence in our kitchen into a void – the closest description of death that I am able to provide.

I am able, by this alone, this terrible flavour of flatness, the taste of death in my mouth, to explain the equanimity with which I accepted Elizabeta's unexpected decision. Some time in late September, perhaps early October – I remember that time during those months had not a shred of meaning – having come home from one of her daily wanderings, instead of her customary terse "Hello", without even a Stevan, Steve, Stephen, and the protracted silence at the kitchen table, this time, in a matter-of-fact, colourless tone, Elizabeta announced, "I'll be leaving for England, Stephen."

I see Elizabeta across from me. I can hear and understand what she is telling me, but still something in me remains dead, untouched, in the universal stupor to which I had submitted in those days. The most I can say for the state of my consciousness at that moment is that at first, only quite briefly, I was startled and confused. Indeed, we had never discussed the possibility of her travelling to England. Earlier on, I knew that she did not want to go back to her birthplace, for reasons I was not able to divine. The last time we had been in England had been in 1939, because we had to go when unfortunate Rašela Alkalaj, so proud of her Jewish adaptability and endurance, didn't wake up one morning. Robert, her father, had died earlier, so Elizabeta really had only her cousin Archibald in England. However, the great shock at Rašela's untimely death and the distance led Elizabeta to limit her ties with him, even before the war, to the exchange of Christmas and Easter cards. Throughout the four war years, we hadn't heard from a single relative that Elizabeta cared about, and then, only a few days before her decision to travel, thanks to Patrick Walker, we learned from Archibald, via a letter that arrived by diplomatic pouch, that, as he said, though "old and not in the best of health", he was alive. I had thought that Archibald's letter had not left much of an impression on Elizabeta, chased into the densest darkness of her cave, because we only exchanged a few words about it, which I judged to be indifferent, without force, like all else we said or did.

All this passed through my mind while I sat silent after her sudden announcement, but I quickly realised that the decision to travel was not, in fact, strange, and that it could, perhaps, be beneficial for her and for the recovery of our lives, so instead of the questions I knew she would be loath to answer (Why England? How? For how long? Is this wise?), after a little while I began to ask practical questions instead. "Should I speak with Ambassador Stephenson?" was the first thing I asked, and I saw right off that she was grateful I wasn't going to torture her with unnecessary curiosity.

"No," she said. "Patrick Walker promised to take care of it. He'll also try to put me on a British plane to London some time next week."

"Fine. I must thank him," I said, and she, after a silence, already absent, somewhere off in herself, said, "Yes, please do."

The month of November 1945. I was alone. Mihajlo was under the earth. Elizabeta had gone. Even I was not here. The last day of my life was beginning, a day that has lasted ever since, for twenty years. I was at its beginning. In our enclave. I planted a hedge, watering it, and every day I saw less and less through the densening thicket. I waited for my wife and wanted what she wanted: to die and live dead. I neglected my life, which became strange and unknown as if it was happening to someone else. We've lived dead ever since!

Propped up on two plump pillows, I have been sitting rather than lying in my regally spacious, old-fashioned bed, which has been, so far as I'm concerned, the central and safest spot in our safe enclave for two decades now. I hear the ticking of the wall clock. Nine fifteen. For a quarter of an hour now, I haven't heard the morning sounds that follow Elizabeta around the kitchen with such predictable bustle that I am able at any moment to say how far she has got in preparing our English breakfast. And though I know that Elizabeta will be angry, though of course she won't show it, that I allowed my laziness to interfere with our funereal ritual of bacon and eggs and porridge, I still cannot fight the sluggishness that has recently, mercilessly, prevented me from making the decisive move of getting out of bed, as if from a throne, into the same twenty-year-long day. I know that Elizabeta is in the kitchen. I know that she is sitting on the chair. Her face is deflated, loose, the way one may look if there's no-one watching, but even then this face does not show what is behind the prominent brow under the reddish grey hair. I must get up. "Just a second," I tell myself, "to let it sink in." I make an effort at the last moment to ascertain whether I am satisfied now that I know I am able to think objectively about the foreign life I just watched gallop by before my eyes. Have I understood what I couldn't understand twenty years ago?

Have I?

I get out of bed and put on my dressing gown. Once more, I gaze around our protracted, twenty-year-long lethargy. I can see it in the palm of my hand: in the middle of a sunlit kitchen, the table covered with a white tablecloth. English porcelain and a silver teapot. Elizabeta and I across from one another. We are silent. We are having breakfast in the enclave. I am hunched over. Thin, though, sadly, not strikingly so; I am not slender, but deflated like people who have suddenly lost weight. My grey hairs are outnumbered by the black, but even they are turning grey, and the white ends have yellowed like the fingers of a heavy smoker. I have shaved off my beard and look feeble-chinned to myself, somehow ashamed by the loss of beard and moustache. I've shrunk. Has Elizabeta also shrunk? She has not. With a white band round her muted red, greying hair, still statuesque, buxom, a former caryatid. She still has that white complexion, with a grid of yellow freckles, now furrowed with a myriad of tiny wrinkles, so tiny that they are hardly noticeable at a greater distance. I, dead, am still not able to watch her, dead, with the indifference that sees nothing of what is familiar.

Alone in our enclave. Two silent pasts in a play from which someone who is uninformed could glean nothing; everything is dead behind our living countenances.

"Some more tea, Stephen?"

GLOSSARY

Albanian exodus: During World War I, Serbian troops were routed by advancing Austro-Hungarian, German and Bulgarian troops in the winter of 1915–16 and forced to retreat, carrying their wounded across the Albanian mountains to the Adriatic, where French and British allies evacuated the survivors to Corfu. Accompanying the troops were thousands of civilian refugees, the Serbian government and the elderly, frail King Petar Karađorđević, who was carried either on a stretcher or in an ox-cart.

Alharos: Haroseth (Hebrew), symbolic bread.

Apis: Nickname of Colonel Dragutin Dimitrijević (1876–1917), one of the Serbian Army officers who assassinated King Aleksandar Obrenović and his wife Draga in 1903. In 1911, Dimitrijević joined the newly founded secret society "Unification or Death" – better known as "Black Hand" (see Glossary) – a militant nationalist organisation that soon exerted significant influence in Serbian politics. During World War I, Apis, then Chief of Intelligence to the general staff, was arrested on trumped-up charges of attempting to assassinate Prince Aleksandar Karadjordjević, Serbia's Regent and Commander-in Chief. Apis and two others were executed in May 1917 after a long court martial at Salonika.

AVNOJ: The Anti-fascist Council for the People's Liberation of Yugoslavia, Tito's wartime government council.

Balkan Wars: Two wars immediately preceding World War I. In the first (1912), Serbia, Bulgaria, Montenegro and Greece fought to oust the Ottoman Empire from its last remaining holdings in the Balkans. In the second (1913), Bulgaria fought a brief, unsuccessful war against its former allies Serbia and Greece, largely over the issue of control of Macedonia.

Battle of Kosovo Polje: June 28, 1389. Long considered to be one of the most significant battles in the Ottoman advance into the Balkan Peninsula, the actual outcome of the battle is unclear. What is known is that both the Ottoman and the Christian forces sustained serious losses, including the deaths of Ottoman Sultan Murad and the Serbian Prince Lazar. Serbia eventually succumbed to Ottoman control, and the battle became a major theme in the Serbian epic tradition. This tradition encouraged centuries of brigands to rebel against Ottoman control and fired the imagination and actions of countless nineteenth-century Serbian revolutionaries.

Black Hand: A powerful secret organisation within the Serbian military during the Balkan Wars. Its official name was "Ujedinjenje ili smrt" (Unification or Death), a reference to its goal of uniting all Serbs into one state. Associated with the assassination of the Austro-Hungarian Archduke Ferdinand and his wife Sophia in Sarajevo in 1914. (See **Apis**.)

Bohus: Unleavened bread eaten at Passover, the Sephardic matzo.

Boza: A non-alcoholic beverage made from millet.

Bregalnica: A battle in 1913 involving a surprise Bulgarian attack on Serbian forces and precipitating the Second Balkan War.

Bundegas: Matzo balls.

Burekitos: Rolls.

Cer: Battle between the Serbian and Austrian armies in August 1914; Serbia's first victory against the Central Powers in World War I.

Chetniks: Originally a term for irregular soldiers who fought Ottoman rule in Serbia and Macedonia (from *četa*, meaning "military detachment"), it was used for the resistance force assembled and led by Draža Mihailović (see Glossary) after Nazi Germany defeated the Yugoslav Royal Army and occupied Serbia in the spring of 1941. The Chetniks were a royalist, Serbian force opposed to the Communist-led Partisans (see Glossary).

Cvetković, Dragiša (1893–1969): Prime minister from February 1939 to March 1941. In August 1937, he signed the Cvetković–Maček agreement with the Croatian leader Vladko Maček (see Glossary), setting up a self-governing region in Croatia. His government was overthrown two days after they signed the Tripartite Pact with the Axis powers.

Debeli: Fatso.

Dedinje: Élite Belgrade quarter.

Degen: Imbecile.

Đilas, Milovan (1911–1995): A member of Tito's inner circle, powerful in the years immediately following World War II, later a dissident who questioned the premises of Tito's new society.

Draško: A character in Njegoš's "The Mountain Wreath" (see Glossary) who returns from a visit to Venice to describe how bizarre and wrong the Venetians seem to him from a Montenegrin perspective.

Drašković, Milorad (1873–1921): Interior minister in the Kingdom of Serbs, Croats and Slovenes, he was assassinated after introducing anti-Communist and anti-terrorist regulations.

Fiume: The Italian name for the city of Rijeka.

Frizaldadas: A flaky pastry dough.

"Gorski vijenac" (The Mountain Wreath): Poem by Montenegrin poet Petar Petrović Njegoš. The poem articulates, indeed defines, both the heroic and the violent ethos of Serbian legend and the Balkan epic. Published in 1847, it tells the story of Montenegrin clansmen who band together to battle the Ottoman presence in Montenegro. The villains of the piece are the local Ottoman dignitaries who had converted to Islam from the Orthodox faith centuries before, and whom the clansmen therefore perceive as traitors. The poem is the source of many of Nanka's sentiments.

Grol, Milan (1876–1952): Belgrade theatre director and leader of the Serbian-based Democratic Party in the 1920s and '30s. After heading the party in exile during World War II, Grol joined Tito's provisional government as deputy prime minister in March 1945, but resigned in August when he realized that the Communists were not going to hold free elections.

Gusle: Ancient Slavic single-stringed bowed instrument used to accompany the performance of epic songs.

Jalija: riverbank (Greek).

Jevtić, Bogoljub (1886–1960): Foreign minister (1932–34) under

Aleksandar II, and then head of the first government under Prince Pavle immediately after Aleksandar's assassination. The government fell after it failed to gain a convincing victory in the parliamentary elections of May 1935 despite unfair voting conditions and repressive measures against the opposition. Milan Stojadinović succeeded Jevtić as prime minister.

Jovanović, Slobodan (1869–1958): Historian and law professor whose many works include a study of British parliamentarism and portraits drawn from Serbian history in the second half of the nineteenth century. He was widely considered, then as now, to be one of Serbia's greatest scholars. Though he had long stayed aloof from active political involvement, in 1937 he formed the Serbian Cultural Club (see Glossary) as an opposition-minded group to discuss and defend Serbian interests within Yugoslavia. After Nazi Germany took control of Serbia in April 1941, Jovanović went into exile with the Yugoslav government, serving as vice-president and, later, prime minister (January 1942–June 1943). Because of his support for the Chetniks and Draža Mihailović, he was tried in absentia by Tito's government in 1946 and sentenced to twenty years in prison. Thereafter, he lived in exile until his death in England.

Kajmak: A rich, aged cheese. Fresh milk is boiled, and as the cream forms a skin, it is skimmed off and set aside in a crock to age. There are salted and unsalted *kajmaks*.

Kalemegdan: The Belgrade fortress overlooking the confluence of the Danube and Sava rivers.

Karađorđe Đorđe Petrović) (*c.* 1768–1817): He led the first Serbian uprising in 1804 against Ottoman rule. The uprising crumbled, and Ottoman forces re-took the briefly freed territory. Karađorđe fled to Russia. When Miloš Obrenović led the second uprising in 1815, Karađorđe returned, only to be killed at Obrenović's orders. Thus began the dynastic feud between the Karađorđevićes and the Obrenovićes that would last until 1903. Karađorđe's son Aleksandar Karađorđević replaced Miloš Obvrenovićes son Mihajlo in 1842 as Prince of Serbia when the governing council called on him to take office. Aleksandar remained in power until 1858, when he went into exile and Miloš Obrenović returned as Prince.

Karađorđević, Aleksandar II (1888–1934): Plagued by ill health, his father, Petar, made him Regent in 1914. Aleksandar was Commander-in-Chief of Serbian forces during World War I and became Regent of the Kingdom of Serbs, Croats and Slovenes, crowned King in 1921 upon his father's death. After Stjepan Radić (see Glossary) was shot in the parliament, the King imposed a dictatorship in January 1929. Aleksandar was assassinated in Marseilles on October 9, 1934. His assassin was a Macedonian man who had ties with the Croatian Ustasha.

Karađorđević, Pavle (1893–1976): King Aleksandar II's first cousin named in his will to head the regency until Aleksandar's son Petar came of age. As Regent he was head of state from 1934 to 1941. Pavle tried to preserve Yugoslavia's neutrality, but under pressure from Germany saw no alternative to signing the Axis's Tripartite Pact on March 25, 1941. Two days later, a bloodless military coup by officers in Belgrade overthrew the government, deposing Prince Pavle and declaring the still underage Petar to be King. Pavle and his family spent the war in Africa under British supervision, then lived in Paris from 1948.

Karađorđević, Petar (1844–1921): Following the assassination of Aleksandar I Obrenović and his Queen, Draga, in 1903, Petar Karađorđević was crowned King of Serbia. He was a popular monarch and encouraged parliamentary democracy. His health was poor, and in 1914 he named his son Aleksandar to act as his Regent. Aleksandar was Commander-in-Chief of the Serbian Army during World War I, but King Petar accompanied the troops, even on their retreat through Macedonia and Albania to the Adriatic coast in the winter of 1915–16.

Karađorđević, Petar II (1923–1970): When his father, Aleksandar II, was killed in 1934, Petar was 11 years old. His cousin Pavle ruled in his name as Prince Regent. After the *coup d'état* of March 27, 1941, Petar was granted majority six months before his 18th birthday and crowned King. Ten days later, he fled the country with the government. He never returned; the Communist Party abolished the monarchy in 1945 as it consolidated power in Yugoslavia.

Karadžić, Vuk Stefanović (1787–1864): Serbian language reformer, ethnographer and collector of Serbian folklore. He laid the foundations for the modern Serbian literary language, based on the *štokavski* dialect of Eastern Herzegovina. This was an essential step in the national awakening of the Serbian people, and yet it also encouraged problems because it assumed that national identity was determined by language. Thus, in Karadžić's view, anyone who spoke *štokavski* was a Serb, even though many non-Serbs found themselves in that category because of their dialect.

Kardelj, Edvard (1910–1979): Slovenian Communist in Tito's inner circle. In the 1960s, he became known for reforms, including that of self-management.

Keva: Serbian colloquial expression for "mother".

Kingdom of Serbs, Croats and Slovenes: The official name of the country in 1918. The name Yugoslavia replaced it only in 1929, and as such was symbolic of the shift away from acknowledgement of the individual nations comprising the triune kingdom towards a unitarist policy in keeping with the dictatorship.

Kolubara: In December 1914, a battle between Serbian and Austrian forces won by the Serbs, though they suffered serious losses.

Korošec, Anton (1872–1940): Leader of the Slovenian People's Party and a Catholic priest. President of the National Council in Zagreb at the time of unification. He was the only non-Serb to head the government in inter-war Yugoslavia. He was prime minister for five months after the Radić assassination, stepping down in December 1928. He served as interior minister from 1935 to 1938, and as education minister from July 1940 until his death in December.

Koštunica, Vojislav: Koštunica was elected president of Yugoslavia in October 2000 after popular protests forced Slobodan Milošević to recognise his loss at the polls. The monograph by Koštunica and Kosta Čakovski mentioned in the Translator's Foreword was published in English in 1985 as *Party Pluralism or Monism: On Social Movements and the Political System in Yugoslavia 1944 to 1949.*

Kumanovo: A battle in 1912 repelling Ottoman forces (First Balkan war).

Lazarević, Dr Laza (1851–1890): A physician and one of the earliest

Serbian short-story writers. He spent several years in Berlin and on his return wrote about his dilemma of whether or not to bring Ana, his German sweetheart, back to Belgrade.

Los de abajo: Lower.

Los de arriba: Upper.

Maček, Vladko (1879–1964): Leader of the Croatian Peasant Party in 1928 after Radić's death, he called for a federalist Yugoslavia that recognised Croats as a sovereign nation. In 1935, Maček headed a single combined opposition list. In 1937, he joined forces with certain Serbian parties to call for a national government to work on a transition to a new constitutional structure. Two years later, he was made deputy prime minister after negotiating the Cvetković–Maček agreement, which set up a new province of Croatia with a substantial degree of autonomy.

Mahala: Neighbourhood, city quarter (Arabic).

Mali žurnal: "Little Journal", a children's newspaper.

Mihailović, Draža (1893–1946): A general staff colonel who defied the Yugoslav Army's capitulation to the Germans in April 1941 and set up an irregular Serbian fighting force properly known as the Chetniks and recognised by the royal government-in-exile as the Yugoslav Army in the Fatherland. Early attempts at co-operation with the Communist-led Partisan resistance movement gave way to civil war. He was put to death as a traitor by Tito's government for his suspected collaboration with the Germans.

Milchbrot: A sweet toast.

Minderluk: A low ottoman.

Minderpuza: A woman who spends all day lounging on her ottoman.

Moriscos: Moorish romantic ballads.

"The Mountain Wreath": See **"Gorski vijenac"**.

Napred: The "Onward" society, a group of left-leaning democratic Serbian intellectuals who began publishing a magazine and brochures in 1937 to promote their views and encourage public debate and education about the issues of the day.

National Council of the Slovenes, Croats and Serbs: A provisional body organised to represent the Slovenes, Croats and Serbs living in the

Habsburg Empire during negotiations regarding the formation of Yugoslavia during and immediately after World War I.

Nedić, Milan (1877–1946): The general appointed by the Germans to head the government of Occupied Serbia during World War II.

Njegoš, Petar Petrović (1813–1850): Poet and bishop of the Montenegrin church and Prince of Montenegro. Author of the 1847 epic poem "Gorski vijenac" (The Mountain Wreath) (see Glossary).

Obrenović, Aleksandar (1876–1903): Assumed the monarchy from his father, King Milan, in 1888. He and Queen Draga were assassinated in the royal palace in Belgrade in 1903 by a group of military officers.

Obrenović, Milan (1854–1901): Succeeded after Mihajlo Obrenović's assassination in 1868. The first ruler of modern Serbia, he was crowned King in 1882. He abdicated in favour of his son Aleksandar in 1888.

Obrenović, Miloš (1780–1860): Led the second Serbian uprising in 1815. He had Karađorđe Petrović murdered and negotiated his way to limited autonomy for Serbia under Ottoman rule. He was made Prince of Serbia in 1838 but abdicated in 1839. He was invited by the governing council to return to the throne at the age of 80 for two more years before his death in 1858. He was succeeded by his son Mihajlo, who had already ruled from 1839 to 1842. Mihajlo ruled as an enlightened despot until he was assassinated in 1868. He was succeeded by Milan.

Obznana: Repressive decrees issued in the spring of 1921 by the Democratic Party leader Milorad Drašković, the interior minister, to combat terrorism.

OZNA (Department for Protection of the People): The Communist secret police run by Aleksandar Ranković (see Glossary) during World War II.

Partisans: Tito's Communist-led fighting force during World War II. At first guerrilla irregulars, by 1944, when they reached Belgrade, they were organised as the People's Liberation Army. The Partisans were the only fighting force in Yugoslavia during World War II that enlisted fighters of all national backgrounds.

Pašić, Nikola (1845–1926): Radical Party leader and prime minister of the Serbian government before World War I. Head of the wartime government. One of the key architects of the Kingdom of Serbs, Croats and Slovenes (see Glossary), he met with the National Council in Geneva to organise the post-war government. Yugoslavia's prime minister for most of the period from January 1921 to April 1926.

Patišpanj: Sweet pastry of flour, sugar and eggs.

Podlo: Vile.

Pribićević, Svetozar (1875–1936): Political leader of Serbs living in Croatia. He was an important figure in the creation of Yugoslavia and led efforts to impose centralist rule in the years after World War I. In an about-face in the mid-1920s, Pribićević declared himself a federalist, and his Independent Democratic Party became a close ally of Stjepan Radić (see Glossary) and the Croatian Peasant Party.

Prst (pronounced "Prrrst"): Finger.

Put Alije Đerzeleza: *The Journey of Ali Djerzelez*, by Ivo Andrić, published in its original version in 1920.

Radić, Stjepan (1871–1928): Leader of the Croatian Peasant Party. An outspoken politician calling for a republic and a federalist programme in the Kingdom of Serbs, Croats and Slovenes. Under his leadership, the Peasant Party grew into a mass movement. After provoking scandals, boycotting the government, calling for recognition of the Soviet Union and even spending time in prison, Radić declared himself a supporter of the monarchy in an about-face in 1925. He was made minister of education. Shot in June 1928 in the parliament in Belgrade, he died of his wounds two months later.

Radical Party: When political parties first developed in Serbia in the late nineteenth century, the Radical Party was a populist, peasant-based organisation. By 1900, it had become the most powerful party in Serbia, although increasingly less populist than its historical platform. The Radicals dominated the political scene in Serbia until the Communists eliminated the multi-party system in the post-war years.

Rakija: strong, purely distilled alcoholic beverage made from fruit.

Ranković, Aleksandar (1909–1979): A member of Tito's inner circle during and after World War II, he was head of OZNA, the wartime security service, and then interior minister until his downfall, in 1966, after a wiretapping scandal and an attack on what were perceived to be Ranković's centralist policies.

Ratluk: Turkish delight.

Ridji: Redhead.

Rināiperos: Dandies.

Samsar: Merchant (Arabic).

The Sandžak: The Sandžak, or *sanjak* (Turkish for "province"), of Novi Pazar is a region inhabited largely by Muslims that lies between Serbia and Montenegro.

Serbian Cultural Club: A gathering of Serbian intellectuals formed in 1937 to discuss and promote Serbian interests within Yugoslavia, a sign of their disillusionment with unitarist Yugoslavism and concern over the decline of Serbian political life under authoritarian rule. The Club grew greatly in prominence and ambition when it became a leading critic of the Cvetković-Maček Agreement (see Glossary) of August 1939. More radical members saw in it the nucleus of a Serbian nationalist political movement, a kind of counterweight to the Croatian Peasant Party (see **Radić, Stjepan**).

Serbian uprisings: The first uprising (1804), led by Đorđe Petrović Karađorđe, and the second (1815), led by Miloš Obrenović, both against Ottoman rule.

Slatko: Fruit preserves. A spoonful, followed by a sip of water, is served to guests upon their arrival.

Slavonia: A Croatian region, part of the Hungarian Crown lands until 1918.

Slivnica: A battle in 1885 between Serbian and Bulgarian troops.

Smrča (pronounced "Smrrrcha"): Spruce.

Sokol: A society for the promotion of fitness, sport and Slavic patriotism.

Stojadinović, Milan (1888–1961): Prime minister under Prince Pavle.

Šubašic, Ivan: A governor in Croatia during the war. King Petar appointed him prime minister in June 1944. He negotiated with Tito on the island of Vis to form a coalition government.

Tito, Josip Broz (1892–1980): Leader of the Yugoslav Communists from the late 1930s; commander of the Partisan irregulars, later the People's Liberation Army, during World War II. In 1943 in the small Bosnian town of Jajce during the first AVNOJ (see Glossary) assembly, he announced the formation of the new Yugoslavia. Tito was president of Yugoslavia until his death in 1980.

Ustasha: A Croatian extreme nationalist organisation first organised as a fringe terror group by Ante Pavelić. During World War II, they were the shock troops for the Independent State of Croatia and conducted genocidal campaigns against Serbs, Jews, Gypsies and those Croats who defied the regime.

Visoki: Nickname for a tall boy.

Živković, Petar (1879–1947): After the imposition of the 1929 dictatorship, the government was led until April 1932 by General Živković as King Aleksandar's agent at the head of a cabinet of royal appointees.

Zmaj, Jovan Jovanović (1851–1890): Serbian nineteenth-century poet famous for his verses for children.